Japanese readers love

HONEYBEES AND DISTANT THUNDER

"The novel is a masterpiece. I applaud the author for her power of description. The author's extraordinary affection for music made this work seem so complete."

"Each character was wonderfully drawn, and I felt moved, as if I were truly hearing each and every musical piece. I also felt the significance of how a competition can create connections between people."

"I felt like I was totally immersed, and there were scenes that brought me to tears."

"This is beyond a reading experience. It felt like some sixth sense was at work. Wonderful."

Honeybees and Distant Thunder

A NOVEL

Riku Onda

TRANSLATED FROM THE JAPANESE
BY PHILIP GABRIEL

PEGASUS BOOKS
NEW YORK LONDON

HONEYBEES AND DISTANT THUNDER

Pegasus Books, Ltd.
148 West 37th Street, 13th Floor
New York, NY 10018

Originally published in Japanese as *Mitsubachi To Enrai* by Riku Onda.

English translation rights arranged with Gentosha Inc. through
Japan UNI Agency, Inc. Tokyo.

First Pegasus Books cloth edition May 2023

ISBN: 978-1-63936-403-9

10 9 8 7 6 5 4 3 2 1

Printed in the United States of America
Distributed by Simon & Schuster
www.pegasusbooks.com

Entry

Theme

WHEN WAS THAT MEMORY FROM? I'm not sure.

I'd just learned to walk, so I couldn't have been much more than a toddler. Of that much I'm certain.

Far away, sunlight shone down, covering the world in its glow – cold, dispassionate, unstinting.

In that moment, the world to me felt bright, endless, forever trembling and wavering, a sublime yet terrifying place to be.

There was a faint, sweet fragrance mixed with the intense smell of greenery found only in nature.

A gentle breeze was blowing.

My body was enfolded in a rustling sound, gentle and cooling. I didn't know yet that this was the sound of leaves on the trees brushing against each other.

But there was something else.

I could see in the air a dense, lively shape that changed from moment to moment, growing smaller and then larger, constantly shifting.

I was still too young even to say *Mummy* or *Daddy*, yet I felt like I was already searching for a way to express something.

The words were in my throat, right there.

But first, another sound began to emerge, capturing my attention.

Like a sudden downpour.

It was powerful, bright.

Something – a wave, a vibration – rippled out.

As I listened, captivated, I felt as if my very being was immersed in it, and a calm settled on my heart.

If I could experience that moment again, I would describe it as the astonishing sound of a swarm of bees buzzing over the top of a hill.

A sublime, magisterial music that filled the world!

Prelude

THE YOUNG MAN TURNED around at the intersection, startled. But it wasn't because a car had beeped at him.

He was in the middle of a major metropolis.

The cosmopolitan city centre of Europe, the number-one tourist destination in the world.

The pedestrians were of all nationalities, all shapes and sizes. A mosaic of different races filling the pavements, the mixture of languages waxing and waning like ripples.

This boy, who, by coming to a sudden halt, had disrupted the waves of passers-by flowing around him, was of medium build, but gave the impression he would soon shoot up even further. He looked fourteen, perhaps fifteen, and seemed the picture of youthful innocence.

He wore a cap, cotton trousers and a khaki-coloured T-shirt, along with a lightweight beige coat. An oversized canvas bag was slung diagonally across his shoulders. At first glance he looked like a typical teen, but there was something strangely free and easy about him.

He had an attractive Asian face beneath his cap, but his striking eyes and white skin made him seem, in a way, unplaceable.

He was looking up.

Oblivious to the traffic, his calm eyes were staring at one fixed point.

A small blond boy passing by with his mother followed the young man's gaze upwards, until his mother tugged him by the hand, dragging him over to the other side of the crossing. The boy looked longingly back at the young man in the dark brown cap, before giving up to docilely follow his mother.

The young man, standing stock-still in the middle of the pedestrian crossing, finally realized the lights had changed, and walked swiftly across to the other side.

He'd definitely heard something.

As he adjusted the bag across his chest, he considered the sound he'd heard at the intersection.

The buzzing of honeybees.

A sound he'd known since he was a child, a sound he could never mistake.

Had they flown over from near the Hôtel de Ville perhaps?

He looked around, eyes searching, and when he spotted the large clock on the corner, he realized he was late.

I have to keep my promise, he told himself.

The young man pulled down his cap and ran off, his stride limber and supple.

MIEKO SAGA WAS USED TO being patient, but she realized with a start that she was about to fall asleep.

She stared about her, unsure where she was, but when she spotted the grand piano, and the young woman playing, she knew she must be in Paris.

Experience had taught her not to suddenly sit bolt upright and look around. Do that and people were sure to know you'd been snoozing. The trick was to gently place a hand to your temple, as if listening intently, and then shuffle a little in your seat, as if tired of holding the same position for so long.

But it wasn't just Mieko who had trouble staying awake. She knew for certain that the other music professors would be feeling exactly the same. Alan Simon, beside her, was a heavy smoker, and to go for so long without a nicotine fix, while listening to such appallingly tedious performances, must be driving him mad. Very soon his fingers would surely start to twitch.

On his other side, she knew that Sergei Smirnoff, sour-faced, would be leaning his large frame against the table, not moving a muscle but thinking of when it would all be over and he'd be released to get to the bar for a drink.

Mieko was with them on that. She loved music, but also life and all its pleasures – cigarettes and alcohol included. All she wanted was to be set free from this painful trial so that, together, they could have a drink and gossip.

Auditions for the Yoshigae International Piano Competition were being held in five cities around the world: in Moscow, Paris, Milan, New York and in the Japanese city of Yoshigae itself. Apart from in Yoshigae, the auditions were all taking place in the concert halls of famous music schools.

Mieko was aware there'd been complaints about her and the other two judges being selected to oversee the Paris auditions, and indeed they had each manoeuvred behind the scenes to ensure this outcome. They were regarded among the cohort of judges as the bad boys, who loved a drink and were always ready with a scathing review.

But they still took pride in their ear for music. Maybe their behaviour wasn't the best, but they had established a reputation for spotting originality. If anyone was going to discover a bright new name among those who'd been initially dismissed, it would be them. Of this they were certain.

But even they were now beginning to lose their concentration.

Earlier on there had been two or three pianists who seemed promising, but the performances that followed had dashed all Mieko's hopes.

What they were on the lookout for was a *star*.

In all there were twenty-five candidates. They were now up to number fifteen, with ten more to go. She began to feel a little faint. It was at this point that the same thought crossed her mind again: being a judge was a new form of torture.

Listening to the endless permutations of Bach, Mozart, Chopin, Bach, Mozart, Beethoven, she felt like she was fading away.

She knew from the moment a pianist began to play if they had a special spark. Some of her colleagues boasted they could tell the moment a performer stepped on to the stage. Indeed, some young pianists did have an aura about them, and even if they didn't, it was easy to discern in the first few minutes the quality of their playing. Dozing off was rude and unfeeling, but if a performer couldn't hold the interest of even a judge who had developed extra staying power, that pianist hadn't a hope of ever bonding with ordinary music fans.

Miracles never happen, after all.

Mieko was certain the other two were thinking the same thing.

The Yoshigae International Piano Competition was held every three years, and this year was the sixth time it had taken place. In recent years, the reputation of the Yoshigae competition had grown. Winners were beginning to move on to scoop prizes in more famous contests. Yoshigae had quickly won a name as an event for emerging talent.

The winner of the last Yoshigae had actually failed the initial application screening. So there were naturally great hopes for the current auditions, as the entrants were well aware of the previous competition's Cinderella story.

But even this winner had come from a well-known music school, and had only been turned down initially because he was too young to have gained the requisite experience from other competitions. In reality there was seldom much of a gap between the application screening and the pianist's actual ability. If someone had, from a young age, distinguished themself through diligent practice, and had been taught by a renowned teacher, they would rise to fame. The truth was that if someone couldn't handle that type of life, then they would never become a noted pianist. It was impossible that some unknown would show up out of nowhere and become a star. Occasionally some prize pupil of a doyen of the music scene would appear, but their pampered grooming only made it harder for them to fly the nest. A concert pianist had to have nerves of steel. The pressures of numerous competitions demanded enormous physical and mental strength, and without those qualities no one could survive the gruelling tours of a professional concert pianist.

But still scores of young hopefuls showed up at the piano, and there seemed to be no end to them.

Having a good technique was the minimum requirement. Even then, there was no guarantee you could become a true musician. Even for those who turned professional, that didn't mean their career would last. How many countless hours had they spent labouring over the keys at the mouth of that terrifying black monster, forgoing the pleasures of childhood, shouldering all the hopes and expectations of their parents? Dreaming, all of them, that one day they would be showered with thunderous applause.

'Your profession and mine have a good deal in common.'

Mieko remembered Mayumi's words.

Mayumi Ikai was a friend from high school who had become a popular mystery writer. Having grown up mainly abroad, Mieko had spent only four years of her childhood in Japan, and Mayumi was one of her very few friends there. Because of her father's career as a diplomat, Mieko had gone back and forth between Europe and South America, and so didn't fit in well in Japan, where homogeneity was prized above all. The only close friendships she'd made were with other loners like Mayumi. Even now they still met up for a drink every once in a while, and Mayumi would make a comparison between the literary and classical-music worlds.

'They're so alike, aren't they?' she said on one occasion. 'You have far too many piano competitions, and there are way too many literary awards for new writers. You see the same people applying for piano competitions all over, to gain prestige, and the same holds true for all these literary prizes. In both fields, only a handful of individuals are ever able to carve out a living. There are tons of writers who want people to read their books, tons of pianists who want people to listen to them, but both fields are in decline, the number of readers and concert-goers gradually shrinking.'

Mieko gave a forced smile. Throughout the world, fans of classical music were indeed ageing, and the profession's daunting task was to somehow lure in younger audiences.

Mayumi went on.

'There's all that banging away at a keyboard too, and the fact that, on the surface, both seem quite elegant professions. All anyone else sees is the final product, the polished pianist on stage, but in order to get there, we have to spend countless hours quietly hidden away.'

'True enough,' Mieko agreed. 'We both spend hours banging away at our respective keyboards.'

'For all that,' Mayumi said, 'both professions have to constantly expand their horizons and bring in a steady flow of new blood, or else you'd run out of leaders. The pie itself would shrink as well. That's why everyone's always searching for that new face.'

'But the cost is different,' Mieko countered. 'You don't need capital to write novels, but do you know how much we musicians have invested?'

Mayumi was sympathetic. She nodded and started ticking them off on her fingers.

'You have the cost of an instrument, music scores, lessons,' she said. 'Expenses for recitals, flowers, clothes. Travel expenses, if you study abroad. And – what else?'

'In some cases you have to pay rental fees for the concert hall, and expenses for the staff. If you put out a CD, sometimes you need to pay the costs for that. Then there's the cost of flyers and advertising.'

'Not a business for poor people.' Mayumi shuddered and Mieko grinned.

'But there's one important part, isn't there, where you have it better than us writers,' Mayumi said. 'Music is understood wherever you go in the world. There's no language barrier. Everyone can share the same emotions. We writers have a language barrier, and I'm so envious of musicians for that universality of language and emotion.'

'You're right,' Mieko said and shrugged. It wasn't something you could explain in words. So seldom did the investment of time and money pay off, yet once you experienced that *special moment* you felt a kind of joy that erased all the struggles you'd made to get there.

Every single one of us is seeking the same thing – craving, thirsting after that magical moment.

There were five dossiers left.

Five more pianists.

Mieko had begun to consider who among the competitors she was going to allow through. Based on what she'd heard, there was only one she felt comfortable passing. And there was one other who, if the other judges recommended them, might also pass. No one else was at the level she was looking for.

What always threw her at this point was the question of the order of the competitors. At first, she might think a pianist had done a good job, but was that really true? If she heard the same performance a second time, would she still feel the same? In auditions and competitions, order was destiny, and had a profound influence, and while she tried to make a clear distinction between order and ability, it still bothered her.

There had been two Japanese competitors so far, both studying at the Conservatoire here in Paris, and both of them had excellent technique. One of them she wouldn't mind passing if the other two judges were of the same mind, but unfortunately the other performer didn't impress her. When the technical level was this high, what you were left with to make a distinction between the competitors was a certain ineffable *something* that tugged at you, that grabbed you, in their playing. Pianists with outstanding technique or an obvious, appealing individuality were one thing, but there was a fine line separating those who passed from those who didn't. Competitors you wondered about, those that caused a bit of a stir, that you couldn't take your eyes off. When she was wavering, she'd rely on these inexpressible, vague feelings. Mieko's criteria came down to this: did she want to hear this pianist again, or not?

As she opened the next folder, the name caught her eye.

Jin Kazama.

Mieko made it a rule not to learn much background info about any of the contestants before the competition.

But she couldn't help examining this dossier closely.

The documents were in French, so she had no idea which characters would be used to write his name, but he did appear to be Japanese. The accompanying photograph showed a young man who looked both refined and a bit wild. He was sixteen.

What caught her attention was that the CV was mostly blank. No academic background, no experience in competitions. Nothing. He'd gone to elementary school in Japan but had then moved to France. That's all that could be gleaned from the CV.

It wasn't so very unusual that he hadn't attended a college of music. In the music world, where child prodigies were a dime a dozen, many who debuted as children didn't go to music college; in fact there were many cases where they only attended as adults, in order to get more of a background in music theory that would enrich their performance. Mieko herself had followed the latter pattern, coming first and second in two international competitions while in her teens – she was seen as a budding girl genius – and attending college later on.

But according to this CV, there was no evidence that Jin Kazama had ever performed anywhere. All it said was that at present he was special auditor at the Conservatoire National Supérieur de Musique et de Danse in Paris. *Special auditor, or 'listener'?* Was there really a such a thing?

Mieko racked her brain as she considered this. The boy had actually passed the written-application stage, and would be taking an audition at the Conservatoire. She found it hard to believe this was made up.

But when she glanced at the bottom of the document, in the column showing whom he'd studied under, she could understand why, despite this joke of a CV, he'd passed.

Her whole body turned suddenly hot.

It can't be true, she thought, shaking her head.

Right at the start she'd seen that bit of the CV, but must have deliberately pretended not to notice.

Has studied under Yuji Von Hoffmann since the age of five.

Her heart began to pound – she could feel the blood racing through her veins.

Mieko couldn't figure out why it had shaken her so much, and that shook her all the more.

That one simple sentence was so very important, and she could well understand why the dossier hadn't been rejected at the initial screening of written applications. Yet he had no performance experience at all, and wasn't at a music school. The boy was neither fish nor fowl, as far as she could see.

Mieko was dying to talk to the other two judges, but managed to suppress the urge. While she normally ignored any background information on the pianists, Simon was the type who always gave it a quick once-over, and Smirnoff made it a rule to glean as much information as possible, so they must have noticed this. To add to the surprise, there was a stamp on the application form indicating that a letter of recommendation was attached.

A letter of recommendation from Yuji Von Hoffmann! Her fellow judges must have been blown away by this.

Come to think of it, at dinner last night Simon seemed to be itching to tell them something. They had a self-imposed rule never to discuss the competitors. She could still picture his expression as he held back what he was clearly dying to say.

Simon had, at the time, spoken of Yuji Von Hoffmann, who had quietly passed away in February. His name was legendary – highly respected by musicians and music lovers around the world – but at his request he'd been given a private funeral with only close relatives in attendance.

But it didn't end there, for two months later, to mark his passing, international musicians held a huge memorial service. Mieko had a recital and wasn't able to attend, though she saw it all on video later on.

Hoffmann had not left a will. This was very like him, since he wasn't the type to become attached to anything, but at the memorial service the place was buzzing because of the final words Hoffmann was reported to have said to an acquaintance of his.

I set a bomb to go off.

A bomb? Mieko asked. Hoffmann was always seen as a mysterious figure, looming large in the world of music, but in reality he had quite an irreverent and mischievous streak. Even so, Mieko couldn't fathom what he'd meant by these words.

After I've gone, it will explode. A beautiful bomb for the world.

Hoffmann's relatives had asked him to clarify what he meant, but he had merely beamed and said nothing more.

Mieko stared impatiently at the almost blank documents.

Simon and Smirnoff must both have read Hoffmann's recommendation letter. What could he have written?

She was so worked up it took her a moment to notice the commotion.

She looked up and saw that the stage was empty. Staff members were moving around, tidying up.

So Jin Kazama wasn't going to turn up after all?

That had to be it – something was wrong with his dossier. And with the letter of recommendation. Just before he died, Hoffmann must have been quite weak. And it was in this debilitated state that he had written a letter.

A staff member in the wings called out:

'We just received a call from the next competitor that it is taking some time to get here and that he will be late. He will perform last today, and the other pianists will be moved up in order.'

The audience fell silent as the next pianist, a young girl in a red dress, made her way on to the stage, obviously discombobulated at the sudden change, her eyes panicky.

Gosh.

Mieko was disappointed. But at the same time, relieved.

Jin Kazama. What kind of performance would he give?

'Hurry up!'

The boy had finally arrived at the audition office, where an official had torn his entrance ticket, and then he had rushed in towards the stage.

'I, um, would like to wash my hands.'

The boy asked a staff member, who looked ready to grab him by the scruff of the neck and hurl him straight on to the stage.

Instead he said, 'Well, fine, but hurry up, OK? You need to change, don't you? The dressing rooms are over there.'

'Change?' the boy asked, looking blank. 'You mean I have to change my clothes?'

The man gave the boy a once-over.

Not by any stretch of the imagination was he wearing anything fit for the stage, he made clear. Was he really planning to go on dressed like this? Competitors usually wore something formal, and if not that, then at least a decent jacket.

The boy looked chastened.

'I'm sorry – I was helping my father with his work and came as I am. Anyway, I'll go and wash my hands.'

He spread his hands wide, and the staff member did a double take. There was dirt stuck to the large palms, as if the boy had been digging in a garden.

'What are you—?' he began, but the boy had already raced off to the toilets, and had disappeared from sight.

The man stood staring at the toilet door.

Had the boy mistaken this hall for somewhere else? He'd never seen anyone about to play in an audition with muddy hands.

He glanced down at the entrance ticket, thinking it might have been for some other kind of certification exam. But there was no mistake. And the boy matched his photo in the application papers.

The man tilted his head in wonder.

WHEN THEY SAW THE BOY appear on stage, Mieko and her fellow judges were taken aback.

He's just a child.

That was the word that sprang to mind.

He seemed totally out of place, partly because of his unkempt hair and his casual outfit, a T-shirt and cotton trousers, but also because of the way he gazed so intently around the stage. There were young musicians who deliberately adopted a punk look as if to provoke the austere world of classical music, but this young man in front of her wasn't that type. He appeared entirely natural, and spontaneous.

He was a lovely boy. And it was a loveliness entirely unaware of its own appeal, without any hint of self-consciousness. And his lithe young figure, sure to grow even taller, was also quite beautiful.

The boy stood there, looking vacant.

Mieko caught the eye of the other judges – they were at a loss for words.

'You're the last to play. Please begin,' Smirnoff said impatiently into the microphone.

They had a mic set up to address the performers, but Mieko realized this was the first time today anyone had actually used it.

The boy stood up straight.

'I'm very sorry for being so late.' His voice was more confident and more charming than you would have expected.

Dipping his head apologetically, he turned to face the grand piano. It was as if he'd only just noticed it.

An odd buzz rippled through the hall, like an electric shock.

Mieko felt it and noticed that her fellow judges had felt it too.

The young man's eyes seemed to sparkle.

He reached out a hand and walked over to the piano. Almost as if he were approaching a girl he'd fallen in love with at first sight.

He settled himself gracefully down on the stool in front of the piano.

The boy's eyes looked joyful. Certainly transformed from a moment ago, when he had been standing there looking so lost.

Mieko felt as if she were witnessing something she shouldn't see. A chill ran up her spine.

What am I so afraid of? she asked herself.

And that fear intensified the instant the boy's fingers touched the first few keys.

Mieko's hair stood on end. The two judges beside her, the staff in the wings, indeed everyone in the concert hall, shared the same fear.

The atmosphere had been slack, and lax, but with those first notes there was a dramatic awakening.

The sound was . . . different. Totally different.

Mieko didn't even notice that the Mozart piece he'd started playing was the same one she'd heard all too many times already that day. The same piano, the same score, and yet—

Naturally she'd had this kind of experience before on numerous occasions. Where an outstanding pianist could play the same instrument as other pianists and yet produce a sound no one else could.

True enough, but this young man—

This sound was fierce, frightening.

Both confused and deeply moved, Mieko greedily took in the tone and timbre of the young man's playing, unconsciously leaning forward so as not to miss a thing. Out of the corner of her eye she saw that Simon's fingers had suddenly stopped twitching.

The stage looked bright.

The spot where the young man was communing with the piano (that was the only way to put it) shone softly, colours seeming to undulate, to flow out from beneath his fingers.

When anyone plays Mozart's refined music, they try hard to raise themselves to that degree of elegance, opening their eyes wide in an attempt to express purity and innocence.

But this young man had no need to put on any sort of show. He simply drew out its essence, staying relaxed, completely natural.

There was both an abundance in his playing, and also a hint at untapped reserves. You could tell this wasn't his absolute best.

Before Mieko knew it, he was on to Beethoven.

The brilliant colour of the piece was transformed into something else, its drive and intent ebbing and flowing.

She couldn't quite express it, but it was as if that unique vector found in Beethoven shot out like an arrow from the boy's very fingers, the sound filling the concert hall.

And now he was playing Bach.

What is this? Mieko thought.

The boy had seamlessly woven together the three pieces,

without a pause. As if unable to hold back the torrent once released, moving on to the next piece as naturally as taking a breath.

The young man controlled the entire hall, the audience giving themselves over to the notes pouring over them.

A powerful sound, Mieko thought vaguely.

Who would ever have imagined that this piano – muttering woefully until now – could emit such an astonishing sound?

The boy's large hands danced over the keys, easy and relaxed.

The music of Bach seemed like some sublime edifice looming over them.

Those fearfully elaborate, meticulous patterns, the layering of melodic lines making up an architecturally perfect whole, had closed in on them all.

He's almost devilish, Mieko thought.

Terrifying. Horrifying.

Mieko was truly shaken, but gradually she acknowledged something else rising up inside her – fury.

THE BOY GAVE A QUICK little bow of thanks before vanishing into the wings, and an eerie silence fell on the hall.

After a moment everyone came back to themselves. They burst into applause, their faces flushed.

The stage was now empty.

The audience exchanged glances. Had it all been a dream?

Smirnoff sat up and yelled, 'Hey, call him back! I have a few things I want to ask him.'

'I just don't believe it.' Simon fell back in his seat.

The concert hall was in uproar.

'Come on! Bring him back!' Smirnoff bellowed.

There was confusion backstage, then someone appeared. 'He's gone. He left as soon as he got offstage.'

'What?!' Smirnoff tore at his hair.

'Hoffmann's letter of recommendation was spot on,' Simon said before turning to Mieko. 'You didn't read it, did you, Mieko? I was dying to tell you about it, but couldn't because of what we'd agreed.'

'This is *unforgivable,*' Mieko said.

'What?' Simon blinked at her.

'I will not accept this. *At all.*'

Mieko glared back at Simon.

He blinked again.

'Mieko?'

Trembling, Mieko placed her palms on the table.

'I will not allow it. That boy is an insult to Maestro Hoffmann. I will not pass him.'

Nocturne

I present to you all Jin Kazama.

He is a gift. *There are no other words to express it.*

A gift from on high.

But please don't misunderstand me.

He's not the one being tested. I *am, and so are all of* you.

He is not simply a sweet gift of divine grace.

He is also a powerful drug.

There will be some who hate him, who are exasperated by him and who reject him. But that's the truth of who he is.

It's up to all of you – all of us *– whether we see this boy as a true* gift, *or as a* disaster waiting to happen.

Yuji Von Hoffmann

'I swear, what a shock,' said Simon. 'You responded just as Hoffmann said you would, Mieko. And it wouldn't surprise me if those Moscow cynics have reacted in the same way.'

Mieko was sitting beside him, wine glass in hand, sulking.

Smirnoff was sipping silently from his glass, staring fixedly at Hoffmann's letter lying on the table.

The night was still young. Pedestrians were strolling past, and cars were streaming by in a blur of red tail lights.

The three music judges were camped out at the back of a bistro on the outskirts of Paris.

The owner remembered this trio, how they would drop in a few times a year to drink and grouse for hours at a time, and had ushered them to this table at the rear.

The meal seemed almost over, or perhaps they didn't have much of an appetite, for there were only a few dishes on the table, though they'd already consumed two bottles of wine.

Mieko's sulkiness was, in part, a way of hiding her embarrassment.

And the source of this discomfort was there, right before her eyes.

That flowing handwriting she'd seen before.

Simon and Smirnoff had been exchanging troubled looks, and at first Mieko had found this odd. In her frustration, she'd told Simon to *give me that letter*, and snatched it out of his hand. Now it silenced her.

Shock. Confusion. Shame. Humiliation.

A jumble of emotions swirled around in her.

The other two looked on sympathetically, hiding their smiles.

Hoffmann, who'd departed this world several months before, had, in his letter, neatly predicted the kind of reaction Mieko would have to Jin Kazama's audition.

So should Hoffmann be praised for his prescience? Or should Mieko be branded immature for reacting so violently, just as he'd known she would? Both, probably. For her part, Mieko inwardly berated herself for being so predictable.

She could picture Hoffmann looking down at her now and saying, *What did I tell you?*

THE WHOLE THING WAS, TO be honest, a complete shock.

Since she was little, people had labelled her wild and

unsophisticated. She was more often than not treated as a problem child. Certainly, she was no star pupil.

So how could I be rejecting this young country bumpkin's musicality? she asked herself. *Before he'd even begun – and after the way all those music professors in Japan and Europe back in the day had called* me *uncouth and uninhibited?*

She felt a sudden chill.

Am I starting to be one of those stubborn, thick-headed people myself? As I've got older, have I turned into a grumpy old woman, and just haven't noticed? I never thought that could happen, but have I – God forbid – become part of the establishment*?*

She started to knock back the wine more quickly.

'OK, so what are you so upset about, Mieko?'

Simon had been teasing her up until then with playfully barbed comments, but now he'd turned serious.

'Sorry?'

'I've never seen you react that way before. It's not how you usually are when you're angry. Usually, you become all sly or – maybe I shouldn't say this – a bit stand-offish. So why reject him like that?'

It did, certainly, feel strange to her now. She no longer felt angry about the boy, and even found it hard to actually recall the performance that had so infuriated her.

What was it that irritated me so much?

'Are you telling me you didn't feel anything yourself?' she asked. 'That kind of horrific – painful – sense of being slapped in the face?'

Simon cocked his head.

'No,' he said. 'I felt a chill, and a sense of elation, and I thought, *Wow, the way this boy can play is insane.*'

'That's what I mean,' Mieko said, nodding. 'There's a fine line separating that from disgust. Isn't it the case that you can feel something but can't decide if it feels good or not?'

'Well, admittedly pleasure and revulsion are two sides of the same coin.'

Auditions had a unique feel about them. Even if you

recorded them, you could never reproduce what you'd felt in the moment.

There's no need for you to go through an audition.

A voice she'd heard somewhere suddenly flashed through Mieko's mind. A gentle voice, with a hint of a smile, yet still stern.

Maestro Hoffmann's voice.

She felt a dull ache inside her, as a long-forgotten feeling was triggered.

Ah, Mieko murmured to herself. *I get it now.*

Maybe I was just jealous.

That one line in his CV might have triggered it.

Has studied under Yuji Von Hoffmann since the age of five.

Just that single line, a line she'd always wanted to have in her own CV.

'I wonder – was he really any good?' Simon muttered, and the three of them glanced at each other.

Mieko knew how he felt.

'It happens sometimes. Everyone gets so worked up, but then they realize it was a passing thing.'

'Well, we're only human,' Simon said.

It happens sometimes – you listen to a pianist and think, *Wow, this person is really promising*, but then you hear them again and are disappointed.

'The problem lies elsewhere,' Smirnoff said.

'Problem?' Mieko and Simon asked simultaneously.

'It's becoming clear to me what Hoffmann meant by a *drug*.'

Smirnoff's expression was solemn, ominous. He leaned forward and the bistro chair gave a threatening creak.

'Meaning?' Simon's right eyebrow shot up.

'We're faced with a terrible dilemma.'

Smirnoff casually drained the wine in his glass as if it were water. He was known for being able to hold his drink, and maybe it did seem like water to him. Furthermore, whenever he was mulling over something, he seemed to speed up and begin to look more alert.

'Dilemma?' Mieko murmured as she gazed uneasily at his now sober-looking face.

Mieko may have been outraged, but after Jin Kazama left the building, the staff were buzzing.

The competition had not even begun, yet they were already talking about how a new star might have emerged. The way he appeared, as the final pianist, before vanishing immediately afterwards, certainly played a part. He left behind a hall filled with excitement. The staff member who had engaged with him explained what had happened.

'His hands were all muddy, and he said he was late because he was helping his father with his work. He didn't go into the green room, but just went to the toilets to wash his hands before going straight on stage.'

'So what does his father actually do?' Smirnoff asked, irritated that the competition office had so little information on the boy, apart from the CV.

Normally the judges would decide swiftly who had passed the auditions, but today they were holed up in a separate room, reviewing the results, and had yet to emerge. From time to time the staff outside would hear loud voices arguing, and exchange curious looks with each other. The whole thing was completely unprecedented.

The reason for the lengthy discussion was obvious: Mieko was dead set against passing Jin Kazama.

The three judges were basically in agreement about who else they would pass, so they spent most if not all of their time debating Jin's merits.

Simon and Smirnoff had both given him almost the highest mark possible in their system of scoring, so even if Mieko gave him a zero, Jin would have just scraped through. They could have ignored her views, and simply passed him, but neither Simon nor Smirnoff wanted to go down that route, and so their discussions dragged on endlessly.

Mieko knew perfectly well that Jin had effectively passed,

yet she argued on, trying to get the others to reverse their decision.

The gist of her argument was this:

If he hadn't been Hoffmann's pupil, she wouldn't have put up a fight. But as he had presented himself as Hoffmann's protégé, and had got an actual letter of recommendation, she would not accept his foolish style of playing, which flew in the face of Hoffmann's own musicianship. It was as if the boy were purposely defying his teacher, deliberately picking a quarrel with him. That was a questionable stance for a musician to take. She could understand it if, after establishing himself as a musician, he decided to adopt a different style, but at this stage not to acknowledge what his teacher stood for was a major issue.

Simon and Smirnoff each indicated that they understood Mieko's position and took turns arguing her down.

'You do admit he has extraordinary technical skills and impact, don't you? If so, then whether you approve of his playing or not is outside our purview. If he exceeds a certain minimum level, then we must give him a chance. Whether we like the candidate's style of performance or not is, at this juncture, irrelevant.'

'In the first place, wouldn't you say it's quite astonishing that he's caused so much debate? The fact that he can inspire such diverse reactions is proof there's *something* about him worth considering. Aren't you the one always saying, Mieko, that if you have multiple judges, you end up choosing bland performers and how that's so uninspiring? Maybe it's just a fluke, but the fact is that he does provoke a strong emotional response, and shouldn't we give that due consideration? To say nothing of the fact that his technique is superb.'

There were no holes in the two men's arguments, and Mieko, feeling outnumbered, fell silent.

What they said next clinched it for her.

'Wouldn't you like to hear him again? Don't you want to make sure that it wasn't just an accident, a one-off?'

'Wouldn't you like the judges in Moscow and New York to hear him? Won't it be fun to see how he raises a few eyebrows?'

The two of them knew which of Mieko's buttons to press. Auditions were taking place simultaneously in several cities, and the judges in charge of each had subtly different approaches. It wasn't as if they were in open disagreement, but Mieko and her two colleagues had dubbed the judges in Moscow and New York *The Authorities* and *The Sensible Ones* respectively (ironic nicknames, to be sure).

Mieko pictured those esteemed judges listening to Jin Kazama and reacting with disgust, then crowding around Mieko and her colleagues, hysterically shouting, *How in the world could you pass such a vulgar performance?*

Forgetting that she had reacted in the same way, the fact was that Mieko found this scenario very appealing. And this alone led her, albeit reluctantly, to agree to pass Jin Kazama.

OK, then – time to notify the successful candidates.

Before she could even nod in assent, Simon and Smirnoff simultaneously rose to their feet and left the room.

Mieko was left feeling a bit stunned. *They fooled me, sweet-talked me into it,* she mused. But by then it was too late.

PERHAPS IT WAS SMIRNOFF, THOUGH, who felt most keenly that the damage was done.

As the waiter refilled her glass from their third bottle of wine, Mieko gazed at her fellow judge.

'I bet he hasn't been having regular music lessons,' Smirnoff muttered. 'The way he behaved on stage, the fact that he ran the three pieces together without a pause – I'll bet he's never played to an audience before. Hoffmann was aware of this, which is why he sent a letter of recommendation. To ensure he attended the audition, and passed.'

'Well, that goes without saying,' Mieko said.

Smirnoff gave an exaggerated shrug.

'Hey, don't pretend you don't understand, you two. You know very well what I'm trying to say.' He gulped down his wine. 'It's as you said earlier, Mieko. We can't very well deny Maestro

Hoffmann's musical legacy. We all respected him so much, he was an astonishing musician. Plus there's the fact that he's no longer with us.'

Smirnoff looked quite stern now. 'We went ahead and passed the boy. You saw how the staff adored him, didn't you? Rumours were rife. About Hoffmann's letter, too, of course.'

Mieko shivered.

'So why include a letter in the first place? To make it almost impossible for us to fail him.' Smirnoff gave an odd smile as he looked at the others.

Simon took over.

'In other words, it's OK to fail someone without a letter of recommendation.'

Smirnoff nodded, looking satisfied.

'Exactly. Because all of us are eking out a living after an established musical education. Having students pay for private lessons all their lives, getting them into music conservatories and making them pay yet more tuition fees. Our pupils, our pride and joy, spend so much time and effort to become great, and so we can't very well treat someone who comes out of nowhere, with no pedigree – someone whom no one ever made a living teaching – in the same way. Hence the letter of recommendation.'

Mieko suddenly recalled a bit of gossip she'd heard.

A local city council in Japan had sponsored a piano competition, and one competitor who seemed like a real musical genius had got the highest marks, yet he had no connections in the musical world in Japan, and had never taken lessons with anyone connected with the competition, let alone with any of the judges. Despite the high marks, the judges ended up picking on some minor issues and disqualifying him.

'Hoffmann's letter had a double goal. The first was to allow this complete unknown to be in the audition, and pass. And the second goal . . .' for an instant Smirnoff's eyes had a far-away look in them '. . . was to ensure that hereafter he would never be ignored. That's why the letter was an absolute must. And dismissing this boy would be tantamount to rejecting the Maestro himself. But there's something even more frightening at work here.'

Simon shot the other two a serious look. 'The fact that this boy has superior technique, and that those who hear him are instantly entranced. Even though he's never been formally trained in a music college.'

Mieko and Smirnoff listened in silence.

Did we commit some egregious error? Mieko thought.

She felt an unseen force at work, and it made her uneasy.

Smirnoff's cell phone rang.

Mieko and Simon both jumped in surprise.

'Excuse me.' Smirnoff reached for his phone. In his massive hands it looked tiny, like a chocolate finger.

'Um – yeah. I see. Is that right.'

Smirnoff murmured into the phone, and hung up.

Mieko and Simon looked at him questioningly.

'It's from the office. They've finally been able to contact Jin Kazama.'

'It took all this time?'

Simon glanced at his watch. It was nearing midnight.

'His father is apparently a beekeeper. He has a doctorate in biology as well, and they said he's researching beekeeping in cities. Today he was at the Hôtel de Ville here in Paris, collecting honeybees.'

'A beekeeper . . .'

Mieko and Simon slowly repeated the word, as if hearing it for the very first time.

'Talk about a different field,' Simon said with a wry smile.

It's up to all of you – all of us *– whether we see this boy as a true* gift, *or as a* disaster waiting to happen.

There was no mistaking it – all three of them could hear Hoffmann's voice ringing in their ears.

Tremolo

THE RAIN GREW LOUDER. Aya Eiden glanced up from her book.

It was daytime, yet outside it was pitch-black, the torrential rain draining the woods of all colour.

I can hear it – horses in the rain.

This was a rhythm she'd heard over and over since she was a child, but when she'd tried to describe it to adults as *horses galloping in the rain*, they'd responded with blank stares.

Now, though, she'd be able to explain it better.

The shed behind their house had a tin roof.

When it rained normally, she didn't hear anything unusual. But when there was a real downpour, she always heard a strange type of music.

A galloping rhythm.

When she was a child, she'd played the Burgmüller piece 'La Chevaleresque', which included such a rhythm, and the rain on the tin roof drummed to the very same beat.

Recently, a video had appeared on YouTube of a fire alarm going off and a band playing in time to its beat. The video caused quite a buzz.

Aya let out a low sigh.

The world's full of so much music.

This sober thought welled up in her as she gazed out at the colourless scenery, distorted by the rain.

Do I really need to add to it myself?

Aya glanced down at the papers on her desk.

'A typical case of burnout.'

'Now she's twenty, she's just an ordinary person like everyone else.'

She was tired of hearing those nasty comments made behind her back.

Every year countless piano talents, boys and girls, appeared on the scene all over the world. They'd play with an orchestra, be extolled as child prodigies, their parents hoping for a golden future for their son or daughter.

But not every one of them would make it. As they reached puberty, some agonized over how warped their world was, drifting back to normal life to spend their youth with others their own age. Others, meanwhile, would get sick of the never-ending piano lessons, upset at their lack of progress, and simply disappear from the scene.

Aya was one of them. She'd won numerous junior competitions both in Japan and abroad, even released a debut CD.

But in Aya's case it was quite clear why her career had been cut short.

When she was thirteen her mother, her first teacher, the person who protected her, who encouraged her, who took care of her, suddenly passed away.

If Aya had been a little bit older, things might have turned out differently. If she'd reached that rebellious stage of teenagers – say, at least fourteen or fifteen – and had started to feel her mother was stifling her, her mother's death might have had a very different impact.

But at the time she loved her deeply, and played the piano to make her mother happy, so when she suddenly vanished from Aya's life, her sense of loss was overwhelming. She literally lost the reason for playing.

Aya was a laid-back person, with little ambition. That said, she wasn't exactly calm in front of a crowd, and confronted by others' competitiveness or jealousy, she timidly shrank back into herself. And so her mother protected her, skilfully working to motivate her big-hearted daughter, guiding her each step of the way – sometimes as her teacher, sometimes as a shrewd and clever manager.

Her concert schedule was fixed for the next year and a half, and so when her mother died a person from the record company hastily stepped in to act as manager.

When her mother was still alive, Aya's grandmother had

handled all the housework, which allowed Aya not to worry about anything domestic, and it took a while for her to fully grasp what it meant that her mother was gone.

The first time she was really aware of her mother's absence was in the dressing room in a provincial concert hall.

The new manager had set her up with a stylist, who advised on her dress for the performance, did her hair and gave her a light touch of make-up. These were things her mother had always done for her. Her work finished, the stylist left the dressing room for her next job.

'Mum,' Aya remembered saying, 'is the tea ready?'

It was then that she realized how alone she was.

Her mother had always given her a cup of sweet, lukewarm tea from a thermos.

Aya was shaken, assailed by a profound sense of loss, as if the floor was giving way.

She actually felt the ceiling moving away from her, along with a strange sensation, warm and tingling, of the blood draining away from her body.

I am all by myself.

This was the moment she fully understood.

Suddenly she was brought back to herself.

What is this place? What am I doing here?

Her eyes flitted restlessly around the room.

White walls. A round clock above the mirror. A dressing room. *It's a dressing room. In some concert hall. I'm about to give a concert.*

That's right – I've just rehearsed with the orchestra. Prokofiev's Piano Concerto No. 2. It went as planned.

I remember how the conductor and members of the orchestra were so impressed. Some were whispering to each other:

'What a relief. I was so worried about her, but she can make it on her own after all.'

'She's pretty amazing. I thought it'd be a bigger shock for her, but she was very calm.'

'Guess the only way to get over it is to perform.'

What did that mean?

She felt a chill in her heart.

The numbing reality of it all overwhelmed her again.

I am all alone now.

The stage manager then came to fetch her and even as she and the conductor headed towards the stage, those words spun round and round in her head.

Aya's heart remained frozen as expectant applause rang out.

All she could see was the grand piano, silently bathed in light.

And she knew.

In the audience, in the wings of the stage, her mother was not there.

The grand piano on the stage used to glisten, waiting, as if bursting with the flood of music that she would now set free.

Quick, she would think. *I have to sit down and release the music.*

She imagined it was all contained in that great black box and always had to suppress the urge to rush to the keys.

Not any more.

Now the piano was like an abandoned grave. An empty black box that had surrendered itself to silence.

There was no longer any music inside it.

This cold certainty became a heavy mass, and in that moment, when she felt it drop with a thud inside her, she turned on her heels and ran.

She briefly glimpsed the shocked faces of the orchestra and the stage manager, but she never looked back. She stepped down from the stage – briskly, then at a trot.

She didn't hear the worried buzz from the crowd, the shouts.

She simply ran.

She pushed open the rear door of the hall, and raced outside into the dark drizzle.

This was how she became the *Genius Girl Pianist Who Vanished*.

That last-minute cancellation of the concert became legendary. Especially since the orchestra reported that the rehearsal had been perfect – in fact even more wonderful than when her mother had been around.

But there were many repercussions that weren't just being sued for damages for breach of contract or complaints aimed at her new manager from the record company. Unless the pianist was some major figure in the music world, they would never be invited to play a concert again. After all, there were plenty of other *geniuses* to go around.

For a while, her name even became a kind of facetious term of ridicule among students in piano departments. 'Do an *Eiden*,' was how they put it. It meant cancelling at the last minute, and the characters used to write her last name – *ei* (glory) and *den* (to convey) – became objects of scorn. Playing on the original meaning of her unusual last name, 'conveying glory', they substituted the character *dan* (to cut off), coming up with 'Ei*dan*' to give the idea of a pianist cutting herself off from all chance of glory.

Surprisingly, though, none of this discouraged Aya.

She knew it made perfect sense for her to suddenly walk out.

If there was no longer any music inside the piano to be released, what was the point of being on stage?

She was absolutely fine about being ridiculed, or ignored, and in fact preferred it to being in the limelight or the object of envy.

Ever since she'd walked out, her followers had begun to vanish one by one, like a receding tide.

Actually, Aya preferred it this way, relieved not to have these hangers-on around her.

From the moment Aya accepted that her mother was gone, she began to live a whole new life. She transferred to a general education curriculum at high school. Most pupils who played the piano and excelled at it tended to have good grades. Aya's grades, too, placed her top of her class. She entered a local high school that aimed at getting its students into university, and thoroughly enjoyed an 'ordinary' high-school life.

This didn't mean she'd dropped music completely. She still loved listening to it and continued playing.

Aya differed from many who were regarded as *geniuses*.

She definitely did have an abundance of musical talent.

There were two people who understood this and knew that in Aya's case it might actually pull her away from the piano: her mother – and one other person.

From the beginning, Aya didn't necessarily need the piano.

Since childhood, when she first heard the sound of horses galloping in the rain as it lashed on the tin roof, she could hear – and enjoy – music from many different sources.

The only reason she used the piano to express music was that her mother had happened to start her on it, and Aya turned out to be gifted, with outstanding technique. But it might well have been some other instrument or means of expression, rather than the piano. It didn't have to be music she herself was performing, since the world was overflowing with performers. In that sense, too, she was a genuine *genius*. All of which explained why her mother had had to supervise her so strictly, making sure to keep her focused so she didn't lose interest.

Was losing her supervisor a good thing for her, or not? Aya no longer knew.

When her mother was still alive, there was just one other person she opened up to, and with whom she shared her concerns about her daughter's talent.

And just around the time Aya was thinking about university, he came to see her.

He and her mother used to be classmates at music college, and with the anniversary of her death approaching, he asked Aya if she would play something for him.

Aya hadn't performed for anyone since the day she'd fled the concert. She'd played an electronic keyboard in both a rock group and a fusion band, but had studiously avoided performing any serious piano pieces in front of anyone. And of course it helped that people now kept their distance.

So, normally she would have turned the man's request down.

But on seeing Mr Hamazaki, for that was his name, Aya felt strangely nostalgic.

The man was stocky and plump, like one of those oversized ceramic raccoon ornaments. Behind his glasses, his eyes were narrow but gentle, reminding her of a high-school principal in a popular TV drama from a few years ago.

Above all, the way he spoke was so relaxed and laid-back, as if he was just asking a casual favour – like saying he'd give her a tip if she'd pick up some ice cream at the corner shop for him – that Aya readily agreed.

'Which piece would you like to hear?' she asked.

'Any piece you like, Aya. Or one that your mother particularly liked.'

Aya thought it over.

'Is it OK to play a recent piece?'

'Of course,' Mr Hamazaki replied.

After her mother passed away, and Aya stopped performing, the whole feel of her piano room seemed transformed.

It was full of CDs and books, stuffed toys and potted plants. It had now become Aya's second living room.

Hamazaki began to look around.

'Sorry it's such a mess,' Aya apologized.

'Not at all,' Hamazaki said, shaking his head. 'It's nice. It's like you and the piano have become one.'

'I suppose so,' Aya said, laughing, as she heaved open the piano lid.

She felt excited, just a smidgen. She'd forgotten how that felt.

It had been so very long since she'd played for anyone.

She dived straight into her piece – a Shostakovich sonata.

She'd heard a young Russian pianist play it once, had found the piece intriguing and practised it just for fun. The sheet music was expensive, so instead of buying it she listened to the recording over and over again until she could reproduce it.

Hamazaki looked surprised, but as Aya played on, he straightened up and his expression brightened.

When she'd finished, he clapped loudly.

'Have you played this for any music teacher?' he asked.

'No, I don't have one,' Aya replied with a forced smile. When her mother was alive, she'd been taught by someone well known, but after running away from her final performance, he'd stopped getting in touch, afraid perhaps of being criticized for how he'd instructed her, and perhaps wanting to show that he had nothing more to do with this problem pupil.

'So you prepared it all on your own?' Hamazaki murmured and then seemed at a loss for words.

'It was excellent,' he continued after a pause. 'What were you thinking about as you played?' Putting a hand to his mouth, as if considering something, he gave Aya an earnest look.

'I was seeing watermelons rolling off into the distance,' Aya said.

'Watermelons?'

Aya explained.

'I saw this funny scene in a Korean movie recently,' she said. 'A load of watermelons had fallen off a cart and were rolling down a road in the mountains. Some split open, some didn't. The tarmac turned bright red, but still the watermelons that hadn't split continued rolling down the road. When I heard this piece, that scene came to me. Don't you get that feeling with this music? Of watermelons merrily rolling down a slope? Can't you imagine a scene where you chase after them and grab one? And the bit at the end is a scene where you clean up all the broken watermelons afterwards?'

Hamazaki's eyebrows raised in surprise, and he burst out laughing.

'I see. Watermelons, is it?'

When he'd finally contained his mirth, Hamazaki sat up straight in his chair.

'Miss Eiden, would you consider applying to our university? I would love it if you would.'

'*Our university* – what does that mean?' she asked, and Hamazaki held out his card.

He was the president of one of the top three private music colleges in Japan.

'You love music, don't you? You love it so much and understand it deeply. That's the kind of student I want at our college. I really feel there's a lot you would find interesting. You should study at a proper conservatory. So – what do you say?'

He spoke in a rush, and Aya's eyes widened.

Hamazaki waited patiently for her response.

I WONDER WHAT MADE ME *decide to take the music entrance exam,* Aya later thought.

Until then I'd been thinking of going into science.

But the truth is that Mr Hamazaki's words touched me.

Even if I'm not going to be a concert pianist, I can never be without music.

But music had been just a hobby for me and perhaps I'd been feeling this wasn't enough?

SHE RECALLED CLEARLY HOW THE moment her performance for the examiners was over, the other professors had looked as one at Hamazaki and broken into applause. And how Mr Hamazaki had smiled at her.

This kind of entrance examination was far from the norm, she learned. Allowing an applicant who had no teacher to take it purely on the recommendation of the college president was a highly unusual step and could even have jeopardized his position.

At first her fellow students in the piano department exchanged *Oh – it's her* type of looks, as if trying to remember something disparaging about her, some even making spiteful remarks behind her back.

But as they got to know how unassuming Aya was, and how unrivalled she was in her technique, they began to treat her as just an outstanding classmate.

And Aya thoroughly enjoyed studying what the college had to offer – the rules and methods of composition, and music history.

As Mr Hamazaki had predicted, studying at a conservatory made her appreciate and enjoy music all the more.

But she never expected at this point to be participating in a competition.

Aya gazed out at the rain lashing at the window and let out another deep sigh.

She couldn't remember much about competing at junior level as a child. Back then it had felt more as if she was giving a recital. This would be her first senior-level competition.

Once she's past twenty, she'll be just the same as everybody else – nothing special.

This spring she'd turned twenty – the age of adulthood in Japan. It had been seven years since she'd stopped performing.

Her present mentor – an eccentric professor, with whom she got on well – had recommended she enter the competition, though it was clear that the college president's influence was also behind it.

Of course Aya was feeling a debt of gratitude to Mr Hamazaki.

She knew that if she declined to take part in the competition, it would embarrass him. And that since he'd taken exceptional steps to get her into his college, she needed to prove her worth.

But, Professor, she murmured to herself, *that kind of music isn't in me any more.*

She loved her college life now. She experienced music outside herself, then played the piano in order to relive it. That was enough for her. Through studying theory, and listening to concerts, she got the sense she was probing deeper and deeper into music.

Mum – what should I do?

Aya gazed at the sheets of rain striking the window ever more relentlessly now.

She laid her book on the desk and slumped down on top of it.

The steady hoofbeats of galloping horses echoed in her head.

Lullaby

'If you wouldn't mind walking one more time with your son towards me? OK, you can start now – please come towards me.'

They were outside the gates of a nursery school. Masami raised a hand, and Machiko, a jittery look on her face, started walking awkwardly towards her with her little son, Akihito, holding her hand.

'Just walk normally. As you usually would. Don't think about the camera.'

Akashi couldn't help but smile.

That kind of comment made you even more conscious of it, he thought.

Naturally Masami had done her best to get Machiko to relax, visiting their home several times and having friendly chats. But in reality, having a camera following you brought on a special tension, and today's filming, especially with the other nursery-school mothers standing to one side watching, put even the normally calm and collected Machiko on edge.

'OK – that's a wrap,' Masami said, cheerily waving a hand.

Machiko looked relieved.

'Thank you, Akihito. I'm grateful for your cooperation,' said Masami.

Akihito looked blankly at Akashi as his father picked him up.

'*Co-op-era-shun, grate-full*,' the little boy repeated with a grin.

Masami lowered the video camera and came over to Akashi.

'After this I'll film a little more of you practising,' she said, 'then in the dressing room on the day you perform.'

'Got it.'

'So how's it going? Have you found time to practise?'

When her eye was at the viewfinder of the camera, Masami was a brisk, businesslike TV reporter, but without the camera she immediately reverted to his former high-school classmate.

'Well – work's keeping me pretty busy,' Akashi answered, hesitantly. 'Honestly, I'd love to have the time to just shut myself away for a while and do some final practice.'

Masami chuckled.

'That's so like you, Akashi.'

'Meaning?'

'You're so unassuming. With you it's never *Me, me, me*.'

'That hurts.'

'*What* does?'

'You've hit my weak point as a musician.'

'That's it?'

'Yep.'

Masami saw his unassuming nature as one of his virtues, that was clear. But in the world of piano soloists, you needed an intense ego and strong sense of your own individuality to thrive, not modesty. Akashi was more aware of this than anyone.

'But I love your playing, Akashi-*kun*. I can't put my finger on it exactly, but something about it puts me at ease. There's an indescribable delicacy to it.'

'Delicacy, eh?' Akashi murmured.

Masami looked at him, her forehead wrinkled in a slight frown.

'Is the filming of the other pianists going well?' Akashi flashed a cheery smile.

Masami nodded in relief.

'Yes, everyone's been very cooperative. I'll be filming a Ukrainian and a Russian pianist who are staying with a local family in Yoshigae. That host family always seems to put up some unique pianists, and people think it's like a spell, that whoever stays there will make it to the finals. Rumour has it that the Ukrainian is pretty amazing.'

'Really—'

Pretty amazing. Well, what did you expect? The classical-music world over there had a brilliant history, so anyone they sent over here was bound to be outstanding.

Akashi sighed deeply.

*

Akashi Takashima, aged twenty-eight, was born in the city of Akashi in Hyogo Prefecture, where his father had been transferred, which is how he got his first name.

Akashi was the oldest competitor taking part in the Yoshigae International Piano Competition, right at the age limit. It was usual for piano competitions to have very young entrants, and somebody Akashi's age was treated like an old man.

When Akashi had been asked to be filmed for a documentary, he'd been surprised to learn that the producer was his old high-school classmate Masami Nishina.

It turned out she was the one who'd come up with the idea, and when she heard that Akashi would be participating, she'd asked to be in charge of filming him.

Yoshigae was one of the more prominent industrial cities in Japan, and one of the main reasons Masami's proposal had been so readily accepted was that, with so many sponsors keen to support the competition, it was an easy matter to secure funding.

Akashi's first reaction was to turn it down. 'Me appear on TV? No way. I don't know if I'll even make it to the second round.' At his age, with a job and a child – honestly, he wasn't exactly in a position to be in a competition. The word *disgraceful* even came to mind.

'No, that's perfectly OK,' Masami said. 'What people want from music is drama. Someone like you, with a wife and child, performing in the competition is sure to arouse a lot of empathy.'

Masami hadn't put this into words, exactly, but the documentary also wanted to go beyond a focus on participants from affluent families. Having someone like Akashi, definitely the odd one out, would make the whole programme more appealing.

It was true that Akashi was from an ordinary company employee's family. His wife was his childhood sweetheart, now a high-school physics teacher, while Akashi worked for a large musical-instrument store. Two generations of an ordinary white-collar family.

A regular dad appears in an international competition! In Japan today, where the trend was to want people to focus more on the family, this could be a real selling point.

For all that, what made him finally decide to appear on the TV programme was the thought that it could be a kind of memento.

It was clear that appearing in this competition would mark the finale of his career as a professional musician, and that afterwards he'd live out the rest of his life as an amateur.

But he also wanted to leave behind proof, so that when Akihito grew up, he'd know how his father had, back in the day, shown real musical ambition. That's what clinched it for him. And that's how he explained it to Machiko and Masami, and to his parents.

But none of that is actually relevant, another voice inside him said.

Those are just excuses, this second self pointed out.

What about the anger and doubt that you – unassuming and gentle, a man of such delicacy – have been suppressing deep down inside. Don't you want to spew this all out at this competition?

Exactly, Akashi said.

I've always thought it strange – are top-flight musicians the only ones to have got it right? Are people who live for music alone the only people who deserve praise?

Is the music of someone who has a routine, ordinary life really inferior to that of a person who makes a living from it?

The heavy door was slightly stuck, but then it opened slowly, and light streamed in.

A square of brightness lit up the dirt floor and projected on to it the shadow of Akashi's head.

He remembered this smell so well.

He pictured himself as a little boy, seated at the piano, still too small for his feet to reach the pedals.

It was so many years ago, yet this smell brought back clear memories from childhood.

'Wow, what a high ceiling. And look at those beams. Old buildings really were built solidly, weren't they?'

Masami's voice brought Akashi out of his reverie.

She was gazing up at the ceiling. The light was on, but their eyes still hadn't adjusted.

'So, there's a mezzanine up there?'

'Yeah, silkworm racks.'

'Oh – so that's what that was.'

Masami, camera in hand, slowly filmed the interior.

The room was essentially empty, the air surprisingly dry.

There in the middle was a baby grand, with a cover over it.

Masami trained her camera on the piano and stood still, filming it.

His grandmother, who'd bought the piano for him, had passed away when Akashi was in his last year of junior high.

Akashi looked over at a small wooden stool in a corner of the storehouse. His grandmother used to set herself down on it, legs tucked neatly underneath her, back straight, as she listened to her grandson play.

'Your playing is so gentle, Akashi,' she'd say. 'The silkworms seem to enjoy it, too.'

'It's strange, but the piano fits in well in a storehouse,' said Masami.

'And the storehouse itself is a kind of soundproof room.'

'Do you come here often?'

'I haven't been in here for quite a while.'

He still had the piano tuned once a year, but after he'd decided to take part in the competition, he'd had it meticulously tuned one more time.

The tuner, Mr Hanada, was about his father's age, and he'd known him for years. When Akashi had revealed he was going to be in the Yoshigae International Piano Competition, he was surprised to see how overjoyed the older man was, and how he had so eagerly and enthusiastically ensured the piano was tuned to perfection.

'I'm so happy to hear that,' Mr Hanada said. 'I've been a fan of your playing, Akashi, since you were little. Because the piano isn't just for prodigies.'

Of course, Akashi knew he hadn't been a child prodigy. But still, it secretly hurt to know that Hanada knew that too. It was, though, a fair enough appraisal of a guy who, at his age, was participating in a competition as a kind of farewell gesture.

Akashi drew strength from knowing that Hanada was thinking along the same lines as him.

The piano isn't just for prodigies.

'Your grandmother bought this piano for you, didn't she?' Masami asked. 'It's a cute little piano. Like in a painting. Takashima-*kun*, would you play something?'

Masami was a visual person, always thinking about what scene would look best on TV.

Akashi removed the cover, lifted the lid, pulled the chair up and sat down at the piano.

He was used to this chair. From long years of supporting him, the seat cushion was moulded to his shape.

This was a small, cosy instrument, nothing like the huge grand pianos used in concerts. When Akashi, a grown man now, played it, it looked even smaller.

It had always seemed so big.

Akashi gently stroked the yellowing keys.

He would never forget the excitement he'd felt when he first sat down at this piano.

His grandmother had come to a recital he'd given and afterwards, inspired by her grandson's performance, went around the neighbourhood telling everyone how he was going to grow up to be a professional musician. Someone apparently told her that if he was going to be a professional, he needed something better than the upright piano he'd been practising on.

And it was true that Akashi had large hands for a child, could master the most technically challenging pieces with ease, and was seen as having enormous potential and promise.

His father's family were the top silkworm-farmers in the area, but by the time Akashi was born this was a dying industry, and his father's older brother, who inherited the business, worked at an electronics company, doing silkworm raising on the side.

But still his grandmother managed to put away some money, bit by bit, and was able to buy the piano, albeit a second-hand one, for her grandson.

That was the first time in his life he'd cried from sheer happiness. For a pianist, having a grand piano was a dream come true.

The problem was that the precious grand piano his grandmother managed to buy him couldn't be kept at home.

His father's work meant they had to move a lot, and the piano just wouldn't fit in an ordinary Japanese apartment. Even if they did succeed in squeezing it in, the neighbours would complain, and his father told him they couldn't keep taking it with them. Akashi cried bitter tears.

So the piano was kept in the storehouse and every summer holiday and New Year's break, and just before recitals, he'd come over and play all day long.

His grandmother, of course, knew nothing about classical music. But she had a good ear, and picked up things by spending time listening to her grandson play. Akashi was often surprised at how keen her sense of hearing was, even in the last years of her life.

She could tell a lot, for instance, about his state of health and mood by hearing him play. After practice they'd be sitting at the dinner table and she'd say things like, 'You seem tired,' or 'Is there something worrying you?' And she was spot on every time. Once she said, 'When your mind's on something else, the notes feel cut off.'

This took him by surprise. Even when he was in a lesson, if something was bothering him, he couldn't get the right phrasing and articulation, and compared to when he was on good form, his playing tended to be more terse, something his teacher had pointed out numerous times. Most people hearing him wouldn't catch the difference, which was minimal, yet his grandmother had.

And when other children in the neighbourhood came and took turns on the piano, his grandmother could always tell who was playing, unerring in her assessment of their personalities.

Akashi's views on music, and the feelings of resistance he

had in him right now, might all be traceable to his grandmother's influence.

'That guy's raising worms in his piano.'

'He practises in a room full of caterpillars. Eww!'

Rumours that he practised in a converted silkworm room in a storehouse soon spread throughout his piano school. The other kids wouldn't let it go. One boy was particularly persistent. Their piano school was well known and had produced a fair share of professional pianists, and this boy wasn't as skilled as Akashi, always coming second to him. Akashi realized the boy must be envious, for besides his piano skills Akashi was good-natured and well liked. In the end, he could only laugh at the boy's unwavering persistence in spreading stories about him.

He'd been friends at college with a young woman who'd graduated from one of the top private women's schools in Japan. It really surprised him when she said that the most common combination of professions for the parents of her fellow students was a father who was a doctor and a mother who was a piano teacher.

Akashi wasn't some exceptional young prodigy, but people did expect good things of him in the future, and so he went on to music college. Yet he felt a growing unease with the warped elitism of the music world and a portion of the people involved in it.

There were people who simply enjoyed music and had a good ear for it, people who lived ordinary lives, like his grandmother. So wasn't it all right for musicians to live ordinary lives as well?

It wasn't as if he didn't have the option to turn professional. It was just a question of whether he wanted to. He loved the piano, but inside Akashi lay a fear: that wide, yet claustrophobic world of music was far from *ordinary*, but *ordinary* was where he longed to be, in the real world where people like his grandmother lived.

'I know this piece. What is it called again—?'

'*Träumerei*. By Schumann,' Akashi said to Masami as he made his leisurely way through the piece. 'You know this one, too, don't you?' He started playing something else.

'Oh – that's the music from the stomach-medicine commercial.'

'It's Chopin.'

'Your playing always *does* sound so gentle.'

For some reason her words startled him.

The silkworms love to listen when it's you playing. It felt as if his grandmother was speaking to him again. A feeling of unexpected warmth welled up from deep within him.

'I'm going to stay here and prepare for the competition,' he said.

'But weren't you going to rent a studio in that mountain resort – Nasu Kogen or somewhere?'

'I've changed my mind. I think here is best for me.'

'Well, I guess for me too – it would be better for filming to be nearby like this.'

Masami sounded a bit hesitant. Which was understandable, given that a few hours ago Akashi had been complaining that he had nowhere to practise and not enough time.

The decision made Akashi feel much more light-hearted.

I'll make the final preparations here, he said to himself. *Do a final run-through for the competition in this converted silkworm room, on the piano my late grandmother bought me, with her listening in. That's what would suit me best.*

'Do you know the movie *Never on Sunday*?' Gently testing the feel of the keys, Akashi looked over at Masami.

'That's sort of random, isn't it? Of course I know it. The one with Melina Mercouri.' Masami's hands were on her hips. Film was her field of expertise.

'There's a line in there I love.'

'Which one? I doubt I'll remember it, though.'

Mozart now filled the silkworm room.

Akashi felt, somehow, happy.

'The movie was set in Greece, wasn't it?' he said. 'Melina Mercouri played a cheerful, vivacious prostitute, and this strait-laced university professor from somewhere turns up and immediately clashes with all the happy-go-lucky locals. The local musicians couldn't read music and knew nothing about classical music. "You call yourselves musicians?" he snaps at them. "Well, you're not." That was a real shock to them, and they become depressed, and say they won't perform any more, that they're not qualified. I'm trying to remember – was there a scene like that?'

'Yep. Since I'm not much of a musician myself, it really left an impression.'

'And then what happened?'

'Melina Mercouri tells them, "What are you talking about? Birds can't read music, but that doesn't stop them singing." When they hear this, the musicians' eyes light up and they go back out into the café and start playing again.'

'Huh.'

'I think that's what it's all about.'

Inside the storehouse the strains of Mozart flowed out and mingled with the lengthening beams of afternoon sunlight.

Drum Roll

Bright laughter bounced off the gently curving domed ceiling above and echoed down to the crowd thronging the lobby below.

Cameras flashed, sober-faced young men and women in dark suits raced around, clutching notebooks – local media and reporters from music magazines, or PR staff from corporate sponsors. Reporters from national newspapers and high-profile music critics were also present, evidence of the growing reputation of the Yoshigae International Piano Competition in recent years.

Mieko Saga, champagne glass in hand, was gazing through the huge plate-glass window of the lobby at the round plaza outside, shrouded in darkness.

The concert hall was part of a multi-purpose facility, including offices and a shopping centre, with the lobby overlooking the stone-paved plaza. It was nearly ten p.m. and the plaza was deserted, while inside, the lobby was buzzing. To Mieko this stark contrast evoked the competition itself – the alternation of joy and sorrow that lurked behind the dazzle of the stage. For a moment she felt as if the late-autumn chill had pierced right through the glass and into her.

She was struck by her image reflected in the glass, the uneasy, stern look.

Goodness, she thought, *what a frightening face I have. As if I'm some music-school student anxiously waiting my turn to play.*

She began to rub her cheeks to loosen the tension, though she wasn't sure it had done the trick.

This was the launch of the Yoshigae competition, which was to continue over the next two weeks. The first round was beginning the next day.

There had been an opening concert, a recital by the winner of the last competition. One of the important benefits afforded the winner was a concert tour of several cities in Japan, and this concert marked the start of their tour.

This winner hadn't passed the written-application stage but had advanced through the auditions and managed to grab first place. He went on to became a world-class star, a commanding presence on the stage, and his appearance at Yoshigae was major news.

One of the special rewards of being a judge was just this: to be able to fully indulge in – from the audience seats now – the triumphant return concert by a star that you had helped discover. Mieko felt filled with energy at the thought of yet another new star being born in the current competition.

After the concert the lobby was used for a party for invited guests only. This was the first time the judges from the auditions around the world had come together, and some of the pianists, too, were there, lending the gathering a decidedly international flavour. The party was in full swing, with dignitaries from the local city council sponsoring the competition, the mayor of Yoshigae and local VIPs, and senior people from business sponsors. Yoshigae was one of the more prominent industrial cities in Japan, home to several world-renowned machinery manufacturers, and the city was blessed with abundant tax revenue despite the worldwide recession.

'You look so lost there, Mieko, all on your lonesome.'

Mieko was still rubbing her face to loosen the tightened muscles when someone tapped her on the shoulder. It was the composer Tadaaki Hishinuma. Mieko shot him a wry smile.

'That's not a very nice way of putting it. You should have said I looked like I was deep in contemplation.'

'Don't make me laugh. Now, who was that young lady who used to miss my lectures because she claimed she couldn't bear having to think too much, and loathed studying solfège? Mm? Seemed more like you were counting all the new wrinkles you've collected over the past year.'

'You're terrible!' Mieko laughed.

The Yoshigae piano competition always commissioned a new piece by a Japanese composer that all the competitors were required to learn, and this year Hishinuma had been chosen to compose it. One of his grandfathers had been an eminent writer, the other a major political figure. He was a handsome man with a decided aura about him, but whenever he opened his mouth to speak, a torrent of crude, old-school Tokyo dialect flowed out, and everyone who met him found the contrast jarring.

'So – what's this I hear about the French contingent uncovering some really amazing pianist?' Hishinuma looked at Mieko with a twinkle in his eye.

'So you heard about that, too, did you?' Mieko couldn't help pulling a long face.

'He's supposed to be the son of a beekeeper? Seems everybody's calling him the Honeybee Prince.'

'The Honeybee Prince . . .' Mieko was at a loss for words. *Jin Kazama*.

The name weighed heavily on her. She and Simon and Smirnoff had recently met for the first time since the Paris auditions, and it was clear that for all three of them the boy remained a thorn in their flesh.

After the audition they'd all been so busy with their own schedules, but in the interim they had gathered a bit more information on Kazama.

What had first surprised Mieko were the characters used to write the boy's name.

She'd imagined his first name, Jin, would be written with the usual character meaning 'benevolence', and was amazed to find it was instead written with the character *jin* meaning 'dust'. Simon was surprised at her flabbergasted reaction, but when she explained the meaning of the character to him, he just burst out laughing.

His laughter made her despair. They'd been caught in Hoffmann's trap, and on top of that the boy's name was *Dust*? Jin's father must be quite the eccentric. Simon found this all pretty amusing, but it only added to Mieko's anxiety.

The rumour that an amazing young pianist had appeared at the Paris auditions had quickly spread throughout the music world.

As always, Mieko tried to avoid gleaning any information in advance about the competitors so as not to have any preconceptions about them, but when it came to Jin Kazama these rampant rumours preceded him, and she heard it all whether she wanted to or not. He was basically an unknown, so there was next to nothing in the way of background details about him, but this only served to stoke the anticipation. With all this build-up, what if his actual performance failed to live up to expectations? Mieko was terrified. If the audience felt let down, they'd certainly turn their irritation on to the judges who'd allowed him through.

'Why the sour face?'

Hishinuma seemed taken aback. He must have thought that Mieko would appear more excited.

'Well, there are a couple of things. Um – even Hoffmann could have made a mistake, couldn't he?'

'There was a letter of recommendation, I heard.'

Mieko had no idea what Hishinuma was thinking – his expression had suddenly turned serious.

'But it does seem true that Yuji taught this – Honeybee Prince,' he said. 'I phoned Daphne the other day, and she said that Yuji had gone on a journey to teach a child.'

'What?!'

Daphne was Yuji Von Hoffmann's widow. Hishinuma and his family were friends with the Von Hoffmanns, and even after Yuji's death, he'd kept in touch with her by phone.

'The Maestro himself went to teach the boy? Unbelievable.'

Hoffmann was famous for taking on very few pupils, since he rarely taught outside his own home.

'Daphne asked him about it, but Hoffmann just grinned, apparently. What a contrarian that guy was. She said he'd smile and say, "I do it because he's a travelling musician."'

A travelling musician. An apt description, since Jin was the son of a beekeeper who had to move around, to wherever flowers were in bloom.

But how did he teach him? The boy had no idea how to behave on stage, and there was no evidence at all that he'd been tutored by a professional.

'So when's the Prince performing? I'm sure he's not here at this party, is he?' Hishinuma looked around the lobby.

'He's scheduled for the final day of the first round. It sounds like he'll arrive in Japan just in time.'

The entire competition spanned two weeks, with the ninety or so performers in the first round playing over five days. Some of the pianists due to play the next day were at the opening-night party, while others were still furiously polishing their performance pieces.

Japan was a long way from Europe and America and so taking part in the competition could be expensive. Even if competitors had arranged to stay with a host family while in Japan, the financial burden was considerable. Those who came a few days early to Yoshigae and stayed in a hotel were mostly pianists from neighbouring countries, China and South Korea, and often they were the children of wealthy families. The rest had little choice but to turn up at the last possible moment. Mieko had no idea if Jin Kazama was well off or not, though it was likely that he was not.

'Uh-oh – don't look now, but the Queen has deigned to make an appearance,' Hishinuma muttered.

'Did you say something, Tadaaki?' a resonant alto voice piped up.

'She always did have a sharp ear,' Hishinuma said to his companion.

An attractive red-haired Russian woman came over, tall, with a voluptuous bust and dressed in a blue suit. This splendid, powerful presence was none other than Olga Slutskaya, a famous pianist, as well as a teacher with an established reputation. Known as a Japanophile, she'd become quite proficient in the language. Nearing seventy, she had lost none of her captivating charm or vitality. She had a wide circle of connections in the music world, possessing outstanding managerial and diplomatic skills, and it was known that, in her role as chair of the judges, she had been key to making the Yoshigae competition a truly international event.

'You wouldn't be badmouthing me now, would you?' Olga shot him a sweet smile and shimmied her shapely shoulders.

'Nonsense,' Hishinuma said with an ingratiating smile.

He wasn't that much younger than Olga, but this old guy was always so self-effacing and polite with beautiful women, Mieko thought, smiling to herself. 'We were talking about how we might see a new star born this year, too.'

'Now wouldn't that be nice,' Olga said with a chuckle. Her eyes seemed to sparkle for an instant.

She'd obviously heard about the Paris audition, and had no doubt taken into consideration the tastes and reputation of that three-member panel. Olga was a strict, by-the-book person and preferred an orthodox performance reflecting a depth of understanding of the piece. She would naturally frown on a colourful eccentric like the Honeybee Prince. Ever the pragmatist, though, she would nonetheless make full use of anything that created excitement and drew more attention to the competition – be it Hoffmann's letter of recommendation, or this Honeybee or Dust Prince.

'It's been ages, hasn't it, Mieko? Please stop by my room later on, would you?' Olga said, casting a dignified sidelong glance in her direction, which Mieko countered with a noncommittal smile as Olga passed by. Heaven forbid, Mieko muttered to herself, quickly scanning around for another flamboyant little group to join.

If anyone was going to view the Honeybee Prince as an enemy, it would be *her*, Mieko thought.

'Apart from the Paris auditions, I heard a rumour there's another superstar waiting in the wings, from New York,' Hishinuma murmured as he followed Mieko's glance.

'Is that right?' *This old guy's a little too quick for me*, she swore under her breath.

Her glance lighted on a tall, slim man – smiling, but with a sharpish twinkle in his eye.

Nathaniel Silverberg.

He had a mass of unruly light brown hair, a veritable lion's mane sticking out in all directions despite his best efforts to tame it. Normally a friendly, candid, charming person, he could be fiery at times, and was unforgiving of both himself and others when it came to music. If you were unfortunate enough to incur his wrath, no one could ever smooth things over afterwards. Mieko had only witnessed this side of him once, when he changed into a completely different person, his hair less a lion's mane than a halo of flames surrounding the head of a statue of some fierce Buddhist deity.

He was of a similar age to Mieko, within shouting distance of fifty, a pianist in his prime, both in popularity and skill, and had recently served as a conductor and stage director – but he was also well known in fields other than classical music.

Nathaniel was British, but he'd been a professor at Juilliard in recent years, so America had become his base of operations.

'What a mound of hair – I'm envious,' Hishinuma muttered, patting his own diminishing crop.

'Well, it's thinned out a lot since the early days, you know. In the past, people used to say, unkindly, that he could be one of those Lion Dance performers with a huge mane swinging around.'

Hishinuma chuckled.

'I heard his divorce lawsuit was a real trauma, but he still has a pretty youthful complexion.'

'His face might just be a little oily.'

Mieko had heard, too, how Nathaniel had got bogged down in the divorce from his present wife.

'When it comes to relationships with women, he's always been pretty slippery,' she murmured.

Hishinuma shot her a questioning look, but then gave his forehead a theatrical slap.

'Damn, that's right. The guy used to be *your* husband, didn't he?'

Seriously? How could he have forgotten, the old fart.

'That's ancient history,' she said.

'Right – so how is your son doing?'

'He emailed me the other day. He got a job this year. He'll be working in government. He takes after his father in everything – including looks.'

After she'd divorced Nathaniel, at her parents' request she'd done a *miai* matchmaking meeting and married a bank employee, a graduate of Tokyo University. Looking back on it now, she could see that she'd basically lost her mind, but at the time she was exhausted after being twisted around Nathaniel's little finger, and honestly felt if she were to marry again it had better be to a serious, dependable type. The son she had had with her second husband resembled him to a tee, as if they were cut from the same cloth; brought up to be so sensible and clear-headed it was hard to believe he was happy-go-lucky Mieko's child.

She and her husband had divorced before Shinya started elementary school and his father had got custody, so she wasn't fully aware of exactly how he had been raised. Her ex-husband had soon remarried, and Mieko's memories of Shinya remained those of when he was little. His stepmother seemed a capable person, and Mieko was truly grateful to her for bringing up Shinya to be such a strong, upstanding young man.

Shinya didn't play the piano but enjoyed music and while at high school had attended some of Mieko's concerts. He'd later write her letters outlining his thoughts. His observations were always perceptive, and she felt an equal mix of happiness and embarrassment when she read them. Nowadays they exchanged emails more often on their phones, and his parents seemed OK with that.

I wonder which parent Nathaniel's daughter takes after? she pondered.

Just as the thought struck her, her eyes met his, and she gave a start.

She detected a hint of embarrassment in Nathaniel's expression.

She knew he'd found it difficult to forget her. The next moment his face hardened, a bad sign. He must be remembering Paris and the whole Honeybee Prince debacle, she was certain.

He walked over, his face still stern.

Mieko forced herself to smile.

'It's been a while.'

Nathaniel looked back at her, his eyes stony.

'You're looking well,' she said. Mieko did her best to sound upbeat.

'You too,' he replied.

Nathaniel's expression remained frozen, though he did shoot one of his winning smiles at Hishinuma.

'Professor Hishinuma, it's been too long. The set piece you have composed is most intriguing. I played it myself and enjoyed it thoroughly.'

'Happy to hear it.'

As she watched Nathaniel enthusiastically discussing the piece with Hishinuma, Mieko sensed his disapproval of her.

He's angry. Incensed with me for passing that boy who had Hoffmann's letter of recommendation.

Why, Mieko? he must be thinking. *Why in the world didn't you stop it?*

She could almost picture Nathaniel's rage when he finally heard him play.

His hair would stand on end just like that angry Buddhist deity. The reason being that Nathaniel had once been one of Hoffmann's tiny, very select group of pupils.

Nathaniel used to fly once a week from England for lessons with Hoffmann, yet Hoffmann never wrote *him* a letter of recommendation.

For those who adored Hoffmann, were in awe of him, even idolized him, the Maestro cast a spell on them, played havoc with them emotionally. *Just as he's done to me*, Mieko thought. *This boy shows up with an unprecedented letter of recommendation from the mentor we admire above all others, and it's honestly floored me – how on earth do I handle this?*

There was nothing I could do about it, she wanted to tell Nathaniel.

This bomb that Maestro Hoffmann primed has already exploded. The Maestro's gift *has already been handed over—*

A shadow appeared in her line of vision, as if slicing through the air.

'Professor Silverberg.'

The shadow seemed enveloped in a soft light.

Mieko couldn't help but blink at this boy's glowing face.

'Ah – there you are, Masaru.'

Nathaniel invited him over, all smiles now.

'Masaru?' Mieko said, wondering about the Japanese name.

'Yeah,' Nathaniel said to her and looked at Masaru. 'He's also of Japanese descent. His mother is a third-generation Japanese Peruvian.'

'Third-generation Japanese Peruvian,' Mieko repeated, her

eyes resting on the young man's face. He struck her as more Latin American; she didn't detect any trace of Japanese blood in his looks. *So several different races mixed together*, she thought, the word *hybrid* coming to mind.

'He's also . . .' Nathaniel had said when introducing him. In the back of his mind, he must have been thinking of Jin Kazama.

This young man was as tall as Nathaniel and dressed in a nicely tailored grey tweed suit. Virile, yet quiet. Wild, yet contemplative. Contradictory elements coexisting, yet not forced together. Mieko would often see someone whose body made her visualize *physical speed*, and Masuru was exactly that. A lithe animal with an explosive power lurking just below the surface.

'I hope you'll be especially nice to this young man,' Nathaniel said, a comical expression on his face as he bowed deeply. He put an arm around Masaru's shoulders and pulled him closer.

'He's Juilliard's hidden treasure. He started competing this year. Your first competition was in Osaka, wasn't it?' he asked Masaru. 'Why Osaka?'

'I thought it'd be a good dry run before the Yoshigae. I wanted to get used to the atmosphere, and the feel of a concert hall. But I wasn't very familiar with the rules and was disqualified because of an infringement.'

The young man scratched his head in embarrassment.

'Eh?' Mieko said in surprise. She narrowed her eyes.

So this was him – the young man who'd got the highest scores by far in that competition, but, without any connections in the Japanese music world to argue his case, had ended up being disqualified.

'His name, Masaru, means "victory", doesn't it, in Japanese?' Nathaniel looked at Mieko. 'Masaru, this is Mieko Saga, an old friend of mine.'

'Yes, of course. It's so nice to meet you finally.' Masaru's eyes sparkled as he held out his hand.

If it's victory *versus* dust, *it's Game Over already*, she thought.

Mieko glanced again through the huge plate-glass window at the plaza outside.

The night was deepening. In just a few short hours, the curtain would rise on the competition.

Eeny Meeny Miny Moe

'I'M THINKING, THIS RED one for the finals?'

Kanade looked so serious that Aya couldn't help but smile.

'But I don't know if I'll even make it to the finals.'

Aya meant it to sound light, like a joke, but Kanade turned around and shot her a scary look.

'Aya-*chan*, are you still talking like that? There are lots of young people in the world who are dying to be in a competition but don't make it. If you're going to look at it that way, you might as well quit right now. You don't need to worry about my dad.'

'I'm sorry . . .'

Aya fell silent and studied the dresses.

The Yoshigae competition was starting tomorrow, and now that they'd finished deciding the order of the performances, Aya was making a quick round trip back to Tokyo.

They were in President Hamazaki's home near the college, an imposing Japanese-style mansion with a lush garden.

Aya and Mr Hamazaki's younger daughter, Kanade, sat in the vast sitting room, now scattered with dresses laid out on the tatami for their inspection.

It was every girl's dream to appear on stage in a gorgeous dress. There are many girls who begin piano lessons solely with that in mind – to wear a beautiful gown at a recital.

But for performers, dresses could also be quite annoying.

They could be bulky, and expensive. And you couldn't wear the same one too often.

In competitions it was usual for a girl to wear a different one for every performance. If you survived to the finals of the Yoshigae, that meant four different outfits.

You could always hire a gown, of course, but if it wasn't comfortable it could hinder your performance, and pianists tended to prefer wearing their own dresses, ones they were used to.

It had been years since Aya had performed in front of an audience, and she had no dresses of her own. Until she was thirteen, her mother had always sewn all her stage outfits. Aya much preferred rougher, boyish clothes and had been thinking of wearing a trouser suit at the competition.

Kanade had casually asked, 'So what are you going to wear?' and when she heard that Aya was thinking of wearing a trouser suit, she was aghast. 'That's absolutely out of the question,' she said. 'A trouser suit would look weird.'

The Hamazakis had two daughters: the elder, Haruka, majored in singing, and was studying abroad in Italy, while Kanade was studying the violin, two years ahead of Aya in the same college. Each of the girls had chosen a field very much in keeping with their given names – Haruka meaning 'pure song', and Kanade 'to play an instrument'.

Mr Hamazaki may have asked Aya to attend his college, but once she started it was his daughter Kanade who took her under her wing. At first it must have seemed like a duty for her, but the disciplined Kanade and the much more laid-back Aya hit it off, and they now felt more like sisters.

The Hamazaki girls had a wardrobe full of dresses, so they made a quick decision to lend Aya the dresses she'd need.

Preferring simple designs in monochrome hues, Aya chose only dark-coloured dresses, but Kanade cautioned her against this. Since the piano itself was black, and at the finals, when she'd perform with an orchestra whose members would all be in black, if she herself dressed the same, she'd be lost on stage.

As it was also advisable for all female musicians, not only pianists, not to have their shoulders constricted, many chose sleeveless dresses. Bustiers were popular as well, but Aya wasn't so keen. With her sloping shoulders, spaghetti straps wouldn't do since one might easily slip off. After much trial and error, she decided to go with sleeveless dresses. She'd heard all the horror stories: about dresses that were beautiful but hard to perform in; of performers stepping on the hem of their dress; of straps sliding down; of girls choosing cheaper, synthetic fabrics and sweating madly during their performance; and of dresses getting all bunched up while girls played until they lost all focus.

After much dithering, they ended up with four dresses: one was a sort of vermilion, one a bright blue, another a deep green and one in silver lamé. The question now was what order she should wear them in.

Kanade could see Aya's confusion. She knew Aya had got into the college on her father's recommendation and that she'd only reluctantly agreed to be in the competition out of a sense of obligation and had no desire whatsoever to win a prize.

'Aya-*chan*?' Kanade said. 'You always thought I was helping you because my father asked me to, didn't you?'

Aya was taken aback. She hadn't imagined Kanade would bring this up now. Or that she would even point it out.

'I was a big fan of yours,' Kanade said. 'Since I was little, my father told me I have an excellent ear. When I went to watch competitions, I could always pick out who would win, and those who would go on to great things. It got to the point he'd always ask me, "So which one is it, do you think?"'

Aya was well aware that Kanade had an amazing ear. This went beyond just having perfect pitch, and included a wonderful mixture of intuition and critical acumen. Kanade played covers from many genres and listened to a lot of indie bands. She'd tell Aya that a certain band would make it big, and sure enough they'd have a major hit. Aya was bowled over by Kanade's unerring musical sense. Kanade's own performances weren't especially standout, but her sound had a maturity beyond her years, and those in the know thought highly of her as a violinist.

'The first time I heard you play, I was blown away,' Kanade said. 'I was used to hearing students who'd come to study with my father, and there were plenty of child prodigies among them, with amazing technique. But you were something else. I was drawn to your musicality – so free and easy, so generous, yet with a haunting insight.'

Aya felt a bit uncomfortable. Was that really her being described?

'You wouldn't believe how excited I was when I heard you play. I remember telling my father, "This girl's going to be a star." I wasn't just confident – I was absolutely *certain*.'

Aya scratched her head.

'And then—'

Kanade suddenly widened her eyes and stared into Aya's. Aya stopped scratching.

'And then you all of a sudden stopped playing. I was shocked. Honestly, I felt humiliated. It's kind of a bit late to say this, but I felt insulted, as if I'd been betrayed.'

'I'm . . . sorry,' Aya replied.

Kanade let out a small snort, and her face relaxed.

'And then years later my father came home one night and told me, "You were absolutely right, Kanade. You nailed it."'

'You mean—?'

Kanade nodded.

'The day Father heard you play the Shostakovich piano sonata.'

Aya looked Kanade full in the face.

'I was so happy when he told me he was going to get you to attend our college. He didn't say, *I want to get her to enrol*, but *I'm going to make sure she enrols*. You know how mild-mannered he seems? Well, he can be pretty tough sometimes.'

'Prof. Hamazaki?' Aya felt a warmth rising inside her. 'So – I guess it's all thanks to you that I could study here.'

'Yep – all thanks to me! So show some gratitude now.' Kanade laughed. 'My father didn't do what he did based just on my intuition. He'd been thinking about you for a long, long time.'

Had her mother, while she was still alive, asked him to keep an eye on her? Aya mused.

'So you've got to do your best at the competition. It's a matter of my pride and honour. Got it?'

Aya nodded.

'All right, then. Which one will be your winning dress?'

The two of them went back to comparing the four gowns.

'I want this one for the finals,' Aya said after a while, pointing to the ultra-chic silver dress.

'Isn't that a bit subdued?' Kanade inclined her head doubtfully.

Aya shook her head.

'No, it isn't. This one is my favourite. The second character in my name, Aya, is the character for "night". This one gives the feeling of moonlight. It's perfect.'

'I suppose you're right, if you put it like that.'

'I'll do my best so I can wear this one in the finals. Thank you, Kanade-*chan*.'

Aya thanked her so sincerely, it was Kanade's turn now to feel a little embarrassed and look away.

AS SHE LEFT THE HAMAZAKIS' house, Aya couldn't help sighing.

The temperature outside had dropped.

It really did feel like late autumn, she thought. The chill air on her cheeks was bracing.

Kanade had made so her happy, had moved her deeply, but now that she was outside, her negative feelings started to creep back.

The competition would begin tomorrow, but she found it hard to get her head around that.

She knew she had to follow what Kanade had told her and pull herself together and focus.

But then, Aya wouldn't be playing until the final day of the first round, for she was No. 88 on the list. Eight was a lucky number – the way the Chinese character spread open, signifying prosperity. But what really bowled her over about 88 was the huge number of entrants it implied.

But why now, at this late date, do I have to have people grade me? Aya thought, mulling over her reluctance about the whole affair. *My musical life the way it is right now is fulfilling. I do want music to be my vocation – that's a given – but becoming a concert pianist is not what I had in mind. Being a studio musician is one thing, but I don't think I'm suited to performing in front of others.*

There was one other matter that concerned her.

Not long ago a request addressed to her from a TV station arrived at the college asking if they could cover her during the competition. They wanted to make a documentary on the entire process from beginning to end. Of all the students participating, they'd singled out Aya. She quickly, and politely, turned them down, but was left with a sour taste.

It was obvious what they wanted to do: capture the drama of the *resurrection of the girl prodigy*.

The girl who'd voluntarily vanished from the stage had made a comeback. Imagine how overjoyed they'd be if she revealed she was dedicating this return to her late mother. It was depressing to think that that's how the world viewed her participation.

She'd never regretted stepping away from being a concert pianist. She still loved music with all her heart, and a life without it was unimaginable. But it was hard to stomach the thought that people were viewing her motives so differently – thinking she'd been dying to return to the stage, or that only now did she feel recovered enough to do so. Aya was an easy-going, laid-back person, though she could be a bit of a contrarian. And this aspect of her personality made her hesitate to undergo this kind of *resurrection* that everyone seemed to be expecting.

Well, she thought, *far from being a* resurrection, *if I don't make it through the first round of the competition, I'll end up a complete laughing stock.*

Aya chuckled wryly to herself.

Perhaps because her college was nearby, her feet naturally carried her in that direction.

It was late at night now, but the school buildings were brightly lit.

As a rule, the practice rooms were available twenty-four

hours a day. When there was a competition coming up, or exams or a school-wide concert, students often pulled all-nighters, practising endlessly.

Aya didn't feel like going straight home. Instead, she decided to take a peek into the practice rooms. She was worn out too, from all the wardrobe decisions. Playing the piano a little might lift her spirits before she went home.

As expected, the practice rooms were almost all taken. She could make out, through the soundproof doors, students doing frenzied run-throughs of Chopin études and Beethoven sonatas. She caught sight of two students who were also in the Yoshigae competition. A palpable last-minute tension, and late-night exhaustion, filled the rooms.

Her favourite piano was occupied, so she set off to find her second-favourite one.

Music flowing out from one of the practice rooms made her stop suddenly.

What the—?

For a moment she didn't know what she was hearing.

An indescribable mass of sound.

She couldn't make out the melody.

Was it jazz piano?

She stood listening.

She'd never heard this touch before. She pretty much knew the sound of every single student in the piano department. Could it be a student from the composition department? Aya went up to the door and pressed her ear against it.

She knew a couple of students had formed a jazz band and often played together.

But as she listened, she felt a chill run through her. Her mouth became dry.

No, this wasn't one of them. Whoever this was, they were exceptional. Truly outstanding. As good as one of the students in her own department. Ha, not quite. She couldn't figure it out, but the sound was incredible.

Above all, it was so *distinctive*.

That was the first thing that had made her stop and listen. Usually the music coming through the soundproof doors was muffled and dull, all individuality and ornamentation flattened out.

But this was rich. It practically pierced right through the door.

There was no way a student here could create such a sound from one of these pianos.

Aya tipped her head back, her heart beating faster.

An amazing passage. Though the pianist was playing in octaves, each note was timed precisely, totally clean. How could they be playing so evenly?

Aya felt the blood drain from her, a shock bordering on fear.

I can hear something completely amazing, she thought. *The day before the competition is due to begin, in a practice room in college at night, I'm feeling something that is stirring my whole being.*

The sound changed, startling her again. That electrifying speed suddenly slowed, replaced by a relaxed mood.

Rhumba, she thought. This was a rhumba rhythm. To the sultry accompaniment of the left hand, the right hand added a melody she knew she'd heard before.

What is this? I know it. There is a lot of improvising going on, but surely this is—

She pressed her ear harder against the door.

'Zui zui zukkorobashi'! The traditional Japanese children's 'Eeny Meeny Miny Moe' song. And played, unbelievably, in a rhumba rhythm! Unable to restrain herself, Aya peered through the little square window in the door.

The first thing she saw was a dark brown cap. The battered cap was swaying back and forth. It was worn by a young boy. He wasn't seated, but standing, moving from side to side as he played. As expected, she'd never seen him before. Aya shifted on to her toes, trying to catch a glimpse of his face.

He's not a student at our school. He's so very young. Maybe . . . still in high school?

He played the rhumba in his own style, suddenly glancing up at the ceiling, then at the wall.

For a second, he stopped playing.

Then just as suddenly he began a Chopin étude.

What the—?

Aya reflexively spun around.

There was no mistake. This boy was playing the opening of the same Chopin Étude No. 1 that another student was practising so earnestly in another room at the other end of the building, timing his playing to match it.

No way! How could he possibly hear it, from inside this practice room?

A chill ran through her again. This boy was playing in perfect sync with the piece she could just make out in the distance. He could actually hear it.

His sound grew muddied, strange, and grating on the ears.

Aya was confused. Was he messing it up?

It was the same melodic line. That glorious phrase washing in like a wave, then receding.

Aya felt goosebumps.

I get it now. He's overlaying the same phrase on top of that other student's playing, but exactly a half-tone up.

He was playing so naturally, so casually. Subdued, dispassionate playing.

Still swaying, he turned towards the door.

His eyes locked on Aya's.

He stopped.

It happened so abruptly Aya didn't have a chance to move away. Her eyes stayed fixed on his. He mumbled something, as if caught in the middle of some prank.

He is beloved.

The moment she first caught sight of the boy's face, these were the words that came to her. This boy was beloved by the god of music.

Why she felt this, she had no idea. But when she saw his

face, the thought sprang up. *Beatific, innocent.* Words she didn't normally use, yet when she glimpsed his face, she had an immediate sense of the image they conjured up.

The boy took off his cap. He grabbed his carryall from the floor and hurried out of the door.

'I'm sorry. I'm sorry,' the boy said to her, bowing his head.

'But why? Why are you apologizing?' Aya asked, but the boy was ready to dash away.

'I'm so sorry. I knew I shouldn't, but when I was walking along outside, I heard the piano and thought it had such a lovely sound, so I just let myself in . . .'

The boy kept on bowing, edging away.

'I . . . haven't touched a really nice piano very often. So I just thought . . .'

'What do you mean?' Aya blinked in surprise. He'd heard the piano, from the road? The sound of a piano in a soundproofed practice room?

'Wait! Who – are you?'

The boy slapped his cap back on his head and dashed out.

'Wait! Tell me your name!'

Aya tried to go after him, but the boy had already slipped through the front door, and she could see him racing not towards the main gate of the school, but towards the wall at the back of the garden.

'No way.'

Aya could only watch as he disappeared into the darkness.

Somehow the boy got a foothold and clambered over the brick wall.

Seriously? He'd been trespassing?

She forgot it all – the competition, the dresses, the filming – and stared blankly from the doorway into the night.

The Well-Tempered Clavier, Book 1, No. 1

MASARU CARLOS LEVI ANATOLE woke up at six a.m. in his hotel room, just seconds before the alarm clock was set to go off. In a flash he pressed the off button.

He rarely needed an alarm clock. He was almost always able to snap wide awake by himself, at exactly the time he wanted, but he'd set it anyway, just to be sure.

After a few days in Japan, he'd overcome his jet lag.

Masaru got out of bed, took off the *yukata* – their largest size of robe, yet still too short for him – and swept open the curtains.

He'd been given a room with a wonderful view of the ocean city of Yoshigae, the Pacific forming a huge arc in the distance. Today was overcast, but still bright, the ocean a sparkling mix of blue and grey. Masaru gave a little yelp of joy.

Even with its unusual colour, the Pacific in Japan looked like a pen-and-ink painting. Maybe because it was viewed through the heavy, humid air. It was hard to believe it was the same ocean you'd see from the West Coast of the US.

Masaru reached up and did some stretches to loosen his limbs, then splashed cold water on to his face. He changed into his running gear, took the lift down to the lobby, strolled outside and began a leisurely jog.

The deserted early-morning streets felt clean and refreshing, the cool air bracing on his cheeks.

Sounds of a dog being walked, its claws clicking on the pavement, the roar of a motorbike as a boy delivered the morning papers.

These were the sounds of Japan. He ran for a while, then

stopped, then ran on. Tall, with a long, bold stride and muscular shoulders, he would be taken for an athlete by anyone who saw him.

In fact he had been a sportsman, a high-jump specialist, and even now, at Juilliard, he considered musicians to be a species of athlete.

The pianos he had to play in different venues were like running tracks, affected by the local climate, while the concert hall was a kind of stadium. Long fingers and large hands were key, but you also needed supple shoulders and wrists, the ability to hold your breath for a long time, to breathe in deeply, muscles that had explosive power, endurance built on a painstakingly trained inner core, all of which made beautiful pianissimos and fortissimos possible. A humble and profound understanding of the music was also required, as well as the ability to play with a generosity of spirit. And Masaru had each and every one of these qualities.

He imagined oxygen filling his whole body, in time with his strides and breathing.

He never listened to music while running. Yet now his head was filled with the music of Bach. Bach was morning music. *The Well-Tempered Clavier*, one of the set pieces for the first round of the competition. This morning it wasn't the Glenn Gould version in his mind, but Gustav Leonhardt's.

'*Ohayo, Nippon*,' Masaru murmured in Japanese.

Good morning, Japan.

MASARU HAD LIVED IN JAPAN for two years from the age of five.

Honestly, he didn't remember it that well. Since he could speak some everyday Japanese, he started at the public elementary school nearby. He didn't last three months.

With his naturally optimistic personality, the experience hadn't particularly scarred him, though he could still remember feeling like an *alien*.

His mother, Michiko, was more shocked by this than he was.

She was a hard-working, third-generation Japanese Peruvian

and didn't look East Asian at all, though she was inordinately proud of her Japanese heritage. She took great pride in the commandments that Japanese-Peruvian society held dear: to honour hard work, to keep promises, to be kind to others, to save money, to study, to live an upright life, to keep themselves and their homes clean and presentable. Her siblings were each outstanding in their own field and held important positions. Masaru's mother was no exception – she had graduated in engineering from the Peruvian national university and went on to study in France. After obtaining a doctorate she worked at a nuclear-power research facility, married a French physicist and had Masaru. All of which explained Masaru's long, complex name.

Under the joint ventures in nuclear power between France and Japan, Michiko and her husband were relocated to Yokohama. It was the first time she'd been to Japan, and she was thrilled with the move. She'd heard that the educational level was high, and so had placed Masaru in a local public school.

Her hopes were dashed.

Masaru was completely rejected by Japan and by the smaller *society* that made up the Japanese elementary school. When Masaru came home each day, his backpack was full of leftover, smelly food. Not only did he not eat his lunch, but it turned out that every morning as he was about to leave, he'd vomit the entire contents of his stomach. Michiko also experienced a wall of rejection because of her Latin American looks. She was a lovely person, lively and animated, and Masaru remembered how unhappy she looked, more than he did, even. The upshot was that he had to be transferred to an international school for the months that remained until they were due to return to France.

For his mother, the experience in Japan was a shock, but less so for Masaru. He was upset that he'd let his mother down. But he also felt that all this was the other side of the coin that was Japan's appeal.

While he'd felt uncomfortable at elementary school in Japan, he sensed schools were basically the same everywhere. France wasn't all that great either. Could it be that the French were more used to seeing a variety of races, and with their long colonial history were more at home with people from other lands? There was still prejudice, even so, like everywhere else. And wherever you went, children were cruel towards anyone different. The only contrast was that in France, with its multi-ethnic population, Masaru didn't stand out as much. After three years in France both his parents changed jobs and, aged eleven, Masaru accompanied them to the US.

'MA-*KUN*, I'M HERE. LET'S GO!'

Masaru turned around.

Even now he could recall that cheerful voice. It was more than ten years since he'd last heard it, yet it remained all the more distinct in his memory.

It was in Japan that Masaru had first set eyes on a piano.

HE RAN BACK ROUND TO the hotel, showered, and made his way down to the restaurant for breakfast.

It was now seven-twenty, and most of the guests downstairs were businessmen. There was a smattering of other competitors too, though not many.

The first round of the competition beginning today would last five days, and since it didn't kick off until the afternoon, it was likely the pianists were taking their time getting out of bed. Anyone performing today would probably come in later, just before the breakfast service finished, and skip lunch. All of them would be practising with their allocated time slot in mind. Some might even be too nervous to eat or sleep and were, even now, studiously running through their recital programme.

Masaru was the type who was fired up by an audience and had never once got stage fright. He thought it was the same for everyone else, so it surprised him to learn there were pianists who lost their appetite completely as the competition neared, growing quite gaunt.

Masaru had found his first competition in Osaka thrilling. It was like a sporting event, an intense, win-or-go-home kind of feeling. He'd felt completely pumped.

What he found he really loved about competitions was the opportunity to listen to all kinds of live performances, from pianists with a variety of skill levels.

'What are you thinking, Masaru? There's no need for you to listen so seriously to these kinds of performances.'

He remembered someone telling him this – most likely another Juilliard student who was also competing at Osaka. Masaru listened to every single performance from the first day onwards, except, of course, for the ones just before and after his own.

'What?' he'd replied. 'But it's fun. We seldom have a chance like this to hear so many different pianists.'

His classmate was astonished. Seriously? Masaru found this all *fun*?

He'd probably imagined Masaru would say something similar to the comment made by another contestant, Jennifer Chan: 'I don't listen to bad performances. It hurts my ears.'

Naturally, some performances were boring, and others a technical horror show.

But Masaru found it interesting to analyse what was weak and how it could be improved.

'Masaru is much more suited than any of us to be a teacher,' his mentor, Nathaniel Silverberg, often remarked.

Nationality, personality, a teacher's quirks – all these influenced a performance, and Masaru wondered how the same piece played on the same piano could come out sounding so different. A competition was a veritable showcase of pianists, and he never tired of listening. When he thought about all the young people all over the world, enthralled by the instrument, willing to spend an incredible amount of time practising, he was struck yet again by its magic. Just as he had the very first time he'd heard the piano.

'MA-*KUN*, I'M HERE. LET'S GO!'

The little girl was a year or two older than he was.

She had big sparkling eyes, and straight, long black hair.

'Ah – OK . . .'

Masaru always dithered at the front door, pretending not to be that interested in going.

Then she would grab his hand and set off. Masaru was waiting for her to do it. The feel of her hand in his as the two of them went for their piano lesson.

The girl had regular lessons, and Masaru was more of a random add-on. He realized now how generous the girl, and her teacher, had been to allow him to join them.

The lessons themselves were unconventional. His teacher's home was always full of different types of music, everything from rock and jazz to Japanese songs and *enka*. There were two songs Masaru particularly liked at the time and he could still sing them: Mina Aoe's 'Isezakicho Blues' and Aki Yashiro's 'Funa uta', or 'Sea Shanty'.

'You like husky voices, don't you, Ma-*kun*. Your tastes are quite low-key.' He remembered how both his teacher and the girl were impressed by this.

They would play along with various types of music, sometimes improvising, then do scales and then a piece played with four hands. They would get more and more into it, and time would fly.

When the girl played, you forgot how young she was. There was something inside her much greater, which felt evolved and mature. Beatific, even.

Masaru thought that if you practised enough anyone could do it, yet the girl's level was so high that she'd already gone well beyond basic practice. She was a prodigy, the first he'd ever met. He was positive that, in the years that followed, she'd become well known.

But he couldn't remember the girl's name, so later, even when he could use the internet, he never searched for her. Her name was a hard one, and they'd only called each other shortened forms of their names – Ma-*kun* for him, and Aa-*chan* for her. Perhaps she didn't remember his name either.

They lived in the same neighbourhood, though she was

privately educated, so they were at different schools and never met there. But he grew used to the sound of the piano filtering through the windows whenever he passed her house.

One day he happened to bump into her as she was coming out of her front door, carrying a bag with a treble clef embroidered on it. He found her face quite different from that of his classmates. She had an inner light and liveliness that immediately struck him.

Before he knew it, he'd asked, 'Are you always playing the piano?'

The girl looked at him, her eyes reflecting an immense curiosity. 'Yes, I am. Who are you?'

'I really like that bit, just after it slows down.'

Masaru sang the phrase and the girl's eyes widened.

'Wow, you have a great ear,' she said. 'That part's hard to play.'

The girl paused for a moment. 'Listen, are you free now?'

'Hmm?' Masaru was taken aback.

'Let's go together to my teacher. I'm sure you'll like it. Right – let's go, Ma-*kun*.'

That was the first time she'd taken his hand, and she strode off immediately.

Showing up with a strange boy didn't faze her teacher. 'Oh, is this a friend of yours?' he asked.

'His name's Ma-*kun*, and he has a great ear for music.'

Very soon her teacher, too, was bowled over by Masaru's ear.

He had perfect pitch and could reproduce any music he heard. The teacher gently led him through the basics, though without a piano at home Masaru couldn't go over anything afterwards.

He and the girl were quickly playing simple pieces for four hands, singing loudly together.

The teacher murmured his approval.

'You're so alike,' he said. 'As if you have some immense musical spirit inside you, powerful and bright, that can't be contained – it's got to be let out.'

'Ma-*kun*'s sound is like the ocean, isn't it?' the girl said.

'The ocean?' Masaru and their teacher both asked.

'Yes, under a deep blue sky, with waves crashing in. Seagulls are flying around, and every once in a while, they rest on the crest of a wave, bobbing up and down. Since it's Ma-*kun*'s ocean, they sit calmly.'

'I like the way you put it,' her teacher said, laughing.

But Masaru couldn't laugh. These words from a prodigy like her weren't just empty praise, for she believed this was *truly* his sound, and it filled him with joy.

When the time came for Masaru to return to France, their teacher said, 'Ma-*kun*, you make a truly wonderful sound. I really want you to continue practising. If you can't, then please continue to love music the way you do. It will be your treasure.'

The girl cried her eyes out. 'You said we'd practise until we could play the Rachmaninoff together!' She stamped her foot in frustration.

When she tired of crying, she turned bloodshot eyes on him. 'Promise me you'll keep playing,' she said, and handed him the bag with the treble clef.

BACK IN FRANCE, HE TOLD his parents he wanted to study the piano.

Until then he'd never clearly stated his wishes about anything, so this took them by surprise, but they agreed. Masaru had lessons at the home of a university music student in the neighbourhood, bringing along his sheet music in his little treble-clef bag.

After only a few lessons, his tutor got in touch with Masaru's parents.

'I'd like to introduce Masaru to my own teacher,' he said. Before they knew it, Masaru was standing out, and after two years he made a name as a child prodigy. As his teacher in Japan had said, he had his own unique sound.

'Listen to me, Masaru,' Nathaniel Silverberg said to him when he'd decided to participate in the Yoshigae International

Piano Competition. 'You are a star. You light up the room. You have an aura. You have an amazing, innate feel for music. And a tough, generous inner strength.'

Nathaniel gave him a serious look.

'I don't say this kind of thing to every student. It would either put too much pressure on them, or make them conceited.'

Nathaniel had a particularly brusque, intense way of speaking. Masaru liked how it seemed at once both clever and a bit awkward.

'I will say this to you,' Nathaniel continued. 'I believe more in your talent than anyone else's. Bring the prize home. Live up to your name, and *win*.'

'Will do,' Masaru murmured.

Masaru finished breakfast, and went back up to his room to change.

He intended to listen to all the entrants in this competition, as he had at Osaka.

This morning he was going to see a friend of Nathaniel, a professor at a music college, to borrow his piano to practise, then in the afternoon he'd enjoy the performances.

He noticed the rolled-up cloth bag in his suitcase, darkened with age.

The bag with the embroidered treble clef that he now kept as a good-luck charm.

Outside the window, the Pacific Ocean off Yoshigae sparkled.

'I've come here, like a vast wave crossing the ocean,' he whispered to the red-eyed little girl of his memory.

'But will this huge wave I bring to the shores of Japan turn into a tsunami?'

He straightened up and put on a white shirt.

The *Rocky* Theme

So when was the *last time I performed in front of an audience?*

Akashi Takashima searched his memory and decided it must have been two years ago when he'd played the background music at a friend's wedding.

He'd become a working adult, got a job in a service industry of sorts, married, become a father and settled down, and though he didn't think he suffered much from stage fright, now, on the morning of the first day of the competition, he was flustered to find himself more tense than he had expected.

No, he thought. *Best to think about it the opposite way.*

I have more to shoulder now in life, more responsibility, and it's precisely because I know more now about the ways of the world that I'm feeling this new sense of dread.

The first day of the competition. The sky was clear and sunny.

Akashi had arrived in Yoshigae the previous day and stayed overnight in a chain hotel in the centre of town. He was the last to perform that first day, so he could have arrived that morning or even in the afternoon, but he couldn't risk some delay on the way. He'd continued to practise until the moment he'd had to leave. A workmate at his music store was from Yoshigae, and his parents had invited him to their home to do some last-minute warming up.

Akashi was twenty-second in the line-up. There were supposed to be eighteen performers per day in the first round, so he'd expected to play on the second day, but as several pianists had withdrawn, he'd been moved up to play last on the first day.

He had no idea if it was a good or bad thing that he'd be the last one to play, though with long hours of waiting ahead of him he knew it would be a challenge to keep focused.

Still, he was glad it was Sunday since that meant that

Machiko could come to hear him. They'd asked her parents to look after little Akihito while she was gone. Machiko would have to teach on Monday, so after spending the night in the hotel with Akashi she'd have to take an early train back the next morning, but all the same she was overjoyed at having the opportunity to hear her husband perform after such a long time. The performance would be recorded, and as Masami would be filming it, she could have watched it afterwards, but Machiko insisted on hearing him play live. If he didn't make it to the second round, this would be her first and last chance to hear him. Getting on for ninety people would play in the first round, while only twenty-four would make it to the second round. Over sixty contestants would fail to advance, therefore. Then only half, twelve, would make it to the third, and only six to the finals.

Akashi had slept soundly last night, surprisingly. With no piano or any other distraction in the hotel room, he could relax. If he'd stayed at home, the piano would have monopolized his thoughts.

He took his time having breakfast and reading the paper.

Today it would all come down to how he was judged for a twenty-minute performance. He'd be in the same boat as all those other young music-department students who practised all day – no, all *year* – each with their teacher close at hand, strategizing their approach to the competition.

It was all rather strange. Not the kind of experience you would find in the normal course of life.

This past year he'd asked his former teacher to critique his playing, and devoted every spare minute to practising, but it was pretty obvious how much more time the other competitors were able to put in compared to him. And he couldn't help but be impatient at this disparity. At his age, simply practising long hours wasn't the only way forward; it was a matter of quality not quantity. When it came to the mental toughness needed for meaningful, quality practice, he knew he compared well, and he prided himself in taking more sheer joy from playing than anyone.

He'd been expecting to be the oldest pianist by far, but when he looked at the programme, he saw that there were others not much younger than him, and breathed a sigh of relief, then found his own reaction comical. There was one competitor from Russia who was nearly as old as him, and two others a couple of years younger, from Russia and from France. Were they all still students? Or working like he was? No matter what country you were from, it was hard to make a living through music. *I'll bet they don't have children, though*, he mused.

It had been awkward to get time off work for such a long competition, but his workmates and boss were supportive. After all, they were still practising musicians themselves. A couple were even coming over to hear him play in the first round. Apparently, the whole staff planned to come if he made it to the finals.

The *finals*. The very word was thrilling.

When still a student, he'd reached the finals of the most prestigious competition in Japan at the time. He ended up in fifth place, the highest level he'd ever attained.

The Yoshigae competition had attracted more attention recently, with winners reaching greater prominence. Musical powerhouses from all over the world were competing here. From China, where hugely promising pianists appeared one after another. And from South Korea, where it was national policy to invest heavily in the arts. The standard of performance in both countries had risen astronomically, and there were numerous competitors from both countries here now. Akashi knew he had only a faint hope of making it to the finals, but still he longed for it to happen, and to play Chopin's Piano Concerto No. 1 with a full orchestra.

At this very moment, all the other competitors must be thinking the exact same thing. Hoping to perform with an orchestra the exact same Tchaikovsky, or Rachmaninoff, or Grieg concerto they'd fallen in love with as a child.

He felt a strength well up in him, and let out a sigh.

'Relax, relax,' he told himself. 'It's going to be a long day. Getting all psyched right now won't help.'

He was about to stand up when he noticed the laces of his trainers were almost undone.

He squatted down to tie them but found he couldn't.

'What the—?' His fingers hovered stiffly over his laces.

'What is *wrong* with me?'

When he was finally able to tie them, it felt like it was the first time he'd ever done it. Nearly fifteen minutes had passed.

He stood up.

Stage fright?

Beads of sweat appeared on his forehead.

He thought back to earlier performances on stage – he'd felt a bit nervous, sure, but couldn't recall ever being this shaken.

He had a frighteningly vivid image of himself seated at the piano on stage, his mind blank, completely unable to recall what notes he was supposed to play.

No, that would never happen. Not when I've practised so much. I mean, that kind of thing has never *happened to me before.*

But then, neither has being so anxious I can't tie my shoelaces.

A cold voice whispered in his ear.

'You're not a musician any more. Working in a music store, with a family at home, you've totally lost your touch. You may have talked confidently about being an ordinary guy with a job, but actually you've run away. You burned your bridges, afraid of taking on life as a musician. You're nothing more than a dropout.'

Akashi had heard this voice so many times. He told himself his music was precisely the product of living an ordinary life, but in the end that was nothing more than sour grapes. If he'd been exceptionally talented, he would no doubt have chosen the life of a professional musician. And if he had become a professional, he would certainly have looked down his nose at those who worked for a living, had a family, and boasted about an *ordinary man's music*.

So, why am I here now? Who am *I, doing all this now?*

A dreadful loneliness took hold of him, his feet seemed to be sinking into the floor.

Every pianist feels a sense of isolation, but the loneliness Akashi was feeling right now could not be shared with any of the pianists about to take the stage, or with his family. It was something closer to extreme despair.

'Good morning, Takashima-*kun*,' a voice called, and it took a moment for him to respond.

Masami had finally arrived to start filming.

Of all the moments to turn up, he thought, almost tutting in frustration as he struggled to not let his feelings show.

'Oh, good morning.'

His voice was strained, his face still showing confusion. Masami gave a little start and glanced away.

I don't want to be filmed. What right does this woman have to come here and aim a video camera at me?

The last few days he'd found her filming depressing, irritating, and he realized he'd even started to hate her for doing it. She must have noticed this too, but it was her job, so she couldn't exactly hold back. Yet a certain awkwardness had sprung up between the two of them.

But today he couldn't handle it. Couldn't handle it at all. If she spent the day, camera in hand, shadowing him, he couldn't begin to imagine what abuse he might end up hurling at her. He didn't trust himself not to say something he would regret.

Akashi took a deep breath.

'I'm sorry, but today's a little—' he ventured, his expression hard, and Masami gave a big nod as if to forestall him. He noticed that although she was carrying her large bag as usual, this morning she wasn't holding the camera.

'Don't worry – I won't film you right now. I'll go to the concert hall to catch the people involved in putting on the competition, and a couple of other performers.'

'I'm sorry.' It was all he could do to get that out.

'But I do want to film you in the dressing room later, and as you wait to go on stage. Without that, the documentary won't work, so I hope you'll understand.' Masami spoke curtly and flatly, making her needs known.

Akashi nodded. 'Sure. I understand,' he said.

'*Good luck*,' she said in English.

She left, and Akashi felt deflated.

Masami knew how on edge he became before performing. Relieved she'd gone so quickly, he also regretted behaving so childishly. *If I'm this nervous*, he thought, *I'm no better than some student competitor*. He'd wanted to play a little differently, give a more mature, adult performance, and felt miserable at how very limited his range was when it came down to it.

Still, talking with Masami had calmed him a little.

He took another deep breath.

Right – I'll give them a mature, adult performance. I'll take this complicated sense of loneliness, and my ambivalent feelings towards music, and express them in my playing. That's the single advantage the oldest competitor in the field has.

He sat up straight, folded up his newspaper and ordered more coffee from a passing waitress.

MASAMI HAD QUICKLY LEFT AKASHI, but still couldn't help letting out a deep sigh when she was out of sight.

It was hard to believe even Akashi could look like that sometimes, she thought.

Reporting on other competitors over the past few days, she found many of them tense, and several had refused to be filmed. Some didn't mind at all (making her wonder why), but many of the entrants from North America couldn't disguise their feelings, with some of their host families apologetically telling her at the front door, 'We're sorry, but today's not a good day for filming.'

She had thought Akashi would be fine, but even he was getting nervous. Close coverage, as she was giving him, meant spending inordinate amounts of time together, and it was inevitable that relations with the subject would feel brittle on occasion.

She had wanted to leave Akashi alone, but she couldn't. It was her job. Today was the first day of the competition, the day Akashi would perform, and she wanted to check on how he was doing, but intuition told her to keep her camera in her bag. If she'd tried to film him now, he would have refused to let her film him actually performing, which was critical to the success of her documentary.

What a demanding, cruel world it was.

Ever since she began reporting on it, she'd been surprised by how unexpectedly harsh the world of classical music, and piano competitions, actually was.

Masami had always imagined the classical-music world as elegant and lofty, but the reality was totally different. Unless you had well-off parents, it was hard to continue playing an instrument. And the housing situation in Japan made it difficult to find a space to practise. Someone might graduate from music college specializing in a wind instrument, for instance, but then find they had nowhere to practise. Some instruments could be muted, but many musicians avoided using a mute since they disliked what it did to the sound. Then there was the cost of maintaining the instrument.

And now piano competitions had become a major industry.

With the audience and all the supporting staff having to stay locally for the duration of the competition, it was an economic boost for a town, and a good opportunity to raise its profile. This resulted in a flood of competitions, big and small, popping up all over the world, with pianists seeking out contests that would bolster their careers, and the organizers seeking outstanding competitors who would win more renown for the competition. So cut-throat was the whole business now that competitions had become like warring fiefdoms.

For all the effort the pianists put in to performing in a competition, the prize money had to be worthwhile, and there had to be a guaranteed concert tour for the winner. Competitions that guaranteed all these perks were the ones flooded with applicants. Sponsors needed to have a promising star who would win, otherwise it wasn't worth the investment. But it wasn't easy to get both sides' expectations in accord, so although competitions might spring up anywhere, many didn't last long.

Piano manufacturers, too, were in fierce rivalry with each other. Having contestants play their pianos was good advertising for vital market share. In the bigger competitions it was the tradition to allow the pianists to select from multiple makers and consult with piano tuners. Every piano maker wanted them to choose their instruments. When one piano manufacturer added its name as a sponsor to a competition, a rumour spread that if you didn't choose their piano you wouldn't win, and so the majority of the pianists did just that. And as this situation continued, other manufacturers stopped providing their pianos.

During a competition each maker would dispatch teams of tuners to take exclusive care of their instruments. With the clock ticking, every second precious, they would fine-tune the piano and adjust the touch to each pianist's preference, which was pressured, physically exhausting work. Many a tuner said they never got a wink of sleep during the entire competition.

With all these outstanding pianists, how could they possibly decide first and second place, let alone the rest?

Masami felt a vague apprehension as she watched the contestants practise their hearts out.

To her, they all seemed amazing, with not much difference between any of them, and she found it hard to believe that all but a handful of these nearly one hundred great pianists would in the end be eliminated. On top of that, ever since they were children these individuals had spent nearly every waking moment at the piano, their lives focused on the single goal of becoming professional pianists.

What a terrifying world.

Masami had voiced this once without thinking, and Akashi had nodded. 'Yeah, it *is* a frightening world,' he'd said, and then murmured, as if this had suddenly occurred to him: 'But that's what makes it so wonderful.'

'What do you mean?' Masami had asked.

Akashi didn't seem to realize that he'd spoken aloud. 'Well . . .' he said, looking sheepish. 'It's not such an achievement to be number one if only a hundred people in the whole world play your instrument, right? But here we have such a broad base, which makes the handful of musicians standing at the pinnacle all the more amazing. Knowing how many disappointed musicians lie there in heaps in the shadows makes music even more beautiful.'

'Really, now?' Masami said dubiously, and Akashi let out a gentle laugh.

'After all, it's just human beings who are playing. That's the way it is.'

Akashi's smile pierced right through her.

Oh, she thought, how she used to love this smile of his.

That was the smile he'd always had. Not a gentleness motivated by a desire to stay in others' good graces, trying not to be disliked or be pushy, but a smile that emerged from deep down, reflecting genuine kindness towards others. She'd been drawn, too, by how exacting and honest he was about himself. Everyone seemed to pick up on this about him, and he'd been popular among the girls, and liked by the boys as well.

If truth be told, Masami had asked to cover him for her TV station precisely because it was Akashi. It made her happy to see how he hadn't changed, how he was still so kind to others, yet so demanding of himself.

For someone like Akashi to become this nervous, the competition world really must be overwhelming.

Masami headed towards the concert hall to interview the volunteer staff. She'd got permission from the sponsors, so they must have decided already who among the staff would speak to her.

It was finally starting.

Masami was trembling with excitement, as if she was walking on to the stage herself.

She spotted a small Inari shrine in the middle of town, where people prayed for good fortune. Praying to the Inari deity was hardly going to make a difference, she told herself, but she went ahead anyway, breathing a prayer for Akashi.

I pray that Akashi can give a performance that will make him happy. And that he makes it to the second round.

A more down-to-earth concern suddenly struck her. If he didn't make it past the first round, her documentary wasn't going anywhere either. She hurried off towards the concert hall.

The looming, multi-purpose facility rose up into the clear, still sky. That afternoon, the long-awaited competition would finally begin.

Round One

There's No Business Like Show Business

Alexei Zakhaev was standing in the darkness backstage. He took a long, deep breath to calm his pounding heart.

Why am I first?! *Why did I have to pick the opening spot in the draw?*

He sighed again, for the millionth time.

He was sure he'd never be the very first to play and had pulled out the first slip of paper he touched. The instant he opened it, his eyes caught that cruel number, *1*.

He passed the paper to the organizer, who gave him a sympathetic look and announced: 'No. 1.' A loud cheer arose from the gathered competitors.

No number was more nerve-racking, or more disadvantageous. It did put a temporary spotlight on you, but it was those who came *after* that everyone was interested in. At most, the lead player would set a certain *standard*. Afterwards competitors would be judged as to whether they were better, or worse, but very rarely would the person who set that bar win the prize. With almost ninety contestants to follow, who would ever recall the first?

What miserable luck.

Alexei had phoned his mentor to relay the news, and his teacher was at a loss for words. The only thing Alexei could do was give a memorable performance so that people would recall how good the first pianist had been.

In the darkness, he limbered up his fingers.

No matter how often he appeared on stage, he could never get used to this unique feeling of tension.

But there is one good thing, he thought. *I'll finish before everyone else and can then take it easy. A lot better than waiting, heart racing, for all those other pianists to play.*

Alexei comforted himself with this thought.

But still – why No. 1?! If only I'd moved my fingers and grabbed a different slip of paper—

The stage manager was telling him something, and Alexei pulled himself together.

The door to the stage swung open.

The lights from the stage.

The piano, black and still, waiting under the lights.

My turn.

Alexei took a breath and steeled himself.

As SOON AS THE COMPETITION began, it fell into a routine. The staff, the competitors and the judges were all in a battle against the clock – to ensure events unfolded smoothly, that performances didn't exceed their allotted time limit, that marks were determined quickly. Each did their job efficiently so that the competition proceeded without a hitch.

First-round performances were twenty minutes each.

They had to play one piece from Bach's *Well-Tempered Clavier*, including a fugue with at least three voices; the first movement from a sonata by Haydn, Mozart or Beethoven; and finally, a piece by a Romantic composer.

Playing all three in twenty minutes might seem simple, but it wasn't. Exceed the time limit and points would be deducted. In the first round, there was no applause between pieces, in order to save time.

The concert hall was about sixty per cent full. The majority of the audience were connected to the performers, but there were also some unconnected, ardent classical-music fans there too, afficionados who enjoyed discovering new favourites among the competitors and predicting who would get through to the second round. Seats to the left filled up first, as they provided a good view of the pianists' hands.

The judges sat in the upper balcony, thirteen judges from

around the world, all assessing the performances. Scoring in the first round was simple – each piece was marked with an O, Δ or X. The first was three points, the second one point and the last zero points. Those with the highest total scores would go through.

'The level of playing is exceedingly high,' Nathaniel Silverberg mused after hearing the first five pianists.

Generally, the goal of the first round was to eliminate any pianists with technical weaknesses. But these days few had any major problems.

Nowadays, when there were so many ways for anyone in the world to access performances, and pianists could tailor their approach towards an individual competition, the technical bar had been raised high.

Until not so long ago, he recalled, pianists would choose the most difficult pieces they could play, but now the programmes tended to be full of safe, steady pieces that competitors could handle without risk, which was a good thing.

Nevertheless, there were clear differences between pianists.

Somebody who *can play* and someone who *plays* might seem the same, but they weren't. There was a vast chasm between the two, Nathaniel thought.

What made it even more complicated was that there were, among those with the necessary technical skills, individuals who could take it to the next level, who had that innate ability, and others who would just spin their wheels, as it were, and end up delivering a performance without real substance. The gap between the two was wide, and if a pianist were aware of it, they might discover the necessary spark to make the leap from one to the other.

In the past, major pianists wouldn't bat an eye at a few thoughtless fingerings, and there were many performers whose eccentric approach went beyond mere individuality. But that more relaxed, more forgiving generation had disappeared.

So the level of the contestants here was quite high, yet none was a match for Masaru.

Nathaniel smiled faintly and nodded to himself.

Masaru was sitting directly underneath the upper-floor

balcony where his mentor, Nathaniel, as one of the judges, was seated.

Like his mentor, Masaru was impressed by the high level of the competitors.

They're all so good, he thought. *A top-level competition like this is definitely something else; it attracts all the best pianists.*

The two girls seated in front of him seemed to be music-college students. They appeared well informed, and Masaru listened in discreetly to their conversation. He wasn't good at writing in Japanese, but he understood the spoken language well enough, and had spent time with Japanese exchange students in New York in an effort to keep up his conversational skills.

He did this in the hope that some day he'd be able to speak again with his childhood friend, Aa-*chan*. He had no idea when that might happen, or if it ever would, but meanwhile his language skills came in handy.

'The showpiece today has got to be Jennifer Chan,' one of the girls said.

'The female Lang Lang they call her, don't they?'

'She's already played concerts. Nakajima – she was ahead of us in school? – went to one in New York.'

This was during a short interval. The two girls were looking through their programmes, discussing all the gossip they'd heard about the pianists.

Wow, they're really all over it, Masaru thought.

'I want to hear this one, too. Masaru Carlos – he's playing tomorrow.'

That took Masaru by surprise.

'I hear he's amazing.'

'He's so hot. He's third- or fourth-generation Japanese or something, but his face doesn't look Japanese at all.'

Masaru prayed they wouldn't turn around.

'The Honeybee Prince is playing on the last day.'

'Right.'

Honeybee Prince?

Thinking he'd heard wrong, Masaru pricked up his ears.

'He's so cute. They say he's only sixteen. That's a shame – he's five years younger than us!'

Masaru searched for the page in his programme that the girls were looking at. He'd been so busy listening to everyone, he'd hardly checked the official programme at all.

'His audition in Paris was supposed to be amazing.'

'It's too bad his home page only has his photo. I wish they'd post some videos, too.'

Jin Kazama.

Masaru wasn't good at reading *kanji* so he looked at the romanized version of the name.

The face of a young, innocent boy. There was no lower age limit for this competition. Masaru had heard the youngest competitor was fifteen, so this boy would be the second youngest. The column detailing competition experience was blank.

Masaru's eye was drawn more to the column listing the boy's teachers.

Yuji Von Hoffmann.

No way! Someone could have studied under Hoffmann?

Masaru's eyes widened. This had been his own teacher's teacher. But what Masaru had heard was that Hoffmann didn't invite Silverberg to be his pupil, and he'd had to fly from London to Hoffmann's home in Germany to specifically beg him for lessons.

Does Maestro Silverberg know about this?

Masaru gazed up at the ceiling.

Masaru liked to hear people's performances, but he had no interest in gossip, so had heard no rumours about the auditions leading up to the competition.

Hmm – so he got into the competition through an audition?

Now he was interested.

I really want to hear him, he thought. *He must be a kind of blank canvas.*

'They say he was helping his father with his work, and when he showed up at the audition he was all muddy. Isn't that weird?'

'The son of a beekeeper would have to move around a lot, wouldn't he? I wonder how he manages to practise.'

'It's all very strange.'

Masaru couldn't quite catch the word *beekeeper* at first but recalled the earlier *Honeybee Prince* and realized what it meant.

Jin Kazama. What kind of pianist could he be?

When the tall girl appeared on stage, wearing a red dress, there was a stir among the audience.

The red was intense and striking, and the girl strode on to the stage with a determined look, radiating great energy.

Pianist No. 12, from the USA, Jennifer Chan.

Today's standout performer.

Mieko Saga stared intently at the dazzling figure. The girl was tall, so it wasn't immediately obvious, but she had broad shoulders and a sturdy frame too. With a splendid build like this, her performance would be something to behold.

Before she'd even heard her, Mieko predicted she was a *GMB* type.

GMB was Mieko's own term for a pianist with transcendent technical skills, who played so well you got that *give me a break* feeling.

Some of the other judges, too, seemed expectant.

Jennifer Chan wasted no time, launching into her first piece the moment she sat down.

A murmur of surprise swept through the hall.

Such crystal-clear, distinct voicing, the huge expanse of her sound – all this was instantly evident.

What an amazingly dynamic Bach, Mieko thought. She was half impressed, half shocked.

Next came the first movement of Beethoven's Piano Sonata No. 21, the *Waldstein*.

Chan's choices were perfect. The tempo of this piece perfectly matched her dexterity and dynamism.

The piano was an amazing instrument if you thought about it, Mieko mused. When Chan played, the piano was like some large, special-edition Mercedes-Benz. Steered perfectly, power surging, the car hugging the road, racing forward with such rock-solid stability. Depending on the pianist, the grand piano could come across as a family station wagon, or a cool but not very manoeuvrable convertible.

Jennifer Chan ran deftly through the *Waldstein*. Its alternating pianissimos and fortissimos had the audience on the verge of breaking into applause, but remembering the stipulation against this, they reined themselves in.

This piece alone took up ten minutes. It would be touch and go if she could finish in the allotted time, and so she launched straight into the final piece.

Chopin's *Heroic Polonaise* in A Flat Major, Op. 53.

Another perfect piece for her. The most gorgeous of all Chopin's polonaises, so well known that, if you weren't careful, it could sound trite, yet she played it with her own unique crisp touch and energy. A robust, moving performance, Mieko decided.

The instant Chan finished, applause broke out. It was clear the audience felt a wave of catharsis, thoroughly enchanted at such a stirring display.

As rumoured, Mieko thought, she'd given a good performance. She really *was* a kind of 'Female Lang Lang', a reputation Mieko was sure that Chan herself was fully aware of.

A wave of apprehension came over Mieko.

The world only really needed *one* Lang Lang. If a second one emerged, how would anyone handle it?

A BOY WAS SEATED IN the very back row of the hall, his pale face and scrunched-down hair visible under his cap.

He seemed to be muttering to himself. No – not muttering, but *singing*.

Tilting his head to one side, he then shook it gently.

'No, that's not it,' he said, so quietly that no one heard.

Two girls hurried into the concert hall through the auditorium door.

'Oh, shoot. We missed her – Jennifer Chan.'

'I really wanted to hear her.'

It was Kanade Hamazaki and Aya Eiden.

'I knew we should have got our hair done yesterday,' Aya muttered.

'There're only three pianists left to play.'

'Let's get a CD of Chan's performance. I think they'll burn a copy for us straight away. If we put in an order, we should get it tomorrow.'

The two girls had come to a halt.

When the boy saw Aya Eiden's face, he flinched.

It was the girl from last night.

The one who'd questioned him about using the music-college practice room. Would she recognize him?

He stealthily pulled his cap down to hide his eyes.

'Where should we sit?'

'I want to hear properly, so let's sit in the middle. The sound balance is good in this hall.'

They passed through without noticing him and sat down in the middle seats. The boy breathed a sigh of relief.

She must be a piano student at the music college, so it makes sense she would come to listen. Or is she in the competition, too?

The boy gazed at the backs of their heads.

He fell into a rapturous reminiscence of the piano in the practice room. The instrument had been wonderful. It was perfectly tuned, but that was to be expected in a music college.

Those guys were so lucky to practise on such a great piano every day.

In his head he was playing it. A superb piano with sublime sound.

Replaying music over and over in his head.

He slid down in his seat to hear the next pianist.

That girl in the red dress had been excellent. Quietly, he began to sing the melody in his head.

*

WHEN THE INTERVAL WAS ANNOUNCED, the boy went out with the rest of the audience.

He decided to go to the practice room. Day one of the competition was almost over. If a practice room was free, maybe they'd let him play. He felt a rush of excitement as he got into the lift.

I wonder where Dad is today. He glanced at his watch. His father would be on his way somewhere new. He felt guilty that he couldn't help out.

I wonder if he remembers he promised he'd buy me a piano if I reached the finals.

His father was a big-hearted, generous man, though he was also quite rough. He could be so painstaking and detailed when it came to his bees, but with anything else he basically couldn't be bothered.

There wasn't a piano in the boy's house.

And it never occurred to him how very odd that was.

Ballade

MACHIKO TAKASHIMA HURRIED TOWARDS the concert hall. She checked the name on the sign and was about to rush into the auditorium when she stopped suddenly and looked up at the sky.

The sun had long set, and it was dark outside. It was the first time she'd been to Yoshigae, but the concert hall was near the station, and there were posters everywhere for the competition, and arrows pointing all the way to the hall, so she'd found it without any difficulty.

The detour to her parents' house to leave her son Akihito with them had taken longer than expected, and she hadn't left Tokyo station until after three p.m. If she ended up missing Akashi's performance, *devastated* wouldn't begin to describe her emotions.

Akashi had sent her the performance schedule, so she knew there was still an hour to go before he was due to play, but his slot had already been brought forward, so Machiko had been fretting since the morning, worried that they would move it up again.

When she reached the right place, she realized how tense she was. The mid-sized concert hall had a glassed-off reception area, and past that was the auditorium itself, the doors shut tight.

THE SIGHT OF THE DOORS alone was enough to make her heart constrict.

Machiko took a deep breath, went towards the hall and showed her ticket.

'There's no admittance during performances, so please wait for a while,' they told her.

She nodded. 'Are they on schedule?'

'Yes, right on schedule.'

Relieved, she had a wander around the lobby.

There were a lot of young women – students from music colleges, she imagined. Chatting casually to each other, they had that look about them as if they were used to all this. For Machiko, who rarely stepped into a concert hall, it was an unfamiliar world, and she gazed restlessly around her. There were others who, like her, were family members, easy to spot since they seemed unsure what to do. *I know the feeling*, she thought.

That older, dignified woman had to be a piano teacher.

Piano teachers were always easy to spot, too. Machiko had learned the piano for a short while as a child, and got the impression that, for some reason, piano teachers always had mounds of hair. Older female piano teachers always seemed to have huge coils of it on top of their heads, and wore mismatched suits – a blouse and short jacket clashing with a longish flared skirt. And you could count on them, too, for sporting the kind of brooch that women Machiko's age would never wear.

I never had any talent for music, she thought with a sigh.

The sound of applause brought her out of her reverie. Machiko hurried inside.

There was a surprisingly large audience. On stage a man in a suit was busily tuning the piano.

Where should I sit?

The rows at the back seemed fairly empty. As she settled down in her seat, she finally felt at ease.

Po–on, po–on, the sounds of the piano strings rang out.

The piano tuner seemed oblivious to the audience as he stood in front of the keys, concentrating on the notes.

There was something calming about this figure, standing in a soft light on the stage.

Akashi finally made it, Machiko told herself, and let out another small sigh.

Ever since she was a child, she'd been told to be dispassionate, and not to reveal her emotions, but at the sight of the grand piano on stage, and the thought of her husband waiting backstage, the phrase *filled with emotion* came to her.

AFTER AKASHI HAD DECIDED TO enter the competition, things got tough.

There was a well-known saying that went: 'Skip one day of practice and you'll know, skip two and the critics will know, skip three and the audience will know.' But after Akashi started work, and Akihito was born, there would be several days each week when he didn't even touch the piano, and it was only about a year ago that he really started to prepare seriously for the competition. A working man like Akashi could, of course, only find time to practise early in the morning, at night or during holidays, and when they did finally build a house of their own, he said he wanted to be able to practise as much as he could, so they made a tiny soundproof room for an upright piano. Even that had cost them a lot, not to mention the price of sheet music, which Machiko had found surprising, or the expense of having her husband's former piano teacher advise him every few weeks so he could regain his touch.

'This is the first and the last time,' Akashi had told her, and she understood how he felt. Rarely did her husband ask for anything for himself, so Machiko, without a word of complaint, cashed in their savings to help pay for it all, but she knew it was hardest for Akashi, for he had to cut back on sleep to carve out more practice time, and when his exhaustion caught up with him, of course it negatively affected his practice. At times he was so frustrated he'd agonized over whether he should just give it all up.

The hardest thing was maintaining his motivation, and every couple of weeks or so he'd go through a period when he found the challenge pointless, muttering in self-criticism that no one had asked him to do this, so why should he, so late in the day? Machiko would encourage him, reminding him how much they'd paid for the soundproof room. 'We at least have to get our money's worth from it, don't we?'

One reason she was so supportive was that she herself regretted not becoming a professional in her own field.

Machiko's father had a doctorate in space engineering, and worked as a consultant for the government, and her two older brothers were research scientists. Machiko herself had hoped to work in research, but when she was a student, she realized she lacked the necessary spark, and couldn't find what she was looking for. She finally chose teaching.

But the desire to be a research scientist like her brothers still smouldered within her.

When Akashi revealed that he wanted to enter the competition, she empathized, knowing that he felt the same way about his own dream and hadn't entirely given up pursuing it. It took Akashi by surprise how enthusiastically she encouraged him.

In a corner of the stage was a white placard with the name and number of the next competitor. The audience grew still and a blonde girl in a blue dress stepped out to applause.

Machiko checked the programme. This pianist was from Russia. Westerners always seemed more grown up than their actual age, but this girl was only twenty.

A graceful sound began to flow from the stage.

Machiko couldn't remember the last time she'd heard a live piano performance in a concert hall.

She'd heard Akashi practising, of course, but now they had a soundproof room, she could no longer hear him.

Wow, she's so good, she thought.

Her earlier nervousness began to creep back.

I guess I shouldn't be surprised that they're so polished, she thought, *and able to play such difficult pieces with so much spirit.* She'd heard how high the standard of performance was in this competition, and that they accepted contestants who were already performing professionally, yet they really did all seem like professional pianists. When Akashi had said how he expected to fail at the first round, she'd assumed that was his timidity speaking, but now she really could see how hard this was going to be. As a student he'd reached competition finals, so she thought he'd have no trouble getting through this time, but that was nearly ten years ago, and it was clear that his age put him at a disadvantage.

What will I say if he doesn't get through?

The worry cut into her suddenly.

You did your very best. It's better to have taken up the challenge than not do it and regret it later. It was a wonderful experience for me as well. Good thing it's over while you still have some days of paid holiday left.

But all she could picture was Akashi, head bent low in bitter disappointment, and she sensed that nothing she could say would comfort him.

'Being a musician's wife can't be easy.'

She suddenly recalled the voice of a former high-school classmate.

They had got together to plan a class reunion. The other woman, who'd had a crush on Akashi back at school, had always been sure to attend his recitals when he was in music college and to present him with a bouquet afterwards.

Boys who played instruments were popular with the girls. Besides being an excellent pianist, Akashi was innately positive and kind, and girls had always liked him.

Akashi and Machiko were childhood friends, had started to

be aware of each other more in junior high, and by high school had gently progressed to going out. Machiko was a born science nerd, not openly friendly and certainly not stylish, and a lot of other girls weren't too thrilled about her dating Akashi, this particular classmate included.

She'd apparently told Akashi to his face how unsuited she thought Machiko was to him, though Akashi, typically, paid her no attention.

After college, when they had reached marriageable age, these girls lost all interest in boys who could play the piano.

'How is Akashi-*kun* doing?' they'd ask. 'Is he still playing?'

'Good thing you're a government employee, Machiko.'

There was no longer a look of envy in the eyes of those former friends who knew she'd married Akashi, but something more akin to sympathy.

Whenever she mentioned that he'd got a job with a large musical-instrument store, their inevitable response was, 'Oh, that's great,' but she could detect their unspoken thoughts: *So he couldn't make a living as a musician, could he?* or, *He wasn't talented enough.*

Being a musician's wife can't be easy.

This seemingly innocent comment was so irritating – the woman herself who back then had appealed to Akashi that she was a far better partner for him than Machiko, had ended up marrying a much older man, a dentist, and had just given birth to her first son – irritating because of the clear note of pity in her voice.

Mind your own business! Machiko said inwardly.

A Korean girl played next, then a Chinese boy, followed by a Korean boy.

Every one of them was excellent. She'd heard that Asian pianists had made great strides in recent years, and these three were clearly more powerful and skilled than the Russian girl who'd come before them.

Superb, all of them, she acknowledged with a sigh.

The opening day of the first round reached its final pianist.

22. TAKASHIMA AKASHI

A new nameplate had been slipped on to the board. With a racing heart, Machiko sat up straight.

When was the last time I felt this nervous? she wondered.

She unconsciously pressed her stomach, the blood pounding in her ears.

If I were playing, I'd be so paralysed with stage fright I wouldn't be able to perform. No – I wouldn't be this nervous even if I *were performing.*

To be able to go out there, alone, on stage, and play, Akashi – you're amazing just to be able to do that.

The heavy door opened, and the tall figure of Akashi appeared.

The applause was especially warm, he being Japanese.

It wasn't just his build, but somehow he looked bigger on the stage.

She was so moved she forgot the ache in her stomach.

He really does have something invigorating and dignified about him, she thought.

It felt as if she were seeing him for the very first time.

Akashi walked briskly, a smile on his face, and seated himself at the piano.

He reached down and adjusted the height of the stool. The previous competitor was very short, and he had to lower it.

He took a handkerchief out of his pocket, lightly wiped the keys and then his hands.

'It's just a little ritual,' he'd explained to her. 'I don't do it because the tuner touched the keys, or because there might be leftover sweat on them. I pretend to wipe them down simply to calm myself.'

She heard his voice.

He laid the handkerchief on top of the piano and gazed upwards. Then he suddenly launched into his first piece.

Oh—

Machiko felt as if her eyes were being opened.

It wasn't just her, but others in the audience felt it too.

They'd seemed tired, because finally they'd reached the last pianist of the day, but Akashi made them sit up.

The sound he produced was – different. The same piano, but a sound totally unlike that of the previous pianist.

Clear, calm, gentle. With a distinct liveliness.

Music, she thought, *really is all about character. This sound is a perfect expression of the personality of the man I know*. Every note, every resonance, rang with the generosity of spirit of Akashi the man. She could see a scene opening up there on stage with him.

The Well-Tempered Clavier, Book 1, No. 2.

He'd fretted for a long time over which piece to choose. Even after whittling it down to a handful of possibilities, he played them over and over, comparing them, wrestling with which to play, until the competition was nearly upon them.

Whenever Machiko heard Bach, she always thought of the word *religious*.

She didn't know much about these things, yet she felt how her heart became still with the music, how it made her understand the meaning of *prayer*.

She wanted to listen to him play Bach for ever. Her own heart grew quiet, and humbled.

But the Bach was over before she knew it.

The next piece was Beethoven's Piano Sonata No. 3, the first movement.

She'd learned that the sonata was a critical musical form. One that tests the composer's abilities and reveals what he is capable of.

Machiko knew Beethoven's *Moonlight Sonata* and *Appassionata*, but honestly couldn't recognize any of his other sonatas.

This one sounded like a composition for the sake of composition, she thought. Not one written to convey something but composed for the sake of the form itself.

As she'd listened to Akashi practise, she'd voiced her unsophisticated impression.

'That's how it sounds to you?' he'd asked, smiling wryly.

'Yes. It's not very compelling.'

'Really. If that's the case, then I'm to blame.'

As he continued to play, he looked up at the ceiling.

'But isn't it the composer's fault?' Machiko responded, folding laundry as she spoke.

'No. There's an inevitability, something indispensable, about all these pieces that have stood the test of time. The pianist who can't draw that out, who can't convince, is at fault.'

She remembered feeling surprised by how stern he sounded.

Machiko suddenly felt tears well up. *I understand what Akashi meant now.*

Each and every phrase of Beethoven's emerging from Akashi's fingertips right now is organically linked, appealing to us in some way.

Akashi's playing is *persuasive. I feel, listening to it now, that I can understand, even a little, what Beethoven was trying to convey.*

She focused her eyes, not wanting to miss a single sound, but his second piece, too, was over quickly.

And now for Akashi's final piece, Chopin's Ballade No. 2.

'What I'd really like to play is Ballade No. 4,' he'd told her. 'But there won't be enough time.'

The opening was quiet and gentle. A simple, exquisite melody, like someone whispering to you. As she listened, an image rose in her mind, of Akashi reading a picture book to Akihito.

Yet with a single, furious phrase, that serenity was abruptly shattered.

A dramatic melody now crashed through, like raging waves, ebbing for a moment only to surge forth even more powerfully, never giving up.

The very intensity, and severity, of reality.

None of the audience knows how hard he has worked to be where he is right now, to be sitting here, dressed in a tuxedo, playing these sublime melodies. How very hard he works to simply make a living, all the endless struggles to support us.

'This will be the first time, and the last, so please, let me give it a shot.'

'I want to be able to tell Akihito that his dad is a musician.'

'Nobody asked me to be in this competition, so I'm trying to figure out why I am.'

'There's so much music I can't perform because of where I am now as a pianist.'

'My fingers just won't keep up. My emotions keep running ahead and the piece is a mess.'

'I really should have given up.'

'An unconvincing pianist is the worst.'

'My colleagues said that if I make it to the finals, they'll all come to hear me.'

Layers of Akashi's words and statements.

Even with all that, how lovely his playing, and this Chopin, is.

Chopin's Ballade No. 2 was the very embodiment of Akashi's gentleness and determination.

When he had finished, for an instant a genuine stillness filled the hall.

Akashi, who'd been looking down at the keys, raised his eyes.

He looked relieved.

He stood up, all smiles, and was greeted with applause and cheering.

As Machiko herself clapped enthusiastically, she murmured to herself.

My husband is *a musician. And I* am *a musician's wife.*

Interlude

'THAT LAST GUY MADE it all worthwhile.'

'Totally. I felt like I'd finally heard some real music.'

Walking back to the green room, the judges, liberated from

the tension and strain of the day, let their true feelings out, and some laughter too.

He really *was* good, that final pianist.

Akashi Takashima. Mieko etched the final competitor's name on her memory.

She'd never heard the name until now, nor any rumours circling about him.

He was, at twenty-eight, the oldest competitor.

In the world of music competitions, where people tended to focus on how young some of the pianists were, twenty-eight made him a veteran. A fine technique and good phrasing were a given. Some pianists entered as many competitions as they could, becoming a jack of all trades, too used to adjusting their playing to fit what they saw as the focus and demands of each competition, losing themselves in the process. But Takashima had avoided these pitfalls. The way his playing sang seemed, on first hearing, quite orthodox, yet it proved, in the end, to be unexpectedly unique; but there was nothing smug or self-satisfied about it, and it clearly called out to the listener.

Mieko felt happy whenever she encountered such a competitor. The impression of beautiful, relaxed playing, but also the sense of having heard something utterly engaging. She felt pulled in by something extraordinary, yet in no way alienating.

Whenever she was listening out for technique, she tried to keep an open mind, but was always left with the feeling that her ears had been somehow besmirched. As if the playing had left behind a sediment stuck in them, a residue she couldn't dislodge, the composition congealing in a lump of sound that could no longer be called music.

But not Akashi Takashima. What she'd heard was *music*.

It felt as if her soiled hearing had been completely restored, wiped clean of all accumulated sludge.

By the audience's reaction she saw that they felt the same way, one of the true wonders of music, for the responses from professionals and amateurs were sometimes totally at odds.

'So – what did you think?' Nathaniel asked as he sidled up to her. He seemed to be in decent spirits.

'I felt, *Right, this is what competitions are supposed to feel like.*'

Nathaniel chuckled. 'That's typical of you.'

'I think it's because I don't serve as a judge that often. I'm always looking forward to the next performance, but then I remember how much of a torment the whole thing can be. I never learn.'

'Best not to get worked up too soon. We have several rounds ahead of us,' he continued.

'I remember you telling me that before.'

It was true. Just as pianists always had hopes that *the next competition would be the one*, so the judges looked forward to each competitor as the next musical star. The two weeks of competition, especially the five days of the first round, were exhausting for those listening, and if they didn't pace themselves, they'd never last the course.

'How about you?' Mieko asked. 'Did any performances stand out?'

'The overall standard is high. I feel sorry for them, since technically they're all about the same. Unless someone really excels, they're never going to stand out from the crowd.'

'And you're saying your prize pupil's someone who actually will?'

Mieko could tell from Nathaniel's placid expression that he had unbounded confidence in his protégé.

'Not at all. A competition's a matter of chance.'

'That's hard to believe, considering how much confidence you have in him. What did you think about today's final competitor?'

'Very nice. He's quite grounded.'

'I agree.'

'Are you free for dinner?'

'All right. Where shall we go?'

'How about the Indian place in the basement?' he suggested.

'Sounds good. Let's have something spicy. It might perk us up.'

Eight straight hours of judging had left them totally worn out and starving. Service ended early in the restaurants of the local hotels, so they ordered as many drinks and as much food as they could. One thing the two of them still shared was a love of food and drink.

After clinking beer glasses, Mieko cut straight to the chase.

'So – is your divorce finalized?'

Nathaniel shot her a sullen look.

'Almost. As soon as we can agree on the alimony.'

'And how's Diana?'

Mieko had met Nathaniel's daughter by his second wife. The music world was smaller than it seemed, and even after she and Nathaniel had divorced, they'd continued to cross paths.

'She's good. I always thought she liked me more than her mother, but I'm not sure any more.'

'How come?'

'Diana's making her debut soon as a singer.'

'Really? Congratulations! What kind of singing?'

'Pop.'

'I always did think she was cute and outgoing. Not like her father.'

'Right,' Nathaniel said without a flicker. 'She *is* talented, musically,' he added. 'A bit green, though. Her mother's the one who understands the show-business world, so she'll be her manager.'

'Makes sense.'

Nathaniel was always jetting around the world and couldn't spend much time with his daughter. His ex-wife, Diana's mother, was a famous British stage actress, who generally confined her jobs to England and could spend more time with her.

'I hate it.' Nathaniel shook his head.

Mieko knew that when he said he *hated* something he wouldn't budge, so she didn't pursue the subject. She changed tack.

'But nothing can alter the fact that you're still father and daughter. Like with my son; we're email buddies now.'

'He's found a job, finally?'

'Yes, he's a civil servant now.'

'Are you still with that guy?' Nathaniel shot her a quick glance.

'Which guy would that be?'

'That much younger studio musician.'

'We live together. We're not married, though.'

Mieko was living with a composer eight years younger than her, a level-headed man who was an outstanding musician, both as an arranger and a performer. Maturity-wise, he might actually be older than her, she mused.

'Will you come back?'

The question was so out of the blue that Mieko, biting down on some tandoori chicken, couldn't respond.

'Come back? *Where?*'

'Back to *me*.'

'What?'

The words put her on edge, but she knew he was always direct when it came to things like this. Quite the opposite of his indecisiveness in the days of their break-up.

That's the kind of man he is. Mieko nodded to herself a few times.

'Well, what about that cute assistant of yours?' Mieko quipped, showing she wasn't taking his proposal seriously. True, she was touched by his very direct approach, much as she'd been back in the days when they'd first fallen in love, but memories of all the long-drawn-out problems that had ensued, and knowing about the massive divorce settlement he would be paying his present wife – a beautiful, talented young Polish woman, fluent in five languages, darling of the music world – convinced her he was merely looking for a way to escape.

Nathaniel smiled wryly. 'She's an efficient assistant. Nothing more, nothing less.'

'I wonder about that.' Mieko shrugged. 'I've heard all sorts of rumours.'

'Ha,' Nathaniel growled. 'Rumours. Rumours everywhere I go.

That I got her pregnant and she went back to her home town and secretly gave birth to our child, that she was made to provide all kinds of questionable services to her careless employer, that she got a huge pay-off to keep her mouth shut. God, I'm always amazed how people talk as if they've seen it all with their own eyes. Thanks to all that, my wife has upped her settlement demands astronomically. I feel like suing someone myself, but who am I supposed to sue?'

Mieko sympathized with his irritation. In her youth, she had been the subject of unfounded rumours herself, often spread just for the sake of it, and had suffered her own share of pain.

'The price of fame,' she said. 'In our world there's always a limited number of seats at the table; people are just jealous of you.'

Her declaration seemed to soothe his self-esteem a little. Nathaniel shot her a half-embarrassed smile.

'No matter – I'm serious, Mieko. I've learned a few things since we broke up. I'm confident things will work out now. Will you think it over during the competition?'

It was Mieko's turn to force a smile.

Now he's pushing it all on to me. And I've never been good at homework.

'By the way . . .' Nathaniel said, his tone changing as he mopped up lamb curry with a chunk of naan. 'Tell me more about this Honey Prince, or Honeybee Prince, or whatever he's called.'

Mieko sighed.

Why am I not surprised he's bringing that *up?*

'I was against him, you should know,' she said, pointedly, but Nathaniel's searching look, and piercing eyes, remained fixed.

'So what is he really like? I want your honest opinion.'

Mieko sensed his impatience.

'How was his performance? Was it like Maestro Hoffmann's?'

He spat this out quickly, curtly. He was trying his hardest to hide it, but she could tell how agitated, even scared, he was feeling. She recognized the highly strung boy genius of old.

He really does see himself as Hoffmann's pupil, she thought.

Even now, whenever he brings up the Master he acts more like a forlorn boy. I suppose most people are like that when recalling the mentor they idolize.

Mieko shook her head. 'He was totally different. What I felt was an overwhelming loathing. It was as if he was denying everything Maestro Hoffmann ever stood for in music. When he finished, I basically freaked out.'

The rage she'd felt in that moment came flooding back, only to vanish just as quickly.

Nathaniel's look was a complex mix of confusion and relief.

Confusion over why the rigorous teacher he adored above all others would choose to teach such a pupil; relief that this pupil wasn't the legitimate heir to his beloved teacher.

'But his letter of recommendation was legit?' Nathaniel asked.

'It was. What's really galling is that in it Hoffmann accurately predicted the negative response of people like me when they hear this Dust Prince play.'

The embarrassment she'd felt came back to her. This feeling didn't go away so easily.

'*Dust Prince?*'

Nathaniel looked mystified, until she explained how the boy's first name, Jin, was written with the character for *dust*, and he finally smiled.

'Seriously, even now I don't get it,' Mieko went on. 'What I was so angry about then, I mean. Smirnoff and Simon both thought he was amazing. How could he provoke such polar-opposite reactions? But they both agreed that provoking such reactions was in itself amazing, and they steamrollered me.'

She decided not to touch on the strongest reason for supporting the boy, that it would shock the music teachers in New York. Nathaniel wasn't really counted among those teachers, though he was a professor at Juilliard.

'Smirnoff and Simon both said the same thing,' Nathaniel said. 'They were seriously excited by his playing, but they only had an impression, and couldn't actually remember much about the performance itself.'

Ah – so Nathaniel had been interested enough in the Paris audition to go around questioning people about it. Mieko looked with renewed interest at the man sitting across from her.

It made sense that he wanted to collect information about any rivals to his prize protégé in the competition. It wasn't hard, though, for her to imagine how very afraid he was to learn the startling fact that in his final years Hoffmann had taken on a pupil.

'The competition office won't let me hear a recording of the audition. Apparently, it's against the rules.' Nathaniel shook his head resentfully.

Mieko had a hunch that Olga Slutskaya must be behind that.

The chair of judges must be figuring that if Jin Kazama were to win the competition or make the finals, the recording would be a goldmine for her. If he blew his chance, well, that would be it, and she could say they'd misjudged him and shelve it. *And that* misjudgement *would no doubt rebound harshly on me and the other Paris judges*, Mieko speculated.

'Professor Hishinuma told me that Maestro Hoffmann definitely considered Jin Kazama as his pupil. He said Daphne had told him Hoffmann travelled frequently to give him a lesson.'

Nathaniel couldn't hide his shock, and Mieko began to regret she'd said anything. She'd been sure he already knew.

'The Maestro? He went out to teach him?'

It was little wonder that Nathaniel was shocked, since that was unheard of – Von Hoffmann travelling to a see pupil.

'So Professor Hishinuma keeps in touch with Daphne, does he?' Nathaniel considered this. He looked around to seek out Tadaaki Hishinuma and grill him then and there.

'Correct. I heard that Jin Kazama is called the Honey Prince or Honeybee Prince or whatever because he's the son of a beekeeper, and he helps his father a lot so they're constantly on the move. I wonder if it's because of his unusual circumstances that Maestro Hoffmann decided to go out to wherever he happened to be for a lesson.'

Nathaniel brooded even more.

'Well, maybe in his final years the Maestro wanted to return to the innocence of childhood,' Mieko said, to console him, but Nathaniel looked up at her with obvious disdain.

'You're not seriously suggesting that, are you?'

His tone was so sharp that Mieko flinched.

She could tell he was flabbergasted.

Nathaniel continued, 'Of course not. He's the last person to behave like that. Until the very end he was more single-minded about music than anyone.'

Mieko turned a bit disdainful herself. She was taken aback at being snapped at when all she'd done was try to console him. And upset at herself for relaying her theory when she hadn't believed it herself.

'Don't worry – I get it,' Mieko said coldly.

'Then don't say it. But – then why would the Maestro take on that kind of pupil?'

Nathaniel was sounding desperate.

Now I remember, she thought. *I really do. This is the kind of man he is.*

She was struck by an overpowering sense of déjà vu.

Nathaniel would work himself up deliberately, hoping for some consolation, but when she did try to comfort him, he'd throw her words back at her and lash out. He'd been that way from the very beginning, and as their relationship had gone downhill, it was an unending repetition of this scenario, day after day.

'Well, he's scheduled to play on the last day of the first round, so you should listen and then decide. You have to hear him yourself.'

Mieko pulled out a cigarette, but remembered it was a non-smoking restaurant.

'Masaru isn't about to lose,' Nathaniel said.

'I suppose not, since he's your blue-eyed boy,' Mieko replied, with a hint of sarcasm, and gulped down her chai.

'How can you say that when you've never heard him play?'

Nathaniel was back to snapping at her, though his anxiety seemed to have eased.

'Well, you've never heard Jin Kazama play either, so I guess we're even.' Mieko snorted.

In point of fact, I'm *the one who wants to hear him play, much more than* you *do,* she thought. *I want to hear him again, to work out who in the world he is, and what Maestro Hoffmann could possibly have meant by singling him out.* I'm *the one who's dying to hear Jin Kazama play.*

A Star is Born

'WHOA – WHAT IS GOING ON here?'

Aya was bowled over by how packed the concert hall was.

'Why is it so full? It's still just the first round!'

The audience was, she noticed, overwhelmingly made up of young women.

'You mean you haven't heard all the rumours, Aya-*chan*?'

Kanade, beside her, looked dubious.

'What rumours?'

'That one of the frontrunners for the prize is playing today. The Prince of Juilliard.'

'Prince?'

It was Aya's turn to look doubtful.

Rumours were flying around about a 'Prince' something or other, and she hadn't a clue who it meant. Aya never kept up with the arts news and was totally oblivious to gossip.

'Aya-*chan*, you mean you haven't checked out any of the other pianists?'

'Well, I figured I was going to hear them anyway, so it's all the same to me.'

Kanade was dumbfounded by Aya's attitude.

'Even *I've* heard about him,' Kanade said. 'Nathaniel Silverberg's prize pupil – part Japanese apparently.'

'Really? I do like Nathaniel Silverberg. These days all he's doing is conducting, but I wish he'd play the piano more often.'

As she gazed at Aya, absorbed in her own words, Kanade wondered what had happened to the girl who, when they were picking out dresses, had vowed to do her very best. Maybe this was what made her so great, Kanade thought. But then this was a competition, and ambition and drive were essential.

It was the second day of round one.

Kanade's father had asked her to chaperone Aya as Aya's teacher had two other students in the competition and couldn't look after her as well.

No, Kanade finally decided, *she's not due to play until the last day of the first round, so perhaps it's best that she seems a bit disengaged at the moment*. People often said the hardest thing for the competitors in a long-drawn-out competition was keeping their cool. Many complained about the lengthy periods of waiting. Their own performance was only twenty minutes, yet the first round was spread over five whole days.

This was Aya's first senior-level competition. Could she cope? Kanade wondered. She looked sideways at Aya as she listened attentively.

Kanade hadn't told anybody this, but she'd decided that if Aya made it to the finals, she would formally switch from the violin to the viola. The decision had nothing really to do with Aya – she could have made that transition whenever she wanted – but she'd decided that Aya's fate in the competition would determine her own.

Over time, Kanade had gradually decided she preferred the viola. She loved its resonance, how it looked and where it sat in an orchestra – it all suited her perfectly.

I trust my own ears, she thought.

She glanced over at Aya again.

AND SO KANADE HAD DECIDED that Aya's participation would mark her own personal turning point. Which was another reason why she'd scolded Aya for her total lack of competitiveness.

But, wow – the standard here is so high! Kanade thought. *How can I even explain it to Dad?*

Each performance was exquisitely musical. Clearly, access now to so many different interpretations and information online had helped raise standards worldwide. It had also led to a certain uniformity of sound, though she was curious to note that the national character associated with various countries did influence the playing.

Chinese pianists, for instance, had a smooth, clean breadth that she thought of as reflecting their *continental* origins. Without exception all the Chinese competitors were from wealthy middle-class families, though the middle class in China was more equivalent to the affluent in Japan, so they were all from families with the financial wherewithal to support their careers. In China these lucky pianists naturally made full use of their advantages, and their powerful, unrestrained playing was very appealing. These days, though, audiences had grown used to this kind of Chinese pianist and their superior technical skills came as no surprise. But what was really enviable about the Chinese contestants was their unwavering self-esteem, something rarely found among their Japanese counterparts. Japanese pianists might talk about *being themselves*, but only as a way to disguise their lack of self-confidence, and anxiety about their identity. This *being yourself* could only be acquired after serious struggle, yet Chinese players seemed to have it from the beginning, like a self-evident birthright, and Kanade wondered if it was the product of Chinese philosophy and a one-party, authoritarian regime. One other factor was the competition within China. Once one had survived that, any struggles over identity were long since sublimated. Compared to the Chinese, pianists from other Asian countries seemed far more naïve. She got the feeling at times that some of them were still asking why they were even here, why they were up on stage playing, still wrestling with basic existential questions that the Chinese contestants had long since put behind them.

What really stood out this time was the contingent from South Korea. Kanade felt similarly when she saw Korean movie stars, that they had a straightforward passion and – she wasn't sure if the term was appropriate or not – a kind of *lovability*.

Their built-in Korean *intensity* and *lovability* worked well with dramatic classical music.

So what was particular to Japanese pianists?

It was something Japanese professional musicians often pondered. Starting with the most basic question: *Why do Asians play* Western *music?* And these thoughts would always veer back to the more personal question of why she herself was playing the violin, and the viola.

Kanade realized that the performance had finished, Aya beside her applauding enthusiastically, her face lit up as she looked at her friend.

'They're *sooo* good! This Korean contingent is incredible.'

This wasn't the moment to be impressed by other pianists, Kanade thought, and smiled wryly to herself.

After the interval, the next pianist was the much-anticipated Prince of Juilliard.

HIROSHI TAKUBO, THE STAGE MANAGER, glanced over at the next contestant.

A tall, dark figure in the shadows. He couldn't help being intrigued.

Some of the competitors were so overcome with nerves he felt sorry for them, but this figure appeared calm.

Takubo was used to seeing professionals and maestros from around the world, ushering all sorts of stars from backstage as they made their entrance. This young man had the same remarkable aura about him as the seasoned pros.

Other staff members seemed to sense it too, and he could tell they felt a bit in awe as they engaged with him. He definitely exuded something quite *special*. There was his attractive physique and features, for sure, but his presence alone was enough to make your heart flutter.

Takubo glanced at his watch.

'It's time,' he said quietly.

Takubo always agonized about when to say this. He didn't want to speak too insistently and put any additional pressure on the competitor. He always tried to sound as casual as he could.

'Best of luck,' Takubo said as he pushed open the door. He watched each competitor closely before deciding whether to give them these final words of encouragement, knowing that in some cases it might break their concentration, or be an unwelcome jolt, but with this contestant he had no such compunction. There was something about the young man that made him want to communicate with him.

'Thank you very much.'

The young man smiled broadly. Takubo couldn't help but be startled by this dazzling smile as the young man stepped out into the lights. As if a refreshing breeze had just wafted by.

The audience also knew in an instant they were in the presence of someone extraordinary.

Aya looked with admiration at this 'Prince' as he bowed.

It was like the moment a movie star greets their fans at a premiere.

The young man was slim and tall, and was dressed in a tasteful, lustrous blue-grey suit. He had on a white shirt, and a chic purple and green tie. Surprisingly few of the male pianists wore ties.

Dark brown, loose curly hair, and calm, deeply chiselled features.

The audience watched with bated breath as he adjusted the stool.

Aya suddenly felt a strange sense of nostalgia.

It feels as if I know him from a long time ago, she thought.

Stars made you feel like that, didn't they? That you'd always known them.

It was because their very aura – how to put it? – set a standard. Like something that becomes an instant classic. A star embodies what the audience has long known, and long been yearning for.

Aya heard a familiar voice in her head. The voice of her old teacher, Mr Watanuki.

My mother taught me the basics, but it was Mr Watanuki, my piano teacher, who taught me to love music. Whenever I opened the door into his home, I could hear all kinds of music. I used to love those lessons.

But Mr Watanuki passed away when Aya was eleven. He said he wasn't feeling well, and died soon after being admitted to hospital. It happened so quickly.

The thought came to her that if only she'd been able to stay on with Mr Watanuki, she may have continued to perform even after her mother died. The teachers she had after him were so skilled at teaching technique. But no one ever taught her to love music the way Mr Watanuki had.

The young man finished adjusting the stool and gazed ahead of him for a moment.

Aya's eyes were drawn to his thoughtful expression.

When he knew he had the audience's attention, he lifted his arms and began to play.

So charming, Aya thought.

He knew then that the audience had fallen for his sound, and for the person who produced it. This was what it meant, she mused, to *entrance*.

But still, how different the sound could be, depending on who was making it.

She'd known this was true, but seeing it play out before her eyes, she found it all the more incredible.

The Well-Tempered Clavier was the most standard of the piano repertoire and, played by the book, could easily end up sounding like background music. *But, my goodness, in his hands it truly sounds alive. Thrilling, even.*

Every note felt profound, not exposed, but shrouded in velvet. And yet it reverberated with the simplicity, and slight cynicism, of the Baroque.

What amazing grace notes, Aya thought. *They don't just disappear, or impede the flow, but feel so precise and integrated.*

He seemed to be enjoying himself so much! No straining, not an ounce of extra effort. As if stroking the keys, producing crystal-clear notes that filled every corner of the hall. Some pianists played with their own idiosyncratic style or pose, the audience distracted from the music as they watched. He was full of a generosity that allowed listeners to give themselves up to the playing.

'There is such expanse, yet there is power held in reserve.'

Mr Watanuki's voice came to her again.

'He has all this music inside him, strong and hopeful – it can never be contained.'

That's exactly what it is, she thought, wondering when Mr Watanuki had said that.

NO WONDER NATHANIEL WAS SO proud of him.

Mieko was in her judge's seat, eyes riveted on the young man before her.

The thirteen judges were spread across the entire balcony, seated in two rows with plenty of space between them. Mieko and Nathaniel were in the upper row, at either end. She knew that, as she and her colleagues listened raptly to this pianist, they were all conscious of his mentor sitting among them.

What *breadth*, she thought, the word coming to her naturally. She hadn't used such an open, simple expression for quite some time. The world was filled with skilled performers, rock-steady pianists whose study of music lacked very little, which made it all the more difficult for a player like this with idiosyncratic *breadth* to emerge, someone who made you appreciate the pregnant pauses and spaces between the notes.

This young man took what were supposed to be intrinsically contradictory elements and smoothly made them his own. A truly astounding scope and range.

Mieko recalled her impression at the party when she first met him.

Wild, yet graceful. Urbane, yet instinctive.

The sounds he produced were at once fresh and youthful, slick and cunning. He was holding back, yet still dignified.

Could it be because he was only part Japanese? No – to be half or quarter Japanese wasn't so unusual.

This boy's amazing touch could be traced to the strength he found in his hybrid individuality, which he used to his advantage.

His sound was sweet and gorgeous, but complex, with subtle ambiguities as well. It evoked classical European resonances, Latin light and shadow, an Oriental poetic sense, and an American frankness and open-heartedness. These elements merged to form an integrated whole. With each piece, he showed a different aspect of his talent. He sparked a mysterious fascination that made you want him to keep playing.

Professionals tended to look down upon young, attractive, technically accomplished pianists, but Masaru would be well received by all.

Mieko noticed the number of women who had filled the stalls below. They had been quick to spot an attractive-looking star. Masaru combined popularity along with all his other qualities.

From up in the balcony the stage could feel very close to her, but when Masaru played, Mieko had the illusion that a pop-up book had opened right in front of her.

The Bach was excellent, as was the Mozart. He had such an exquisite sound, yet didn't rely solely on this; he had clearly understood the music deeply. Nathaniel would never allow a pupil of his to do otherwise.

Just like Maestro Hoffmann.

She was suddenly taken aback.

Wasn't Nathaniel convinced that Masaru would be the one to assume Hoffmann's mantle?

She wanted to glance over at him but stopped herself.

Maestro Hoffmann was a hybrid himself, now that she thought of it. His grandmother had married into a Prussian noble family, his father was a famous conductor, his mother a well-known Italian prima donna. He'd travelled the world since he was young, been looked after by various relatives. It was his fierce individuality, created by this diverse background, that produced the monumental musician that was Yuji Von Hoffmann.

Nathaniel may have discovered in Masaru a Hoffmann for a

new generation. Which may have explained why he was so shaken to learn that Hoffmann had a pupil in his last years.

Masaru certainly was a pupil who could live up to his own expectations.

Mieko looked fixedly at Masaru as he came to the end of his second piece.

HIS LAST WAS LISZT'S *Mephisto Waltz* No. 1, the same piece Aya had chosen to play.

Kanade had coolly appraised the situation.

Since it was hard to make a performance of the first two pieces, a Bach fugue and a classical sonata, stand out, many pianists had chosen a more challenging piece to end with. Usually by Liszt or Rachmaninoff. That final work would typically be eleven or twelve minutes long, and so as many as five pianists had chosen the *Mephisto Waltz*. Someone had played it yesterday, but Kanade had missed it. She read audience members' responses online, but didn't see any direct references to it, so it probably hadn't been anything especially memorable.

Kanade sat up straight to pay careful attention to Masaru's performance.

This 'Prince' had played the Bach very precisely and had expressed the purity in the Mozart to the max, but now, suddenly changing gear, he switched to a more brilliant, glorious mode.

It was as if they'd swapped pianists. His entire being was filled with the cold passion of Liszt's waltz, with its dynamic motifs.

When less powerful pianists played Liszt, it could sound like a noisy clatter, yet the Prince's fingers danced lightly over the keys.

Playing the piano with such force meant the pianissimo passages were all the more effective, the dynamics unbelievably stirring.

Perfect glissandos, casually dispatched. Sweet, heart-rending, transparent tremolos.

She was used to technically outstanding players, so she didn't expect to be surprised, but this young man's technique was extraordinary. Electrifying, crisp articulation. A superb voicing that grabbed the audience's hearts and led them wherever he wished.

The final chord rang out, and the Prince rose to cheers and screams of approval.

He smiled, put a hand to his chest and bowed deeply. At the sight of this beautiful, open face, the audience's adoration swelled all the more.

'Wow – that was totally *amazing*! He really might win the prize.'

Aya was applauding so excitedly that Kanade felt crestfallen.

This *Mephisto Waltz* had set a new standard. *Doesn't Aya realize how this puts her at a disadvantage?*

The Prince beamed as he headed offstage. Even after he'd disappeared, it was as if his dazzle still lingered behind him.

He is simply incredible, Kanade thought.

He's already *a star*.

The wave of cheering surged on and on.

It's Only a Paper Moon

Akashi Takashima remained riveted to his seat.

The audience had erupted in a storm of applause, but Akashi, against the tide, felt dragged down, sinking deeper and deeper into the seat.

All that he could hear was the frenzied cheering, along with what felt like some manga sound-effect – the persistent, heavy *bong* of a bell reverberating deep inside him.

A female pianist had emerged, and all he could think was *that poor girl*. She could play for all she was worth, and though the audience's eyes were vacantly trained on her, they were still steeped in the afterglow of Masaru Carlos Levi Anatole. They weren't seeing her, but *him*.

It wasn't until the third competitor after Masaru that the audience was able to focus on the performance at hand.

Today marked a fault line, thought Akashi. Time henceforth would be measured as *Before Masaru Carlos* and *After Masaru Carlos*.

Akashi had felt the response to his own performance the previous day, and he'd come away with a good feeling.

If I play like this, he'd thought, *I can't lose. Even I'm a contender*.

He'd tried not to dwell on this too much, since they were all in the same competition, and anyone could be dropped, but it was impossible to completely ignore this inner voice telling him he had a decent chance.

The moment Masaru had appeared, that small inner voice was blown away.

He tried his best not to gather any information about the other competitors. To be honest, he just didn't have the headspace. But he did happen to hear titbits from his network of friends from music-college days, rumours about some of the more notable competitors.

One thing he'd heard: an outstanding pianist would be coming up, Nathaniel Silverberg's prize pupil. What he found hard to believe was what a colleague who'd heard the pianist play in New York had said. He asked him what he was like and was surprised to hear it wasn't the piano he'd played, but the trombone. Come to think of it, back in college this friend had studied jazz and played bass, so it made sense that he'd happened to find the pianist in a well-known jazz club in New York.

The guy was amazing, his friend had said. He played this kind of hardcore, radical solo à la Curtis Fuller. He was still only fifteen or sixteen, but he'd seriously put the pros to shame.

He looked into the boy's background and was astonished to learn that the trombone was just a hobby and that he was a full-time piano student at Juilliard. Word was he was also not bad on guitar and drums.

Ah – the type of genius who effortlessly mastered everything, Akashi thought. The guy had so much talent he could explore an entire orchestra.

He'd envisaged an eccentric, precocious child prodigy. A boy raised lovingly, and who appeared otherworldly.

The child prodigy was a long-established concept in the music world. From a very early age they could see things ordinary people couldn't, and gain access to the mystery that was music.

The thing was, they didn't see what ordinary people *could*. Ordinary people longed to produce some godlike music one day, felt joy as they set off at the foot of the mountain, from sea level, hoping to reach its sparkling heights, found sheer pleasure in overcoming failure as, step by step, they drew closer to the music. Prodigies didn't experience this joy.

Ordinary people sometimes had a distorted sense of superiority towards geniuses.

Which is why Akashi never felt threatened by them, or jealous. But once Masaru Carlos appeared on stage, Akashi's image of his own meagre *genius* was crushed to bits.

Such maturity, such immense musicianship, such a clear sense of the bigger picture. It was a miracle that he could possess all that at only nineteen. He truly was a genius.

Akashi was both inspired and devastated by it. Despite all the qualities Masaru had obviously been blessed with, Akashi still sensed in him the earnest, profoundly considered sound, the stoicism of someone seeking more.

That was surely why he was trying so many other avenues – the guitar and the trombone. It was his desire to grasp a complete vision of music, to probe the meaning of music to its very depths.

Akashi was filled with despair. *Why wasn't* I *born this way? Why am I trying to compete with a person like this, on the same instrument, at the same time, in the same competition?*

Why am I? Why?

As these thoughts swirled around in his head, the competitors *After Masaru Carlos* came and went as if on fast forward. Masaru had appeared about halfway through today's first-round performers, yet the second half of the programme seemed over before Akashi knew it, and he suddenly realized the day was over, the audience heading towards the exit.

Why?

Akashi finally managed to drag himself to his feet. He knew he should start practising for the second round, but it all seemed too much. He slowly made his way up the sloping aisle in the now deserted concert hall, like an old man struggling against gravity.

'YOU KNOW SOMETHING? *THAT* GIRL's going to play on the last day of the first round.'

'Yeah. Aya Eiden. That'll be something to see.'

Aya was in a stall in the women's toilets and had been yawning. Startled by the voices just outside, her hand unconsciously flew to her mouth.

'There's a lot of buzz around her, right?'

'I wonder. I mean, what could she be thinking? Someone who once played a concerto at Carnegie Hall and everything.'

It seemed to be two young women talking, chatting in front of the mirror as they touched up their make-up.

Aya hesitated. She was stuck. If she came out now, would those girls realize she was Aya Eiden? Her hairstyle was different from the photo in the programme. She wore it in a short bob now, so maybe they wouldn't recognize her. Especially if she looked nonchalant.

'How many years was she away?'

'A lot. Seven, maybe eight?'

'Where do people like that go, anyway? There are so many of them. Child geniuses who debut playing a concerto with an orchestra at age ten or twelve. But I get the feeling there aren't many who go on to a big career.'

'They burn out, don't they? Piano's all they've known. When you don't know anything else in the world, you're limited, right?

Like famous child actors where there's like a wall keeping them from becoming adult actors.'

Aya felt a chill run up her spine.

Once past twenty, an adult, you're nothing special. A case of burnout. Some of the merciless things people had said about her all came rushing back.

'It will be hilarious if she doesn't make it past the first round,' one of the girls said.

'That'd be hard to live down. Isn't she nervous? With all those years away? I mean, a solo concert to revive her career is one thing, but in a competition you either pass or you don't. If it were me, I'd be too frightened to go on.'

As much as to say that Aya was being reckless. She felt cold sweat trickling down her back.

'You think she'll really show up?'

'I want to see her.'

'What if she cancels again at the last minute like before?'

The voices faded. Silence fell.

Aya still couldn't bring herself to come out.

HOW LONG SHE STAYED INSIDE before opening the stall door and peeking out, she couldn't say. No one was there.

She washed her hands and left the toilets.

The lobby was deserted.

She was relieved Kanade wasn't with her today. Her friend had had some things to do back in Tokyo and had left straight after Masaru Carlos's performance. Aya didn't want Kanade to see how she looked right now.

She practically ran out of the concert hall. *It's not like I'm in this competition because I want to be.*

These thoughts ran through her mind all the way back to the hotel.

Was she feeling embarrassed? Sorry? Sad? Angry? She wasn't sure what her emotions were right now.

But that's the public *– the image, and impression the public has of me.*

Up until now she hadn't cared at all. The vast world outside the hall was noisily targeting her with vast quantities of spite.

The public *hasn't forgotten me. They've never forgotten I was the pitiful former girl prodigy who, on a last-minute impulse, cancelled a concert.*

Those voices she'd heard earlier spun around and around in her head.

'Aya Eiden. That'll be something to see.'

'What could she be thinking?'

'Where do people like that go, anyway?'

'It will be hilarious if she doesn't make it past the first round.'

'Isn't she nervous? If it were me, I'd be too frightened to go on.'

I agree – it's reckless and shocking to do what I'm doing. To take part in a competition after all these years. What was *I thinking? Exposing for all to see this pitiful shadow of my former self, the ex-child genius. Mixing with all these stars-in-the-making.*

The image of Masaru Carlos popped into her mind, and that magnificent *Mephisto Waltz*.

She hurried into her hotel room, shut the door and leaned her back against it.

That's why I didn't want to be in any competition.

Why did Prof. Hamazaki want me to do something so humiliating? For his own reputation? Because he made an exception when he let me into the school?

She knew full well, deep down, that was a baseless accusation. But at this moment she couldn't help but abuse, attack, curse all of them – Prof. Hamazaki, Kanade and herself – for deciding that she should do it.

Maybe I should just not play.

If I leave now before anyone's heard me, I'll remain the genius young girl who suddenly vanished.

But then one of those earlier voices came back to her.

'You think she'll really show up?'

'What if she cancels again at the last minute like before?'

She broke out in a cold sweat.

A white sign on stage that says: '88. AYA EIDEN'.

But no one appears on stage. And a stir runs through the audience.

The staff begin to whisper among themselves. Someone comes out on stage and removes the sign with her name. An even greater stir sweeps through the hall.

Someone laughs, and there is more whispering.

'What? She withdrew?'

'No way – I was looking forward to hearing her. Aya Eiden.'

'She's run off again. She must have been too scared.'

'And she was here until now, listening to the other first-round performances.'

'That's why. She realized how high the standard was. She must have thought it was better not to go on.'

She could picture another scene as well.

Kanade sees the sign has been removed and rushes out of the hall, her face pale. She hurries to Aya's hotel room, and rings the bell, but there's no answer. Kanade jumps into the lift and races to the front desk. They inform her that Aya has cancelled her reservation and checked out. In a panic, Kanade phones her father.

'Aya-*chan*'s run away.'

'*What?!*' Kanade hears her father gulp at the other end.

News about Aya's sudden withdrawal from the competition quickly spreads through the college. It is a real blow to Prof. Hamazaki's reputation. She hears the other professors talking about it.

'I feel sorry for Prof. Hamazaki. He took such good care of his old friend's daughter and now look what's happened.'

I can't leave. I can't withdraw, thought Aya.

She realized the room was pitch-black.

She slowly lifted her hand and slipped the key card into the slot for the lights.

Laid out on the bed was the bright blue dress she and Kanade had picked out for her to wear in the first round.

The Hallelujah Chorus

THE LAST DAY OF the first round.

Since the morning, Masami Nishina had been visiting the host families in turn and had now arrived at the concert hall. Immediately following the end of the first round, the successful competitors would be announced, and she couldn't miss it – she had to capture their expressions in the moment. As she couldn't be in two places at once, she'd asked the host families if they'd help by taking a video of the competitors staying with them. Given that these families were used to having pianists in their home, and some of the pianists were already making videos for their parents to show them what things were like in Japan, they were all happy to comply with Masami's request. Masami's main focus here, of course, was Akashi Takashima, so she made sure she could be with him when the results were announced.

Akashi's wife had to teach today, so she wasn't around. Not that Masami was aware of it, but when Machiko was with him she couldn't relax.

Masami was by now used to the concert hall, but she was still amazed by the number of people gathering to hear the results. And there was a tension in the air that hadn't been there before. A suppressed excitement might be a better way of putting it.

'This is incredible, don't you think? There're so many people here today.'

She was speaking to Akashi, who was waiting for her at the entrance.

FOR THE COMPETITORS IT WAS a fateful moment, but for the audience it was more of an exciting spectacle.

Akashi put up a good front, though he'd been nervous ever since he'd woken up.

Will I make it to the second round? he wondered. *Was my*

performance good enough? In seven hours from now will I be smiling, or phoning Machiko to relay the bad news?

An image sprang to mind of him calling his wife, hiding his disappointment, trying to sound like the whole thing didn't bother him. He brushed the thought aside.

'There are a few pianists still to play.'

Masami glanced at the programme. 'You're right.'

'There's the – what do they call him, Honeybee Prince? And that Russian pianist who came third last time.'

'I forget what they call him – Honeybee or Honey. His audition in Paris was apparently spectacular.'

'The winner last time followed the same path, didn't he?'

Masami flipped through the programme until she got to the page she was searching for. Akashi peered over her shoulder to take a look.

Jin Kazama.

The section on his competitive background was blank. He was only sixteen, so it was very possible that no one had heard of him until now.

'Wow, he looks cute. And so young. Sixteen. Imagine that!'

'Stop sounding like some middle-aged fan girl.'

Akashi smiled, though his eyes shot straight to the paragraph about Jin's music teacher. Anyone would have had the same reaction, he thought. It was hard to believe that he'd listed himself as Hoffmann's student. In the end, would that turn out to be a good thing? Or a liability?

Akashi quietly turned the page. He had his eye on another competitor.

There was something in the photo that ignited shards of memory. The unaffected, large, piercing eyes looking right at you.

Aya Eiden. Age: 20

She's twenty already. She's still only twenty. The two thoughts collided in his head.

There hadn't been the same buzz around her that there had

been for the Honeybee Prince or the Juilliard Prince, yet Aya's return to the stage was a hot topic of discussion.

What kind of performance would she give? And why was she back?

Akashi had been a fan of Aya in the past. He'd heard her recordings and gone to her concerts. He always thought of child prodigies as 'Rug Rats Got Talent', finding them a bit creepy, but Aya had been different, entirely natural. He remembered very clearly thinking, when he'd first heard her play, *This isn't a* child prodigy. *This is a genuine* genius.

Music was an entirely flowing, natural part of who she was.

When he heard Aya had suddenly cancelled her concert after her mother died, he was completely stunned. In a sense, he felt betrayed. That a girl endowed with such a gift could give it all up was a profound shock.

Time passed, however, and he began to think that maybe it was precisely *because* she was a genius that she could give it up like that, so decisively. That sort of abrupt farewell may well have been in keeping with who she was.

Since he'd mythologized her in his mind, he had very mixed feelings now about her return to the stage. It was something akin to the disenchantment when a pop idol who'd left the stage for a 'normal life' afterwards decided to restart their showbiz career.

Now there was also the fear of being disappointed and not knowing how to react. Other pianists in the competition would actually want to be disappointed. *Ah, so that's all she has,* they might think. It was hard to deny the temptation to show contempt for a former idol.

Akashi continued to stare at her photograph, his feelings decidedly mixed.

MASARU PASSED THE SIGNED PROGRAMME back to the young girls and they squealed in delight.

This scene repeated itself every time there was a break between performances, and he was happy about it, but also a bit disconcerted, as it interrupted him while he was scanning the particulars of the upcoming pianists.

The programme listed all the pieces the competitors planned to play, from the first round all the way to the finals. It was highly informative and Masaru enjoyed studying the detail – choice of repertoire revealed much about the pianists' technical prowess and preferences, as well as their strategy in the competition. The first and second rounds had to follow certain guidelines, so the choice of works was somewhat restricted, but the third round was a one-hour recital, and here a pianist's personality could really emerge. There were all-Chopin recitals, all-Rachmaninoff ones, programmes spotlighting contemporary composers and others taking a more academic approach, all revealing the repertoire a pianist felt would show them in their best light.

Honestly, in this first round the choice of pieces seemed either amazingly inspired, or amazingly stupid.

Masaru had opened the programme to the next performer, Jin Kazama, and his choices for the first round:

Bach, *The Well-Tempered Clavier*, Book 1, No. 1,
Prelude and Fugue in C Major.
Mozart, Piano Sonata No. 12 in F Major,
K. 322, first movement.
Balakirev, *Islamey: Oriental Fantasy*.

The choice of *Islamey* he could understand. The Bach and Mozart pieces were technically not very challenging, so the *Islamey*, one of the two most difficult pieces in the entire piano repertoire, was the strategic choice for displaying technique.

Technical standards had shot up in recent years, and though *Islamey* had seldom been performed, here in the first round there were several pianists who'd chosen to play it.

But still – why *The Well-Tempered Clavier*, Book 1, No. 1?

It was such a super-famous piece that even those unfamiliar with classical music had heard it at one time or another. Every time you did, you had to filter it through various other famous performances. Playing it was a brave decision.

The Mozart, too, was a bold choice. Another famous piece, which made it hard to address square on. The choice had either been made quite naturally and innocently by the pianist, or he had done it intentionally.

Masaru considered this.

No – hold on, he thought. These weren't necessarily pieces Jin Kazama had chosen himself. Since this was a newcomer's first competition, and the first round, it was more natural for his teacher to choose what he would play.

If this choice was made at Yuji Von Hoffmann's direction while he was still alive, it had to be a deliberate tactic. If so, then he must have great confidence.

Masaru nearly let out a whistle.

The audience began to applaud, and Masaru was surprised to see a woman in a yellow dress on stage bowing. The performance was over before he knew it, and he'd failed to hear any of it.

DEEP IN THE WINGS, THE piano tuner Kotaro Asano fidgeted.

In his mind was the figure of that young boy. *It's his turn very soon. And my turn, too.*

Of the three piano tuners dispatched by the piano makers, Asano was the youngest. Tuning pianos in a competition was gruelling work, but for a tuner it was also a huge honour. He'd been hoping for his chance for a long while, and had finally been allowed to take part. He was fired up when he arrived, but the atmosphere in the hall was more tense than he'd ever imagined. He understood why tuners said they couldn't sleep during a competition. Physically it was tiring, but also emotionally draining with so many competitors to meet, and trying to understand, despite the language barrier, what sort of sound they were hoping for. He took detailed notes but was still uneasy, and his head was filled with all sorts of sounds and images as he worked out how to reproduce what they wanted. Relaxing was out of the question.

Some of the pianists were highly strung, and their nerves seemed to rub off on him, making him feel agitated.

One particularly hard-to-please girl from France had kept insisting, 'This isn't my sound,' which had completely drained him. It was at this point that the young Japanese boy turned up: just being able to speak the same language was a great relief.

'Hello. My name's Kazama. Very nice to meet you.'

The boy bobbed his head in a quick bow.

'My name's Asano. I'm so happy to meet *you*. I'll do my very best to make sure the piano is exactly the way you want it,' Asano said, his typical greeting to competitors, and he bowed.

'Uh, I'm fine with anything,' the boy said. 'I know it's an incredible piano.'

Asano couldn't believe his ears. 'When you say anything's fine . . .'

Asano scratched his head. He'd heard this boy was sixteen, and that this was his first competition. He had to know how important the correct tuning was, but should he explain it to him?

'Everyone has a different touch, and their own sound preference, and the sound of a piano changes far more than you might think. There's a tuning that works best for your repertoire, so could you try playing something for me?'

'Hmm.' Now the boy was scratching his head.

He hesitated, then strolled over to the piano, adjusted the stool, sat down and began running through some scales.

Asano's attention was caught.

Could this be the same piano the French girl had played? Do our pianos really sound like this?

The boy began to sing 'Love Me Tender'. The staff in the wings stared, wide-eyed.

It was improvised. Not a trained voice, but one that was free and easy.

Asano had never heard of a pianist playing and singing when the tuner had arrived for a consultation. Normally pianists would run through the climax of a piece they were going to play, or a section whose resonance they wanted to check.

The boy suddenly halted. 'Hmm,' he said again.

'Is something wrong?' Asano couldn't help but ask.

'Hmm,' the boy repeated, stood up, then fell to his knees and pressed his ear to the floor.

'What's the matter?'

Asano was about to hurry over, but the boy held up a hand. He was still for a while, and then stood up again.

'Right,' he said, and walked to the back of the stage. 'Mr Asano, is it OK to move this piano?'

The boy pointed at the grand piano on the right.

At the back of the stage were three pianos from three different makers, so the pianists could choose which one they wanted to play.

At the boy's direction, he and Asano moved the piano thirty centimetres.

The boy sat down again and ran through some scales.

'Um. It's good now.'

He nodded and looked back at Asano.

'Mr Asano, when I play could you make sure that piano is over there?'

The boy stood up, as if done.

'Oh – one more thing. This key *here*, and over *here*, is out.'

The boy pointed, and quickly left.

Asano checked the keys. And sure enough, the pitch of one key was a little high, the other a little low, the difference so slight most people wouldn't notice it.

Asano broke out into a cold sweat. Neither he nor the French girl with all her complaints about *my sound* had picked this up. He took some tape out of his pocket and went over to where they'd moved the other piano. He stuck a strip of tape to the floor, wrote the boy's competition number on it with a felt-tip pen, and reminded himself to make sure the person in charge of that make of piano knew about it.

A NEW NAME SIGN WAS placed in the corner of the stage; a stir of excitement trilled through the audience.

81. KAZAMA JIN

Recently they'd taken to giving the names in the style in which they appeared in the various countries the competitors came from, so with Japanese performers that meant family name first.

Mieko felt uncharacteristically tense. Simon, Smirnoff and Nathaniel must all be feeling the same. Olga and the rest of the judges, too, must be immensely curious and full of expectation, some of them surely waiting with considerable cynicism to hear the boy unearthed in Paris by this trio of *upstarts*.

Would they be found guilty? Or mocked?

But beyond what people might actually think of them, Mieko wanted to find out what the boy's music was all about.

Was my first impression mistaken? She had to find out.

THE EXTRAORDINARY ATMOSPHERE in the concert hall put Hiroshi Takubo, the stage manager, on edge.

Taking a quick peek into the auditorium, he saw that, though the interval between performances was only halfway through, people were already streaming into the hall. It was standing room only.

He glanced over at the boy waiting offstage; he seemed oblivious, poking around in one ear with his little finger.

The boy blended into the background so that you barely noticed him. He was more relaxed than the staff. He was wearing a white shirt and a pair of black trousers that looked one size too big for him. His school uniform, perhaps.

The problem was that with the hall this packed, the piano would sound totally different. All those bodies would absorb the sound. And all the people standing along the wall and in the aisles would affect it too. Should he let the boy know?

Takubo was afraid that giving him some last-minute, gratuitous advice might add to the pressure of the moment, but decided to count on the boy's laid-back nature. Plus, he'd heard that he had amazingly sharp ears.

'Kazama-*kun*?' Takubo said, motioning him over. 'The hall is packed. I'm thinking that all the people standing in front of the walls will absorb a lot of the sound. I suggest you play more firmly than usual.'

The boy seemed startled.

'I see. The audience? Makes sense.'

He looked through the peephole at the audience. Out on the stage, Asano was carefully tuning.

'I'm sorry, but could you get a message to Mr Asano for me? Please tell him to put the piano we talked about back in its original spot and then move it over thirty centimetres in the opposite direction.'

Takubo pulled out a memo pad and ballpoint pen from his breast pocket and had the boy repeat his directions.

The boy drew a diagram with a message for Asano.

Asano scanned the message dubiously as Takubo explained about the unusually packed auditorium. A murmur ran through the hall as the tuner, in the middle of tuning one piano, suddenly began to move another piano over.

'I'm sorry about the sudden request.'

The boy quickly bobbed his head to the piano tuner when he came backstage.

'Is that positioning OK, then?' Asano glanced back at the stage.

The boy peered through the peephole. 'Yes, I think that's fine.'

Takubo looked at his watch.

Thank God – we made it in time.

The door opened and the boy strolled out into the light.

There was a storm of applause. The boy gave a little nod of his head, raising a roar of laughter.

NATHANIEL FOUND HIS BREATH TAKEN away by this simple boy. A *child of nature* – that was the only way he could describe him.

I only hope the audience's expectations don't crush him.

When the boy raised his head from his little bow and turned his gaze to the piano, Nathaniel was startled by the look on his face.

Jin Kazama sat down a little clumsily, and started impatiently to adjust the stool. Then he launched straight into his piece.

Nathaniel could sense the other judges, too, giving a start.

The whole concert hall was unnerved, bewildered, unsure what was going on.

What *was* this sound? How in the world could he produce that?

It was as if rainwater was trickling down, one drop at a time, each drop unable to support its own weight. A special tuning? The tuner had moved the other piano over from the back – could that have some connection?

Nathaniel shook his head.

You can't change the sound like this just by tuning. And the competitor who had performed before the boy had played the very same piano.

Why this impression of sounds descending from on high? The musical theme surfaced again and again, as if the piano – from both far away and near – was simply playing itself. Nathaniel heard it in stereo, as if multiple pianists were playing.

This was not an ordinary sound, but something far more three-dimensional.

Nathaniel felt his own shock, a realization that in itself was a shock.

A *Well-Tempered Clavier* prelude and fugue that sounded heavenly. He'd never heard a performance like this.

AKASHI TAKASHIMA, TOO, WAS ASTOUNDED.

How could each and every sound linger and resonate for so long? Was it the tuning?

The hall was packed, with people standing along the walls, even. So how could the sound reverberate like this?

Akashi felt a sudden chill.

An unknown genius taking a totally unexpected direction. Utterly different from Masaru Carlos.

Before he knew it, it was no longer Bach but Mozart, the colouring of the piece brighter, more brilliant. The lighting on the stage literally felt more dazzling.

The entire audience sat thunderstruck.

He felt unsettled, a throbbing excitement, a heat radiating up from deep within him. *This* was the piercingly supreme melody that Mozart intended. No hesitation, no doubt, like a pure white lotus bud, blossoming out of the mud. As if it were only natural, and one had only to receive, both hands wide open, the descending light.

From the moment this boy sat down, he'd been smiling, Akashi noticed. He didn't look at the keys at all. It felt less like he was playing the piano than that the piano was playing *him*. As if he called out to it, and the piano was happy to respond.

Akashi was always deeply moved by the phrase in the first movement of the Piano Sonata No. 12, the bars that best displayed Mozart's genius. Every time he heard this miraculous melody, written hundreds of years ago, he would tremble, but now he had gooseflesh.

This Mozart – how far is he going to take it?

The boy began the final piece, *Islamey*.

How is he making the piano sound like this?

MASARU, TOO, WAS ASTONISHED, TAKEN in by the illusion that the piano was ringing out before the boy had even touched it.

The Well-Tempered Clavier.

Spare, yet sensual, even a bit sensational.

It was as if he were improvising. That famous phrase from the Mozart summoned up an emotional response as if he'd only just thought of it.

And then there was the *Islamey*.

Masaru had the gut feeling that maybe Jin wasn't even aware that this was supposed to be one of the hardest pieces in the piano repertoire.

Most pianists who are about to play a hard piece steel themselves, as if to say, 'OK, now for something *really* hard.' Even pros do that.

This was the first time Masaru had ever felt the *Islamey* could be this much – well, *fun*.

Wasn't this perhaps the first time he'd ever heard it played correctly, every note held down?

Masaru felt his skin crawl.

As the number of notes to be held down increased along with the tempo, the sound necessarily grew thinner, less distinct. Yet the chords the boy played weren't muddy at all, but well defined. In fact, as he got to the second half of the piece, his playing grew even more forceful.

Masaru noticed one other surprising thing.

He'd practised the piece a bit himself. Because of the structure of the melody and the rhythm, even if you kept the correct tempo there were parts that sounded sluggish, as if you'd slowed down. It was an illusion. But with this boy, you'd didn't feel that at all.

The piece thrust onwards, racing towards a climax, a wall of sound leaping out, as if from the piano – no, from the entire vast rectangular space of the stage.

The audience desperately braced themselves in their seats to keep from being blown away by that acoustic pressure, by that sound hurtling towards them. The substantial tremolos, like the earth rumbling, were a series of blazing fastballs striking your face, eyes, ears, indeed your entire body.

Masaru withstood it, indulging in the pleasure of it all.

Jin's music was something you experienced with your entire being.

The final notes rang out, and as if propelled by them, the boy stood up, gave a nod of the head and quickly exited the stage.

The audience were slow in realizing it was over. For a moment an awkward silence held sway over the hall. But in the next instant, everyone emerged from their spell.

With feverish yells and shouts.

There were no encores in the first round, but the audience weren't buying that.

More applause, the sound of stamping feet. The door from backstage didn't reopen, until a staff member emerged to put out the name board for the next performer.

You'd Be So Nice to Come Home to

THE JUDGES WERE THROWN by Jin Kazama's performance. *This is exactly what panic looks like,* Mieko thought as she gazed around her.

No sooner had Jin disappeared than everyone began talking at once.

She looked over at Nathaniel, who was lost in thought.

As Mieko had expected, reactions were split right down the middle.

Unbelievable, fantastic, miraculous.

Vulgar, pointlessly inflammatory, a circus.

For Masaru Carlos there had been unified praise and blessings, so what was different here?

Mieko took a deep breath and gathered her thoughts.

Hearing Jin a second time now, she felt she understood things a little better.

When you heard him play, you couldn't help but react emotionally. His sound touched a soft, delicate part deep in your heart that people had forgotten they even had.

A small room within that everyone possessed.

When someone became a professional musician, the presence of that small room grew elusive. There in that room was the essence of the music they *truly* loved, present since childhood. An innocent yearning for music symbolized by a child's face.

When a pianist became a professional, their being was permeated with practical knowledge, as if the music they loved, and what was considered superior music, were two different things. As you became used to delivering music as a part of work, as a product, it became increasingly difficult to pinpoint what music you really loved. And you became painfully aware of being unable to give a performance you were satisfied with, your ideal performance. The longer the career as a professional, as the hurdles grew ever higher, the further away you moved from your ideals, and the more sacred and holy that little inner sanctum became. If you weren't careful, you opened that little room only rarely, forgetting, in fact, that it even existed.

But Jin Kazama's performance blew open the door to that inner room. Suddenly opening that door triggered extreme, polar-opposite, reactions – a feverish gratitude at having the room opened, and a repudiation of it as a rude invasion of one's private space.

Maestro Hoffmann must have realized all this.

A defenceless audience, that soft part of their inner selves not locked away, would display an enthusiasm bordering on frenzy when their emotions were ambushed in that manner.

Mieko could analyse his music objectively like this, yet she remained confused, unable to focus on how she herself should process it all.

There was one other strange thing.

Hearing Jin Kazama a second time, she no longer felt such an aversion. This time she'd been genuinely drawn in, full of admiration.

Was it because it came after she'd read Maestro Hoffmann's message? Did the letter now bias her in Jin's favour? One thing was very clear. There was something overpoweringly emotional in the boy's performance.

How in the world was he able to generate music like that, so intense and alive?

He communicated the score with impeccable technique, yet retained a fresh, unspoiled sound. She couldn't believe he'd been practising it a mind-numbing number of times.

Maybe this was precisely why his performance invited such a harsh response from some of the judges: it did not seem at all the product of intense effort and study.

Recently it felt as if the key issue in music had become the performer's ability to convey the composer's intention, with emphasis placed on how they interpreted the score and took into consideration the social and personal context at the time of the composition. It was the trend these days not to welcome a free interpretation or performance by a musician.

But Jin Kazama's playing was unencumbered by such strictures. It was truly free, brimming with originality, and made you wonder if he even knew the name of the composer. You got the impression that it was just him and the piece, boldly confronting each other, one on one. For all that, the performance was impeccable – tough indeed for those involved in music education to accept.

'I wonder what Yuji had in mind.'

Mieko heard Olga muttering. As expected from the chair of judges, her calm demeanour gave no indication of whether she was with those who applauded Jin, or those who rejected him.

Clearly she was thinking deeply, though. Noticing Mieko looking at her, Olga turned to her with an odd expression.

'Intriguing. Very intriguing, this boy,' she murmured.

She appeared not to be seeking Mieko's agreement, but instead gave a small shake of her head and made her way towards the judges' retiring room.

'AYA-*CHAN*? AYA-*CHAN*, WE NEED TO go.'

Kanade tapped Aya on the shoulder, startling her.

She needed to go to the practice room, change her clothes and await her turn.

'Aya-*chan*, are you OK? Shall I go with you?'

Aya looked vacantly at Kanade and shook her head.

'No, I'm good. You stay here.'

Aya stood up, garment bag in hand.

Feeling feverish, she made her way down the aisle and out of the hall, Jin Kazama's playing reverberating in her head.

She was oblivious to her surroundings, but her body remembered the route.

Yet still Jin Kazama's music didn't leave her. Bach, Mozart and *Islamey* in an endless loop.

What a shock. That brilliantly coloured music.

Music filled with the joy of life.

This boy is beloved by the musical gods.

She'd felt this, instinctively, from the moment she'd run across him at the college in Tokyo.

The instant he appeared on stage, she knew it was him.

AYA HAD GREETED THE MORNING on this, the final day of the first round, with despair.

She couldn't shake from her mind that conversation she'd overheard in the toilet a couple of days earlier. She felt nauseous; she felt like screaming.

Kanade interpreted Aya's behaviour simply as excess tension; acting nonchalantly, she invited her to come and hear the so-called Honeybee Prince play.

Today's the end of the line for me, thought Aya. The curtain was going to fall quietly on the story of the girl genius. A trite, stupid ending for the girl who, once she reached twenty, was, like they said, just a nobody, unable to make a comeback after all.

This cold premonition shook Aya to the core. *I'm sorry, Kanade. I'm sorry, Prof. Hamazaki.*

She knew she couldn't apologize enough to the Hamazakis, father and daughter. She felt awful for letting down Kanade. Would they still want to have anything to do with her after this? They'd be more hurt by this than she would. She pictured them worrying about her.

'Wow, what an audience. This Bee Prince really does draw the crowds.'

Aya raised her head and saw Kanade gazing around her. The audience did seem boisterous. People were even lining the walls along the outer aisles.

Aya, too, was wide-eyed at this unusual scene. She knew the boy was a Japanese pianist whom people had been talking about ever since the Paris audition, but this fever-pitch audience left her vaguely apprehensive. It wasn't really her business, yet she still felt sorry for him, for being the object of so much attention.

AYA SIGNED IN AT THE registration desk and was shown to the rehearsal rooms.

As she walked down the corridor, she heard another pianist frantically running through a piece.

She went into a room and sat down in front of the grand piano.

She closed her eyes and listened to Jin's playing in her head.

The god of music. God was . . . present there.

Aya would remember many times that strange sensation.

What rose up in her mind was that scene from childhood. Of rain striking a tin roof, and of a girl tapping out a rhythm with her fingers in time to the sound.

Her mother, her teacher Mr Watanuki, the bag with the embroidered treble clef on it.

The performances she'd given all came back to her, one after the other, with frightening clarity.

Different concert halls, pianos, conductors and players.

The pieces she'd played, the reverberations of the different pianos, all flowed through her head.

That's right – back then there was always someone waiting inside the piano. When she walked out on stage, someone was always calling out to her from inside the instrument. Someone was always waiting for her.

Jin Kazama seemed so . . . happy. Just as I was.

God was waiting for him. Like he was for me.

I've completely forgotten how much fun that was.

No, that's not actually true.

I ran away.

She felt a dull pain in her chest. The urge to cry welled up in her.

Hot waves pounded relentlessly at her temples.

I want to play. Like I used to. Let me play, joyfully, one more time.

In the rehearsal room, Aya kept her eyes closed. She did not touch the piano once.

A passing staff member peeked in and knocked on the door, telling her she was on soon. It was time to change into her dress.

The hall had emptied after Jin Kazama's performance, but now it was filling up again. Now, a very different feeling ran through it, a kind of ominous expectation.

Kanade found the atmosphere disquieting, painfully so.

When she herself performed, she always knew she'd practised, and was doing her absolute best, so she could bravely face anything up on stage.

But when it was someone else's performance, you felt so helpless.

The audience's eyes were filled with a kind of stark hostility as they waited to witness this former girl genius's comeback – or perhaps to see how, after all, she was just a shadow of her former self.

Kanade found it hard to breathe. A painful stab of sympathy ran through her.

She took a deep, soundless breath.

People were still noisily trooping down the aisles.

'WELCOME BACK.'

Hiroshi Takubo confined himself to a simple greeting.

He wanted it to sound heartfelt.

The girl in the wings looked over at him. She seemed absorbed, as if considering something, but then, apparently satisfied, beamed at him.

Takubo smiled back.

He had, indeed, seen her from the wings in the past – and he remembered what she'd played then. A Ravel concerto.

He remembered it as if it were yesterday – listening backstage, his heart trembling.

Remembering her beatific face as she returned to the darkness of the wings.

Takubo noticed that a different atmosphere now filled the concert hall.

Looking at that girl quietly waiting there in the dark, he felt as if some of her natural calm had rubbed off on him.

'Eiden-*san*. It's time,' Takubo said, glancing at his watch.

She stepped forward, into the lights, her face no longer that of a young woman, but as he'd seen it before: a face filled with the dignity of a goddess.

Masaru listened carefully to the buzz around him, hoping to pick up on why the next competitor was drawing such a crowd. He soon gathered the necessary background information from a couple of girls nearby.

Ah, he thought, that explained the mix of curiosity and ill will, the mood around him.

A complicated, ever so uncomfortable feeling.

The poor girl, he thought. A half-baked performance wasn't going to cut it here.

These thoughts were running through his head as the stage door swept open.

A petite young woman emerged. The look of her startled him.

He felt drawn to her face, but wasn't sure why.

It felt like a refreshing breeze had blown in with her.

She wore a simple, bright blue dress. Her hair in a short, angular bob.

Her gaze stayed with you. As if light was radiating from within her – and Masaru realized he'd had the same sort of feeling long ago.

When he was a child. Here in Japan.

Eiden Aya. Aya—

He couldn't believe it. All the while he'd been picturing that worn-out cloth bag in a corner of his suitcase in the hotel room.

Coincidences like this surely don't happen, he thought, yet his heart wouldn't stop pounding. In fact, the pounding only grew louder.

When the girl settled on her stool, the hall grew almost painfully still.

Masaru stared intently at her profile, the look in her eyes, not wanting to miss any of it.

The girl, seemingly unaware, gazed up into space.

Her eyes narrowed as if it was too bright, and a faint smile broke on her lips.

She lowered her hands to the keys.

The whole audience snapped awake.

We're on a different level *here*, Akashi Takashima thought.

This was a true professional up on stage. A person born to make their living as a musician.

Akashi was a bit disgusted with himself when he realized how comically relieved he suddenly felt.

The girl was an idol. Back then, and even now.

Nathaniel Silverberg remembered Hamazaki's words.

'There's one girl you'll have to wake up for,' Hamazaki had told him with a wry smile.

Hamazaki, an old friend of his, now the president of a private music college, had been responding to his enquiry about the Japanese pianists.

He hadn't mentioned who it was, but now Nathaniel had heard her, it suddenly clicked. Maybe Hamazaki was just being modest, but where on earth did this pianist emerge from, anyway?

Nathaniel felt a twinge of exasperation. And then he smiled.

Outstanding playing, and so mature, he thought. This was the *real thing* – as if an experienced, mature adult had somehow slipped in among a bunch of children. Her technique was already such an integral part of the music, you didn't notice it. You could only appreciate the music, not sit in judgement on it.

In the Beethoven sonata, her interpretive skills shone in intriguing ways. She already had a solid grasp of her own style, and there was an inviolable dignity to her performance.

He felt a cold sweat breaking out.

Jin Kazama wasn't Masaru's rival. *This girl* was.

She began the *Mephisto Waltz*, casually, quietly.

The audience was now wholeheartedly enraptured, and devoid of malice.

Kanade was afraid she would weep.

The thrill she'd felt ten years ago when she'd first heard Aya play came rushing back.

This performance was totally different from Masaru Carlos's.

Quiet, yet dramatic. Noble, and heart-rending. Layers of energy gradually building. Her *Mephisto Waltz* made your heart tremble – you couldn't help it.

This girl really did seem to be soaring. A goddess taking wing.

'Welcome back, Aya-*chan*,' whispered Kanade. 'You're finally – *finally* – back where you belong.'

AT THE VERY BACK OF the auditorium was a boy in a well-worn cap.

He was staring hard, eyes wide, face flushed, at the girl on stage.

AYA STOOD, BOWED DEEPLY, AND the hall erupted into applause.

She looked up, grinning broadly, and hurried off the stage.

There was no foot stamping or cheering, just rousing applause, on and on and on.

'Hmm.'

'That was – incredible.'

'Just as I thought. Aya Eiden is something else.'

'She's in a class of her own.'

Masaru leapt to his feet. He was so excited he didn't realize how desperate he was to get out of the hall. But the aisles were so packed with people eagerly sharing their reactions, he could barely move.

Let me out. Let me get out.

He stood impatiently behind the audience members inching their way along.

*She's here. My Aya-*chan.

Masaru felt like bursting into tears.

'Excuse me. *Pardon*,' he said, elbowing his way through, and then taking a leap out into the lobby.

Romance

BACK IN SWEATER AND jeans, Aya sensed her old self had returned.

How incredibly relieved and refreshed she felt – as if her vision had cleared, as if a bad spell had been broken. *Hard to believe,* she thought, *when, until this morning – no, actually until I heard Jin Kazama – I'd been so despairing.*

Wearing a dress really does make me tense.

Aya gave a big stretch, and left the green room.

It already felt like a dream.

There were two more competitors after her, and soon after that, those who had got through would be announced.

Why did I do it? She felt calm enough to ask herself this.

No – she'd always been calm, even when she was performing. There had been a part of her that would listen to herself play. That had never changed, ever since she was a child. She'd always felt the presence of another self quietly surveying from on high what lay below.

But what was that urge I had earlier? she wondered.

It was the only moment when she felt a chill, when she tried to recall that feeling.

That urge that drove me to want to play like Jin Kazama, beloved of the god of music. What was *that?*

She hadn't felt a compulsion like this in years. In truth, she hadn't even felt it as a child. She'd never even known such feelings lay within her.

That boy, that boy's music, is what triggered this urge.

Jin Kazama. Should I be grateful to him? Or maybe—?

She made her way to the lift and pushed the button for the concert hall. The next performance had already begun.

One thing was certain, she thought – this feeling of fulfilment, of catharsis, only came about because she'd been on stage. This wasn't something she could experience during practice.

The question is – do I want to taste it again? Do I feel like making a complete comeback to the front lines of music? Hold on. I already have *made a comeback, as far as the world is concerned. But am I prepared to face them again?*

Could she take the gossip and expectation? Laid-back, carefree Aya who'd always done what she wanted to do?

Aya shook her head.

One thing's certain. I enjoyed every minute.

In a corner of the deserted lobby was a lift to the floor of rehearsal rooms.

When she stepped out of the lift, as expected no one was there. As she was looking up and down the corridor, a tall figure loomed.

Gently curling dark brown hair. A nicely tailored blue shirt and trousers.

Goodness – it's the Juilliard Prince, Aya realized with a start.

He was so big, she thought, when you saw him up close. With an amazing aura about him. A true prince. He seemed to belong to a whole other species.

She was struck with admiration.

Is he waiting for someone, standing here like this?

Aya glanced behind her.

The Prince continued to stand – he was looking at her, but she couldn't read him. Maybe she was imagining it, but his eyes seemed a little teary. She went past him and stood with her back to him, by the door of a practice room.

His voice called out behind her.

'Aa-*chan*?'

THE WAY PEOPLE'S MEMORIES WORKED was unfathomable.

When he said her name, time instantly rewound, and a drawer in her brain she'd never opened was yanked ajar.

This voice, this way of calling my name—

She spun around and saw a slim, dark-skinned, Latin American young man with curly hair.

'Aa-*chan*, I have to go back to France.'

The voice of a perplexed boy.

'I'm sorry,' the boy had said, hanging his head as Aya stood weeping.

He had always been reserved, a little sad-looking, not the type to rush into anything – yet he produced a sound that was as boundless as the sea on a sparkling day.

'Ma-*kun*? Are you really Ma-*kun*? Is it really *you*?' She stared hard.

The face of this boy – not a boy any more, but an imposing young *man*, well over six feet tall – lit up. He nodded.

'Yes, it's really me, Masaru. Aa-*chan*, you know – I still have that bag with me, the one you gave me with the treble clef on it.'

'No way!'

Aya had always laughed at girls who talked like that at the drop of a hat. Girls her age, flitting about like so many butterflies, with all their trite little reactions: *No way! You kidding? Seriously? That sucks*.

But now one of those pathetic phrases was all that came to her.

They were meeting again after more than ten years, so what other reaction could she have than to scream out loud and rush over to hug him?

Masaru's chin was way higher than the top of her head, she found, as his arms wrapped themselves around her. He was twice her size.

'Ma-*kun*, I can't believe how big you've got.'

Aya lifted her head to gaze up at his face. When he was a child, he seemed clearly Peruvian, but his skin and hair colour were lighter now and it was hard to pin him down to any particular nationality. His chiselled features reminded her of a philosopher, or a Buddhist priest, slightly aloof and unapproachable.

Masaru burst out laughing.

'Stop it, Aa-*chan*! You sound just like my grandmother. When you came out on stage, I knew who you were in an instant. *You* haven't changed a bit.'

He grabbed her hand and squeezed it.

'Tell me, Aa-*chan*,' Masaru said. 'How's Mr Watanuki? You know, I kept my promise to both of you. I started studying piano immediately after I arrived in France. A student introduced me to a professor at the Conservatoire and I studied with him. Then I enrolled at the Conservatoire and graduated in two years.'

'You really were a genius, weren't you, Ma-*kun*,' said Aya.

'Really?' Masaru shook his head. 'I always thought you and Mr Watanuki were the geniuses!'

The true genius was Mr Watanuki. Their teacher who, when she showed up one day with Masaru in tow, was all too happy to give him lessons too. The man who recognized Masaru's talent and marvelled at it. And now here that boy was years later, a wonderful young man that people had such hopes for, a star in the making. If only Mr Watanuki could be here, how happy it would make him.

'Ma-*kun* . . .'

Aya felt a wave of sadness welling up.

'Mr Watanuki passed away. Less than two years after you went back to France. He had pancreatic cancer, and they discovered it too late. He didn't even last a month after he was hospitalized. He was always thinking about you, Ma-*kun*.'

Masaru's face fell. His smile vanished, and he blanched.

'Sensei—' he said. 'He . . . he really died?'

Aya nodded. 'He's buried in Zoshigaya.'

'I'd . . . I'd like to pay my respects at his grave.'

'Let's go together. I know that'll make him happy.'

Now Masaru's hand was in hers – it all felt like they'd gone back in time. Except she had to look up at him now since he'd grown so much, and his hand was twice the size of hers.

But, she thought, his hands were big even back then. They said that children with big hands and feet grew really tall. With hands this big he could easily cover the whole keyboard, and Rachmaninoff should be no problem. In fact, as children they'd talked about playing a Rachmaninoff four-hands piece, Aya recalled. Well, with hands like these, that should be a cakewalk for him.

People were streaming out of the hall – a performance must have ended. She realized that Masaru had been deliberately waiting for her.

'Ma-*kun*, can you still sing that song you used to like, "Funa uta"?'

She looked at him teasingly and Masaru swelled with pride. 'Of course! When I sang it at karaoke in Tokyo, the Japanese were all so surprised.'

She pictured Masaru, looking as he did now, belting out that Japanese tune and felt laughter welling up inside.

'But my teacher's even more amazing. He sings the one by Kiyoshi Maekawa. "Tokyo Desert".'

'What? Nathaniel Silverberg does?'

She knew Silverberg had been married to a Japanese woman, but still – she tried to picture him, with that lion-like mane of hair, standing ramrod straight, belting out the tune.

She burst out giggling, and Masaru pulled her by the hand.

'Aa-*chan*, you laugh too much. Let's go and listen to the final pianist. After that, we'll hear the announcement of who's got through.'

Aya was startled out of her laughter.

THE COMPETITION. THEY WERE RIVALS. Only twenty-four would get through to the second round. And only twelve to the third.

Masaru seemed to be thinking the same thing.

In this nodding, smiling face there was no trace of the boy she'd known. His voice was confident. 'I don't think you and I need to worry, Aa-*chan*. Let's do our best in the second round.'

She managed a lukewarm reply.

Masaru would most definitely get through the first round – no doubt about that, she thought. With that superb, charming performance, how could he not? They were already talking about him as a possible winner. There were rumours that the judges had given him a really high score.

But what did they think about *her*?

'MISS EIDEN?' A VOICE FROM BEHIND.

She turned around to find a man and a woman wearing press armbands. Reporters.

'Congratulations on finishing the first round. Your performance was wonderful.'

'We're from *Classic Stream*. Do you mind if we ask you a few questions?'

By the look of these two, she must have done all right. But the request was so sudden, and she hadn't been interviewed in a long time. Her mind went blank.

'How was it being back on stage for the first time in so long?'

'Did you feel anything special, actually playing again?'

'Well, uh . . .'

'I'm sorry, but we're going to listen to the next performance, so if you'll excuse us,' Masaru said, smiling at the reporters but firmly cutting them off.

He tugged on Aya's hand and led her into the concert hall.

Our roles are completely reversed now, she thought.

From behind she heard: 'Wait – isn't that guy with her the one from Juilliard?'

'Yes, you're right.'

For a second, she worried what they might say.

Masaru dropped down quickly in a seat at the back of the hall.

Aya had planned to rejoin Kanade, but Masaru had led her to another seat, and she couldn't say anything.

The first round would soon be over, and she could rejoin Kanade then.

'Thanks for rescuing me,' Aya whispered and smiled.

'If you don't want to talk to anyone, it's best to turn them down flat.'

'You must have a lot of requests for interviews, too?'

'I don't accept any during the first round. I'll do some after they announce the results. And I'll do the same during the second round.'

'I see.'

Exactly what you might expect of a future virtuoso, to be

good at handling the media. *I wouldn't be surprised if he's already signed up with a management agency*, she thought.

She opened the programme and studied Masaru's page again.

'Your name is really long, isn't it?'

'And yours is hard for me.'

'So you're representing the US. That's why I didn't notice you were in the competition. Aren't you a French citizen?'

'Either one is fine now. Juilliard asked me to enter as an American. Before long I might have to choose one over the other.'

He was a year younger than her. She was stunned at his age in the programme: nineteen.

He's so grown up, yet still a teenager.

She was about to turn the page but realized Masaru still had a tight grip on her right hand.

He hadn't let go of it since he first took it.

'Ma-*kun*?' Aya said. 'Could you let go of my hand?'

'No.'

IT WAS THE EMOTIONAL SHOCK of meeting up again after so long apart that made Masaru keep a grip on her hand, and the nostalgia that feeling triggered. But at the same time he had an unconscious sense of something else—

That if they didn't stay tightly connected here, she might once again turn away from the piano. That this muse, with no regrets about leaving anything here on Earth, might desert Masaru and go somewhere far away. Never to return.

Somewhere inside, Masaru couldn't shake this unease and anxiety.

Ode to Joy

MASAMI FOCUSED ON AKASHI whose face was creased with tension.

Through her viewfinder he looked forlorn, somehow.

'How are you feeling?' she asked. Akashi glanced over and smiled.

'Well – pretty tense, I have to say. I haven't felt like this since the day my son was born.'

He patted his chest playfully.

The lobby was filling up. Lots of people from the press, and a few with media armbands, cameras at the ready.

Of the ninety or so competitors, roughly three-quarters would be cut.

Masami was aware of how merciless competitions were and how tense it made everyone.

But there was also an excitement. A thrill. For music fans, no other spectacle could be so compelling.

Akashi was wandering around, his eyes gazing over the crowd, unfocused. Would he pass, or would he fail? His mind must be filled with trepidation, dwelling on how this moment could decide his fate. Masami found herself growing nervous.

Squinting through the viewfinder, she panned her camera across the lobby, as if gently stroking the scene. As it did with most filmmakers, looking at the world through the viewfinder immediately calmed her. You felt in control, as if excising a small slice of the world.

There was a buzz among the crowd, and cheers.

The judges had started to descend the staircase from the upper floor.

Wow, they're so many of them, Masami thought.

This was definitely a highlight, this group of thirteen international judges drifting towards them.

Spotlights came on, and a row of cameramen swung towards them, turning the scene into theatre. A hush descended.

In the middle of the first row stood Olga Slutskaya, chair of the judges. She was smiling broadly, but there was a penetrating look in her eyes, an inner fire burning within, and it wasn't just the orange trouser suit she was wearing – she was an unmistakably forceful presence. Novels often described people's hair as red, but Olga's, lit up in the harsh light, was a true vermilion.

Olga picked up a cordless microphone.

'To our pianists, and to those supporting them, thank you for all your efforts during the first round of the competition.'

At her voice, speaking in fluent, careful Japanese, the room grew still.

All eyes were trained on her hand, at the sheet of white paper clasped between her fine long fingers.

'The standard of the competition has risen with each event,' Olga noted, 'with this year's participants being the best ever. I hope those who don't make it will not feel discouraged, but will continue to forge ahead.'

As she carried on making remarks along these lines, the packed lobby grew restless.

That was all very well, but who was through and who wasn't?

Olga smiled.

'I can see you're all eager for the main event, and so without further ado here is the list of pianists who will be going through to the second round.'

Olga unfolded the piece of paper.

'No. 1, Alexei Zakhaev.'

'*Yay!*' a shout rose up.

Everyone turned to look towards the back. In a corner of the lobby, a young Russian man and his friends were hugging each other.

'That's unusual, for the first performer to get through,' murmured Akashi.

'Really?' Masami asked.

'Usually the first performer is at a real disadvantage,' he explained.

'No. 8, Han Hyonjon.' Another shout of joy. This was a Korean woman, apparently.

'No. 12, Jennifer Chan.'

An even louder cheer.

Cameras flashed around an Asian girl. An American pianist, said to be a contender for the top prize.

Names were read out in quick succession; every time people would cheer, but Masama couldn't capture them all with her camera. The crowd was also growing ever more boisterous.

Akashi had grown pale. They were getting close to his number.

Masami trained her video camera on him. His eyes were wide and unblinking.

She held her breath.

'No. 22, Akashi Takashima.'

For a second, Akashi looked totally blank.

But then his face grew visibly flushed.

'*Yes!*' he called out in a small voice and pumped his fist. He looked at Masami for support, a shy, genuine look of relief washing over him.

'I did it. Thank you. Thank you.'

It was unclear who he was thanking, but he bowed repeatedly to the camera.

'Congratulations,' Masami said, a feeling of warmth flooding her body. Camera in one hand, she managed to shake his hand.

I'm so happy, she thought. *Now we can carry on filming*.

Since Akashi was the first Japanese pianist to be named, reporters came over to get his reaction.

'Oh – I need to call home,' Akashi said, and he hurried over to a corner of the lobby. Masami followed.

Akashi breaking the happy news to his wife. That was a scene she had to capture on film.

But when she saw Akashi talking animatedly to his wife on his cell phone, she couldn't help feeling a kind of loneliness.

'No. 30, Masaru Carlos Levi Anatole.'

A cheer rose up, and everyone in the lobby applauded. Masaru had made fans not just of the audience but of his rivals, and among the staff as well.

Masaru beamed and bowed, and as Aya watched from a distance, she was astonished all over again at his star quality.

'Talk about popular,' Kanade whispered to Aya.

'He is pretty cool-looking, isn't he?' Aya said. She still hadn't told Kanade about bumping into Masaru a little while ago, or that they were childhood friends. As soon as Kanade had spotted Aya, she started to say how awed she was by her performance, looking as if she was about to cry. The timing hadn't seemed right.

'Amazing. There were a lot of Asian entrants to begin with, but I'm thinking they might make up more than half of those who get through,' said Kanade.

A lot of the successful entrants were from South Korea and Eastern Europe, and Aya was concerned how many Japanese contestants would pass. When they'd reached the halfway point in the announcements, only three Japanese pianists had been named: the man who was the oldest competitor among them, a teenage girl and a twenty-year-old music-college student.

Before Aya knew it, the list of those reaching the second round had exceeded twenty names.

Available seats are running out fast. The phrase suddenly came to her.

If they called her name, it would be last, or maybe second to last, Aya predicted. Being one of the later numbers wasn't good for your heart, she mused.

Olga seemed to take a deep breath.

Was Aya just imagining it, or did Olga hesitate?

'No. 81, Jin Kazama.'

'*Oh!*' Another wave of excitement rippled through the crowd.

That boy. The boy beloved of god. Had Olga really hesitated before announcing his name?

But that thought was interrupted by a roar of applause.

People scanned the crowd to catch sight of Jin Kazama, but soon doubtful voices were heard: 'What? He's not here?' The boy seemed to have skipped the announcement. He wasn't the only one, of course, since they also posted a list of the successful competitors in the lobby and online.

'And No. 88, Aya Eiden. That concludes the list of twenty-four pianists.'

Aya was so absorbed in speculating about Jin Kazama's whereabouts that it took a moment to register what she'd just heard.

Kanade let out a cheer and hugged her, while others turned to her, smiling and applauding, and she understood.

She'd made it to the second round.

'Congratulations! *Congratulations*, Aya-*chan*!'

Now Kanade really was crying.

The two of them hugged each other, yet Aya's heart remained unmoved.

Feeling someone's gaze upon her, she looked up and saw Masaru in the corner, giving her a thumbs-up.

Didn't I tell you we'd both pass? his eyes told her. *Let's do our best next time too.*

The show would go on – and so would her contest with Masaru.

IN THE LOBBY WERE PHOTOS on the wall of all the entrants. Staff members were attaching little flowers made of ribbon to the ones of the successful competitors. Every time a pianist got through to the next round, another little flower would be added to their photo.

'That was a close call,' Alan Simon said. They were inside the smoking room, and he was gazing through the glass at the beribboned photos.

'*What* was? You mean your nicotine withdrawal?' Mieko asked.

Puffing away herself, she glared at him for a second.

'Well, that too,' Simon said. 'But what I meant was Jin Kazama.'

'So he succeeded in breaking through.'

'As we expected.'

Judges each gave entrants one of three scores – O, Δ or X, essentially three, one or no points – and pianists were then ranked by their total.

Jin Kazama's scores were clearly divided between high and low marks – threes and zeros. This system allowed pianists to pass even if they didn't receive a lot of threes but managed to get a uniform middle scoring. Simon and Smirnoff had been panicky about the results, yet because of the way the scoring was devised, Jin Kazama had got through, though only just.

'It helped a lot that you changed your mind, Mieko,' Simon said, a little sarcastically, and shot her a glance.

'It's not as if I changed my mind. I just finally understood.'

Mieko shrugged. She'd given Jin Kazama a three this time.

'At any rate, his technical skills are more than enough for the first round. What I find more amazing is that someone could give him a zero,' she continued.

'I really wonder what kind of lessons he's had. Who's teaching him now? And what are his ambitions? Is he planning to become a concert pianist?' Simon moved his head from side to side, as if singing.

'I'm a little concerned about that myself.' Mieko looked upwards and exhaled a puff of smoke.

'Somehow I can't imagine him as a concert pianist.'

'I know, right? But I can see him turning into a tremendous musician, a kind we've never seen before.'

A vision suddenly came to her, of a small truck bumping down a narrow track between rice fields, the boy in the truck bed playing an upright piano.

'What are you talking about? No one's about to break out into the "Internationale" these days,' Simon said.

'In Japanese we have an expression that goes *Farm while it's sunny and read when it's raining*. It means live a quiet, peaceful life. For this pianist, it would mean playing the piano while keeping bees. In our environmentally concerned world, people might appreciate that.'

She'd said it as a joke, but Mieko could see Jin Kazama living a life that embraced both. And she had a faint premonition that that sort of musical life might go down well. The clearest image, though, was of the boy strolling in the hills, singing.

'He is intriguing, for sure.' Mieko realized she was repeating Olga's line. 'Very intriguing.'

AKASHI WAS STARING AT THE pink flower pinned next to his photograph.

Masami had gone off to get more footage. They'd promised to meet up later for dinner and to celebrate. But before he began to prepare for the second round, which started tomorrow, Akashi wanted to have some time to himself, to savour the joy.

All his work up until now came down to this: a single little ribbon-flower.

He felt tears rising.

His family and friends' support had made this little flower possible. And it had all been worthwhile. Sure, it was just a flower made out of ribbon, but for him no other flower could have ever made him happier.

'Let me add one more flower to this,' he said, and took a photo with his cell phone.

Then he held the cell phone out at arm's length, turned it round and angled it for a good selfie. It was awkward getting the distance right, and he couldn't quite capture himself and the flower in the same frame.

This is harder than I thought.

As he kept on trying, he heard a laugh from behind.

He spun around to find Masami, doubled up in laughter.

'Oh, my goodness. What're you trying to do? Let *me* do it.'

They looked at each other and hooted with laughter.

He couldn't remember the last time he'd laughed like this, with such a light heart.

The tension he'd felt at the judges' announcement made him realize how much he'd been suppressing his emotions, how little he'd been feeling all this time.

Catching their breath again, they pushed open the double doors together and headed outside.

Round Two

(Part One)

The Sorcerer's Apprentice

THE SECOND ROUND OF the competition – lasting three days – began the next morning.

In the second round, the size of the audience for each performance was more consistent. It wasn't just friends and family listening now but many more regular audience members who planned to catch as much as they could. One could sense a greater intensity of focus, not only up on stage but among the audience as well.

Second-round performances were set at forty minutes, twice the length of the first round. Pianists were to perform the following:

1. Two études from two of the following composers: Chopin, Liszt, Debussy, Scriabin, Rachmaninoff, Bartók, Stravinsky.
2. One or more pieces by one of the following: Schubert, Mendelssohn, Chopin, Schumann, Liszt, Brahms, Franck, Fauré, Debussy, Ravel, Stravinsky.
3. The piece *Spring and Ashura* by Tadaaki Hishinuma, specially commissioned for the Yoshigae International Piano Competition.

What particularly worried the competitors was where in their programme to put the single new piece, the modern composition *Spring and Ashura* (Ashura being the name of a Buddhist guardian deity, a warlike figure).

As the title indicated, this piece used poetry by Kenji Miyazawa as its motif and was almost completely atonal. It took about nine minutes to perform, nearly a quarter of the allotted time, so where to position it was a major decision.

No matter how you looked at it, this piece stood out, and

didn't feel right coming in the middle, so the majority of pianists placed it either at the very beginning of their selection, or at the end.

'Well, it's simple. You either play it first, or last . . .'

Seated in a corner at the back of the auditorium, programmes in hand, Masaru and Aya were whispering to each other. Masaru was due to perform on the second day, and Aya on the third.

The first competitor, Alexei Zakhaev, back on stage after some ninety others had performed in the first round, looked relaxed after delivering a polished performance, and exited the stage to generous applause.

Kanade had gone back to Tokyo, and planned to return the following evening.

I'm sure she'll report back to Prof. Hamazaki, and I'm relieved she'll have good news for him, thought Aya.

She studied Masaru's choices.

'Your recital starts quietly, so I think it's good, to put *Spring and Ashura* first.'

'I knew you'd get it.' Masaru looked pleased.

'But Ma-*kun*, aren't you going to be pushed for time? It's hard to know how long those variations are going take.'

Masaru had included, at the end of his recital, a lengthy set of variations by Brahms. Play them in too leisurely a way and they'd take nearly twenty-five minutes. It would be touch and go if he could stay within the forty-minute time limit.

'It might be faster, but never slower. I hardly ever go over time. I see you put *Spring and Ashura* right in the middle. That's bold. Right after Liszt's *Will-o'-the-Wisp*.'

'It's as if they're all connected up with our universe, or maybe the climate. That was the idea.'

'Hmm. You're doing Mendelssohn's variations. I love that piece, too.'

She and Masaru shared a similar approach to their pieces, and how to build a recital. They loved listening to others play, and to enjoy, as much as was ever possible, their competitions. She couldn't put it into words, but their outlook was very similar.

'I see you picked Prokofiev's Concerto No. 3 for the final, Ma-*kun*.'

'And you're going with No. 2, Aa-*chan*. That's unusual.'

'You think?'

She recalled with a chill that Prokofiev's No. 2 was the piece she'd been due to play the day she walked off the stage.

Had it been an unconscious choice? Aya suppressed the thought.

'I like all Prokofiev's concertos,' she said. 'You can dance to Prokofiev.'

'Dance?'

'Yeah. Even with his non-ballet music there are parts where I can visualize dancing. When No. 2 premiered, it was panned, apparently, but you've got to hand it to Diaghilev, since that's why he went on to commission Prokofiev to write for ballet after that.'

'When I hear No. 3 it makes me think of a space opera, like *Star Wars*.'

'I totally get it! It's outer-spacey. No. 2 is more noirish.'

'Exactly. Like some gangland fight.'

They looked at each other and laughed.

'I can really picture you playing Rachmaninoff No. 3, Ma-*kun*.'

'Hmm. Nos. 1 and 2 are one thing, but No. 3's not really my style. In the second half, it's as if there's this leakage of the pianist's self-consciousness. When No. 2 became so popular, Rachmaninoff must have decided to outdo it with a concerto that could trap its performer in his own spell.'

Aya raised her eyebrows.

'Ma-*kun*, where did you learn the word *leakage* in Japanese?'

'From a student at Juilliard. I borrowed a lot of manga from him and studied them so I wouldn't forget my Japanese.'

Thanks to which he was able to speak the language so well now, though his vocabulary often took Aya by surprise.

'Check this out – if he gets to the final, the Honeybee Prince is playing Bartók's No. 3. Bartók fits him perfectly, don't you think?'

The Honeybee Prince. Jin Kazama. So Masaru was keeping his eye on him too.

'The guy's amazing,' he went on.

'You're right. I've never heard such an electric sound before.'

'Absolutely. But there's a rumour floating around that some of the judges weren't too keen on him at all.'

After all the excitement around his playing? Aya couldn't believe it.

'I guess some don't like his vibrancy, that he was sensationalizing Bach or something. It will all come down to the scoring system of point deduction.'

Masaru was calm about it. But Aya was feeling uneasy. In a competition, public opinion was a factor. But if a stupendous, creative performance wasn't recognized, then what was talent, anyway?

'I was thinking about doing a Bartók concerto myself,' Masaru murmured, 'but you have to consider the orchestra.'

'The orchestra?'

Masaru scratched his nose.

'I ordered a few CDs of the orchestra that will be playing for the concertos, but their brass section is a bit weak – Japanese orchestras tend to be.'

'Even when more people than ever are joining brass bands?'

'With Bartók you need a really strong brass section or there's no impact. You can add players, but they have to coordinate their playing over a long time, or you just don't get the sound you need.'

Aya couldn't believe he'd gone so far as to investigate orchestras for the final round.

He wasn't just an attractive personality, but quite the calculating tactician as well. For most competitors, just making it to the final round would be all they could ask for. If truth be told, they weren't too concerned about the orchestra they'd play with if they made it that far.

'Speaking of brass, didn't I hear that you play the trombone, Ma-*kun*?'

He turned to her, looking surprised.

'Who told you that?'

'Somebody at music college.'

The information network at music colleges was formidable.

'I thought I'd try something other than keyboard. I have long arms and was told I'd be able to handle the slide well, so I gave it a try. What about you, Aa-*chan*? What did you do after you stopped the piano?'

Masaru seemed to know something about her own background too, which surprised her. *Well*, she thought, *it's a pretty well-known story in the music world, so I guess it's only to be expected.* She shrugged.

'I quit performing, but not the piano. I played keyboard in fusion and jazz bands, and I was really into the guitar for a while. Though these days I haven't been playing it at all.'

'Classical guitar?'

'No. Jazz. Kind of faddish of me, but I copied Pat Metheny, Joe Pass, guys like that.'

She remembered that time in her life, before she started music college, when she was totally into guitar.

'I'd love to hear you play.'

'I'm not that good. I've found the guitar is a guy's instrument, really. Especially rock and jazz.'

'You think?'

'Yeah. As they say, when you play guitar, you feel like you can really get, for the first time, how guys feel when they *come*.'

Masaru snorted.

'Then if you come to New York, Aa-*chan*, we can play a session, too.'

'I guess we could!'

Masaru suddenly looked at her with a serious expression.

'You really should visit. After the competition,' he said.

'To Juilliard?'

'Not just for Juilliard.'

'Not just for that?'

'Never mind,' Masaru said and turned to face forward.

Not just for Juilliard.

Aya decided not to think too much about it, and changed the subject.

'The next pianist's a friend of yours,' she said.

'Who's that?'

'Jennifer Chan. Isn't she one of the competitors they think might win this whole thing?'

'Well, she's definitely good,' Masaru said. 'She's got serious power and technique. She's the perfect type for competitions.'

Masaru seemed to be implying something else.

'I'd love to know what you think of her, Aa-*chan*.'

The stage door swung open and Jennifer Chan, tall, in a bright red dress, emerged. A cheer went up from the audience.

'Whoa. A red dress again. She looks good in it.'

'Apparently she wears a different shade of red in every competition.'

'Must be her lucky colour.'

Chan strutted boldly over to the piano, glaring for a second in the direction of the audience.

Chan's programme, too, began with *Spring and Ashura*.

Like Masaru, she'd decided to kick off with this work. What was interesting was that she gave the impression it was an awkward piece she just wanted to get out of the way. Programmes really could display each pianist's personality.

This was the world premiere of *Spring and Ashura*, and people were curious to hear how Chan would play it. With an untested composition there was no precedent to follow, so it was helpful to hear others perform it.

I want to hear as many performances as I can, Aya thought.

Chan's reading seemed spot on. Aya was impressed by her crystal-clear interpretation.

When performing a piece by a Japanese composer, Japanese pianists tended to accept any impressionistic sections as just that, playing in a sort of indeterminate, nebulous way, while Westerners strove to convey Zen-like imagery.

Chan read the music dispassionately, with nothing random or wilful about it, making utterly sure to interpret it in a very particular, concrete way. It was as if you could hear her explaining the meaning of every note that expressed Kenji Miyazawa's view of the universe and his whole-of-creation theme. Chan's rational approach to every situation, and her personality, were more than evident.

This is one model for how to play it, Aya thought.

Next to come were the more challenging études by Chopin and Liszt, which seemed to be Chan's forte.

Aya felt herself snapping out of her sense of awe.

A dynamic performance, yes, but there was something flat and monotonous, she mused. Though Chan's technique was beyond reproach, it was like being stuffed so full of good food you couldn't take another bite.

Aya thought she could understand what Masaru had been trying to say.

She seldom analysed other pianists' performances like this. Instead, she sat back like any other member of the audience and let the music wash over her. Masaru's comment about wanting to hear what she thought was one encouraging factor, but not the only one.

An odd image had been taking shape in her mind for a while.

An image of tall men playing volleyball. A scene of an ace hitter making some amazing offensives from the back, but the other team predicting the trajectory of the ball in advance and blocking every move.

There was something in common between music and a top athlete's balletic agility; indeed, sometimes as Aya watched sport, she could hear music in her head.

It wasn't clear why Chan's performance had conjured up this image, but in it the pattern of offensives became so predictable that the other team were able to time their blocks perfectly so that no spikers could win a point.

Impressive physical ability, yet the spiker would never score. In a word, you weren't moved.

Why, Aya wondered, when her playing was so clearly well shaped and passionate?

The whole thing was puzzling.

She recalled what a film director had once said, that Hollywood movies weren't entertainment any more, but *spectacles*. That's how Chan's performance felt.

Since the beginning of the twentieth century, so many European classical musicians had fled to America or emigrated there. Talent naturally gravitated towards wealth and power. After prosperous America became a huge market for music, classical music became popularized. The demand was to showcase music that was easier to understand.

For orchestras this meant the inclusion of pieces that were neatly constructed, and for the piano, pieces where the notes were neatly arranged, all performed with a clear-cut, transcendent technique. This was quite different from the music of historical salons, where works were played before a select, privileged audience. What was required now was a dazzling, expansive sound that could fill the huge concert halls built to house growing audiences. Musicians needed to respond to the expectations of the market, and performances evolved to meet these demands.

People no longer wanted musicians to improvise. Instead, audiences went to hear the famous tunes they were already familiar with. They were less keen on challenging or new work, and idiosyncrasy was avoided.

The growth of the CD market only speeded up this trend.

CDs, as was commonly known, excluded the highest and lowest registers, sounds on the edge of audibility. And so the kind of indigenous, European nuances of performance that had for so long been a tradition, were eroded.

Chan was the perfect embodiment of the audience research conducted by the American market, exactly the kind of pianist that audiences now hoped for. Whether this was good or bad wasn't the point. This was the type of pianist produced by the demands of the times and the public.

Chan came to the end of a splendid forty-minute recital.

The audience responded with enthusiasm, sending up rousing cheers.

Encores were permitted from the second round onwards. Chan left the stage for a moment, then reappeared, responding with a relaxed smile to the applause. Her tall figure, in its red dress, bowing graciously, couldn't have been more brilliant.

'So – what did you think?' Masaru whispered in Aya's ear as the clapping went on.

'She can play anything. Such amazing power.'

'Right?'

'I felt like I was at Disneyland. Riding on the Big Thunder Mountain Railroad.'

Masaru was silent. 'You say some scary things sometimes, Aya-*chan*.'

'Do I?'

Masaru looked lost in thought. 'But you're right. She's an attraction.'

'The audience loves it, and she's so popular.'

'If you told her that, though, she'd be pissed off. But you've got to admit it fits.'

'Don't tell her I said that, OK?'

'Of course not. I'd never do that.'

'Her performance of *Spring and Ashura* was really good,' she said. 'I feel like I understand its structure for the first time.'

'Me too. She's good at giving a three-dimensional interpretation – that's her strong point.'

'I liked her cadenza, too. I wonder if she wrote it.'

'No, I'm sure her teacher did. Boleyn. Chan can't really improvise. Lots of pianists find it hard.'

Spring and Ashura had an improvised section, marked *Freely, giving a sense of the universe.*

Freely, giving a sense of the universe?

Aya herself had tried out many approaches to the *Spring and Ashura* cadenza, but still hadn't settled on how to interpret it.

But that boy – Jin Kazama – for him *sensing the universe* would be quite natural.

She pictured him. Not on stage, but when she'd bumped into him at her music college, in a cap and casual clothes.

'Ma-*kun*, your cadenza's your own composition, isn't it?'

How could you ask such a thing? his eyes said. 'Of course,' he replied. 'Yours too, right?'

'Yeah. Did you write yours down?'

'For now. Lots of people have heard it, and I've really thought about how I should play it.'

Aya paused. Masaru gave her a look.

'Are you telling me you haven't written yours down?'

'No. I'm still playing around with a few versions. I can't decide, so I was thinking I'll just go with how I'm feeling during the performance.'

Masaru looked flabbergasted.

'But it's a competition, Aa-*chan*. Wow – you really *do* come up with some scary things. Didn't your teacher say anything?'

'He did.'

Aya recalled the moment. Even when the score indicated an improvised section, in the classical world the majority of pianists played a published cadenza.

When she had discussed with her professor how to approach the cadenza in *Spring and Ashura*, he had no problem with her writing her own. But when she told him she'd go with her feelings in the moment, he tried to dissuade her.

'You can't take a risk like that in a competition,' he'd warned.

'I know, but . . .' She'd paused. 'Some days it rains, some days it's windy, and the music tells us to sense the universe. Doesn't it go against the score's directions to practise a cadenza over and over again? Like this, for instance,' she said, before running through five different versions of the cadenza – with titles like 'Rainy Day', 'Clear Autumn', 'Stormy Day', 'Night of the Leonid Meteor Shower'.

Masaru was momentarily at a loss for words.

'I knew it. That's the Aya I know.'

He was smiling, though there was a hint of pain in his face.

'Wow,' he said. 'If only we weren't in the same competition.'

They fell silent.

'Competitions are really absurd,' Aya said after a while, and Masaru laughed.

They each directed their gaze again at the stage.

'Let's keep that to ourselves,' Masaru said. 'We all knew that when we entered.'

The two of them settled in their seats as the bell rang, signalling the end of the interval.

Spring and Ashura

FEELING MORE RELAXED IN the second round, Akashi limbered up his fingers, clutching his hands and pressing his fingertips together.

The tension in the first round had been unbearable. He couldn't recall anything in recent years that frightening. Yet being up on stage, even just the once, had changed him.

I became a musician, he told himself. *It made me realize I have always been one*.

That feeling bubbled up inside him.

What an incredible sense of fulfilment. His ordinary life now seemed so remote. The feeling of being on stage, the grand piano lit up, the sensation as he stepped towards it, the moment all eyes were trained on him as he lifted his hands, when both the intimate and the sublime collided into a single entity. And then the impassioned applause. The sense of having shared something with the audience.

Akashi relived his elation as he'd walked off the stage.

This *is where I belong*, he thought. *This is the moment I've been thirsting for*.

As he stood in the wings now, he was certain of it.

But as the second-round performance grew closer, he'd begun to feel a heaviness in the pit of his stomach. As if he had a second consciousness that was now hovering above his physical self.

The forty minutes of the second round would feel long. Keeping your concentration wasn't easy. And it was even harder to keep the audience with you.

Building a programme was a stimulating yet arduous task.

The first thing Akashi did was to buy recordings of some canonical performances and choose his favourites, rearranging the order, slotting in other pieces, so that they would fit in the forty-minute limit, and listening to them repeatedly. Then he played through them himself to get a feeling for whether they were a good technical fit for him, whether he felt comfortable playing them. Consultations with his former teacher followed, and a long while later he finally settled on a programme.

And now I need to practise.

Your repertoire. The eternal question for musicians.

Did you want to be known as a musician with a wide-ranging repertoire? Or establish a reputation as a specialist in a certain composer, become someone, for instance, whose forte was Schubert, or Mozart? No matter what kind of musician you wanted to become, the important thing was to have a substantial repertoire.

You might spend months polishing a piece, but if you stepped away from it for a while you would forget the detail. Getting up to speed again might not take as long as it did the first time, but dedicated practice was essential or your performance wouldn't be convincing.

The pianists would play over ten pieces during the competition. Those who got through to the finals, seventeen or eighteen. The longest pieces were nearly thirty minutes; the technical demands of different pieces varied, and likewise the amount of time needed to polish them. It was next to impossible to maintain every piece at the same degree of perfection.

How many times have I said to myself, 'If only I'd been a genius'? Akashi thought. There are an unbelievable number of geniuses who can reproduce a piece after just one hearing, or sight-read a piece without practising. Who was it he'd heard about? A pianist travelling to a concert whose programme included a piece he'd never played before, and he merely reviewed the score on the train and then proceeded that day to perform it flawlessly on stage. And another pianist who asked, 'Why do you have to practise? I don't get it. Once you know the music, all you have to do is make your fingers move.'

Akashi believed he was good at memorizing, though never to that kind of level. Unless he practised a lot, he always felt anxious.

For a busy working man with limited time to practise, the only way to manage was to cut down on sleep. The past year, preparing for the competition had been a constant battle with sleep. Even when he did actually drop off, he'd pop awake again, unconsciously moving his fingers over a difficult phrase that muscle memory couldn't let go of.

THERE WERE MANY WAYS TO practise, but after much thought Akashi decided to do it in three-month blocks. First, he'd play all the pieces he was due to perform – in his case, twelve – in order until he felt they were polished. Over the next three months, he would refine them further, starting from the very first piece. And then repeat that process. In that way he could, after an interval, practise the same piece again. This way of playing a piece over a long period gave him confidence, and deepened his interpretation of the music.

Things didn't always go as planned. Two pieces had taken up way more time than he'd intended – Stravinsky's *Three Movements from Petrushka*, a technically challenging piece he'd keep for the end of the second round, and Schumann's *Kreisleriana*, which he'd placed in his third-round programme.

On the other hand, he discovered that some pieces he'd found hard as a college student were much easier to play now. There certainly were things only experience could teach you. Happily he found his technique at least had not declined, and he was confident he could compete against the younger entrants.

And then there was the concerto he'd have to play if he made it to the finals. He found it hard to begin practising that.

Reaching the finals was an added bonus, he thought, and on top of putting off practising his concerto, he struggled to find someone to play the orchestral part for him on the piano. When he finally did, though, another problem arose – finding a place with two pianos where they could practise. He'd thought it wasn't allowed, but he asked the staff in the piano section of the music store where he worked, and they let him and his accompanist rehearse there after hours. That was the extent of their dual practice, though.

It felt like a dream now, to be actually about to perform.

I've made it this far, he told himself. *The time to show the fruit of my long hours of practice is right here. This very moment.*

A sudden apprehension took hold of him.

But what about afterwards? What comes next? Once these tense days are over, what's waiting for me then?

Applause snapped him out of his reverie.

He unconsciously took a deep breath. There was an interval now.

This could very well be my final performance, he thought. *I've done everything I possibly could. I'll do my best, the very best I can do at this point.*

He shut his eyes and conjured up an image of himself playing on stage.

The first piece, *Spring and Ashura*, was key. If he could give a convincing performance of that, then the rest were familiar pieces he'd played any number of times.

The hardest thing for Akashi about not being a music-college student now wasn't the concerto as much as this brand-new piece.

If he were in music college, he could pore over the composition with his professor, minutely examining the structure and interpretation. There would be other teachers to consult with, too, and he could exchange information with other students. When it came to the cadenza, he imagined that most of the pianists had their instructors rewrite it.

But Akashi began to see it could actually be an advantage to be an older pianist.

He'd always loved literature, and there was a time when he read a lot of Kenji Miyazawa's work. A more mature pianist was bound to have a deeper understanding of the writing.

He started rereading Miyazawa's poems and stories while commuting, as well as commentaries and critical studies, endeavouring to grasp Miyazawa's world view, his vision of the universe. He made a quick visit to far-off Iwate, Miyazawa's home, touring the places said to be the settings of his works.

Miyazawa was hard-headed, idiosyncratic, detached, dreamy, yet also a bit disreputable, self-pitying and miserable – a complex mix of realist and visionary.

As he bumped along in the train, Akashi mentally superimposed images from Miyazawa's literature on to the musical composition.

This bit was reminiscent of the beach in England, he thought, and this bit must be 'The Night of the Milky Way Railway' – an image of soaring through the night sky – while this section must be from the poem 'The Morning of Eternal Farewell'.

A sudden idea flashed through his mind. *That's it*, Akashi thought. *I'll make the cadenza melody fit lines from that poem.*

Brother, will you bring me some snow?
Brother, will you bring me some snow?

These were especially memorable lines from the poem 'The Morning of Eternal Farewell' Miyazawa had written about the death of his younger sister, Toshi. The lines, written in a thick northern dialect, evoked his sister, suffering from a high fever, begging her brother to get her some snow and feed it to her. Poignant words, but at the same time rhythmic and melodious.

Akashi wasn't particularly skilled at improvising, though he'd always been told since childhood that he had a real feeling for poetry. He'd studied composition and didn't find composing too difficult.

He decided he'd write it so the right hand would play the melody, based on Toshi's words, expressing her voice calling from heaven after she had died, while the left hand would portray Miyazawa's day-to-day life, gathering ice crystals while contemplating the world and the cosmos.

This decided, he was lost in thought as different melodies came to him. He added all kinds of extras, ending up with a five-minute cadenza. He'd have to pare it down to three minutes.

One day he played the cadenza for his wife.

'Too intense and chaotic.' His wife's reactions were those of any ordinary listener, honest, free of any preconceptions, and her response often took him by surprise.

Agonizing, he went ahead and jettisoned the parts he was unsure about and played it to her again.

'Now that's nice!' she said, and when he heard her humming the 'Brother, will you bring me some snow?' melody as she tidied up, he was sure this would stay with the audience too when they heard it.

Once his cadenza was under his fingers, he knew that his own *Spring and Ashura* was ready.

Other than the one he'd done for his wife, this performance at the competition would be the first, and probably the last, time anyone would hear it.

And so he both looked forward to the performance and feared it. The composer himself would be seated with the judges and the plan was to award the best player a prize named after him, the Hishinuma Prize.

So – what would the composer, and audience, think about his *Spring and Ashura*? His cadenza?

As these thoughts swirled around interminably, the bell rang signalling five minutes to go.

My turn.

Akashi straightened up, ready to go.

ONCE HE WAS IN THE wings, he felt calm.

From experience he knew he often felt elation just before a

performance. Excited, eager, a feeling of great power and possibility filling his body.

The minute he began to play, he'd know if that elation was real or not. There were times when he discovered it was actually an illusion, to escape the pressure of performing.

But what about now? he wondered. Was this exultation for real?

Akashi clasped his fingers together.

Let me believe in the music.

He wanted to burn into his consciousness the darkness of the wings where he stood, the feeling in his fingers as he clasped them together.

He felt a whoosh of cool wind. He looked towards the stage. The door was closed, the staff members still.

Just my imagination?

He looked down at his fingers again.

Light filtered in through a gap in the door frame and through the peephole.

A strange feeling came over him, a sudden premonition.

Beyond that door lies my grandmother's mulberry orchard, where I'll find scores of mulberry trees. It's early summer, and the rain has just eased.

AKASHI COULD SEE THE SCENE CLEARLY.

The hazy sunlight, tinged with the colour of summer, illuminated everything.

The ground was carpeted in mulberry leaves, raindrops poised on the branches above, waiting to fall.

A bluish mountain range loomed in the distance. Inky clouds floated across the sky.

Akashi had just got off the bus and was standing by his grandmother's mulberry orchard. The wind threatened to carry away his cap, but the elastic under his chin held it in place.

Beyond the mulberry orchard, Akashi spied his beloved grandmother's house.

And the grand piano Akashi loved more than anything.

He began to run.

Bathed in the scent of mulberry leaves, and the sensation of wind and sun on his cheeks, he raced as fast as his legs would carry him down the narrow dirt track that ran through the mulberry orchard.

'Grandma—'

Akashi could hear his own voice calling out.

A BURST OF THUNDEROUS APPLAUSE jolted him; a Korean pianist was coming through the door from the stage.

A blaze of light streamed in.

His turn had finally come, and even while on stage the sensation persisted.

Stage fright? he wondered. *I'm like a traumatized child making up an imaginary friend, an alter ego.*

Yet Akashi was aware that he was beaming and calm as he patiently adjusted the stool.

He spotted his wife, Machiko, sitting by the aisle on the left, five rows from the front.

It surprised him how quickly he found her.

The first piece, *Spring and Ashura*.

He began to play, as if he'd known it for years.

Ah – I get it, he realized as he played.

That mulberry orchard – it was about this. And about Kenji Miyazawa's English coast, his home town of Hanamaki in Iwate, his universe.

Akashi felt the Iwate scenery filtering out into the darkened auditorium. The murmur of a river at night. The stars twinkling above.

He was walking along the riverbank.

Miyazawa was walking with him too. A few steps in front, head bowed, as in the photo of the poet Akashi had seen.

This was all of creation for Miyazawa, for all of us. Everything turning, everything returning. We are here for but a brief moment. Not even a blink of an eye to the universe. The shortest of moments.

Before he knew it, he was playing the cadenza.
Toshi's voice, calling from heaven, over and over.

Brother, will you bring me some snow?
Brother, will you bring me some snow?

Miyazawa continued walking along the riverbank, head bowed, as if he couldn't hear Toshi calling.

Her voice was beautiful, crystal clear. Like a distant echo, like the little bells on a mendicant's staff, ringing out over and over in the sky far above.

Brother, will you bring me some snow?
Brother, will you bring me some snow?

Everything came and went, and then vanished in the stillness of time. And the cycle repeated. The circle closed, returning to the longed-for days gone by, a renewed past.

Akashi's final chord rang out.

He held his fingers over the keys, watching as the traces of sound faded.

The hall was hushed.

Now for the Chopin étude. Popularly known as the 'Black Key Étude'. A piece his hands were so used to that they seemed to form the shape of the sounds all by themselves.

His fingers practically glided across the keys.

Is this OK? Akashi had his doubts as he played.

It felt like someone else was playing. As if a second self were looking down from above.

This nimble, vibrant 'Black Key Étude'. *I'm making it look easy,* Akashi thought. *A little mischievous and not bad at all.*

Next came the Liszt étude.

Variations on a theme by Paganini, Liszt's Étude No. 6.

A bright, modulated piece freely developing the famous theme.

Good, I'm playing it dynamically. My fingers are moving nicely. Paganini's theme has so much drama every time I hear it. It's possible to make it as pretentious as you like, but I'll dial that down here, he told himself.

Strange how my fingers are following my thoughts this closely. It doesn't seem like I'm playing, but rather that someone is playing me. *But the sounds are coming out just as I want them to, so there's no doubt* – I'm *the one playing*.

He was on good form. Playing it comfortably, yet as tight as it needed to be. Such an efficient, balanced architecture to the piece – its *jo-ha-kyu*, you could say?

What did they call *jo-ha-kyu* – introduction, development and climax – in a Western language? Japanese artistic terms managed to capture something essential.

The audience was listening so intently, as if with one pair of ears. Those ears and his had merged, as if he and the audience had become one, breathing in sync.

He came to the end. *A pretty smart finish, if I say so myself*, he thought.

Next was Schumann's *Arabesque*. A little breather after Liszt's flamboyance.

Still, the *Arabesque* was a difficult piece. It was simple, in a way, but that made it all the harder to blur any passages. *Every time I play it, I discover something new, the piece growing harder the more I play it.*

I love Schumann. Some day he wanted to really perfect his *Fantasie*.

For some reason, Akashi thought, whenever he played the *Arabesque* he remembered moments from his childhood. Beginning the piano, which meant going to Grandma's house, being afraid of the sound of the silkworms chewing on mulberry leaves. And strangely, this made him feel like crying.

Ah – the Schumann is over. A short piece, but whenever I get to the end, I feel sad. Four pieces finished, and so quickly.

On to the final piece.

Stravinsky, *Three Movements from Petrushka*.

A bold, glorious intro. Let the harsh, rigid notes ring out as clear as a bell.

The glissando was brittle, yet smooth.

So colourful, so tricky.

Akashi steadily fell into a strange frame of mind.

Wow – I see colours around me! The colours of *Petrushka*. Bright, modern, stylish, full of vivacity.

Is this me *playing? Or am I being* made *to play?*

What is it I'm seeing? It's as if I'm on a journey from a mulberry orchard, to an English beach, then to Europe.

A splendid, glorious sound resonating through the hall.

Akashi and the audience experienced these bright colours together, breathing in the tremolos and the chords.

Then the climax.

At that moment, Akashi and the audience flew straight up to the heavens. And with a rush of tempestuous chords, the music cascaded towards its finale like a surge of raging waves.

Done.

Even when he stood up, Akashi still couldn't feel as if it was really him.

When he heard the applause, and saw Machiko with tears pouring down her cheeks, it finally hit home. The second round was really over.

Rondo Capriccioso

A BOY SAT IN A corner of the hall, swaying ever so slightly as he listened to the performance. Dressed casually, sunk back in his seat, he was totally inconspicuous, like a local kid from the neighbourhood who just happened to be passing by and had wandered into the auditorium. No one seemed to realize this was one of the pianists, Jin Kazama.

To be honest, the first thing he'd felt when he learned he'd be going through to the second round was relief.

Because now there was a greater possibility his father would buy him a piano.

Not that he was brimming with confidence. He'd hardly ever played in front of anyone, let alone in a competition, and he hadn't the slightest idea how his performance would be received. When Yuji Von Hoffmann was still alive, he'd told him, 'Just be yourself, Jin. There's value in who you are. Don't worry about what others say. Just play the way you want to.' And in that sense there was no confusion. All he needed to do was follow his teacher's instructions.

Jin was astonished by the performances, how excellent they all were, their outstanding technique. Even so, he didn't have any doubts about his own performance, or a sense of inferiority. He had absolute faith in Maestro Hoffmann. He'd put the seal of approval on Jin's playing, and that was enough for him.

If your attention wandered while listening to performances, they could flow right through you without leaving any impression.

Jin Kazama reacted to music in some visceral way, and when he heard pianists playing like that he reflexively fell asleep.

When he was beginning to doze off, his body swayed slightly, although sometimes it was because he was into the performance. So anyone watching him might think he was napping throughout, while others might conclude he was eagerly listening.

'Listen,' his teacher had told him. 'The world is overflowing with music.'

JIN HAD LISTENED RAPTLY TO Jennifer Chan's performance, but before long had begun to doze off.

Truly the world was overflowing with music, but there were some things that passed by unheard.

Though it does feel good, the boy thought, rubbing his eyes.

It was amazing how every piano could sound so different. Since he was young, he'd never had his own piano, though he had played all sorts of pianos in many different venues. Out of necessity he'd learned the basics of tuning, too, and could draw out his own sound from any instrument.

He could spot a good piano at a single glance.

He recalled how entranced he was by the piano on stage, shining and distinct, so that he couldn't help wanting to stroke it, hug it tightly to himself.

He could also tell a good piano by its voice, even from far away. To him it sounded like it was calling out to him. *Here I am!*

He'd heard the call of a piano, that time he'd sneaked into the music college. He never expected that girl would catch him, and certainly never dreamt they'd be competing in the same contest.

He swayed silently from side to side, steeped in the music.

A competition was such a strange affair, he thought. To be immersed in so much music – it was like a dream.

To allow it to permeate your body – to breathe music, and exhale it – you completely lost all sense of time, your heart just floated away.

His teacher's advice came to him.

It was critical to understand the structure and historical background of a piece; how it sounded when it was first performed. Though no one knew for sure if the way it originally sounded was what the composer actually expected to hear.

An instrument's timbre, too, changed through usage. And there were changes in performance style over time.

Music always had to be of the *now*. It couldn't just be something preserved in a museum, and it was meaningless unless it was *alive* in the *present*. If you were satisfied with merely unearthing a lovely fossil, then music became no more than a relic from the past.

Jin felt a breeze brush his cheeks.

You know, he thought, *the performance by that guy Akashi Takashima was really captivating*. Jin had pictured ripples on a river, the wind whistling, the pitch-black universe above. That man must be living his own music, as well.

Jin thought he could see a green field, too, and wondered what kind of field it was. The vast field seemed to ripple in the wind like some living creature.

Brother, will you bring me some snow?

Jin could pick up even the dialect pronunciation of the phrase from the Miyazawa poem Akashi had woven in.

He remembered how he and Maestro Hoffmann had played an electric piano sitting on the back of a bouncing truck.

Taking it in turns to improvise the melodies they heard in their heads.

How many hours had they played, never tiring?

The truck rumbling along, the scenery changing by the minute. The wind whipping through the forests and rolling hills, stroking their hair and lifting their caps.

Wouldn't it be amazing if they could do the same here, on that stage, with that incredible piano?

It was a shame they couldn't.

At first he was moved and awed: by the wonderful acoustics, the beautiful piano, as if, like a present in a shiny box, tied up with ribbon, it was quietly held out for the listener.

But after a few days it all began to feel stifling.

He wanted to be able to liberate the music from this dark container, from this thick-walled jail where it was comfortably guarded.

Lead this flock of notes outside to a more vast and open space, like the Pied Piper of Hamelin, luring notes to the great outdoors.

Out there, of course, the sound would be absorbed, dispersed, disrupted by all kinds of other sounds, yet still they could romp and play with all the music found in nature.

After a few more days, the boy's thinking changed again.

Maybe, he thought, *nature is* here *too*.

That nature lay inside the performers. Mental images of scenes of their home towns nestled together, accumulated in their minds, in their fingertips, their lips, their internal organs. As they played, their own bountiful nature bound up in these memories was expressed.

So we are *all connected*, he thought.

Akashi Takashima's performance truly made him sense this – it caught him by surprise.

In a competition, though, the programme of pieces was prescribed. That was the only thing that left him dissatisfied.

Wonderful, famous pieces he never tired of hearing. All incredible stuff, but, somehow, limiting. Some freedom still remained in how you played it, though – the endless ways of interpreting it.

It's true, he thought. *The world has become quite restrictive*.

As the boy floated, half dozing in a sea of sound, he searched through his memory.

I remember talking with my teacher about something similar.

It was after Jin had been to the Paris Conservatoire for the first time.

'I wish we could take it outside,' Jin had commented. 'All this music tucked away inside this impressive building, posing in such formal attire and all lit up.'

The Maestro had chuckled.

'OK, Jin – *you* take it outside,' he said.

Hoffmann's eyes had looked a little frightening, like two bottomless pits.

'It's very difficult, you know, Jin – in any real sense – a difficult thing to take music to the world outside. You understand, don't you? What encloses music isn't the concert halls and churches. It's people's *minds*. Simply taking it outside to some pretty space doesn't mean you've *really* taken hold of the sound. That won't free it.'

To be honest, the boy couldn't follow what his teacher was getting at, though he could tell how serious he was.

At that moment his teacher was giving him a tremendously heavy burden.

It was not long afterwards that he'd raised the idea of Jin participating in the competition.

And it was around this time that Hoffmann fell ill and was laid up at home.

When news broke that Von Hoffmann was sick, musicians from around the world hurried to his bedside, but the Maestro refused to see them. He probably didn't want anyone to see him so weak and helpless.

The boy was frantically worried. Hoffmann was his only teacher, but also he represented all the wonderful music that occupied the greater part of his experience.

He travelled so much with his father that it was hard to fit in visits to the Maestro. When he was finally able to get to the Maestro's house, he rang the bell over and over only to find no one at home, the interior dark. The boy began to tremble.

He plunked himself down outside their door like a forlorn puppy and sat there waiting.

'Jin!'

Fortunately the Maestro and his wife came back the following day. When they spotted the boy at their door, they cried out as if they'd seen a ghost. 'Waiting here, you'll catch your death of cold,' they said, scolding him.

The boy began to sob, shoulders heaving.

'I'll make us a nice cup of cocoa,' the Maestro's wife Daphne said, heading to the kitchen.

'Thank God it was only a short stay at the hospital for routine checks,' the Maestro said. 'I am not afraid, Jin.'

Eyes glittering mischievously, Hoffmann patted the blubbering Jin on the shoulder.

'I'll go ahead of you and take all those notes *outside*,' he said, and pointed up at the ceiling. 'You're my parting present, Jin. My beautiful gift to the world.'

'No, Maestro. Don't leave me.'

Jin dropped to his knees, and Hoffmann smiled. 'Don't kill me off quite yet,' he said and burst out laughing.

He flashed his signature smile, as if he'd just come up with an impish thought.

That smile had now melted into a sea of sounds.

Maestro – what should I do? What should I do to make all this music a part of the wider world?

Tears were now welling in his eyes.

Half asleep, he whispered, 'Some day I will keep my promise to you – and take music out into the world.'

A Sound Picture

'THE STANDARD THESE DAYS has become exceptional,' mumbled Tadaaki Hishinuma as he stuffed his mouth with naan.

'Were there any performances of your composition you particularly liked?' Nathaniel threw this out casually, his expression bland.

Hishinuma managed a smile. 'I suppose,' he said, parrying the question.

'It must be interesting to hear these pianists play a composition in front of the person who wrote it. Quite a unique experience, something no one else can feel.'

Mieko's comment left Hishinuma shaking his head.

'Interesting, yes, but stressful. Since I put everything I had into that score and most of the time they don't grasp my intention. Though I can't very well tell them, "Hey, that's not it, you idiot – stop what you're doing."'

'I can see that,' Nathaniel said. He worked on composing and arranging for movies and the stage. Mieko had seen him in rehearsals, how detailed and critical he was, urging performers to do better. When it came to his own work, he agonized over the nuances of every single note.

'How freely do you allow performers to interpret a piece?'

'It all depends on how you interpret the term *free interpretation*,' Hishinuma said with a shrug.

Nathaniel looked displeased. 'If it's for the satisfaction of the musician, then it shouldn't be allowed,' he said. 'Though most free interpretation is exactly that.' He had clearly endured a lot of *free interpretation* of his own music.

'But here's the thing,' Hishinuma said, leaning in. 'Do you think a composer really understands his own work?'

He might be smiling but the look in his eyes was intense, and Nathaniel sank into silence for a moment.

'Of course they *think* they do. That they know what each sound means, each phrase. They composed it, after all. We think, *I created this*.'

Hishinuma munched on some more naan. For someone his age, he had quite an appetite, and as he sampled generous portions of four different varieties of naan, tearing off pieces and stuffing them into his mouth, they were quickly depleted.

'Well, there are types who think they're omnipotent. As in "you must pay careful attention to every single note I wrote, I know this work better than anyone, my intentions are absolute" sort of thing.'

Nathaniel was looking a little uncomfortable. He was quite clearly the type of composer being described.

'But you know, as I've grown older, I've got the feeling that we're nothing but, you know, mediators.'

'Meaning?'

'Composers, performers, everyone. From the beginning, music is everywhere, and we capture it and write it down as notes. And then perform it. We don't create it – we merely translate it.'

'So we're prophets,' Nathaniel said.

'Yes. A heavenly being entrusts us with their voice, and we pass it along. In the presence of music, a famous composer and an amateur performer are equals – individual prophets. I've come to think that way. Wow – this naan is terrific. OK if we order some more?'

'Let's get another garlic naan too.'

Nathaniel motioned the waiter over.

'Now that you mention it, it's because music is a reproducible art that it always has to be made new. These were Yuji Von Hoffmann's words.'

At the mention of Hoffmann's name, Nathaniel and Mieko exchanged a quick glance.

The first day of round two was over, and Nathaniel had grabbed the opportunity to invite Hishinuma to dinner. The last time they'd shared a meal it had ended badly, so this time Nathaniel had asked Mieko to join them. She wanted to find out more about the relationship between Jin Kazama and Maestro Hoffmann, and so, albeit reluctantly, here she was again dining on curry and naan.

'I'm guessing you both want to hear about that young man, am I right?'

Hishinuma hadn't missed the glance the two had exchanged. Probably from the moment he was invited, he'd known they were dying to ask him something.

Nathaniel and Mieko looked at each other again. 'That's right,' they replied, nodding.

'Is it true that Maestro Hoffmann went to Jin's home to teach him?' Nathaniel locked his fingers together on the table.

'Yes, it's true,' Hishinuma said. 'I heard the kid's performance in the first round. Blew me away. I had to call Daphne and tell her. Ask her where on earth they found him.'

'What did she say?'

Mieko noticed she and Nathaniel had leaned forward expectantly. She found it comical. Anything that had to do with Maestro Hoffmann got them acting like little children.

'I heard that the boy is a distant relative of Yuji.'

'*What?*' the other two chorused.

Hishinuma fluttered his hand to downplay the notion.

'A very, very distant relative. Almost not related at all. You know that Yuji's grandmother was Japanese. The boy's a descendant of a branch of his grandmother's family.'

'Really—'

'So almost not related at all.'

Nathaniel looked relieved. Mieko wondered if her face reflected the same response.

'Daphne said she had no idea where they'd met. All Yuji said was that it was a *strange twist of fate*.'

A strange twist of fate.

Mieko found the phrase odd, but also convincing.

'Everyone knows by now that the boy's father is a beekeeper, but did you know they are constantly on the move? They apparently keep an apartment in Paris but are hardly ever there.'

'What about school?'

'Sometimes he goes, sometimes he doesn't. His father has a teaching qualification, and so he teaches his son.'

'Hmm.'

So maybe that was where the boy got that sense of freedom about him, of nothing tying him down.

'And what's really interesting—' Hishinuma suddenly lowered his voice. 'Apparently the boy doesn't own a piano.'

'*Seriously?*'

'You mean he doesn't have a piano at home?'

Hishinuma nodded. 'Exactly,' he said. 'But he knows where he can find one when they're on the move, and he's allowed to play. That's the way he's always done it, playing in his own style, until he met Yuji.'

'Unbelievable,' Mieko said.

Perhaps that's exactly *why* he could play so spectacularly. The thought suddenly came to Mieko: it's paradoxical, but if you weren't sure when you could play next, that would surely make you focus on your practice when you had the chance.

If an empty stomach was the best sauce, as they say, then a craving for a piano might very well create the optimal environment for practising.

'Yuji was surprised too, at first. The boy could apparently make any piano sound exquisite. He could tune pianos, too. He learned out of necessity, I suppose. That really piqued Yuji's interest. He enjoyed visiting the boy wherever he happened to be, using whichever piano was around. Which is why he decided to go to him.'

'I see – so that's why he went.'

'Anyhow, the boy doesn't have any music to read from, so he got in the habit of memorizing pieces after only one hearing. Or else he'd improvise on the spot. Daphne told me she heard them playing together once. Back and forth, improvising on two pianos – she said it was as if they were in conversation.'

Nathaniel and Mieko were speechless.

Maestro Hoffmann improvising? Neither had ever heard such a thing, and possibly nor had anyone else who'd known him. Impossible! The Maestro? And in his later years, playing an improv session with a boy young enough to be his grandson?

Mieko's feelings were in turmoil – with an intense jealousy, and a sense of humiliation that the Maestro had not wanted anything to do with her. No doubt Nathaniel beside her was experiencing a similar, if not more traumatic, internal struggle.

Even stronger was the desire to have heard those improv sessions, and a profound regret that the opportunity was lost for ever.

'I wonder if any of those sessions were ever recorded,' Nathaniel murmured.

'No idea. They've only just started getting his affairs in order. The guy tended to be lackadaisical about recordings, so who knows – maybe there are some recordings, and maybe not.'

Nathaniel and Mieko both sighed in disappointment.

One thing they did share was a sense of how great a loss Von Hoffmann's death had been.

'Listen, you people should worry more about your own situation,' Hishinuma said pointedly, and the two of them gave him a look.

'What do you mean?' Mieko asked.

'Here's the thing,' Hishinuma said with a wry smile. 'Are you guys actually able to mark that boy?'

Mieko was startled. She recalled the ominous prediction Smirnoff had muttered immediately after the Paris auditions.

She was steadily coming to understand the meaning behind Hoffmann's words *powerful drug*.

We are faced with quite a dilemma, she thought.

'You're saying we can't?' Nathaniel countered in a quiet voice.

Of course he knew what Hishinuma was getting at. Not that he fully understood the dilemma she, Simon and Smirnoff faced. Intellectually he got it, but he didn't really *feel* it.

'Well,' Hishinuma admitted. 'I was just wondering who could

score such an original talent. If you look at piano competitions historically, unconventional virtuosos have always been sidelined. Because they exceeded what the judges could comprehend.'

Hishinuma looked pensive, and tore off another chunk of naan.

'The sending out of that boy was a premeditated crime. A challenge thrown to you judges, and to all of us. It is *we* who are being tested.'

'I wonder about that.' Nathaniel seemed ready to counter anything Hishinuma said.

It was often said that judges, while judging others, were being judged themselves. Each of them had their own musicianship and their biases unmasked in the process.

Intellectually, at least, Mieko thought she'd known what a frightening thing it was to be a judge; how much your own musical sensibilities and character were exposed.

But like Nathaniel, until now she'd never really understood what that actually *felt* like.

Ride of the Valkyries

HE REACHED OUT FROM his bed, as always, to turn off the alarm clock just before it rang.

He was a moment too late getting up as he tried to retrieve the dream he was having before he awoke.

Masaru had been playing *Spring and Ashura*. It felt good. He wasn't on stage, but somewhere outdoors, in a lush green space. This was how it should be, he felt.

It was hard to grab hold of a dream – akin to grabbing a fish in the water only to have it slither through your fingers.

He gave up, scrambled to his feet and drew open the curtain.

Down below, the horizon was a mix of grey and blue. As soon as he caught sight of the sea, his dream dissipated. Only a trace of it lingered within him.

He did some light stretches and went out for a jog.

The cold air felt good. His days in Yoshigae had become routine.

Masaru was always good at relaxing wherever he went. Adaptable, yet doing things at his own pace. This was Masaru's forte, reconciling the contradictory as if it were only natural to do so.

He was the first performer on the second day of round two, but he didn't mind where in the running order he was placed. He figured playing first wasn't bad, because once he finished, he could sit back and enjoy the other recitals.

As he'd told Aya, it was helpful to have heard the performances of the new piece the day before. Everyone's interpretation was different, but hearing eight of them helped him understand what the composition was all about.

But it was the *Spring and Ashura* played by his mentor, Nathaniel Silverberg, that had left the strongest impression. Nathaniel never wavered in his faith in Masaru. As if challenging him, he played him his own idiosyncratic version, inspiring Masaru to interpret it in his own way.

Nathaniel knew the composer, Tadaaki Hishinuma, personally, and gave Masaru a lecture that analysed in detail his personality and the special features of his compositions.

Meeting Hishinuma in the flesh was a welcome experience. Masaru was quite confident in his ability to read others. The composer's expressions, gestures, voice told him a lot. Even if it was just for a few minutes, nothing was better than meeting and talking to him.

The second round was the only occasion when all the pianists would play the same composition. There were several goals here – to see how they handled contemporary music, and how they would approach a brand-new piece, as well as to promote the image of the competition as truly international. But it was also a unique opportunity to compare the different performers.

This was one of the important aspects of the second round, but not, Masaru had decided, the pivotal one. It was important to demonstrate that you took the piece seriously, but you couldn't allow it to stand out too much from your overall programme. It had to be incorporated into a forty-minute recital, and sound like part of the complete flow of the programme.

He checked his breathing as he jogged, imagining the whole sweep of his performance.

He loved working out a strategy. At high-jump competitions, too, he enjoyed figuring out a strategy to take on rivals, how high to raise the bar, and so on, all the different game plans the competition could allow. But you also couldn't let tactics be your downfall. It was hard to abandon a plan you'd worked on for so long, but when the competition began, you had to be flexible and adjust to each new situation.

Now that he looked back on it, his disqualification at the Osaka competition may have been a blessing in disguise, since in terms of competition experience, he could come to the Yoshigae contest fresh, as a newcomer.

Competitions were interesting, and he thought of himself as a tough competitor, but Masaru didn't feel he was the type to keep performing in them. His strategy was to enter only two or three prominent events. The Yoshigae would be his debut, and his first real battle.

He was breathing harder than usual. He'd begun to speed up, and was now running faster without meaning to.

This is not good, he told himself. *I've got to pace myself.*

He took a few deep breaths, and did some deep stretching.

His *Spring and Ashura* would be—

He shut his eyes and tried to visualize it.

The opening piece in the second round. The first piece in the programme that he'd purposefully put together, to flow from stillness to movement. He imagined softly touching the keys to impart the opening notes.

Suddenly the feeling he had from his dream that morning came flooding back.

Warmth, sunshine filtering down through leaves. *I'm feeling all of creation in this piece—*

He remembered thinking that. *The same feeling I have right now.*

Masaru gazed around him, as if viewing the world for the first time.

A small park nestled between buildings. The air was still cold, the pre-dawn tension unabated. Dawn quietly broke, and before you knew it, the world was filled with signs of awakening. The call of birds; the ground trembling with the rumble of cars on a distant highway. Ever so gradually, morning permeated the world.

All of creation.

Masaru felt a hushed flow of energy. He sensed the wind before it started to blow, the colours of trees about to glisten in the sunlight. His whole body absorbed it all.

He ran back to the hotel and had a hot shower.

The water struck his head and shoulders, and flowed down his back. In everyday life every nook and cranny, he thought, was filled with the wonder of creation.

Spring and Ashura. What he wanted to convey, Masaru decided, was the beauty of blank space, of the *in-between*. Not like Jennifer Chan, who gave a clear-cut explanation for every single note.

The atmosphere of the piece was serene, modest, uncomplicated. Yet the world it portrayed was vast. Like a miniature indoor garden or a tea house. Where a part could evoke the whole. Where, from a tiny fragment, you felt something massive and endless.

Or perhaps you could say it inspired a paradoxical view of the universe, where the whole world was contained in it precisely because of its smallness.

Hishinuma had left much unexplained, allowing every single note to suggest a separate world.

The composer, a dyed-in-the-wool Tokyoite, was basically a shy person. He didn't ramble on, and believed not everything needed spelling out, that to attempt to do so was vulgar. This was a traditionally Japanese aesthetic sensibility.

Still, Hishinuma's intention in his composition was not to convey some clear representation of Japan. Masaru wanted to ensure that was understood. To the last, this was Kenji Miyazawa's vision of the cosmos and a reflection of Hishinuma's character.

The question was how to communicate this.

As he ate breakfast Masaru pondered the journey so far. His strategy towards the piece was simple. Not to over-explain things in sound. Not to use any overly verbose passages. That was it. The task was then to inspire the listener to imagine the huge world behind all this restraint.

It was clearly a contradiction, but there had to be a way, which Masaru pursued through a lengthy process of trial and error. Until he found it.

I won't explain, he told himself. *I'll let them* feel.

The theme of his *Spring and Ashura* would be the expression of blank space.

It took an unexpectedly long time to determine this, but he was convinced it was the right approach. But how do you express *blank space*?

He tried out all kinds of things, until finally he landed on it. The *cadenza*.

Masaru gazed at the directions written on the score.

Freely, giving a sense of the universe.

The notes were arranged to create this sense of the cosmic. It was only in the cadenza, which didn't contain any at all, where you could catch a glimpse of the real *substance* of the cosmos.

I can use the cadenza to complete this expression of blank space.

Masaru was excited. For the first time in his life he felt that he'd discovered the *secret* of the music contained in a score, the *secret* of the world itself.

With this, he thought, his performance of *Spring and Ashura* would be complete.

Masaru keenly remembered the instant when he knew this for sure.

I was truly happy, as if the world had opened itself up for me.

Now, he thought, *let me reproduce that sensation.*

Masaru breathed slowly and began to change his clothes.

The day had arrived when he would perform this piece for the first and possibly last time ever.

THE SECOND DAY OF ROUND TWO.

It was ten-thirty a.m., and for the opening performance of the session, the hall was packed.

It was obvious why. Masaru was up first.

All this attention didn't make Masaru cocky, or tense. He merely accepted it as natural. Well aware of his popularity, he had no problem enjoying it, accepting the fact he really was a star.

He stood in the wings, collecting his thoughts. *Where is Aa-chan sitting?* he wondered. *Will she like how I play?*

Aya's comments about Jennifer Chan's performance had startled him. He was a little nervous to hear what she'd say about his, but decided he'd go ahead and ask her afterwards.

'But the two of us are disciples of Mr Watanuki,' Masaru had said to Aya when they were sitting in the audience. 'He was our first teacher, he taught us all kinds of music, from Yashiro Aki's *enka* to rock. He instilled in us a love of music. So there's no way our performance could end up as an *attraction*. Am I right?'

Who am I playing for?

This was what he asked himself as he hovered in the wings.

Do I play for the audience? For myself? For the god of music?

I don't know. But one thing is clear – I am playing for someone. Or not someone, *but more for some*thing.

A competition was such a strange experience, he thought.

A COMPETITION WAS EXACTLY THAT, people competing against each other, but it was also a one-man show, a solo recital. It was weird to have to compare what were essentially different solo recitals.

But during these forty minutes, the audience and the stage are all mine, Masaru thought. *All eyes will be on me alone, every ear attuned to my playing.*

The very thought thrilled him. The pale face of a classmate flitted through his mind.

'You're so talented,' his classmate often told him.

'You're a star,' people told him. 'The complete package.' People had said this, at the Conservatoire in Paris, and at Juilliard, their faces a mixture of envy and admiration. The ones who said it were themselves talented, in their own way, their technical skills not so very different from his.

So how should one respond?

Take the humble approach? Be modest about it? *No, not really . . . I still have a long way to go.* Or simply thank them?

Both reactions left Masaru uncomfortable. It's true he stood out. Something about him was unique.

But in the end that was how others evaluated him, not how he evaluated himself. There were things about himself he didn't understand, and things only *he* could understand.

So when people complimented him, all he did was grin. He didn't reply, didn't give a self-assessment.

The only thing he understood was that he could express whatever he wanted, something he'd known since he first began to play. Back when he and Aya had played a four-hands version of 'Little Brown Jug', when he'd made an early attempt at a Mozart minuet, he knew that, one day in the future, he would be able to communicate whatever he wished.

When he began lessons in earnest, he soon developed technique. It felt as if he was recalling knowledge he already had. He grasped the essence of the pieces he played, took up other instruments, listened to all kinds of music, absorbing it all so swiftly his mind almost couldn't keep pace.

'You're an unusual case,' Nathaniel Silverberg had told him. 'I wouldn't call you precocious. Or a child prodigy, either.'

'Then what am I?' Masaru couldn't help but ask.

'You just *know*. From the very beginning, you've *known*.'

His teacher then told a story.

'A long time ago in Japan there was a sculptor,' Nathaniel began. 'He left behind some Buddhist sculptures, the sort that would these days be designated National Treasures. He was said to sculpt incredibly fast. He never hesitated, working so fast it was as if his hands could barely keep up with the idea he had in his head. One day someone asked him how he did it.

'"I'm not making it," he replied. "I'm only unearthing the Buddha that's buried within the wood."

'When I watch you, Masaru, I remember that story,' Nathaniel said.

Masaru listened in bewilderment.

Of course, he didn't view himself as a finished work, but rather a work in progress, still rough around the edges, with much he still needed to practise and enhance. Even if he exerted himself for the rest of his life, he knew he would never be totally satisfied.

But still, I can *do what I'm capable of right now.*

Masaru had this odd conviction.

The one thing he found hard to grasp was that other people didn't seem to feel the same way. So many were filled with anxieties and fears: *I might forget the notes, I might freeze, I might make mistakes*. They felt so much pressure that the stage became a terrifying place. Masaru took it for granted he *could do it*. If this was talent, then he supposed he must be talented.

THE STAGE MANAGER, MR TAKUBO, stood like a shadow in the wings, smiling.

The best concert halls around the world almost always had amazing stage managers, people who were well known to the musicians. A skilled stage manager gave you a sense of calm, just to look at them filled you with confidence.

Takubo exuded calm, he kept just the right distance, yet his deep empathy for the musicians was clear. He trusted, encouraged, was there for their every need.

I'm so lucky, Masaru thought.

'It's time.' The manager gave a nod.

Masaru nodded back.

'Best of luck.'

Masaru stepped on to the stage.

An explosion of wild applause enveloped him, lifting his spirits. The audience's expectations always lent him power.

OK – and now for *Spring and Ashura*.

MASARU'S SECOND ROUND BEGAN QUIETLY.

Aya and Kanade were listening from the back of the hall.

Aya's eyes were riveted to the stage, which was bathed in light.

It isn't just the spotlight, she thought. *There's a definite aura around him.*

In an instant he had stilled the air, pulling the audience into his world.

Masaru's performance would determine how *Spring and Ashura* would be seen hereafter.

Aya knew Masaru's approach was different from all those who had played it the previous day. It was so natural, so unaffected.

She felt a rush of gooseflesh along her arms.

You could see darkness – the universe.

Faint stars, a forlorn, endless empty space.

He has so many resources he can call on, she thought. *He can bring out so many stories, so many scenes, letting us see them, depicting them right before our eyes.*

The term *visual music* had become so familiar, but that's exactly what Masaru was making. Each visual element was one of a kind, filled with emotion, convincing. Masaru possessed his own unique voice, and used it to convey so very much.

Short, whispered sentences, modest, mysterious. Masaru found the perfect touch and dynamic. Only he could bring out that stillness and breadth.

What about Spring and Ashura? Aya thought. Was it reckless to improvise? Could it take her anywhere near Masaru's studied level of perfection?

Aya hadn't considered it this way before, and the realization startled her.

*

The much-anticipated cadenza.

Nathaniel felt power flowing into the boy.

This was Masaru's first display of emotion as he exposed the *hidden* parts of the piece.

A cadenza with transcendent technique, making use of octave passages and complex chords.

Nathaniel had feared Masaru's cadenza was far too difficult and would stand out too much from the rest, but Masaru had insisted. 'I'll make it a part of the piece. No one will notice the technique.'

He actually pulled it off, making the cadenza an integral part of the whole.

Nathaniel's pupil was truly evolving day to day. The performance that Nathaniel was hearing right now was totally different from what he'd heard only a week before. He'd made exceptional progress.

Part of Masaru's genius was this inexhaustible room for growth. He never set limits for himself; every handicap was just fodder for further development.

Nathaniel was full of admiration and pride.

It was said that a pupil can't choose their teacher, but that wasn't necessarily true. In the case of great talent, Nathaniel felt it was more that the pupil *does* choose their teacher.

He didn't say this out of vanity. Masaru was possessed of major talent, of this he was certain, but this wasn't in any way because he himself was an outstanding teacher.

He was, though, skilled at helping deepen and develop Masaru's talent.

They must have both felt this in their gut, the moment they first met. Masaru chose Nathaniel, believing he was the one who would help him grow. And Nathaniel had felt the same – here was a pupil in whom he would invest all his skill, and who would then surpass him. He was a pupil who had no problem using Nathaniel as a stepping stone. And as a teacher this was his most cherished hope. Nathaniel had seen too many sad, pitiful cases of pupils who could never outclass their teacher. For a teacher this could be dispiriting, for no matter how wonderful you might be as a performer, you also needed to bring up the next generation of musicians.

Naturally there were plenty of genius pianists who never took on pupils, who weren't suited to teaching. They would leave behind only their performances, in that way teaching others who listened to them.

But when you did decide to take on a pupil, you had to see results. From the moment Nathaniel became a teacher, developing his student's gift became proof of his own.

A sudden thought struck him.

If only Maestro Hoffmann could hear Masaru play.

THIS CADENZA IS AMAZING.

Aya felt gooseflesh rising again.

A single ray of light shining amidst the faint stars.

And from that light, a glimpse of infinite colours.

His phrasing is incredible, she thought. All that experience improvising on the trombone was showing.

Young classical pianists weren't used to improvising. There was always, in their cadenzas, a sense of embarrassment and unease. With a brand-new piece, a piece whose reputation had yet to be determined, a performance often sounded unconvincing, dazzling technique alone catching your attention.

Aya could imagine how impressed Mr Watanuki would be.

Ma-kun *is every bit as amazing as you said.*

AND THEN, FLOWING SEAMLESSLY FROM *Spring and Ashura*, Rachmaninoff's *Études-tableaux*, Op. 39, No. 6.

An ominous beginning, something was squirming in a pit of darkness.

Quicker movements, a tense tremolo piercing the dark.

Fast passages displaying his attention to *detail*.

He'd done a fantastic job of ordering his pieces, Kanade thought.

*

The programme was neatly presented like a scrolling image, with each piece an extension of what came before.

AND WITH THE THIRD PIECE, Debussy's Étude No. 5, *Pour les octaves*, they were suddenly out in the open. Coupled with Debussy's unique sense of scale, Masaru's dynamism brought an incredible emotional expressiveness.

Then a further gear change as he shifted to the final piece, Brahms's *Variations*.

Paganini's theme was presented boldly, confidently, served up surrealistically.

Omnidirectional, impeccable, yet with a sense of something still in reserve, the whole imbued with a breathtaking freshness.

Kanade marvelled at Masaru's confidence, he looked as if he was thoroughly enjoying himself.

His talent actually sparkled.

It was hard to sustain the right tension throughout such a lengthy set of variations – much like a series of films that used the same actors in each. You had to have just the right pace, grab the audience's attention, pull them in.

Rachmaninoff had written his own variations on Paganini's theme, but it was said that even he, when he sensed the audience getting bored, skipped some of them.

The whole piece, its melodies and development, was written using various devices in order to keep the listeners' interest, but when you played it, other challenges arose. It was much more difficult than people imagined to repeat the same theme over and over and have it still sound fresh. You had to be laser-focused and employ a wide range of expressive tools.

Masaru was an entertainer, yet he didn't chase after popularity. Brilliant and charming, yet he also gave you the sense of some chillingly deep abyss.

Kanade had been intending to analyse his personality, but before she realized it, she found herself completely captivated by his music.

PLAYING VARIATIONS WAS FUN, THOUGHT Masaru. It felt like jazz improvisation and arranging.

Even a short, four-bar theme had endless possibilities. The composer had proved this long ago. Weaving a tapestry out of kaleidoscopic variations, you could trace the composer's thought process.

Playing these Brahms variations, Masaru imagined steering a canoe downstream, moving at a fair clip, a pleasant wind caressing his cheeks and pushing on his back. He could see himself paddling at a nice tempo, heading towards the mouth of the river, passing scenery that was changing by the minute.

Each stroke of his oar carried him forward, his canoe arriving finally at the mouth of the estuary – no need to rush. Take it one stroke at a time. Tamping down any impatience, waiting for the premonition of the climax. Keeping both the excitement and the calm under control, trembling with joy as he forged ahead. *I'll emerge soon.*

A broad space waiting for me to arrive, a scene I've never experienced.

Masaru felt a strange shiver run up his spine.

That's *what I'm searching for. I'm playing to reach that unseen place.*

WHEN HIS PERFORMANCE WAS OVER, and he stood to thunderous applause, it felt to Masaru as if it were happening to someone else, as if he were watching it all from some perch high above.

Love

MASARU WAS SO OVERCOME with the astonishment of experiencing that new sensation that by the time he got back to the concert hall after a breather, the doors were already shut.

Damn it, I've missed the next performance.

He had to make do with watching it on the monitor in the lobby.

The sound quality wasn't good, but he could get a sense of it.

Engrossed in what was happening on the monitor, he didn't notice a tall figure come up to him.

'You played so well, Masaru.'

Oh no, he thought, *this is the last person I want to see right now*. He tutted in frustration at being ambushed.

The girl was tall, with distinctive features, and dressed in jeans and a dark Bordeaux-red, loose-fitting sweater.

It was Jennifer Chan, from the same piano department at Juilliard.

'So you came back. I was sure you wouldn't until the next judges' announcement,' Masaru said, a touch of sarcasm in his voice.

'I might try to avoid bad playing, but I always make sure I catch good performances. Including yours, of course.'

He wasn't surprised Chan hadn't picked up on his little dig at her.

Ever since they both started at Juilliard, Chan had felt a rivalry with Masaru, one that had become well known. It made everyone curious to see how Chan's competitiveness would play out. She had recently made her debut as a concert soloist and seemed to be ahead of Masaru, while he was busy playing jazz trombone.

Masaru had never viewed Chan as a rival. To him the whole idea of it, competing over something so incomparable, was nonsense. And he disliked it when others cited her as an example.

Back when Masaru was fourteen or fifteen, when he started to grow taller and his many gifts began to show, girls began to get interested, and Masaru had tasted both the happiness and unhappiness of being the object of so much one-sided affection, learning that if he trod on their feelings, he could also get badly hurt.

'Your *Spring and Ashura* was very smooth, wasn't it? Did Silverberg OK that?' Chan suddenly turned to cross-examining him, and Masaru shrugged.

'I thought about it a lot and that's what I finally came up with. My own interpretation of it.'

'Ah – I remember. Silverberg's pretty close to Hishinuma, isn't he? So is this the composer's own interpretation?' Chan's eyes widened as if suddenly recalling this connection.

'No, you're wrong. Mr Hishinuma didn't provide any interpretation beyond what's written on the score. That's just how my *Spring and Ashura* turned out.'

'Seriously?' Chan looked dubious.

This illustrated how the two of them weren't on the same wavelength, Masaru thought. If Chan had been in Masaru's shoes, she would have got Silverberg to sound out Hishinuma about what kind of performance he was expecting to hear. She would do anything to gain an advantage. For Chan that was the way things were done, her own way of showing her commitment to the music.

How would that have played out? Masaru wondered.

If he had approached Silverberg to ask him for Mr Hishinuma's personal interpretation, would Silverberg have complied? He tried to picture the latter's face in that scenario.

It could have gone either way. Silverberg was quite aware of how much of a strategist Masaru was, and that never bothered him. He might have gone along with it if Masaru had wanted to take that route. But it was possible he might have reacted otherwise, telling him it was unfair, that there was no need for it.

It's an interesting question, Masaru thought. *I'll have to ask him.*

'By the way, that girl you were with is a Japanese pianist, isn't she? How come you're hanging out with her?' Chan's voice interrupted his thoughts.

Ah, Masaru thought. *This is what she really wanted to know.*

'Oh, she's someone I knew when I was younger. It's a total coincidence that she's here.'

'Seriously?' repeated Chan. 'You mean you've lived in Japan, Masaru?'

'Yeah, for a short time. We lived in the same neighbourhood and went to the same place for piano lessons.'

'Wow – pretty amazing that you'd both be good enough to perform in an international competition.'

'I know, right?'

Chan lowered her voice. 'You'd better be careful,' she said.

'Huh?' Masaru couldn't believe his ears.

'Wasn't she a professional as a child, and then burned out?'

You really know all about her, Masaru thought, half astonished, half impressed. *What a world we live in. Way too much information and gossip*.

'If you're with such an unlucky girl like her, it might jinx you. Don't you think maybe she found out you're one of the leading prospects to win, and wanted to use you to help her comeback?'

Masaru looked at her blankly. 'You're not seriously saying that, are you?' he shot back, and Chan frowned.

She was proud of her logical and rational outlook, and despised others for allowing emotion to influence their opinion. Yet here she was going on about *luck*.

'Thanks for the warning.' Masaru made it clear he had no intention of continuing this conversation.

Chan glanced at her watch and said that she had to go.

'You're not going to listen to the other performances?' Masaru asked.

'No, I have a lesson now for the third round,' Chan said lightly. 'I listened to you play and that's enough for today. See you!'

She gave a small wave, and hurried off, scrolling through her cell-phone screen as she did so.

A bit dazed, Masaru watched her go, before turning back to look at the monitor. He'd missed most of the current performance.

Liszt's *Mazeppa*. Everyone plays such difficult pieces. He focused on the pianist's fingers.

But he couldn't shake off the serious look in Chan's eyes.

It surprised him that she knew so much. People were always

*

watching you, weren't they? Aa-*chan* would hate it if she knew what people were saying behind her back.

It was only to be expected, but at a competition there were people from all backgrounds. The pianists were at their most impressionable age – teenagers to twenty-somethings – and Masaru knew that bringing everyone together for such an intense experience inevitably led to hook-ups, though most of these relationships didn't last.

There was also a kind of suspension-of-reality effect at work. Young musicians-in-the-making were usually quite lonely, and a competition was the ultimate solitary experience. You travelled to some foreign place you'd never been to, feeling so much stress your stomach hurt, and went out on stage alone. Since you met people who'd been put in the same extreme situation, where your very being and musicality were exposed for all to see, it was no wonder that empathy and attraction would blossom.

And there arose the age-old question of whether a couple playing the same instrument could ever have a successful relationship.

Musical couples were far from rare, but one half tended to come from a different field than their significant other – a conductor and a pianist, or a composer and a singer.

There were plenty of couples who were both pianists, but Masaru's impression was that usually both, or at least one, was more likely to be a teacher or critic than a practising musician. He'd rarely heard of a couple where both were major performers.

Certainly playing the same instrument must lend a kind of unity to a relationship, but mightn't differences in their approach to music be a source of friction? And disparity in musical ability might give rise to unwanted emotions that could threaten the relationship.

*OK – so what about Aa-*chan *and me?*

Before he knew it, Masaru found himself sinking deep into thought.

Get a grip, boy – we only met again two days ago. I can't let myself get distracted.

He gave a big stretch.

It was all Chan's fault, he decided, a little resentful. But still he couldn't forget that look in Chan's eyes. Maybe there was some truth in what she'd said?

An unlucky girl, Chan's voice echoed.

Not that he believed Aa-*chan* was particularly unlucky, he thought. But bumping into her again at this competition might hold some significance for him. Though what, he didn't know.

Masaru folded his arms and gazed at the monitor. His thoughts were no longer on the performance, but far away.

Round Two

(Part Two)

Clair de Lune

THE AUDIENCE WAS STREAMING into the lobby.

It was already dark outside and even in this heated space you could feel how the temperature had dropped. Aya sighed deeply. Her whole body felt in knots.

The standard of playing on the second day had been high, but none of the pianists had matched Masaru's *Spring and Ashura*. They had played well, to be sure, but most had attempted to project some vaguely Japanese image that she found unconvincing, and none of them had come close. The content and power of his cadenza, too, elevated it far above the rest.

A major factor might have been the running order, since he had gone first. If he had played later, perhaps she would have judged some of the others more highly. That's how impactful Masaru's performance was, how his rendition was the lasting takeaway the audience had from that second day.

Aya's impression of Masaru's cadenza was so overpowering that she had to struggle to wipe it from her mind when she listened to the others. She remembered every single detail of it, and if it happened to start playing in her mind, she couldn't help but replay it to the end.

Can my cadenza be as persuasive? she wondered. Could an improvised cadenza really reach that level of perfection? She felt driven to try playing her version.

This was a first. Since the competition began, she'd not once felt so motivated to play as she felt now.

Kanade could tell how on edge Aya was.

'What's wrong, Aya-*chan*?'

'I want to try playing my cadenza.'

'Shall we go to Ms Harada's, where you can play without bumping into any of the other pianists?'

Ms Harada was a friend of Aya's teacher who ran a piano school in Yoshigae. Neither of her students had made it to the second round.

'I really like that idea, though I feel like I'm imposing.'

'No, don't worry about it. She'll be happy if you use the piano.'

Ms Harada's home, which doubled as her school, was in the city centre, within walking distance of the concert hall.

'I'm fine by myself, Kanade-*chan*. You can wait in the hotel. If you're hungry, go ahead and have dinner if you like.'

'OK, then text me when you're on your way back.'

'Got it.'

As a fellow music-college student, Kanade knew you could practise so much better if you were on your own, so she said a quick goodbye.

AYA HURRIED ALONG, CHECKING HER map; Masaru's cadenza still played, endlessly, in her head, and it irked her.

I have to overlay his performance with my own, she told herself. But then something suddenly brought her to a halt.

She spun around.

She was just outside the main city-centre area near the shopping district, and there were a lot of pedestrians.

Aya had the feeling someone was following her, though she figured it was just her imagination playing tricks. She looked around, but nothing seemed out of the ordinary, so she started walking again.

With her bright eyes and plump cheeks, Ms Harada was the type that made you instantly feel relaxed. 'I'm sorry I came empty-handed,' Aya apologized, to which Ms Harada smiled.

'Don't worry,' she said. 'You should focus on your performance. It's so much easier to practise away from the competition.

'Here's the key. It's a little cottage; feel free to play as much as you want. And adjust the heater to however you'd like it. The toilet is by the front door. I've left out some snacks for you. Have you had dinner?'

'I'll think about that after I've done some practice.'

'If you're hungry, let me know. That's what I'm here for. Just push the intercom button.'

Ms Harada handed her the key and pointed to a box-shaped little soundproofed building.

Aya quickly thanked her and skipped over to the cottage.

It must have been a wonderful place to give piano lessons.

There were two grand pianos, an audio system and a side table with chocolates and cookies piled on a plate. There was even a thermos with hot tea.

There was only one small window, double-glazed, with white blinds.

Aya adjusted the stool and ran through some warm-up scales. Long years of practice made these second nature, and she raced through them, raising them by semitones as she went.

Masaru's cadenza still ran on in her head. Before she realized it, she was playing it herself.

Whoa – this is tough, she thought. *I'll have to practise it if I want to articulate all the notes*.

She pictured Masaru up on stage.

The stillness. The darkness. The faint starlight shining through—

She reproduced his cadenza, but at a certain point added her own arrangement, taking it in a different direction.

What about – *her* cadenza? Her *Spring and Ashura*? Just then her ears picked up a different sound.

What was that, that sound? A vibration – like something tapping—

She stopped playing and went to look.

Bang bang bang.

Someone was knocking on something. But where? She walked around the room, then raised the blind at the window and let out a yelp. There was somebody right outside.

Just before she dropped the blind, she caught a glimpse of a hand waving.

'What the—?'

She'd seen that person before. Aya stepped towards the window and raised the blind again.

Outside a young boy doffed his cap and bowed.

'Jin . . . Kazama?'

The boy grinned and made a little pleading gesture. He pointed to the door, apparently asking her to open it. Aya went over and unlocked it.

'Sorry for interrupting.' The boy nodded an apology and, cap in hand, stepped inside.

'How did you – get here?'

'I climbed the wall.'

'No – I mean, how did you know about this place?'

'I'm sorry. I followed you.'

Aya stared at the boy's slightly blushing face.

'But why?' she asked, and Jin chuckled.

'I figured you were going somewhere to play the piano on your own. And I knew that wherever you were going, there must be a good piano there.'

Aya blinked in surprise.

'Where are you staying for the competition?'

'At a friend of my father's. A florist.'

'But what about practice?'

'I don't like using the pianos in the competition practice rooms. I prefer the pianos in people's homes, where you feel the fingers of the people who play, where their presence hovers.'

Jin gazed into Aya's eyes, nervous.

'So – can I play the piano here with you?' he asked.

Aya didn't know what to say.

People used to call her a bit of a space cadet, but this boy was on a whole different level. This was a first – a pianist following a fellow contestant in the middle of a competition and asking if he could practise with her.

'You were playing that guy's piece, weren't you? That big guy? The one who looks like a prince?'

He sat down at the other piano beside him, opened the lid and played an A.

In the practice room in college, Aya now remembered, he'd been playing in unison with another pianist playing a Chopin étude in a different room. What a frighteningly acute sense of hearing he possessed.

Jin played a furious octave phrase. Masaru's cadenza.

He performed it so perfectly it was as if Masaru himself were playing.

Jin stopped and grinned.

'This was running through your head all this time, wasn't it?' he said. 'As soon as you got outside, you wanted to reproduce it – right? I bet. Me too.'

He had a lilting voice.

'So you thought you'd go and find a piano?'

Aya felt gooseflesh again. *He sees right through me*, she thought. *Everything. How I felt, that impulse I had to play.*

He really was beloved of the god of music.

What about me? Aya surprised herself at how intensely she felt.

Does the god of music love me *too?*

In Aya's eyes, for a moment she could see a single spotlight illuminating him, bathing him in a yellow glow.

I didn't choose you.

I chose Jin Kazama.

An awful pain pierced her chest, sharp yet spreading. Something bitter caught the back of her throat. *Why is this causing me so much agony?*

She felt like she'd known the answer for a long time – she'd been holding on to a vain conceit, that deep inside she wanted to carry on performing, and knew that better than anyone. The feeling of looking down on others. The deep-down terror of being told that she had no talent, that after turning twenty she would become simply average.

Shards of that pain in her chest still lingered.

'My teacher told me to find someone to help me take this sound outside.'

Aya had zoned out for a moment and had missed what the boy just said.

'I was thinking you might be that person.'

'Might be what?'

'Nothing,' he said, waving his hand. 'The moon's so lovely,' he added, turning to the window.

The blind was now raised, and Aya realized she'd been so preoccupied that she hadn't looked up at the sky.

The boy's fingers fluttered over the keys, for all the world like butterflies floating in the light.

Debussy's 'Clair de lune'.

Whenever she heard it, she pictured the night sky outside her window. The moonlight pouring down on a silent world.

Aya sat down beside the boy and they began to play 'Clair de lune' together.

They played around with their arrangement, giving themselves up to the surge and roll of the waves under the moon.

Jin Kazama was laughing. Mouth wide open, he was laughing.

Before she knew it, Aya was laughing too.

Suddenly, the piece had changed.

'Fly Me to the Moon'.

Which of them had started it? It came out of nowhere – that's all she could say.

This was, after all, the boy who even did a rhumba version of the children's song 'Zui zui zukkorobashi'.

They took turns playing the bass line, exchanging solos. Now 'Fly Me to the Moon' transitioned into the second movement of Beethoven's *Moonlight Sonata*.

I see, she thought. *The opening* is *a bit similar*.

And then the third movement.

They launched into it in perfect tempo, in complete unison.

Aya felt as if there were two of her, that she was hearing herself in stereo.

A motorboat gliding along the water's surface? Was that what this felt like? No – more like the thrill of speeding along on water skis, spray flying up. The nervous excitement of knowing that one false move and you'd be smashed to pieces by the waves.

The next moment, Aya was segueing into 'How High the Moon', while Jin carried on with the Beethoven. He joined in with an accompaniment: a flowing, dizzying version in 1/16 time. Aya threw in some supersonic glissandos.

I can fly. Fly anywhere.

Aya looked up at the ceiling, then at the moon.

I really can fly. She found herself gazing at a faint star twinkling far away.

Her own *Spring and Ashura*. It was there.

Over the Rainbow

THE THIRD, AND FINAL, day of the second round.

Masami had spent the whole night reviewing the video. She'd taken a lot of footage, so if she didn't review it now, it would make things harder for her down the line.

If Akashi got through the second round, she'd keep filming him, but since he'd passed the first round, she now had a better idea of how this would all translate into a documentary worth watching. If he'd been eliminated at the first hurdle, the programme would inevitably lose impact, so as the film director, she breathed a sigh of relief when he succeeded.

She'd spotlighted some of the other pianists, from Russia and elsewhere, but none of them had got through to the second round. The host family for one of these pianists had told her, 'None of the competitors who stayed in our house made it past the first round. It's a fine line, isn't it? We feel sorry for them.'

They seemed to take it harder than the pianists themselves. The host families had taken them out to eat *kaiten* sushi, to cheer them up. Even though they'd failed the first round, they had scheduled a mini concert at a local elementary school, and Masami had got permission to film it. The Yoshigae competition encouraged contestants to play in local concerts, and she heard that some other events were also taking place, including lessons for children.

There was still some time before the announcement at the end of the second round, so Masami decided to film some of the volunteer staff members. Perhaps because she worked behind the scenes herself, she felt a lot of empathy for the staff who did such valuable work in the background. The Yoshigae competition in particular relied heavily on local volunteers, and their enthusiasm and dedication were inspiring. Some had been taking part since the very first Yoshigae competition, and she could tell how much all of them looked forward to the event. They told her how they'd pick a pianist they particularly liked and eagerly cheer them on. And if their pick ended up winning and going on to a career around the world? Well, all the better.

Masami understood how the bittersweet drama of an international piano competition could captivate people.

What she found strange, though, was how often certain pianists she was sure would progress in the competition failed. There seemed to be many instances of audience favourites being dismissed by the judges. How did the judges even compare such elite pianists? It was all quite puzzling.

Whenever she asked people which of the day's pianists were most promising, besides those from Russia and South Korea, the names that came up most frequently were Jin Kazama and Aya Eiden.

Kazama was an unknown high-school student who'd passed the Paris auditions. When Masami saw Kazama's photo, she'd said she thought he was cute, which prompted Akashi to tell her to stop sounding like some middle-aged woman swooning over a pretty face. As for Aya, Masami heard she was a child prodigy who'd played professionally, only to suddenly give up performing, and that she was hoping for a comeback. Both had appealing backstories.

Akashi had mentioned that he used to be a big fan of Aya. Masami had now seen her perform, too. When she'd come out on stage she'd looked so small, yet when she began to play, her power and presence had magnified her.

It was still early days, but when Masami asked anyone to predict a winner, the first name they gave was that of the young American man, Masaru Carlos Levi Anatole, whom Akashi had heard play too, and was blown away by. Another name that popped up was Jennifer Chan's, also an American and at Juilliard. Both of them were superb, wide-ranging pianists. Jennifer had already made her professional debut in America.

There did seem to be quite a few who were US citizens with Asian roots. Jennifer Chan was of Chinese background; with Masaru it was hard to tell just by his appearance where he was from, for he was part Japanese, Peruvian and French. He was hugely popular, and it was clear he'd already captured the hearts of the audience. Even to Masami's untrained ear it was obvious he had star quality, and to put it bluntly, he was a looker, too.

No matter how they appeared, to play in a competition these pianists had to spend endless hours practising. Masami found it overwhelming to think of the incredible amount of time that was invested. You might practise over ten pieces, only to find you were eliminated in the first round. For many, it was all over in twenty minutes.

Akashi had skipped sleep to allow more time for practice. He might be a good pianist, but his wife didn't have an easy time of it, working hard as a teacher for them to make ends meet.

But how joyous Akashi looked when his performance was over. It sent shivers through her. *Have I ever felt that much happiness and fulfilment in* my *work?*

She was positive this was the profession meant for her, yet had it made her happy? She'd never thought about it before.

Masami was standing in front of the wall of competitors' photos outside the concert hall.

Some photos had ribbons affixed to them. But far, far more did not.

Her eyes found Akashi's image. A black and white shot of him, with his typical gentle smile. She chuckled when she recalled him wrestling with his camera to take a selfie with the beribboned photo. But when she thought of how much struggle he had gone through to win this single ribbon, she felt like crying.

This piano competition really was the most absurd and cruel event.

Yet she also realized how seduced she was by the whole thing.

Cruel, yes, but intriguing and fascinating in its own way.

And could you really score art? Most people would say you couldn't rank some art as superior and some as inferior. Intellectually, everyone knew that.

Yet she longed, emotionally, to see that very distinction made. To see the chosen ones, the winners, the handful of people granted this great gift. And the greater the struggle, the more exciting it was, the more moving the joy, and the tears.

Masami wanted to witness the human drama, the journey to that point. To see people reach the pinnacle, but also to glimpse the tears of those who didn't make it.

She'd love to come to this competition one day as an ordinary member of the audience. She'd like to come with a friend. How wonderful it would be to listen to music together, experience the drama, witness those moments.

The previous performance was now over, the hall doors had opened and a crowd was spilling out.

Today, though, I'm listening to the performances as part of my work, as someone on assignment. Masami composed herself and, video camera in hand, strode into the hall.

Rite of Spring

IT WAS THE THIRD and final day of the second round. The hall was already bustling. People were vying for good seats, and the section on the left facing the stage, which gave you the best view of the pianists' hands, was becoming packed.

As Kanade entered the hotel buffet, she came to a halt.

Aya was seated at the other end of the restaurant, and the sudden glimpse of her face pierced Kanade's heart.

*Aya-*chan*, have you – changed?*

Kanade couldn't pinpoint what or how she'd changed, but something about her was different. She seemed totally focused on something, staring fixedly into space, completely lost in thought.

What's behind this new expression on her face? Kanade wondered. It was as if something had been concentrated, distilled. Something . . . mature. As if, in a single night, she'd become the very image of a contemplative philosopher.

'Morning, Aya-*chan*,' Kanade greeted her, plunking her bag down on the chair opposite her friend.

'Oh – good morning,' Aya said, looking startled.

Kanade was dying to ask her what had happened, but held back. Something inside her warned her it was best not to interrupt this moment of concentration. Aya stirred her coffee with a spoon.

'Did you sleep well?' Kanade asked, taking advantage of the moment.

'Not exactly.' Aya let out a big yawn. 'I had so many things in my head. I want to play *so much*.'

'I know,' Kanade said. 'It's hard being last in the running order.'

'If I have any more time to think, it'll make me even more confused.'

'Eh?' Kanade asked.

'Things might change again after I hear Jin Kazama play.'

Kanade understood – Aya's impatience wasn't because she was going on last.

'Are you perhaps talking about the cadenza for *Spring and Ashura*?'

Aya nodded. 'I've wiped Ma-*kun*'s cadenza from my mind, but since then, I've been batting around all kinds of ideas.'

'I see . . .'

Kanade was half shocked, half impressed. Not a bad kind of trouble to have. She couldn't imagine there was any other competitor who was struggling like this – about *which* of many cadenzas to choose from.

Well, this was what a competition was all about, she told herself. Walking your own path was all well and good, but not if you ended up somewhere all by yourself.

'Jin Kazama and I both put *Spring and Ashura* in the middle of our programme, so our approach is a bit different from those who put it either at the beginning or the end,' Aya said.

Ah, so it's Jin Kazama who's on her mind.

Jin with his free and easy, spirited playing. She could understand why Aya, the apparent genius, should be attracted to that. She could feel a kindred spirit.

Kanade had picked up, from rumours and the atmosphere in the hall, that more traditional pianists and judges treated Jin as some form of *added colour*. It would make more sense for Aya to be concerned about the likes of Jennifer Chan and Masaru Carlos.

'The talk at the moment is all about how great the Juilliard Prince's cadenza was,' Kanade said.

'Yeah. Ma-*kun*'s a real genius. Such limitless potential,' Aya said, lightly putting the subject to rest.

'I'm going to get a refill of coffee,' she added, getting to her feet.

Kanade watched her go. *She really has no idea how others feel sometimes*, she thought.

EARLY THAT SAME MORNING, JIN Kazama was dozing in a sleeping bag.

Instead of staying in a hotel, he had been introduced by his father to a well-known florist in Yoshigae. The son of the owner had gone to college with Jin's father.

'An international competition? But we don't even have a piano here.'

When Jin showed up, unpacked his sleeping bag, and spread it out in a corner of the sitting room, the owner was a bit rattled. 'I've prepared a bedroom for you,' he said. But Jin was used to a sleeping bag on the floor, and slept more soundly in it than elsewhere.

His father had phoned and explained to his friend that he should just let Jin be, since that was what he preferred, and the man relented.

As days went by, the florist grew used to Jin sleeping like a log in a corner of the sitting room, then eventually getting up and setting out for the day. He simply let Jin do his own thing.

The flower shop's day started early.

At about the time the sun had risen and was officially announcing the beginning of a new day, the staff were already arriving back from the flower market.

As Jin sensed the morning light creeping in, he enjoyed the sounds of the flower-shop staff busily buzzing around. The scent of cold water, the bracing smell of freshly cut flowers, the fragrance of life. Japanese plants, with their vibrant green, gave off a singular, almost decadent smell.

The florist was a businessman, but also an artist, a celebrated practitioner of traditional Japanese flower arrangement who tutored a number of pupils.

This was a type Jin knew well. Farmers and horticulturists, people working with nature, and especially with plants, shared an astonishing patience. When dealing with the natural world there really was little humans could do. You could make an effort, yet there was scant guarantee of reward.

As Yuji Von Hoffmann joined Jin and his father on their travels, advising Jin on different pianos in various locations (most of the people offering their pianos were scholars of natural science or farmers, acquaintances of Jin's father), the Maestro had voiced a similar impression.

'Maybe this is the real face of music,' he'd said.

His words came back to Jin.

'You give water to help things grow, and you adjust your work according to the rain, and changes in the wind and temperature. One day the flowers unexpectedly bloom, and you can gather them. No one knows what sort of fruit their labours will bear. You can only see it all as a gift, one that outstrips human understanding.

'Music is action. Habit. If you listen carefully, you'll find the world is always filled with music.'

Last night was so much fun, Jin thought, a smile rising to his face.

The *Moonlight Sonata*, 'How High the Moon'. They could fly as far as they wished. That girl was amazing. He'd never met anyone like her before, someone whose feelings were so in tune with his own.

How far will we fly today? he wondered.

Jin suddenly felt wide awake and famished.

Maybe I should have some rice and egg, he thought, sitting up and wriggling out of his sleeping bag.

A sudden memory came to him and he tried to slip out of the sleeping bag without disturbing it. The night before he'd placed his trousers, his best outfit, under the sleeping bag to keep them pressed while he slept, but when he'd rolled over they had apparently slipped out of place and were now wrinkled.

I'll have to borrow an iron, he thought.

Scratching his head in frustration, Jin stretched and got up.

KANADE WASN'T THE ONLY ONE to think Aya's expression had changed.

The moment Masaru saw Aya in the breakfast area, he'd had the same thought – *Something's different about her*.

'Morning, Ma-*kun*. Kanade, this is Ma-*kun*.'

'It's a great pleasure to meet you. Aa-*chan*'s told me all about you.' Masaru grinned and bobbed his head.

'My – your Japanese is so polite. I'm impressed.'

Masaru chuckled. 'I'm OK with speaking, though writing is another story. But being back in Japan it's slowly coming back to me.'

'Maybe that's how it is with people who have a good ear.'

When they reached the concert hall, Kanade asked, 'Where are you going to sit? At the back again?'

'Um,' Aya said. 'I like being where I can make a quick exit. But you and Ma-*kun* can sit at the front if you like.'

The three of them found seats at the back, in the middle.

'What a huge audience.'

'Yeah. The Yoshigae audience is always so dedicated. There're people who even take notes as they listen.'

'Maybe because there are a lot of piano teachers among them?'

'Aa-*chan*, what did you think of how I played?' Masaru asked, a bit hesitantly. He'd been dying to ask her.

'You were amazing, Ma-*kun*.' Aya looked him straight in the eye.

She *had* changed, Masaru thought again in that instant. How, exactly, he couldn't say. Was it something to do with her make-up? But that couldn't be it, since Aya didn't usually wear any.

'Everyone uses the same brush and paints to create their picture. They have their preferred colours, certain brushes that are easier to use. No matter the piece, they paint with the same strokes. Some see that as individuality and, actually, sometimes it is.' Aya's eyes suddenly turned dark.

That's it, thought Masaru. *Aya's eyes today are more sombre. There's an enigmatic, cold darkness to them. As if she's witnessed something beyond human understanding*.

'But you, Ma-*kun*,' Aya continued, 'can choose your brushes and paints. You have so many tools to choose from. If you want to create an ink painting, you have India ink and a Japanese-style brush at your disposal. You can paint on a canvas, or on a board if you want. Such a pianist could easily end up as simply a technician, but not you, Ma-*kun*.'

He understood what she was trying to say. She was referring to the type of pianist who played everything quite well and ended up a mere generalist. You had to admire their versatility – it was useful – but it was hard to respect them.

'But the really amazing thing is that no matter what tools you use, Ma-*kun*, whatever you play always has your unique signature. To me, *that's* true individuality.'

Aya's expression remained serious.

There was no higher praise, and Masaru felt a warmth filling his heart.

Vivid memories came to him of when they'd been studying piano as children and Aya had told him his playing was like the ocean.

*I'm OK. I'm going to be OK. Because Aa-*chan *believes this.*

Other than his teacher, Silverberg, whom Masaru greatly respected, there was no one else whose praise he now sought more.

'That makes me so happy.'

Masaru was all smiles, and Aya looked a bit taken aback.

'Don't get that excited,' she said. 'It's just my personal impression. You should ask your teacher what *he* thought.'

'If *you* tell me it's good, that's all I need to know.'

Kanade, watching all this, chuckled.

'You two are like children. Makes me wonder if this is how you were when you were at piano school together.'

'Maybe so.'

'Aa-*chan*, you know something's different about you today. Did something happen?'

Masaru's words caught Kanade by surprise. *Ah, so something is up.*

Aya looked puzzled.

'I don't know what it is, but you're different today.'

'Yeah, I thought so too,' Kanade agreed.

Aya looked back and forth between the two of them. 'Really? I didn't sleep that well, so maybe I look worn out?'

She tilted her head and rubbed her cheek.

'No,' Kanade said. 'It's as if your expression has changed. More grown up, maybe?'

'Hmm.' Aya seemed to be considering the idea. She looked up.

Ah – there it is again. That dark look in her eyes.

'I see. Maybe because it's become so much fun.'

'Fun?' Masaru and Kanade asked in unison.

'Yesterday when I heard Masaru's cadenza, it really made me think. It took for ever to get it out of my head. But as I was thinking, it just struck me as – so much fun!'

'So much fun,' Masaru repeated.

Fun. Music? Or the competition?

'I know it's late in the day to say this, but I started to find it all so gratifying. The new composition, the competition. All of us gathering like this, playing the piano. Maybe that's why I seem different.'

She let out a small giggle. Masaru's and Kanade's eyes met.

This girl sitting here was so extraordinary. How much could they ever really know her?

THE COMPETITION HAD BEEN GOING for over a week. And with sound washing over you in the same concert hall day after day, you got used to it, or maybe even tired of it. The fact was that as time passed, it got harder and harder to distinguish a good performance from one that wasn't.

There were even some performances that made you wonder how the pianist could possibly have made it to the second round.

People were talking, too, about how there were several pianists who had made it to the final round of a prominent competition earlier in the year, yet here had been eliminated in the first round.

Sometimes you were in the zone, and sometimes you weren't.

If you happened to hit it just right you'd pass, if not you wouldn't. Which is why it was said competitions were a form of gambling. Even if there was a buzz about a certain pianist, if their performance wasn't up to scratch, it was game over.

Akashi Takashima thoroughly enjoyed hearing the other pianists perform.

He hadn't been in a competition for years, and he loved to catch up on performance styles and which pieces had become popular. It was exciting to plug into the latest in the music world.

As it was the final day of the second round, naturally Akashi had the announcement of the successful pianists on his mind.

He was especially looking forward to the back-to-back appearances of Jin Kazama and Aya Eiden, the final two pianists of this round.

He recalled Kazama's earlier performance, how totally unique it was.

If someone had asked him what was so memorable about it, he'd find it hard to answer.

All Akashi remembered was being bowled over, that it moved him, that he'd never heard a performance quite like it before.

Everyone recognized Jin's creativity, yet a rumour was circulating that the judges found him less than stellar. Akashi could sort of half understand this, and half not.

Creativity. Every musician today wanted it so badly they could taste it, but what did it mean when creativity was seen as a negative? Akashi had thought he understood the ins and outs of a competition, but he recoiled from this news of how some people viewed Jin.

If he were honest, as a fellow competitor of course he welcomed anything that reduced the number of rivals. Yet as a music fan, he hoped they would value a performance as unique as Jin's.

And then there was Aya Eiden.

Every time he looked at the brochure, he couldn't help feeling an innocent excitement, as if he'd met his very first love again.

Her performance had been so buoyant, so striking.

There was a completely different air about her. A sense of

unwavering conviction, of a person walking her own path. It made his heart tremble.

He was sure she'd rank high, but what about after the competition? Would she resume performing? Others, too, must have asked themselves the same question. Was this a statement that she was coming back? Or a kind of exam taken without really caring about the results?

Either way, he was ecstatic that he could hear her perform once again.

And then there was *Spring and Ashura*.

Many of the competitors had treated it merely as an unusual showcase piece, but Akashi thought it might play a far bigger role than most of them expected. Proof of this lay in how most of his impressions of the second round so far were all about how this piece had been performed.

Masaru's entire recital had been brilliant, but Akashi had a particularly vivid and intense impression of his cadenza for *Spring and Ashura*. Depending on how it was approached, this piece could have a broad appeal.

And this was Akashi's hope as well. He was confident about how he'd played *Spring and Ashura*, positive he'd done a better job than anyone of interpreting the poetry underpinning the composition. But the question was – would anyone recognize this?

This was his secret hope.

I have a realistic chance of winning this thing, too.

Akashi felt his competitive spirit well up inside.

THE HALL WAS ALREADY BURSTING, and when the doors opened yet more people crowded in.

Takubo cast a glance over his shoulder at the boy standing behind him.

Jin Kazama looked totally relaxed.

'Kazama-*kun*, it's standing room only again today, so what would you like me to do?'

The piano tuner, Asano, was about to go on stage.

The boy tousled his hair as he considered.

'The piano is fine where it is. Just make it sound a little softer.'

'Softer?'

'Right. Don't make it sound too bright.'

'But – there are more people out there than when you played before. They're standing two-deep in the aisles,' Takubo couldn't help explaining. 'Such a big audience will swallow up the sound.'

The boy shook his head.

'The audience is tired, the hall is stagnant, the air is tired, too. There's a lot of accumulated humidity with so many people breathing.'

Takubo and Asano looked at each other.

'Plus, after me, that lady will be playing, and her performance is crisper and brighter than anyone's. She'll wake them up.' The boy smiled.

'So you're really OK with a softer sound?' Asano wanted to make sure. He shuffled quickly out on stage and, ignoring the buzz from the audience, began tuning.

The boy listened, giving a little nod from time to time.

'That's it,' he said. 'That's what I meant.'

An unusual young man, indeed, Takubo thought as he watched Jin.

A dark horse. The expression sprang to mind.

'That's really a great piano,' the boy said, staring out at the stage.

There was a startling, almost wanton look in his eyes. This boy was totally unpredictable, Takubo thought.

Asano continued tuning right up to the last moment of the interval, surely feeling the pressure of Jin's instructions to make it sound *soft*.

He came back into the wings, looking a bit uneasy. 'Does that sound OK?'

'Yes.'

The boy grinned and held up a hand.

Asano looked unsure for a second, but then nodded and gave him a high five.

Takubo noticed that the audience was hushing itself. He cleared his throat.

'Well, Kazama-*kun*, it's time.'

Jin Kazama walked out on stage, for all the world as if he were just setting out for a stroll, with a dog, in the local park on a sunny afternoon.

For an instant, Takubo thought he'd glimpsed a flash of sunlight and a green forest on the stage as the boy walked on.

Jin gave a little bobbing bow, and sat down on the stool as if he couldn't wait another second to begin. The audience fell immediately silent. Everyone knew he liked to jump right in.

Masaru was struck by the illusion that all the seats in the hall seemed to rise upwards.

It was so strange, but the moment you heard him you felt as if all your cells were taking a breath, your body growing lighter.

He focused on every note, eager not to miss a thing.

Debussy, Étude No. 1.

An audacious choice, Masaru thought. Bold, yet totally in keeping with him.

As the subtitle – 'After Monsieur Czerny' – suggested, the piece put one in mind of a child just starting to learn the piano. It began with an awkward, impish ascending and descending scale for five fingers, but this impression of a basic piano-practice session soon evolved into something else. Timid fingers took on a surer, more powerful touch, the uneven right and left hands now moving in dynamic unison until this *practice piece* drew to a close as a stunning *performance*.

So dazzling. So redolent of Debussy's colouring. Masaru was astonished.

EVERY PIECE THIS BOY PERFORMED sounded like he was spinning out his own improvised phrases.

Kanade strained not to miss a single expression on his face, or the way his fingers moved.

Was he just some *added colour*? Or was he the *real thing*?

Her first impressions were usually spot on, but with Jin her critical ear had let her down. One thing she could say was that she'd never heard a classical musician like him.

Maybe Friedrich Gulda? Or Fazıl Say? No – there was something about him fundamentally different from these genre-crossing pianists. The sense of live-wire improvisation. It was something no one else could imitate.

The second piece he played was from Bartók's *Mikrokosmos*. Bartók's somewhat earthy tones, the jazzy, whimsical melody suited the boy well. Wild, could you call it? Animalistic? It felt like children romping around outside.

Nathaniel Silverberg surprised himself by feeling a genuine interest in the performance.

This was not Maestro Hoffmann's choice of programme. Intuition told him this. The boy had an instinctive ability to edit – a skill musicians nowadays absolutely had to possess. The ability to *produce* yourself, to show what sort of musician you wanted to become. Only those who possessed that objectivity stood out from the crowd and survived. Playing live on stage was like compiling an album, and through others' pieces, from every historical period, you had to pull listeners into your inner world, to display your unique world view.

Maestro Hoffmann had treated Jin as an equal.

This thought brought a slight twinge of pain.

There were plenty of self-styled pupils of Hoffmann, or people so called by others, but not a single one who'd played an improvised session with him.

Only this boy up on stage.

Maestro, how did you plan to mentor him?

Silverberg couldn't help asking the question.

Would you be satisfied so long as the gift *you have bequeathed to us* explodes? *You must have anticipated all too well the shock for all of us involved in music education. What happens to him* after *he explodes? What should we do with him? Who will mentor him?*

Bartók. His *Mikrokosmos*. Bartók was a man who adored the folk melodies of his native land and devoted much of his life to researching them. Yet he was forced to abandon his homeland and ended his life in disappointment, in a far-off country. A wandering composer – and now this boy was playing his rustic melodies.

Maestro, no one can mentor him. Do you wish him to be a wandering pianist? You wouldn't mind that? Nathaniel continued asking these questions, to no one in particular.

Akashi Takashima awaited the next piece with bated breath. He felt odd, as if he were praying, or perhaps wanting to cry.

What performance am I hoping for? The kind that will encourage me about my own? That will make me relieved, knowing that my interpretation was excellent? Or – am I hoping for something that will blow me away?

Jin Kazama's *Spring and Ashura* began quietly.

A casual beginning, as if a continuation of the previous piece, *Mikrokosmos*.

The piece evolved with simplicity. Everyday life. Your usual path. Open the window and the new day has begun. Nature. The laws of the universe that surround human activity. Taken for granted, they fill our lives.

So far, his interpretation followed the score. A straightforward approach, sounding like his own improvisations but still quite smooth. Not all that different a reading from others.

But the moment it plunged into the cadenza, this impression was smashed to bits.

The audience froze.

The cadenza that Jin Kazama spun out was cruel and brutal to an absurd degree.

The frightening, clamorous tremolos stabbed you right in the chest, and were painful to listen to. Persistent chords in the lower register.

A shrill scream, a low rumbling, a raging wind. An openly threatening, irresistible menace.

A violent cadenza, nothing like the other pleasant, natural, innocent performances.

Akashi realized he was barely breathing.

This was *Ashura* indeed.

Akashi felt as if his own more indulgent take on the piece had been thrown back in his face.

Jin was using his cadenza to express the *Ashura* part – the notion of struggle and strife.

Nature didn't just softly envelop humans. Rather, since ancient times it had beaten them down, driven them to the point of near extinction.

The poet Kenji Miyazawa was painfully aware of this. In Tohoku in northeastern Japan where he lived, he had witnessed one natural disaster after another. Freezes followed by crop failures, volcanic eruptions and earthquakes. People raised their eyes towards the heavens, sobbing, gasping, suffering. Children and the elderly starved to death. It was a reality that was cold and heartless. Yet even so, spring arrived, and the seasons came and went.

The child of a beekeeper; the ferocity of nature that humans were no match for – Jin had no doubt experienced that himself. It was the cosmic, Zen-like images of beauty in the piece that Akashi and the rest had read and attempted to express. But Jin Kazama had confronted and presented them with its violence, with the true *Ashura*.

Akashi felt a tingling irritation that turned into both an intense pain and an indescribable happiness. He didn't know what he was feeling, or what he should be feeling.

Jin Kazama's style didn't allow room for applause between pieces as he moved swiftly on.

For his fourth piece, he launched into Liszt, *Deux légendes*, No. 1, 'St Francis of Assisi's Sermon to the Birds'. It was more common for pianists to choose No. 2, 'St Francis of Paola Walking on Waves'.

But No. 1 was the piece that suited Jin Kazama.

Mieko felt a strange sense of awe at his including this directly after the stormy cadenza of *Spring and Ashura*.

St Francis was a Catholic saint who lived in the twelfth and thirteenth centuries. Born to a rich merchant family, he gave up all his wealth to live a mendicant life, and the legend has it that he could communicate with birds and other animals. The piece illustrated the twittering and flapping of their wings as St Francis conversed with them.

The endless trills and tremolos from Jin Kazama's fingers conjured vivid pictures for Mieko – birds fluttering and frolicking with the ragged young man in the wilderness.

How had Jin mastered such expressiveness, as natural to him as breathing?

It was as if he were trying to erase the score—

Erase the score. What could that *mean*?

To tease out, up on stage, the exposed, naked face of music—

For an instant, Mieko felt she had latched on to something.

It felt to her as if her heart had been grazed, fleetingly, by a vision of what Maestro Hoffmann had been hoping for from this boy.

But it all vanished before she could put it into words; Mieko tutted to herself in frustration. There was a glorious shift in gear as St Francis's words transformed into revelation, light shining on a renewed world.

Jin Kazama and St Francis were as one.

Now that she thought of it, she could see the resemblance. Jin had no piano, carried the music in his head, moving restlessly from one place to the next, speaking with the bees. Free and unfettered.

Mieko stared at the boy up on stage, bathed in light.

MASARU HAD NEVER HEARD KAZAMA play Chopin before, and looked forward to his final piece, Chopin's Scherzo No. 3 in C Sharp Minor.

To Masaru, playing Chopin, that melody-maker with his sweetness and popularity, revealed the performer's true essence.

The Scherzo No. 3 was very much in keeping with Jin, flowing perfectly from his previous piece, 'St Francis of Assisi's Sermon to the Birds'.

Then the tone changed. Masaru smiled despite himself. Now that was a sensationalist version of Chopin if ever there was one!

In Italian *scherzo* meant a joke or a prank, and Jin Kazama's scherzo was exceptionally tricksy.

Jin seems to love playing so much, Masaru thought. *Listen to him and you end up dying to play yourself, racing to the nearest piano to enjoy yourself as much as he did.*

Assessing him was a waste of time, since as a member of the audience your response was simply the desire to hear more.

Masaru realized that a part of him was coolly analysing how the judges would evaluate them both.

Perhaps Masaru would have the advantage, since the judges would find his performance easier to grasp, to evaluate. If they disliked the direction Jin had taken, he most likely wouldn't make it to the next round.

But if Jin did make it to the third round – well, then things would get interesting.

Masaru was curious about Jin's next programme. He really wanted to hear it.

In a few hours, they would learn the results.

But first, Aa-*chan* – the final pianist of the second round.

As he gazed at the genius up on stage, Masaru wondered: *So, Aa*-chan, *how are you going to play?*

She was in the green room, waiting to go on, but Masaru addressed her in his head.

Jin's *Spring and Ashura* had been astonishing. Masaru had no idea he would take that approach. *Now that you've heard it, Aa*-chan, *how will* you *play it?*

JIN'S RECITAL WAS DRAWING TO a dazzling close. He struck the final chord of the scherzo with a flash of brilliance, then sprang to his feet as ardent, half-crazed applause filled the hall.

Members of the audience, faces flushed, rose one by one in a standing ovation.

People stamped their feet and whistled.

Jin Kazama grinned and shambled off into the wings.

The cheers were so loud that those leaning up against the back wall had to shout to each other to be heard. Someone noticed a girl standing quietly by.

She had on a green evening dress. She was holding up the hem of the gown, and gazing fixedly at the stage. It was Aya Eiden.

She hadn't gone to warm up for her own performance, but instead had chosen to listen to Jin Kazama play live. When people finally started to move towards the exits, she gazed around her, looking startled, and tottered out of the hall, still holding the hem of her dress up high.

Will-o'-the-Wisp

A COOL WIND WAS BLOWING from the stage.

The excitement over Jin Kazama's performance still lingered but it was clear – the air had changed.

The girl in the deep green dress strode on to the stage.

The audience picked up on the strange dignity this girl possessed, different from all the previous competitors.

AS AYA STEPPED TOWARDS THE piano stool, her eyes half closed, an ethereal expression on her face, Masaru felt he had just seen Aya's shadow self floating above the stage and projecting on to the floor.

Applause brought back the tension and anticipation – the audience eagerly awaiting her performance.

Aya settled herself and, for a moment, gazed upwards at a point in space, her thoughts elsewhere.

She's doing it again, Masaru thought. *She gazed up at the same spot in the first round.*

Masaru wished he, too, could see whatever it was Aya was looking at.

She dropped her hands on to the keys.

The dramatic world of Rachmaninoff erupted, like a violent slap in the face, a huge presence that suddenly made itself known.

Masaru felt goosebumps. She had evolved.

Études-tableaux, Op. 39, No. 5, Appassionato in E Flat Minor.

Overnight she'd evolved.

It's become so much fun. He remembered her words from this morning.

She must have been evolving all the while she was listening to Jin Kazama. But now, in an instant, that vibrant performance had been erased from the audience's minds. Yet it gave her a starting point as she built her own castle.

This voice, so utterly confident – she was creating an enormous painting in sound.

SUCH AN INCREDIBLE AMOUNT OF information, Akashi thought.

What separates a professional's sound from that of an amateur is a difference in the layers of information. Every sound she made was infused with a kind of philosophy and world view, but it was also lively and new. These layers never congealed, but vibrated continuously, hot, kinetic ideas flowing like magma beneath the surface. The music became a *living*, organic being.

You had a sense of a higher presence glaring down. Aya herself was like a shaman or spirit deploying the piano as its medium. As if it were using Aya as its vessel.

Aya's focus never waned. She closed her eyes briefly before launching into her second piece: Liszt's Transcendental Étude No. 5, the *Will-o'-the-Wisp*.

As the name implied, it put you in mind of flickering, pale flames. A densely packed score, it was known as one of the more challenging pieces in the piano repertoire.

In contrast to the Rachmaninoff, this piece was extremely delicate. Playing it was like stringing together many tiny, multicoloured beads with the finest of threads.

You could see it – you really could – the will-o'-the-wisp, wavering in the dark. And almost catch a whiff of phosphorus.

A multitude of dazzling pale lights flickering and flaring, only to fade away.

Amazing, though, that so much modulated dynamism could come from such a tiny body. Jin Kazama's touch was so powerful, but here was such a terrific clarity of sound, as if amplified by a speaker.

Akashi recalled a teacher saying that only talent could produce such an immense sound.

Aya's fingers came to a halt and the flames disappeared.

The hall was still.

She closed her eyes. The audience held their breath.

Next was *Spring and Ashura*.

Akashi swallowed hard.

JIN KAZAMA'S VERSION OF THE piece had been so shocking to Aya that, from the moment she heard it, something inside her had begun to spin around at high speed, desperately seeking the answer.

Aya realized her fingers had begun to play the opening melody of *Spring and Ashura*.

The universe.

She turned her gaze to the spot somewhere above the piano.

And saw a darkness unfold before her.

The rustling of a meadow at her feet. She could feel the grass beneath her bare soles, the cool blades tenderly tickling her. The wind blew up from somewhere, making her hair flutter, the hem of her dress flap up and down.

Who's there?

Aya felt someone standing behind her, watching, *watching over* her. Giving out a warm, slightly frightening aura.

Who are *you?*

Her back was burning, tingling from a cold light. Someone was physically present.

A presence she used to know well, warm, nostalgic.

Her fingers were playing *Spring and Ashura*. A plaintive, yet witty, melody.

The cadenza was coming up. *Freely, giving a sense of the universe.*

Aya had the illusion that she was expanding, like Alice in Wonderland. Swelling into the dimensionless pitch-black universe.

Her fingers began to seem so far away, way below her. Yet the sensation in them was sharp, acute. Every part of her body told her precisely what sort of sound she was making.

Was this what they meant by being *in the zone*?

She felt she had split into many selves – one self was coolly appraising, another playing the melody, another considering her programme, another floating in space.

And behind her was—

Mother

The realization reverberated in her mind, shaking her to the core.

Aya's mind went blank.

Goodness, it took you long enough. You silly girl.

She could hear a voice – no, it was more as if it was welling up in her heart.

Aya was a bit disgusted with herself.

Why didn't I notice who it was before? I was closer to her than anyone. The person I've longed for, who watched over me, who gave me everything. My mother, who suddenly left me.

No, she didn't leave me. She was always at my side. All I needed to do was turn around to see her.

Mother, forgive me.

Aya felt something warm running down her cheeks. Some intensity was rising from deep within her.

Spreading her fingers wide, she pushed down into the opening chord of the cadenza.

Kanade's eyes widened.

Where had this cadenza *come* from? This wasn't any of the ones she'd been practising.

And were those tears? Or sweat? Kanade saw that Aya's face was wet.

But her expression was unchanged. Her eyes were still half closed.

This wasn't the performance I'd ever imagined.

Kanade took it all in.

Sturdy, yet loose and comfortable – generous and solid. The kind of touch Aya had never shown before. Not brilliant or radical as she always had been, but with something that encircled everything – like – the Earth itself.

Mother Earth.

The words slipped out despite herself.

The horizon stretching out for ever. Children running. Someone far off, their arms spread, waiting. All living creatures striding across the Earth.

She could sense a green meadow opening out deep inside her. She could smell the fragrance of the grass. The comforting aroma of supper wafting on the breeze.

An indescribable sense of security. Of peace. As if she'd returned to the carefree days of childhood.

Ah – so this is Aya's return. Kanade felt sure of it.

Aya had listened to the intensity of Jin Kazama's *Ashura* and had responded to it. Hers was not a depiction of the cycle of slaughter and violence, but of an Earth that enfolds everything and swallows it all up. An Earth that then gives birth to, and nurtures, new life.

Aya's music had grown, and matured, like never before.

JIN KAZAMA WAS ENSCONCED at the very back of the hall staring intently at Aya up on stage.

From there, he could feel the wind blowing.

He knew where she was.

A fresh green meadow, the light shining down.

You can soar even higher, you know.

Jin closed his eyes and flew through the air with Aya.

SO THIS MARKED THE RETURN of the girl genius.

Mieko studied the girl, her feelings a mixture of empathy and relief.

She'd heard all about Aya Eiden indirectly. As a former child prodigy herself, Mieko recalled clearly how devastated she had felt for Aya after she had so abruptly retired from concert performance.

So young, yet so accomplished – Mieko remembered how awful it was. Day after day on concert tours, the loneliness and moments of emptiness, the despair at thinking it would never end. The pressure of constantly living up to being a child prodigy.

Here I was thinking Aya would be behind, trying to catch up, when in reality she's overtaken everyone. Lapping one and all.

Her cadenza went far beyond brilliant. It had an unexpected maturity, a ripeness, about it.

Masaru and Jin Kazama's cadenzas had a proper youthful ardour, but Aya had passed that stage long ago.

So how far will this young lady go? She's a worthy rival for your blue-eyed boy, isn't she? Mieko thought, and shot a glance at Nathaniel.

AYA REMAINED TOTALLY FOCUSED. SHE moved on to the fourth piece with, as before, no room for applause.

Ravel's *Sonatine*.

A three-movement piece, a bit old-fashioned, and Aya played it meticulously.

What she does is give us a fresh reminder of the joy of hearing great music.

For Nathaniel Silverberg, too, Aya's ability was a given, and now he was simply enjoying the *Sonatine* as one of the audience.

At this rate, it might come down to a play-off in the final round. The real competition had only just begun.

As he analysed her, how she compared with Masaru, Nathaniel realized how much Jin Kazama remained a worrisome factor. Nathaniel was perplexed by him, about how hard it was to compare him with the others, how difficult he was to score.

He was well aware of the contradictory nature of competitions. This was nothing new, for back when he was young he'd endured some trying times, and later on had made his pupils go

*

through the same. There was so much in a competition you had to come to terms with. Still, after Aya's recital the results would be announced, and that would determine what direction this competition would take.

THERE WAS AS USUAL NO applause between works, and now Aya had launched into her final piece. Mendelssohn's *Variations sérieuses*.

A quiet opening, with ripples washing in and out. The waves grew higher and began to roar. The theme came back. And then, like raging surf, the variations expanded outwards.

Aa-*chan*'s performance was, in the truest sense, *dramatic*, Masaru thought, steeping himself in it.

Any number of performers were dramatic in a showy way, but few could be genuinely dramatic while making the piece really speak. Especially young pianists, many of whom tried too hard to express themselves and put on too much of a display.

He'd felt betrayed, in a sense, by her cadenza. He'd been fully expecting a tricksy, cutting-edge passage that would outdo Jin Kazama's. If Aya had wanted to, she could have easily come up with any number of perplexingly intense versions.

But her cadenza had been almost disappointingly generous and warm, which took him by surprise.

Masaru was shocked to acknowledge that her cadenza was a kind of ode in reply to Jin's.

She really did play, as the score indicated, *Freely, giving a sense of the universe*.

Didn't Aa-*chan* care about the outcome of the competition? Didn't she have any ambition? What about becoming a concert pianist? Was she not planning on that? Even though her playing could be this superior?

Even though she could produce such a haunting, chilling sound? Masaru closed his eyes.

A tempestuous passage was coming to an end, the piece racing towards its climax.

The conclusion of the second round.

Masaru opened his eyes.

Aya, who'd kept her eyes half closed the entire time, opened them wide, smiling generously, and stood up.

The hall shook with thunderous applause. People leapt to their feet.

Masaru and Kanade looked at each other, as if they'd woken from a dream, and, smiling through tears, they stood up too.

Aya's expression as she reappeared for an encore was shy, embarrassed even.

The second round was now officially over.

And the results would soon be announced.

Heaven and Hell

CAMERA IN HAND, MASAMI found herself bowled over by the strangely feverish atmosphere of the crowd.

The lobby was overflowing, not just with competitors, but their family and friends, and no doubt peers from their music schools. She recognized some of the faces she'd seen up on stage. Back in casual clothes, they blended into the crowd, though when she looked closely, she saw how strained and flushed they were.

Masami took a deep breath and trained her camera on Akashi Takashima, standing beside her.

Like the other competitors, Akashi appeared tense and stiff.

'How are you feeling? Nervous?' she asked, noticing her own voice was more on edge than she'd thought it would be.

Akashi didn't seem to hear her, and stood for a while, looking vacantly ahead of him. 'What? Yes – I *am* nervous. *Very*.'

'It's so nerve-racking,' Masami said. 'Like when you're waiting for entrance exam results. No – actually I feel more excited than that.'

Akashi nodded.

'Yeah. When they did the first round, I was so preoccupied it was like I was waiting for the results without really feeling I was in the competition myself, and had lucked out. But now it feels like I'm on the *inside*, and when I think how my fate's about to be decided—' Akashi fell silent.

Fate. This was when the results of all that effort would come out. Would he get a chance to stand on that stage ever again?

It's a good thing my performance is over, he thought. *If they asked me to play right now, I'd fall to pieces.*

The judges had not appeared, yet cameras were flashing everywhere, trying to capture the pianists before the big moment.

Akashi realized that Masami was filming him, and the thought flitted through his mind that he had no time or energy to worry about cameras.

His eyes darted about the room: the tall figures of Masaru Carlos and Jennifer Chan, both looking ethereally calm. *I envy them*, Akashi thought. *The kind of musicians whose talent is a given*. He wished he wasn't the sort of run-of-the-mill person constantly worrying about trivial things such as whether he had talent or not, agonizing over whether he had a fifty–fifty chance – or were the odds lower than that? – of making it to the next round.

There was a sudden cheer.

He looked to one side and saw a crowd of judges gliding down the stairs from the upper floor.

Blood coursed through his body.

The judges were descending calmly, relaxed looks on their faces.

Akashi felt a sudden flash of hatred towards them, these people who were to decide everything. He knew this hatred was misdirected. He was well aware their judgement reflected the bias of countless people who, though nothing special, desired nonetheless to be a part of the musical universe.

Like him. One of those countless, nothing-special people in the world. Viewed from the sky, he might not even be visible, just a speck, one of a multitude of nameless musicians.

A staff member handed the microphone to the chair of the judges, Olga Slutskaya, and the lobby suddenly hushed.

Olga smiled coolly and began to speak.

Her opening comments went in one ear and out the other for the competitors, since they were pretty much a repeat of the first-round announcement.

'The level of playing was quite high,' she said, 'very technically competitive – and failing to advance to the next round does not mean that a competitor's musicality is being diminished. We have seen a promising trend here in terms of sound programme management . . .' et cetera.

People observed her vacantly as she spun out her remarks.

The twenty-four who'd made it to the second round would be whittled down to twelve for the third round.

'And now, I would like to announce the names of those pianists who will advance to the third round.'

Maybe Akashi was imagining it, but it felt as if everyone was leaning forward as one.

'First – Alexei Zakhaev.'

A cheer rang out, and a man jumped with joy, no doubt Alexei Zakhaev himself.

The unlucky first batter had made it through again. It was clear everyone was surprised by this.

A second pianist's name was read out. A Korean girl. The next pianist was also Korean. A man this time. With Korean names Akashi couldn't tell if it was a man or woman and had to see them to know.

There was a stir in the crowd and a bit of a commotion, and at first Akashi couldn't figure out why. People were whispering, shooting glances in one particular direction.

He followed their eyes to a stunned-looking Jennifer Chan.

Jennifer Chan had been cut.

No! Akashi thought, yanked back to reality.

Yet Olga forged on.

'No. 30, Masaru Carlos Levi Anatole.'

Akashi saw Masaru Carlos, smiling as he acknowledged the congratulations.

His mind went blank.

'No. 22, Akashi Takashima.'

Olga's voice announcing the first-round results rang out in his head.

No. 22, Akashi Takashima.

This time his name wasn't read out.

It took a while before it sank in.

He noticed that Masami beside him had frozen. I must have the same blank, stunned look on my face as Jennifer Chan, he thought.

Running through Akashi's mind in that instant was a phrase from Schumann's *Kreisleriana* that he always flubbed, an imagined scene of himself replaying that phrase again and again.

The *Kreisleriana* he was supposed to have played in the third round.

But now he wouldn't, wouldn't have to play it, wouldn't have to worry about messing up that phrase.

Yet still it played over and over in his head.

Cut. I've been cut.

Time flowed on, leaving Akashi behind. The names of pianist after pianist were read out, and as he took in the reactions, the joy of some, the disappointment of others, it all seemed like something behind a pane of glass, a scene from another world, not his own.

None of the names registered, only the reality that his was not among them.

'No. 81, Jin Kazama.'

An intense, almost violent cheer went up. This too seemed to be greeted by a strange stir and surprise among the crowd, or was he just imagining it?

'And finally, No. 88, Aya Eiden.'

Akashi felt himself break into a smile.

I've always been her fan. She's been an idol of mine. As a musician she's the real thing. I'm glad.

The clamour flowed around him. The noise and commotion. People shouting excitedly. Congratulations and laments, bitterness and confusion – he could calmly observe all these emotions now.

'Immediately after this will be a get-together with the judges,' a voice announced, 'and we do hope all the competitors will take this opportunity to speak with them.'

'I'm so sorry.'

Masami's voice brought him back.

'Yep. I guess I got cut.' Akashi was surprised at how upbeat he sounded.

Masami seemed to feel the same way, her expression both dumbfounded and relieved.

Akashi gave a big stretch. 'Thank you for everything, Masami. I'm sorry I couldn't make the programme more interesting.' He really meant it.

Masami shook her head.

'I'm the one who should be thanking *you*. I know having the camera in your face all the time was a pain, but thank you so much for cooperating. Really.'

Was Masami crying? Or was he imagining it?

'Not at all. Shouldn't you be filming the others now?' Akashi motioned to those around him.

'Yeah. Right. I'll be back.'

'Go for it.'

Akashi could go home now.

He remembered he should call Machiko, and headed off to the deserted lobby.

What tone should he use when he called her? What should he say?

He rehearsed the conversation in his mind as he pulled out his cell phone.

The get-together after the second-round announcement turned out to be quite stormy, as Jennifer Chan protested volubly and vehemently about the second-round results.

Even if she hadn't, there was often a complex, strange feeling to these gatherings with the judges, owing to some smouldering sense of dissatisfaction and resentment about the decisions.

This time Jennifer Chan walked right up to Olga Slutskaya, and made her objections known loud and clear, taking everyone aback.

Certainly one of the main functions of these gatherings was to assuage any dissatisfaction, but seldom did someone protest so openly.

'I just can't accept it,' Chan argued. 'Explain to me exactly where I fell short.'

In a sense her objections were admirable, but before long her father, a rather wealthy, well-known businessman in America with close ties to the US Secretary of State, and her teacher, both got on the phone to the judges, throwing the party briefly into an uproar.

In the end, Nathaniel Silverberg took Chan aside and talked her down.

'Your technique is impeccable,' he said, 'and no one denies your obvious musicality. Still, the fact remains that several judges – and I don't mean just one or two – felt you shouldn't go through to the third round. I think you should take a step back and consider what that means. Your inability to understand the reasons might be one of the factors that has kept you from advancing, don't you think?'

Chan screwed up her face and burst into tears. Her mother, who'd accompanied her, tried to comfort her, and by the time Chan left the venue it was nearly midnight.

'About ready to call it a day, I imagine.'

Mieko had watched all this from a distance, and when she offered the gloomy-looking Nathaniel a glass of wine he muttered, to no one in particular, 'She's already debuted at Carnegie Hall, and I'm sure she wanted the prize here as a boost to her career.'

'Well, it's something she needs to discover on her own.'

'She was impatient. She really hated how people were comparing her to her predecessors, calling her the female Lang Lang and the like.'

'I see.'

Mieko had been thinking the same, for when she heard Chan perform, she'd thought, *One Lang Lang is enough*. The other judges seemed to share this opinion, and Jennifer Chan herself had probably sensed the same thing.

'Her teacher probably told her something along the lines of *Be yourself*. She's overly sensitive to the word *originality*, the poor girl.'

'Good grief. The concept is an illusion, after all.'

Raising her glass to her lips, she saw Masaru walking over.

Nathaniel cocked his chin in his pupil's direction.

'She must have felt a lot of pressure. She has an intense rivalry with him.'

'Hmm. That can't be easy for her.'

Mieko had also picked up on a romantic interest, too, from Chan's side. She hoped it wouldn't get too complicated.

'Good evening, sir,' Masaru said.

'How's Chan doing?'

Masaru gave a forced smile. 'She went back to the hotel with her mother. But she's calmed down. She's OK – she's not the type to brood.'

'Did you console her?' Mieko asked, and Masaru waved a hand.

'Not at all,' he said. 'I don't think consolation from a fellow competitor is very comforting.'

'True enough.'

'By the way—' A girl was standing behind Masaru.

Hmm? Mieko thought.

A petite girl with a bob cut. Dressed casually – a sweater and jeans – but Mieko had seen her somewhere. One of the competitors?

'Ma'am, I'd like to introduce you. This is Aa-*chan* – I mean, Aya Eiden.'

Nathaniel and Mieko both nodded. *Is this really her?* Mieko wondered. The child prodigy making a comeback. Mieko had known the name, but this was the first time she'd seen her up close.

She seemed so fresh, so unaffected. Hard to believe she'd gone through all that in the past. Above all, her eyes were amazing. Large eyes that sucked you in.

'Congratulations on making it to the third round,' Mieko said, smiling.

Masaru, red-faced, turned to Nathaniel. 'Do you remember I told you about how I started the piano? Aa-*chan*'s the girl I was talking about, who first took me for piano lessons. I never imagined we'd meet up again here. Never,' he repeated.

Mieko could tell that Nathaniel was taken aback.

'*Seriously?* The one you played "Little Brown Jug" with?'

Mieko didn't know the background, but these two were apparently childhood friends.

Masaru grinned and nodded. 'That's right. I knew it the second I saw her. The instant I saw Aa-*chan* on stage.'

'I didn't recognize you, though.'

They shared a look.

'You really haven't seen each other since back then?'

Nathaniel looked incredulously at each of them in turn.

The two of them were so completely different as musicians, yet both shared a certain charisma.

'Well, your performances were amazing,' Nathaniel said in a gentle tone. 'The Beethoven in the first round, and the rest.'

'Thank you,' Aya replied, bowing slightly.

Mieko thought Nathaniel might start trembling any minute now, for it was obvious how in love Masaru was.

Fall for another competitor? One of your closest rivals? This is a critical competition, not the moment to fall madly for a girl.

Mieko could almost hear Nathaniel's silent plea.

He surely must be remembering how, when he was just a little older than Masaru, he'd fallen head over heels for Mieko. Aware, too, that the woman herself was standing next to him, eyeing him.

Nathaniel cleared his throat. 'It's late, so you two should rest. Competitions take more out of you than you think.'

'Yes, we're going to head back. Maestro, see you tomorrow.'

The two young people bowed repeatedly and left. Nathaniel watched them walk away, his expression ambivalent.

'You kept yourself in check nicely,' Mieko joked.

'What do you mean? I wasn't holding back.' His voice, though, was sullen.

Mieko burst out laughing.

'It's as if a young couple have come to announce they're getting married, and you're an old man wondering if you should strike them with a bolt of lightning.'

'Absolutely not.'

Nathaniel reacted defensively, but then he began to feel a touch of melancholy.

'How wonderful to be young.'

'I was thinking the same thing,' Mieko said. 'Well, I'm going to call it a day too. Like you said, a competition does take more out of you than you think.'

Nathaniel set his wine glass down on a nearby table and headed with Mieko towards the exit.

'I never imagined he would make it past the second round,' Nathaniel said.

'Jin Kazama?'

'I was seventy per cent sure he wouldn't.'

For Mieko it was both surprising and expected.

'One thing's certain,' she said. 'More people are looking forward to his next performance. About the same number who thought Jennifer Chan shouldn't get through.'

Nathaniel gave her a look.

'You heard?'

'I'd just like to know how you convinced her to accept the judges' decision.'

Mieko was surprised how the judges who'd been so negative about Jin had slowly come round to accept him, though since she herself had had the same experience, perhaps it wasn't so hard to understand. But there were still judges trenchantly against him, and this time, too, Jin had only just made it over the line to the next stage.

This was going to be interesting, she thought. How many more fans would Jin be able to bring with him? Would the judges who completely rejected him now succumb to his appeal?

Mieko and Nathaniel stood waiting by the lifts, and she shot him a glance.

What about Nathaniel?

The doors slid open.

And what about me? she thought. *Do I really accept his musicianship? Do I understand what he's doing? And Maestro Hoffmann's intentions?*

As she mulled this over, a huge yawn crept up on her.

Nathaniel was right – this really was more exhausting than she could have imagined.

I'll put these thoughts on hold, she thought, *until I hear his third-round performance. I'm just thankful I can hear him play again.*

She stretched and stepped into the lift.

Round Three

Interval

'IT'S FREEZING OUT HERE.'

'Whose idea was it to come, anyway?'

'Wasn't it Aa-*chan's*?'

The coast in November was brutal, deserted, devoid of all appeal.

They'd spent most of their time in hotels and the concert hall, and weren't used to the temperature change. Aya regretted wearing only a thin jumper and an equally skimpy coat.

She pulled her collar up, hunched over and winced.

It was Aya, indeed, who'd suggested that an outing to the coast might be a nice change of pace. The shore outside her hotel window looked warm and calm, and she'd never expected the wind to be so biting.

'Let's head back. If we let Masaru catch a cold, Nathaniel Silverberg's going to wring our necks.'

Kanade glared at Aya with a grim expression.

'Hey – Jin! What're you up to over there?'

Masaru was waving his arms wildly at Jin, who could be spotted in the distance squatting low, his head bent as he inspected something.

'Let's go back!' Aya called out.

The boy jumped to his feet and jogged over.

'I found these conch shells. The spirals are in a Fibonacci sequence,' he said, holding out a small shell.

'Fibonacci sequence? Just what we'd expect from a genius.' Masaru laughed.

And in fact Jin Kazama's grades in science were outstanding, though he'd hardly been to school. He'd attended the music conservatory as an auditor, he'd said, because everyone had strongly advised him to enrol in a science and technology university.

'Music really must follow the order of the universe,' Aya said. 'Music and mathematics do have a close affinity. Your grades in science must be good too, right, Ma-*kun*?'

'I suppose.'

'I'd always thought the laws governing the universe were sort of random.'

'Random?'

'I'd always thought that the smallest unit of matter would be totally different, depending on which galaxy you were in. But I recently read that research shows water is water everywhere, oxygen is oxygen, wherever you are. The universe turns out to be simpler than I'd imagined, with the same laws applying everywhere. I found that really curious.'

'Hmm. I think I know what you're getting at.' Masaru nodded.

'At its root the universe is the same wherever you go. There might be stars that are cold all year long, and ones that are always hot, but the components are all the same.'

'That's strange. I thought there was an infinite number of basically different things, but even if the processes and results differ, the basics of life turn out to be the same.'

'So as long as certain conditions exist, life forms just like humans are possible.'

'Yeah. They used to say that they wouldn't necessarily look like us, but even if a few details might be different, it's weird that they would end up looking like this.'

'You're right. It's interesting that the old theories turn out to be right. The power of intuition, I guess. You know, if matter is the same throughout the universe, it also proves the Big Bang theory, doesn't it? That everything started from one point?'

'I wonder if they have pianos.'

'What?'

'OK, suppose there's a planet on the edge of the galaxy with the same air, and sound waves carry in the same way, then I think music will develop there. And if it does, then similar types of musical instruments will develop, too. In some far-off corner of the universe there might be someone playing their heart out on something like a piano.'

Masaru came to a halt. 'It's possible. Then that planet might have its own Mozart or Beethoven.'

'Maybe it would!'

'I'd love to see the scores. I want as many pieces as possible, if they're Mozart's or Beethoven's.'

'Me too.'

Another Mozart at the far end of the universe. What kind of music would it be?

On the horizon sunlight poured down from a break in the clouds, lighting up a single path.

Aya had a sudden feeling of déjà vu. Masaru walking beside her.

Jin in front, eyes glued to the ground, studying it with curiosity.

Kanade, in a hurry to get back.

The greyish sea and the beach.

The biting wind and the rhythm of the tide.

For some reason I feel strangely nostalgic, Aya thought. *Makes me tremble.*

As if I'd always known this moment – the four of us, at the beach in Yoshigae, on this day, walking together in the cold wind. This moment will be etched into my heart, this almost painful feeling. I'll remember it for the rest of my life.

THE FIRST AND SECOND ROUNDS had been eight straight days of battling, but now there was one day off before the two-day third round began.

Aya had no idea how the twelve remaining competitors would spend their time off. Have a rest? Or perhaps spend the entire day practising?

A gap in time.

She'd got up late, and after some warm-up practice in the

afternoon, Aya and Kanade had decided to go for a walk, and they'd bumped into Masaru. Since they were staying in the same hotel, it wasn't hard to see each other. She'd thought of sending him an email asking if he was planning to take it easy on their day off, but hesitated to, and Masaru had hesitated to email her, too, about her plans. But when she learned he'd been considering a change of scene, they decided to go out for a walk together.

'Let's go to the sea,' Aya had said.

Just as they were setting off, Jin Kazama appeared. 'Is that Jin?' When Masaru spotted him, Jin strolled over.

'Where are you staying?'

'At my father's friend's house,' Jin said.

'You really do pop up everywhere, don't you?' said Masaru.

Aya and Kanade found it curious, but Jin just responded with a grin.

'Ah – I find this free time kind of stifling,' Masaru said, and stretched.

'You think so, too, Ma-*kun*?' Aya looked at him in surprise.

'I do. I don't need a day off, and I wish they'd just do it all without a break.'

'Yeah. If you aren't careful, you waste your time thinking about all kinds of useless things.'

'The ones who really need a day off are the staff. And the judges, too,' Kanade said, cutting in on their muttered complaints. 'Running a competition is exhausting. The pianists have it hard, but those behind the scenes have no time to sleep.' She'd seen what a tough time her father had managing competitions, and couldn't help putting in her two pennyworth.

'That makes sense,' Masaru said. He seemed a little abashed that it was only now occurring to him. 'The staff really have worked hard for us. My Juilliard friends said the host families, too, have been so nice to them. And these competitions in Japan are run like clockwork.'

'How many times have you been in a competition, Ma-*kun*?' Aya asked as they walked along.

'This is my second. I've also been to one in Osaka. I don't know what competitions are like in other countries.'

'I hear all kinds of rumours about how tough they are.'

They'd set out for the beach again, but the unexpected cold turned them around quickly and they decided to stroll through town.

'I'd love some *unagi*,' Jin Kazama said. *Unagi*, grilled eel, was, after all, something this town was famous for.

'But it's so expensive,' Aya whispered to Kanade.

'Once is completely fine. Papa will allow it,' Kanade whispered back.

They didn't want to make Masaru and Jin have to pay, since they'd travelled so far to be here.

'I hadn't noticed all the shops selling Japanese musical instruments. This is the first time I've walked into town.'

They'd passed several stores with a shamisen in the window. Even in Tokyo there weren't many of these.

'Aa-*chan*, have you ever tried the shamisen?' Masaru asked as he peered through a window.

'Not yet. I'd like to try, though.'

'In New York I went to a performance of Tsugaru shamisen. I was surprised how good they were at improvising.'

'Really? Who were they?'

'Those two brothers who play together,' Masaru said.

'I know the ones you mean. Tsugaru shamisen sounds like solos based on standard numbers. Have you ever heard Shinichi Kinoshita and Roby Lakatos play duets?'

'You mean the guy they call "the devil's fiddler", right?'

'Right. He's awesome.'

'The Tsugaru shamisen sounds like a whole trio playing. As if the guitar, bass and drums were all being played at the same time.'

'It does have a melody and bass line and rhythm percussion all rolled into one. But what I want to play isn't the Tsugaru shamisen, but the kind that accompanies Japanese ballads.'

'That's different from Tsugaru shamisen?'

'You don't play it so percussively, and it has a duller sound, as accompaniment to a recitation.'

'Hmm. I didn't know there was that kind too.'

'It's not tuned in equal temperament, and the time signatures are totally different from Western music, which is why I want to try it.'

'I want to try the shakuhachi,' Jin said.

'Shakuhachi?' Aya repeated, eyes wide in surprise. 'They say it takes three years just to master how to make a sound on a bamboo flute, right? That's an unexpected ambition.'

'I think it's the closest thing to the real sound of the wind,' Jin said.

KANADE WAS LOOKING ON QUIETLY – THEY were at the crucial point of a competition, and here were three contestants who'd got through two rounds, yet they were totally relaxed and enjoying themselves.

Geniuses, she thought. *What can you do?*

She was feeling a tad left out, the same sense of isolation she often felt in this world where talent vied against talent.

Do these guys have any idea how blessed they are?

What about all those who tried to make it as a musician, practising hour after hour, unable to sleep, their stomachs in knots wondering if they'd be able to perform without tripping up, beaten down by their own mediocrity yet unable to walk away? What about *them*?

OK – enough of the negative thoughts, she said to herself.

People labelled as geniuses had their own problems. Aya understood her status as the fallen prodigy. She'd had countless insults thrown at her.

No one knew how their life would work out. Even for Masaru, who seemed to be on the road to stardom, the future wasn't guaranteed. So many prodigies had been toyed with by fate. The world was littered with tragic, fallen stars.

And then there was Jin Kazama. What life lay in store for this unusual young man?

Kanade watched as he studied the shamisen in the window.

She unconsciously took a step back. The three of them together like this at this moment.

Her hand touched the cell phone in her pocket.

I've got to take a photo. She stole a quick snapshot of the three of them, casually chatting. Maybe some day this photo would fetch a high price, Kanade thought.

She imagined herself as an old woman being interviewed about it.

'That's right, I just happened to take a photo. I never imagined they'd all become such stars – that photo is pretty valuable now, isn't it?'

Kanade blinked in surprise at how vivid this imaginary scene was.

The three of them might never be together like this in the same place ever again. This premonition grazed her mind for a second.

It suddenly dawned on her – these three never take any photos.

Which again made Kanade feel a bit left out.

I guess there's no need for them to record their lives. Others will record their lives for them and keep it for—

AYA TURNED AROUND AND SAW she was taking their picture.

'You're taking photos?' Aya said.

Kanade stuck her tongue out in a sign of embarrassment.

'Sorry, it's just that when I saw you three pianists looking at a shamisen, I thought what a great photo opportunity.'

'You're right. How come I didn't think of that? I've got to get a shot of Ma-*kun*. And Kazama-*kun* too. A photo of these future great pianists.'

She rummaged around for her cell phone.

'Can – I join in?' Masaru said. 'I thought it would be a little rude.' He took his phone out. 'I want to send it to my friends.'

'Take one, take one!' Jin was delighted.

'Kazama-*kun*, don't you have a cell phone?'

'I do, but I left it behind.'

'A cell phone isn't much use if you don't have it with you.'

Kanade watched the three of them posing for each other. *Maybe I overestimated them a little*, she thought.

Promenade

THE NATIONALITIES OF THE remaining twelve competitors in the third round were: American (1), Russian (2), Ukrainian (1), Chinese (1), South Korean (4), French (1), Japanese (2).

Because of the geographical location of the competition, it was only natural that there were a lot of Asian pianists, but Mieko found that this list was representative of trends in the classical-music world. A competition that drew top-notch entrants would naturally reflect which countries had the most musical energy and ambition.

Which in and of itself showed how the level of this Yoshigae competition had ramped up, didn't it?

Mieko stretched and then took her seat among the judges.

With six performers per day, each playing for one hour, and including the intervals, there was a long, hard session ahead.

The first day would begin at noon, with the final performance due to finish at nine.

No sooner had the staff opened the doors to the hall than all the seats were taken. When they reached this stage, with the number of competitors whittled down to twelve, audience members had their favourites, and the hall was filled instantly.

The judges would be more attentive too.

Up until now it was really nothing more than a process of weeding out. A pianist might be able to focus for twenty or even forty minutes, but an hour-long performance required a level of concentration demanded of professionals. Getting an audience to listen to your music for a full hour was no easy task. You had to have a compelling recital programme, and your own distinctive voice.

One other consideration was that this would be the third time the judges had heard each competitor and so they'd be listening with an even more critical ear.

By this point, it was do-or-die for the pianists.

DESPITE HER DAY OFF, MIEKO felt tired, physically and mentally.

As the first pianist, Alexei Zakhaev, appeared on stage, the judges and audience quickly noticed that something was not right.

Where was that smile of his?

The ever mischievous Zakhaev wore a grim look.

He was unusually pale, and when he sat down, he seemed stiff.

As he adjusted the stool his hands appeared clumsy.

He took a deep breath and plunged right into his recital, but it was as if he were someone else. A confused murmur rippled around the hall.

My goodness, he seems so awkward, Mieko thought. Zakhaev, aware he was no longer his normal soaring self, became more and more out of joint.

Word was that when he heard his pupil had made it to the third round, Zakhaev's mentor had rushed over to Japan, and they'd spent the night before in an intense lesson.

Probably neither teacher nor pupil had anticipated he would make it this far. Excited and worked up, it was likely they had overdone the last-minute practice session.

I know how you feel, Maestro, Mieko thought, *but you should have just left well alone*.

Zakhaev had drawn the first position, and up until now he'd turned this to his advantage. Never thinking he'd make it to the third round, he'd played how he wanted to, his performances full of his naturally open-hearted generosity of spirit.

But now his self-consciousness got in his way. It was no wonder, what with his mentor flying halfway around the world, rushing to his side.

At any rate, out of nearly one hundred pianists, he had made it to the exclusive group of twelve, among whom memories were still fresh of the previous winner who had been propelled to stardom. He could see winning as a real possibility now, could taste it.

But he now struggled to remember the advice his teacher had given him yesterday. *Keep calm*, he told himself repeatedly.

The more he did so, however, the more the word *win* flickered through his mind. He moved his fingers, trying to play better, trying to show what he could do, but he ended up overplaying, and losing the generosity of sound for which he was known.

The more desperately he tried to connect his phrasing, the more he strained, misfingerings littering his performance.

Zakhaev was totally shaken, and those listening could tell.

This was no recital any more, but more like a runaway car, brakes shot, careening down a mountain road. The audience listened breathlessly, waiting to see where this terrifying performance would end up.

Even when the piece was over and the audience applauded, Zakhaev still looked blank.

As he began the centrepiece of his performance, Mussorgsky's *Pictures at an Exhibition*, things began to really slip away from him.

He must have been planning to start it at a fair clip, taking an aggressive, youthful approach, but a look of panic came over him, for he seemed to have begun at an even faster pace than he'd intended.

The opening 'Promenade' was rushed. His fingers slid over the keys, the voicing weak, not grasping the core of the sound.

Hang in there, Mieko, on edge, silently called out to him.

You can still pull it together, she thought. Calm down at the 'The Old Castle' section.

Pictures at an Exhibition was structured like a short-story collection, with the 'Promenade' motif repeated between each part. They were in a variety of tempos, and some had a leisurely, calm tonality. There should be plenty of chances to pull it together again.

But Zakhaev's brakes remained shot. Or more precisely, the concept of contrast had gone out of the window. He raced on, ignoring the road signs and bends, as if his performance wouldn't end until he crashed. And thus he charged on, pitching forward, head over heels.

Though he should be praised, Mieko thought, for managing to hit almost every note even at that breakneck speed. *But if he's playing 'The Market at Limoges' this fast, what's he going to do when he gets to 'The Hut on Fowl's Legs'?*

Mieko felt a twinge of pain in her chest.

He might actually fly off his stool, mid-performance.

If *she* was feeling this way, she sympathized, imagine his piano teacher, seated somewhere in the hall. This young man up on stage must be about to give his teacher a heart attack.

Zakhaev's face, deathly pale in the first half, now turned bright red.

And it was no wonder. Straining so much to get through the first half, his arms must be swollen by now with the sheer effort.

He'd already lost it – his mind, as they say, was a complete blank.

Mieko remembered the term *spinal reflex*. He was playing now completely by muscle memory.

She could tell members of the audience in the front row were literally frozen. She felt sorry for them, caught up in Zakhaev's panic.

An ascending scale, a roller coaster clattering its way up a steep rise, an instant of sheer fear and panic as it reached its zenith.

As if leaping off a cliff into the void, Zakhaev avalanched his way into the final section, 'The Bogatyr Gates'.

An avalanche was exactly what was happening here. Strangely enough, perhaps he was now relieved that the end was in sight, since his sound suddenly became calm, as if he'd finally relaxed.

Mieko breathed a sigh of relief, and she could tell that the audience, and Zakhaev himself, had all done so too.

Totally thrilling, she thought, *though it's shaved years off my life*.

The judges around her, too, clearly felt a sense of release.

A lot of old guys among us, she thought, *so make sure you don't kill them, OK?*

Zakhaev's innate open spirit returned all of a sudden, and he sat back a bit and raised his head as if taking a breath.

Goodness, if only he'd played this way from the start.

Mieko leaned back in her seat.

This boy naturally had a clean, good sound, a breadth of vision.

And now she finally could afford to *judge*.

His delivery took on more colour, a more pronounced voicing.

The audience could relax and enjoy what they were hearing now. They'd had enough thrills for one day. The final chord rang out.

Zakhaev, blushing, stood up, looking deeply relieved, as he was enveloped in the equally relieved and encouraging applause of the audience.

'Thank God,' Mieko said.

AFTER BEING THROWN INTO A vortex of thrills and suspense, the audience found themselves instantly drawn in by the next competitor, a young South Korean who carried with her none of the jolt and stir that had preceded her, but instead gave a calm and limpid performance.

Ah, one of Schneider's pupils, Nathaniel Silverberg thought as he gazed at the girl on stage. She was studying at a conservatory in Ireland.

Just as in sport a famous player doesn't necessarily make a great coach, in the music world there were teachers in every country who, though not themselves distinguished performers, displayed a real talent for spotting and mentoring young pianists.

Schneider was one of these, and for the last few years

Nathaniel had seen some great pianists who, it turned out, studied under him.

Perhaps it was the way Schneider taught them to use their hands, but there were moments when you thought, *Ah, of course – this is one of Schneider's pupils*. And in this age of increasingly homogenized performances, it was interesting to detect these traces of the teacher in their style.

All of Schneider's pupils shared a kind of fidelity to the music, a way of reading and interpreting it. You always felt secure listening to a Schneider student.

You also got an occasional unexpected glimpse into Schneider's own musical ideas, moments when the listener would think, *So this is how he approaches things, so this is the kind of pianist he is.*

And there was so much that a pianist could understand only after they tried teaching, moments when they grasped for the first time what they, themselves, considered good. And it was possible, through their pupils, to actually make their ideal performance a reality.

This was true of Schneider, and maybe he was performing *through* his pupils. He was, in a sense, continuing as an active musician.

So this is how music is passed down, Nathaniel mused.

Even if it was diluted, diffused, to the point where you couldn't determine what the original was, the prototype forgotten, somehow the scent of it, the touch, the essence, remained.

So – does the Maestro's essence remain within that boy, Jin Kazama?

He'd never thought of it before.

He'd been so distracted by the carefree, boundless style of Jin's performance that he hadn't looked for Hoffmann's touch somewhere in it.

So was the Maestro hoping to leave a trace of himself behind? Did the Maestro live on within this boy?

Silverberg felt as if a tiny light had lit up inside his chest.

By the time you reached this level, it boiled down to a question of taste.

Akashi, now back in the audience, listened admiringly to the third competitor from South Korea.

He had enjoyed particular pianists in the second round and was sure they would make it through. He found it hard to accept the news that they had been eliminated, so he bought their CDs to review them.

His findings surprised him. What really caught him off guard was how fastidious the judges were as listeners. Akashi had always prided himself on having heard a lot of piano.

But he was taken aback by how different his impression was between hearing them play in the concert hall and hearing them on CD.

He discovered there was a reason why they had been eliminated.

The clearest reason was the pianists' inability to sustain tension. Instead, they muddled through. Listen carefully and you heard how the theme might be obscured, or where the piece got away from them. Akashi found himself shaking his head, wondering how he could possibly have been so impressed when he'd heard them live.

He was surprised at how even Jennifer Chan's performance, which sounded so dynamic in the concert hall, now came across on CD as monotonous.

I need to work on my listening skills, he thought.

The pianist currently on stage had struck him as too unadorned and simple, yet with his solid performance of Beethoven in the third round his abilities gradually revealed themselves.

On the other hand, in the second half of his recital the pianist began to display another side, with a gorgeous rendition of the ever-challenging concert piece *La Valse*, by Ravel.

The judges had recognized all this, the pianist's true worth. Akashi was floored.

Wow, he thought, a little belatedly, *what an amazing glissando*.

How easily the pianist pulled it off, as if simply brushing the keys, all the while looking so nonchalant.

He remembered when he'd first tried a glissando, how he'd cried at the pain of it.

Performing a glissando meant sliding across several keys with the backs of your fingers – simple enough, but it could also be incredibly painful.

He gazed at this carefree young man on stage. *I want to play that piece, to play like that*, Akashi thought.

To think that everyone was playing such demanding pieces. Pianists were truly amazing, with their superb technique.

Making progress was like ascending a staircase, not like walking up a gentle slope.

There were times when he'd play and play, and be at a complete standstill, not making an inch of headway. There were countless times when he'd despair, thinking he'd reached his limit.

And then, one day, from out of nowhere, there'd come a moment when he reached the next step, when he knew that, for some reason, he was suddenly able to play something that had stymied him.

I'm so glad to have been a part of this, Akashi thought.

I'm glad to be one of the countless pianists in the world.

He was so touched by his own thoughts, as if these feelings were reward enough, that he almost felt like crying.

Still, there were people who at this point had far outstripped him, who were on such a higher plane that he could never fully empathize with them.

Presences he could only look up to, whose experiences he could never share.

The pianist finished *La Valse*, and as Akashi enthusiastically applauded, he pictured the next competitor up – Masaru Carlos.

Sonata in B Minor

An hour-long programme, the content of which was limitless, since they were free to play whatever they wished. Free to choose any combination of pieces.

Modern pianists could choose from any period. From eighteenth-century Bach to twentieth-century Shostakovich, from the heritage of the past three hundred years.

Yet even professionals – or maybe you should say *because* they were professionals – weren't always able to play the programme they wanted.

This was even more pronounced with popular pianists as they expanded their fan base. To sell more tickets and fill larger concert halls, you had to play the music that the audience wanted to hear.

At a competition, though, you could in principle try out an experimental programme without worrying about ticket sales. It might, in fact, be the one place where you could be the most daring.

Random thoughts flowed through Masaru's head as he stood waiting in the wings.

I want to be the kind of pianist, he thought, *where the pieces I want to play, and those the audience wants to hear, are one and the same*.

Meaning the kind of pianist who got the audience to enjoy the pieces *he* found interesting. The kind of pianist who extracted the maximum fascination and charm from every piece, and could communicate this.

Masaru had yet to talk about it with anyone, but he had a secret ambition.

An ambition to create *new* classical music. To be a new kind of composer-pianist.

Chopin, Liszt, Schumann, Brahms, Rachmaninoff, Scriabin, Bartók.

All were distinguished pianists *and* composers. That being the case, shouldn't there be more composer-pianists nowadays?

Not that he ever compared himself to any of them. Just doing justice to their work would take more than a lifetime.

There were tons of pianists with amazing technical skills, but why didn't any composer-pianists emerge from among these virtuosos? Masaru had long found it strange.

That said, most *contemporary music* operated in an exceedingly small field, the music existing mainly for the sake of the composers themselves, and for critics, and this wasn't work you felt like playing, or listening to.

Couldn't there be a pianist who linked all these?

Even Friedrich Gulda, a kind of freewheeling genius who transcended musical barriers, began playing his own work as a jazz pianist. Though he was one of a rare breed who embodied the orthodox Viennese sound, he was treated as an outlier, outside the realm of the classical pianist. That's how strong a spell his predecessors had cast, how high the hurdles were.

Even so, Masaru thought, *I'd like to try some day*. That's the dream he held within.

He suddenly heard the bell signalling the next performance. He smiled. *First things first. I have to do my absolute best over the next hour*.

Perhaps noticing Masaru's wry smile, the stage manager looked at him wonderingly for a second.

'It's time,' Takubo said. 'Good luck.'

The third time Masaru had heard these words.

'Thank you very much.'

For the third time, he gave Takubo a warm smile, and walked out on stage.

MASARU HAD DECIDED SOME TIME ago that Bartók's Piano Sonata would be the first piece he played.

Starting off with this avant-garde piece would grab the audience, and overturn the sweet image people had of him.

During his lifetime, Bartók had often said that the piano was a percussion instrument as well as a melodic one. Few people ordinarily thought of the piano that way. Look inside, though, and you do see the hammers striking a string at lightning speed, clear evidence that yes, *percussive* is indeed what it is. But look only at the keys and you'd never know.

By starting off with Bartók, you'd be reminded fully of the piano as an instrument that *strikes*.

Which is why Masaru didn't so much *play* the piano as *pound* it.

In his head was the image of striking a marimba, his fingers like ten long mallets, his wrists snapping smartly as they struck the keys.

He tried imitating the unique flexibility and effortlessness of a marimba player.

With percussion instruments you can't hesitate before you strike them. If you do, even for a fraction of a second, the core force is weakened, the intensity of sound diminishes.

That's why, to play Bartók, you have to strike with urgency, even violence, which is only to be expected, seeing as how the piano is a percussion instrument.

For all that, what a cool piece this was!

Masaru's heart soared as he played.

Yes – this was much like the joy of playing drums. The sensation as the vibrations rebounded through your body, the pleasure of rhythm surging through you. A primal joy.

The drum is an instrument from ancient times, in every country and people.

In that sense, he thought, the piano is an extension of the drum.

After trying all sorts of instruments, one of Masaru's acquaintances had settled on drums. One drum is equivalent to an entire orchestra, he claimed.

The same was true of the piano. With a single piano you can reproduce an entire orchestra. Instead of drumsticks, the hammers struck internal wire strings.

Beating. Beating.

Humans possessed this basic desire – to express their feelings by striking something to make a sound. The drum was what they hit first to satisfy that desire. And over time, the piano emerged. And this piece by Bartók.

How extraordinarily Bartók had developed his sound, so refreshing and pure; hearing it was like coming upon a lovely vista, a euphoric feeling like a blue sky opening up before your eyes.

Whenever Masaru played Bartók. he smelled a forest, grass, a complex gradation of green, drops of water falling from the leaves.

Wind wafting through the forest to an opening, where a log cabin stood.

Bartók's sound was like a thick, rough-hewn log. Unvarnished, unworked, the beauty of the grain visible. A solidly built structure in the midst of nature, a sound like the materials themselves.

The sound of an axe ringing out somewhere in the forest.

A robust, regular rhythm.

Striking. Striking. A vibration rings out in the forest that you can feel in your gut.

The beating of a heart. The rhythm of drums. The rhythm of life, of emotion, and the interplay between the two.

Beating. Beating.

Finger mallets striking wood.

You could fall into a trance as you beat out the sound, gathering strength, striking with even more vigour. Totally absorbed, giving it everything you have. Until you go blank.

A final blow and the sound stops.

Then silence. The utter stillness of the forest.

WHEN MASARU STOOD UP, HE was enveloped in a swell of applause.

Grinning and bowing, he felt relieved, and at the same time an indescribable joy.

I want to be the kind of pianist, he thought once again, *where the pieces I want to play, and those the audience wants to hear, are one and the same.*

And what about the next piece? Masaru asked himself.

This, too, is surely a piece that both the audience, and I, want to hear.

Sibelius. *Five Romantic Pieces.*

As the name indicated, it was a complete about-turn from the Bartók work, a series of five short, melodic pieces. Unashamedly beautiful, well-ordered melodies.

Nothing technically difficult, you could play them as sweetly as you pleased.

Yet for Masaru placing this second in his programme was a risk.

In his one-hour recital, the second piece played a key role.

The contrast with the Bartók added balance, and aimed to release the audience from any tension. It also provided, and satisfied, the audience's desire for the kind of tenderly enrapturing music they hoped for from Masaru. But the main goal was to lay the groundwork for the major work that came next, a Liszt sonata.

But this Sibelius is harder than I imagined, he thought, keenly feeling this every time he practised it.

It was technically simple and he mastered it quickly. But the sweetness also bordered on the tacky, an excessive self-consciousness (the phrase *leakage of the pianist's self-consciousness* expressed it well). It was hard to find a convincing balance that neither made it sing too much nor, in contrast, sound too brusque. If he strained too hard to emphasize the gear shift from Bartók, it might warp the entire thing, and since the ending was fairly nonchalant, it could leave the audience feeling unsatisfied.

What does Romantic *mean, anyway?*

He had stared at the title, wondering what Sibelius meant by it.

As the representative Finnish composer, Sibelius projected a sense of *whiteness*. Snow covering dense, spiky coniferous forests, ice, glaciers, deep blue lakes. An elegant, refined white.

This really is Romantic, he tried whispering to someone.

But how does it make you feel? He shut his eyes.

Lovers gazing at each other. Shadows drawing closer.

A beautiful night. Flickering candlelight.

A little embarrassing, a little bittersweet, a little tearful, the feeling of floating in the air.

Since the melodies themselves were more than romantic enough, he aimed to play them straight, and rather stiffly, the chords uniform, the arpeggios precise, with no pretentious ritardando.

Crystal light, of the kind seen in a Baccarat glass.

Singing was difficult. Sometimes you might be pleasantly singing along only to find it sounded like someone belting out karaoke. You had to be patient and humble to give yourself up to the natural flow of the piece and grow close to the voice of the piano. Otherwise the performer's smug side would soon show its face.

To make a gorgeous melody sing, the sounds themselves had to be exquisite.

Masaru polished and refined his touch even more, searching for ways to make the transition from one sound to another smoother, more flowing.

As he focused, he felt as ever how very challenging it was to play at a consistently even volume, to ensure each particle of sound was in alignment.

You had to let the sound emerge rather than try to force it. He practised minutely, seeking that kind of sound.

All his work and research led to this conclusion: a Romantic sound needed the sense of something being held back.

A weak sound, or one where you played to your limits – neither of these approaches would work. It had to be more like a fluffy, plumped-up quilt, cushiony, as well as slightly damp. There had to be moistness to it, like the liquid eyes of lovers, but to convey that dewy feeling the pianist needed to be calm and composed.

You needed muscle strength not to make it any louder than necessary. It was like placing a cup gently on a table, you needed the strength to hold the cup still in the air before setting it down.

Staying power was necessary to get a Romantic sound. Both physical, and emotional.

Similar criteria to being an *adult*.

I have to be stronger, thought Masaru.

A tenacious body, a strong spirit. That's what created a truly *Romantic* sound.

Of course, he couldn't be thinking all this while performing.

Memories of all the trial and error he'd gone through merged, and flitted through a corner of his heart like a shadow.

Masaru had been absorbed in expanding the *Romantic* performance he'd been after. A superb sweetness of tone.

In reality, he simply let his desire to sing run free, his feelings fresh and honest.

A silent euphoria lingered, then Masaru smiled and rose to his feet as wild applause erupted. He felt the temperature of the audience shoot up, sensed how they had shared in his joy in the music.

MASARU BRACED HIMSELF FOR THE third work, today's main course.

Franz Liszt's major piece, the Sonata in B Minor.

Composed from 1852 to 1853, it was first performed in 1857. Liszt had by then already retired as a pianist, and it was his pupil Hans von Bülow who performed it.

Renowned as a masterpiece, it had an unconventional form. Since it was billed as a sonata, when it was first played there was a heated debate over whether it fitted that form or not. Because of its novel structure, it was, famously, subject to intense criticism.

Its main feature was that, unlike the usual sonata form, divided clearly into exposition, development and recapitulation, this sonata was played as one continuous piece.

It was almost thirty minutes long, technically very demanding.

Masaru had studied its delicate, complex structure, yet every time he heard it, it struck him, with its meticulous foreshadowing, as very much like a carefully plotted novel.

It was like a magnificent story written in musical notes.

Both the writer and the reader needed tremendous tenacity.

Like a troubadour, you had to physically absorb the entire piece to be able to relate it up on stage – its story with all its twists and turns, written in such wonderful language.

It was a famous piece he'd heard over and over since he was a child and had practised it numerous times. He'd memorized the score long ago.

Yet in preparation for the competition, he'd painstakingly studied it all over again from the beginning. The score was a kind of blueprint, a mass of parts constructing the vast edifice of the Sonata in B Minor.

Where did all the parts go, and what role did they play?

As if viewing a huge building in 3D, Masaru studied every nook and cranny of the score.

And the more he read, the more he marvelled.

With famous compositions you were struck by the beauty of a score just by looking at it. Even children who couldn't read music would discern its lively, attractive patterns.

There were, of course, varying versions, and minor questions remained as to whether this was the original as Liszt wrote it, but even if parts had been added and revised by later generations, the impression and balance of the score convinced you how exquisitely constructed it was.

This was created from human imagination, written down, and performed over hundreds of years – a truly astonishing, miraculous thing.

The composition – the story – began casually, with an enigmatic scene.

A YOUNG MAN IS QUIETLY walking, lightly stepping through grass along a desolate, wintry track. He is smartly dressed, an intellectual, his eyes dark, smouldering.

The sky is overcast, covered in thick cloud, the air biting. It is utterly still, with not even the call of birds disturbing the silence.

The crisp snap of a broken branch underfoot.

The man notices a crumbling gravestone half buried in the

grass. Dates are carved on to it, but the inscription is worn away and all that's conveyed is the futility and fleetingness of life.

The young man steps over the gravestone.

Before him appears a village on a low-lying hill, a church steeple, the walls of an old castle; it's clearly a place with a rich history.

The young man's expression is forbidding, his eyes fixed on one spot in the distance, hinting at a troubled past, for what unfolds is a tragic tale of multiple, ill-fated generations, one that explores the complexities of human motivation.

Following this ominous introduction, the first theme arrives, with members of a land-owning family making their appearance.

We're told of the despotic father, his younger brothers vying to succeed him, and his sons, with their tangled relationships. Intrigues have been set in motion, the seeds of discord already sown.

After a lengthy narration, the second theme arrives.

A new protagonist makes her appearance, a fresh-faced young heroine.

Though part of the ruling clan, she was orphaned early, and has been sidelined. She was raised by her strict but loving grandmother, and lives a simple, frugal existence on the outskirts of the village.

The beautiful, intelligent heroine. One look in her eyes and you can see she possesses true courage.

Her theme suits her personality, an emotive melody that is warm and brimming with affection.

On her way back from the parsonage, she encounters the young man standing on the outskirts of the village, still staring at a fixed point.

He is with an official who is explaining something at length.

The heroine gazes at the young man.

She's never seen him before, yet something stirs in her, and she has the feeling she's known him from a long time ago—

Chance brings her and the young man together several times. A child is injured in a pasture and the two of them speak as they come to the child's aid.

The young man tells her he is a lawyer, ordered by his client to visit the village to prepare a lawsuit. They are attracted to each other, though the occasional chilling look in his eyes concerns her.

People gradually learn about the new man in the village and rumours abound.

It seems he has been assigned to sue the landowning clan, people gossip.

Before long, news of his arrival reaches the ears of the clan's head.

The clan's theme is filled with tension.

Gradually, this mysterious young man corners the clan. Murkier family members meet with sudden accidents, or die off, one after the other, in foolish quarrels.

The scene quickly changes, and the men of the clan are thrown into panic.

What is happening? Is this a vendetta against them? And is the young man involved? Who is pulling his strings?

They start to suspect each other.

One scene after another passed through Masaru's imagination.

He felt as if he could even hear the people talking.

He could see the light of their candles at dinner, the dull glint of a coin being paid to an informant at the back door, the rainwater pooling in the ruts made by the carriages.

It was a tale filled with magnificent characters – the beautiful strong-willed girl, the grandmother with her gift of foresight – and offering detailed descriptions of scenery and states of mind as it moved towards its tragic denouement.

Fate cannot be escaped. Step by step the gears of time turn, drawing characters together, leading them to places where they will meet.

The young man opens up his heart to the heroine, but when he learns who she is, he is beside himself. And the heroine tries to discover why.

The young man confesses he is there to take revenge against the clan, to destroy them.

The story reaches its climax.

It is finally disclosed by the clan that the young man is the child of the youngest son, who was murdered before he could reveal the malicious intent of his fellow clansmen. At the time, the man's wife tried to escape with her newborn child but was cornered and cut down. Her child was nowhere to be found. It was a cold winter night and the chances of survival for a baby were slim. They were sure he'd expired somewhere along the way—

The clan let loose assassins on the visiting young man.

But with mutual suspicion running rampant in the family, the clansmen turn on each other instead.

The young man fights back, there is blood everywhere, dead bodies scattered all around.

The young man, burning with the desire for revenge, tries to capture the heroine.

And just then, there's a scream.

The grandmother, sick in bed all this time, totters to her feet, calls out a name, and the young man is filled with astonishment.

They are brother and sister!

The darkness is split by the scream of the heroine, as a clan member stabs the young man.

The final scene: the heroine notices a gravestone, half buried in the grass. It carries the name of her mother, the woman who had been murdered that cold winter night.

The heroine, unable to bear her grief, gazes up at the sky, and walks away into the distance.

MASARU FELT HE COULD SEE the word *Fin* marking the end of the score. But no, what was that in German – *Ende*?

He closed the score. A bit of a clichéd story, but this was the nineteenth century, the age of the Grand Romance.

And this was also the tale Masaru could *hear* in the music.

What remained was to convey this complicated narrative through his performance.

THE WORK OF COMPLETING A piece was, he found, a lot like cleaning a house.

Cleaning a house entailed endless physical labour. And so did playing.

It was difficult to keep a house clean.

If it was a small house the cleaning was easier, and not so time-consuming. You could make it spick and span in a short time, and just a little tidying up was all that was needed for it to be neat again.

But cleaning a large house wasn't easy. To keep it always looking its best, you needed to be constantly vigilant.

The Sonata in B Minor was a huge house. The structure was complex, layers upon layers of elaborate design. Countless people had come in and out and kept the place spotless.

But if you're asking one person to clean up this entire huge house?

Just opening the heavy door was difficult. Just getting to the porte-cochère you had to sweep away piles of leaves, and you had to constantly think of how the place had originally looked when it was all pristine.

There were so many parts you weren't sure how to tackle – the old wallpaper, a brass handrail.

You first needed to consider the amount of time and effort you'd need to clean it, and how you'd go about it. Only when you had thoroughly prepared could you begin.

Masaru was confident. He had the very latest cleaning implements, and stamina besides.

Yet once he began, he realized the task was much harder than he'd first envisaged.

There was no way he'd be able to reach every corner of the verandah. It was just too large, and he was soon out of breath.

He scrubbed here and there, but left many places untouched, including the windows. He didn't have the strength left to sweep away the soot from the ceiling. In the beginning it was all he could do just to mop the hallways.

Focus on one spot, and the dust would soon pile up in another place in his absence.

The composition was tougher than he'd ever imagined.

Masaru went outside the mansion once more and thought things over.

He knew now that cleaning at random would never get the whole place in proper order.

He was determined to deploy every ounce of strength he had, and all his technical resources, in an all-out battle.

He tried all sorts of efficient approaches, but in the end concluded that the only way was to simply clean up and polish each room, individually, making a thorough, careful job of it.

In doing so, he made all sorts of discoveries.

Wonderful designs in places no one had noticed before, and drawers inside wardrobes that no one had ever tried. Rear windows that revealed refreshing views, and which had never been opened.

As he practised every day, he came to understand the correct timing for waxing the floor of the entrance hall, and when to take a break from cleaning.

Bit by bit the mansion grew tidier, and the orderly appearance of the building when it was first constructed emerged.

The balustrade on either side of the stairs leading to the great hall tended to get dusty, so he diligently wiped them down.

Occasionally he'd throw open all the windows and let the breeze blow through the mansion.

He came to know less accessible places where he still wanted to clean. Places that guests might notice and remark on, admiringly, how even these out-of-the-way areas had been well looked after.

He even noticed how the morning sunlight streaming into the hallway on the east side showed the flowers next to the windows at their very best.

And finally that day had come.

The day when every corner of the mansion had been renewed, with the building appearing in all its original glory.

He understood the changes wrought in the house by every season, what was needed to manage each.

This mansion belonged to him. He remembered each and

every tree and blade of grass in the garden, and if he closed his eyes, he could clearly picture how they were swaying.

That day had come.

The moment when he knew everything there was to know about this composition.

The time when the music permeated every corner of his being.

It was a moment of supreme joy, when he felt that, no matter how he played, he and the music were truly *one*.

He could do whatever he wanted – decorate the entire mansion with flowers, or have an all-night party—

Though Masaru could still feel all the hours and hours he'd worked on it, right now, as he flew at the Sonata in B Minor, it felt utterly new, as if it were the first time he'd played it.

Forget all the hardship.

And present this dazzling drama to the audience, and to myself.

What is coming next? Where's it going? He was like a member of the audience himself, waiting with bated breath for what would unfold next.

All ears were trained on the story Masaru was telling. The audience's attention was painfully focused on him alone up on stage, and he knew that their excitement and tension were balanced on the edge.

The solemn final scene was nearly upon them.

He played it vigilantly, steadily. Making it as full and complete as he could. Leaving nothing out.

Telling it all, yet leaving strength in reserve – a suggestion of something lingering.

The heroine slowly fading into the distance.

The now deserted scene.

The empty plain, only the grass swaying in the wind.

He felt like he could actually see the word *Ende*.

The concert hall was hushed.

Masaru rose to a storm of applause. He bowed deeply.

Thank you so much.

For some reason, words of gratitude came to him. He didn't know who he was grateful to.

Thank you for letting me play this magnificent narrative piece. Thank you, truly, for letting me perform it here, today.

He bowed again and again to the endless applause, and it wasn't until he seated himself once more that it died away.

MASARU WAITED A LITTLE LONGER for the hall to settle down, and then began his final piece.

A short waltz by Chopin.

He'd chosen the piece as a kind of encore to his hour-long recital.

Waltz No. 14 in E Minor. A posthumous work by Chopin.

A romantic waltz, bittersweet and heart-rending.

A casual piece. A farewell – Masaru had long before decided it would be his last piece.

The quiet final curtain. He never did like drawn-out endings.

Masaru finished the waltz and quickly stood up, once again enveloped in thunderous applause.

He took in, with his entire body, how excited and moved the audience were as they stamped their feet.

He bowed, eyes closed, and savoured the feeling. *It's over.*

Even after he withdrew to the wings, the applause showed no sign of letting up.

A Masked Ball

RIVETING. AS EVER, MASARU'S performance had captured the affection of the entire audience, and they were still buzzing. This was the phrase that sprang to mind for Aya, seated in a corner of the concert hall.

Not *wonderful*, or *amazing*.

Riveting.

Aya had understood that Masaru had related a grand drama. She hadn't known it was some nineteenth-century tale, but the sense of a tumultuous human drama came through vividly.

They shared mental images of certain works – Prokofiev's Piano Concerto No. 2 as a noir piece, the No. 3 like *Star Wars*, so Aya felt like she could picture the image Masaru had of the Sonata in B Minor.

I get it, she realized. *This feeling of the piece being so* riveting *is because it's performed by a friend, someone I'm close to.*

It had only been a couple of days since they'd met after so many years, yet Aya felt she knew what made Masaru tick.

When performing with others, she'd often felt as if she'd touched their essence when something resonated deep down – at the level of the soul. She knew that as a listener grew to know the personality of a performer, an understanding of their playing deepened.

But this *riveting* performance from Masaru was unlike anything she'd previously experienced.

Part of it was Masaru's wealth of originality. He was an exceptional and charming pianist. His interpretations were vivid and well defined, and always interesting.

But that wasn't all. Aya pondered this as she looked around at the audience, excitedly discussing their impressions.

Masaru was special. *To me*, she thought, *he's like a second self, a part of me. And I've never felt that way about anyone else before.*

Is this love I'm feeling? Aya tilted her head and thought about it, trying to be objective.

Masaru was attractive, no doubt about it, and popular with women. Any woman would be happy to get to know him better. Maybe she was just getting worked up because an attractive, wonderful guy was being nice to her.

Of course she felt a stirring of love inside.

But the certainty she felt was dispassionate. Not a thrill of emotion. It was the same certainty she had when she was performing and sensed she was observing herself from above.

This was the first time she'd ever experienced this – that someone's performances were so completely different from hers yet made her feel as if *she* was the one performing. Performances that made her believe, *I know him. I understand what he is feeling.*

When she compared this to how she'd felt when listening to Jin Kazama, she understood how special this was.

She sensed a closeness, an empathy, to Jin as well.

Especially the other day as they played the *Moonlight Sonata* together, she'd felt a oneness with him, a dizziness and drive as they vied to outdo each other.

But that was momentary. Just a passing sensation that filled her while performing with him. Something close to accidental, really.

When she wasn't with him, she felt distanced from him. To Aya, Jin's genius was mystical, something she could never grasp. Masaru's genius and Jin's were worlds apart.

A genius you could understand, and a genius you could not. What was *that* all about? Their aims were different? Or was it their way of thinking?

There was something elusive about Jin Kazama, an unaffected quality, even an occasional glimpse of a certain coolness, detachment. God's mercilessness must be something like this, she imagined.

At any rate, she'd never known how entrancing it could be to listen to a performance by someone she knew.

Aya had a feeling she might get addicted to this new discovery. She'd always loved listening to other pianists and suspected now she'd love it even more.

ANYONE FOLLOWING MASARU WAS UNLUCKY. That was the only way to describe it. The impression Masaru left was so striking that most of the audience could barely recall who had come after.

But in the third round these were, one and all, highly skilled pianists. The Frenchman who followed Masaru put on a fine performance.

Through colourful compositions by Debussy and Ravel he created a unique atmosphere, and succeeded in drawing in the audience. The structure of the programme revealed a clear, well-considered vision.

I can sort of understand French pianists, Akashi Takashima thought.

Maybe it's my own preconceptions, but French pianists have a translucent feeling, as if swathed in pale pastels.

A bit simplistic to say this, but it felt as if you were inside an Impressionist painting. Not just the ambience, but as if you could hear Impressionist colours glimmering in the sounds they produced.

The world seemed borderless these days, but there was no escaping one's roots. The scenery and features of the land where you were raised were indelibly imprinted on your body.

When people listen to me, do they see a green mulberry orchard, and feel the wind blowing through it? wondered Akashi.

Before he knew it, the first day of the third round drew to a close with the final pianist.

It was a tall, slim young man from China – handsome and highly educated.

He too was carrying the soil of his homeland, the great rivers, the mountain ranges, the boundless plains.

Hmm, I don't recall this competitor.

Jennifer Chan had grabbed all the attention, and few had noticed the pianist who was now enthralling the audience.

A robust version of Beethoven, with a generosity of spirit, and a determined core, expressing Beethovian struggle.

The programme said he'd studied at an American conservatory. Considering his age, he must have spent most of his life in the US. And yet what he carried with him wasn't the North American continent, but Eurasia. It was Asian blood coursing through his scalp, his eyes and beneath his skin.

Interestingly, in the first and second rounds Akashi hadn't detected much of the pianists' backgrounds in their performances. Instead, he'd felt how the world had become more homogeneous, the performances flattened out, all resembling each other.

But now, in the third round, he sensed the *background* of each and every performer.

When only the most technically advanced competitors remained – or to put it another way, the strongest ones – the more their essence, their roots, began to shine through.

Music is truly a universal language, thought Akashi.

The fact that he himself had been eliminated no longer occurred to him.

People streamed out of the concert hall, the lobby was now steeped in a feeling of both exhaustion and satisfaction, of having had one's fill.

BUT I DON'T DISLIKE THIS *sort of atmosphere*, Kanade thought. That feeling of a long competition entering its last stages and approaching a climax. The thrilling sense when the number of competitors has been whittled down. The sensation of how very tough and unrelenting it all was.

Putting aside the question of whether it was right or wrong to reduce music to a battle, the fact remained that that was part of what made a competition so compelling.

'That was so much fun, wasn't it?' said Aya, seated next to her. 'I get it now, why they say the semi-finals in the national high-school baseball tournament are always the best to watch.'

'High-school baseball?'

Kanade raised her eyebrows, but she understood what Aya was getting at.

By now the audience knew all about each pianist and their personality. They could ponder how they ranked against each other, with each audience member becoming, in effect, a judge. It was fun trying to predict the outcome. It might sound insensitive, but you couldn't deny that one of the pleasures at this stage was betting on which performer would come out on top.

'Which performance did you like best, Kanade-*chan*?' Aya asked.

'Honestly, they were all good.'

Kanade pictured the faces of the pianists.

She felt sorry for what had happened with the first performer, Alexei Zakhaev, but everyone since had performed exceptionally.

'I always feel sorry for the pianists when the standard is this high. Though of course winning a low-level competition wouldn't make anyone all that happy.'

'True enough.'

It was hard to tell if Aya was even aware that she herself was one of the competitors.

'But I think anyone would have to say that Masaru is the real star. You feel like you want to hear him again, want to see him, to go to his concerts. Part of that's just simple charisma.'

'Yeah, that's important for a musician,' Aya agreed. 'For people to want to hear him again, to hear him play more.'

'Every piece was great. I'd never heard the Sibelius played live before; it's the kind of choice you'd expect from him. Though a bit risky, perhaps.'

'It could end up sounding a bit forgettable if you didn't play it well.'

'The last pianist, too, the Chinese man, was really good.'

'A lot of potential there, for sure,' Aya concurred. 'Oh, and speak of the devil, here's our star right now.'

Kanade looked out at the lobby where Masaru, a head taller than most, was surrounded by his fans.

'He is popular.'

'No wonder.'

It wasn't just girls who were after his autograph, but older audience members too, including quite a few older men who seemed to have a good ear for music. Masaru's popularity spanned all age groups.

'Aya-*chan*, how about practice? Would you like to borrow the same piano as before? Shall I call Ms Harada?' Kanade glanced at her watch.

Aya looked at a loss. There was silence for a moment.

'Um . . . Not today.'

'Are you sure? The other day you couldn't wait to play.'

'I know,' Aya said. 'That day I couldn't wait to start playing the cadenza.' Her eyes darted about. 'For some reason, though, I just don't feel like it today.'

Her expression showed she found it odd herself. Looking at her, Kanade felt a cold sense of misgiving.

Was Aya perhaps enjoying the competition *too* much? Enjoying it so much as a spectator that she'd lost all sense of tension? It was all right to perform without fearing the results. But the way she was behaving now – was it really OK? Tomorrow was a critical point in the competition, after all.

In the first- and second-round performances, Kanade had grown more convinced than ever that her own ear had been spot on in recognizing Aya's genius, but with this attitude of Aya's today she couldn't decide how things would turn out.

Aya had not yet made a complete comeback to playing on stage.

Kanade studied her friend's face, the vacant, uneasy look in her eyes. It was a look Kanade knew well, the expression Aya had when she was unsure of herself.

She'd had that look in her eyes so many times. When she'd decided to be in the competition. When she was choosing which dresses to wear on stage. When she arrived at the concert hall for the first time. In those moments Aya's mind was elsewhere, somewhere Kanade knew nothing about. Kanade wanted to chase after her, but knew she'd never catch up.

If this was part of the music world, of the artistic world, all well and good. But something about this seemed different.

Kanade felt a vague impatience and unease well up in her.

'AA-CHANNN!'

Masaru had spotted them and was waving as he made his way over.

The shining prince. Every time Kanade saw him, she was bowled over by his aura. Maybe this was just momentary, yet what he radiated right now was the kind of light that only someone who was promised everything could have.

'Ma-*kun*, you were great!' Aya exclaimed.

'Really? I'm glad.'

'I knew it when I first saw your programme, but when I heard you play I thought, *wow*, these pieces are perfect for you.'

'That's what I was hoping. How was the Sibelius? Not too sugary?'

'You gave it the perfect amount of sweetness. Pianists often hold back on that, but some things have to be made sweet.'

'I knew you'd get it, Aa-*chan*.'

Kanade felt a little of the envy and sadness she'd had towards these musical geniuses when they were all at the beach, but mingled with it now was a sense of compassion. The innocence that they possessed – was this a kind of blessing they received for being unable to grasp the emotions and subtleties of those who were *not* geniuses?

'Aa-*chan*, I'm starved. Let's grab dinner.' Masaru stretched.

'And me. Just listening to music makes me famished. Kanade-*chan*, what should we eat?'

Kanade was lost in her own thoughts. 'I don't know . . . Curry, maybe?'

'Sounds good.'

'But not too spicy. That'd be overstimulating.'

'Come on – I'm up for something good and spicy!'

'So you like spicy food, Ma-*kun*?'

'I do. Before I go home, I want to try out the super-spicy ramen I read about, at a place in Ebisu in Tokyo.'

As they were about to leave, Kanade stole a glance at them.

Masaru showing up again was a good opportunity for Aya. There were people it would be better for her not to meet as fellow competitors – since Aya wouldn't feel any inspiration from a half-hearted connection. But these two were geniuses whose paths had crossed as children. And Masaru was so obviously an appealing, wonderful young man, both as a musician and as a boyfriend. Reconnecting with him, Kanade hoped, might entice Aya back to the stage.

Part of that had already happened, but perhaps they were a little *too* much alike?

Kanade observed them, as if checking out their mutual empathy.

Aya saw Masaru as her alter ego, not as a rival. That much was clear. Even though there was a part of Masaru that viewed her as a rival.

Could it be that Aya felt satisfied that her alter ego had delivered an exceptional performance? Wasn't she, in part, entrusting her own music to him? And planning to return to being simply a spectator?

'Hey – what about Jin Kazama?' Aya said, as if suddenly struck by this. She came to a halt and scanned the lobby.

'I don't see him.'

'Was he in the concert hall?'

'Now that you mention it, I didn't see him. Which is strange, since I was sure he'd come to listen.'

Aya paused to look around.

Kanade was startled.

Just maybe, the person to persuade Aya back to the piano, who really could get her back on stage was—

An image came to Kanade, of the boy in his cap.

While Aya and the others were enjoying their curry, Jin Kazama was with his host. He was in the tatami room, ensconced with the florist, Mr Togashi, not moving a muscle as he watched him expertly clipping flowers with a pair of scissors, as if the scissors were an extension of his fingers.

'Jin, have you had any dinner?' Togashi asked, and shot the boy a glance. The boy's gaze was fixed on Togashi's hands.

Jin didn't realize he'd been spoken to.

Togashi suddenly felt something alarming about this boy before him, as if all the air in the room was being sucked up by him.

'What? Oh. Yes – I did eat.'

The boy's eyes, like clear mirrors, flickered to life. He looked over at Togashi.

Togashi heaved a sigh of relief.

TOGASHI WAS OFTEN AWAY, AND even when he wasn't, he was occupied with his business or the flower-arranging studio. Which meant that he'd had hardly any time for this son of an old friend. Togashi had let his family and staff look after the boy, and was relieved to learn that Jin, used to staying in other people's houses, wasn't a high-maintenance guest at all. Yet still he felt bad about not having enough time to spare for him.

Early one morning as he was about to leave, he bumped into Jin, who asked him if, when he had time, he could teach him about flower arranging. It seemed that he'd peeked into their shop and studio and had seen Togashi putting together flower arrangements.

Did Jin really have time? But Togashi was happy that the boy was interested and readily agreed, though his busy schedule was like an intricate puzzle, and it was going to be hard to find a slot.

He was aware of the high level of the Yoshigae International Piano Competition, and how stars came out of it, but he didn't know how good Jin Kazama was, nor how he'd become so talked about at the competition. He'd only heard from his family that Jin had made it to the third round. *This boy's performance must have been amazing*, Togashi thought.

If Jin had been eliminated earlier in the competition, he might very well have travelled straight back to France, and they wouldn't have had the opportunity to be together like this.

One of Togashi's clients had suddenly cancelled, and so Jin had come back as soon as the first day of the third round was over. He had picked up a rice ball at a convenience store on the way back and was still munching on it as he hurried into the house, so in that sense it was true he had eaten dinner.

As he sat down, with the luxury of spending a few hours with Jin for the first time, Togashi sensed what a remarkable person he was – someone who, a bit like himself, possessed an atypical talent.

There weren't many people like Togashi, able to be both a skilled practitioner of Japanese flower arranging and the owner of a thriving floral business. Most flower arrangers had florists that supplied them with flowers, but Togashi saw the floral business as his main occupation, and thus was viewed as a bit of an outlier in the *ikebana* world. It would be as if, instead of a musician adopting the piano and playing it, a piano maker also had a career as a professional pianist.

Togashi didn't refer to his work as *ikebana*, the usual term for flower arranging, but rather as *noike*, literally 'field arranging'.

His family's line could be traced back to Kyoto and a school of flower arranging that was very rare these days, known as *keshiki-ike*, or 'scenic arrangements'.

As the name implied, these arrangements reproduced in miniature hills and fields, and famous scenic spots, with some compositions replicating Heian-period scenery, giving a sense of how Heian-period gardens would have looked, so much so that historians used them as reference material in place of written documents.

They occasionally had the opportunity to prepare larger-scale landscapes, and were preparing one now for an event nearby. Jin had seen this and shown an interest.

Togashi explained, simply, to Jin the three basic principles of flower arranging – *ten-chi-jin* – and demonstrated these in a flower arrangement for him.

The techniques of *noike*, though, were used to extend the lives of plants without overburdening them. You needed to know basic methods of how best to cut and bend flowers, and how much water and heat a plant needed and the best environment for it. When you had an overall grasp of these aspects, you were doing *noike*.

Jin listened closely. 'May I try cutting some?' He looked at the scissors in Togashi's hands.

'OK. But these scissors take a lot of strength to use. You're a pianist and you have an important performance tomorrow, right? It's hard on your hands, so you'd better take it easy.'

Despite Togashi's warning, Jin reached out for the scissors

and started clipping away, testing their sharpness and how they worked. The look in his eyes was earnest and intense, like that of a researcher, and it was clear his powers of observation were considerable.

'Jin, show me your hands.'

Togashi found it hard to believe the boy had never used this kind of scissors before – his skill with them was impressive – and he took the boy's hands in his own.

'Oh.' Togashi unconsciously expressed his admiration. *What beautiful hands*, he thought. Large, fleshy and soft.

Not the delicate hands of an artist, but more generous hands, fit for practical work. Hands that combined those of a craftsman and businessman, that could pick up anything. Hands involved in something larger scale.

Togashi had an odd feeling of déjà vu.

In this vision he was older, and he and Jin, now a vigorous young man, were carrying handfuls of branches for an international event where they were arranging flowers.

There was a grand piano in the hall, too, and Jin had lifted the lid and was tuning the piano as Togashi prepared the flowers.

Togashi was perplexed by this image and shook his head.

What was *that?*

'Um, Mr Togashi, when you arrange flowers, what are you thinking about? You arrange them so fast. As if you already have the final arrangement in your head.'

Jin picked up the scissors and traced the curve of the blades with his fingers.

This was a common reaction. Almost everyone, when they saw Togashi arrange flowers, was amazed at the speed with which he worked. He completed the compositions at lightning speed, as if every second counted.

'Well, doing it quickly puts less of a burden on the flowers. That's one of the things I aim for.' It was a question he was often asked, and this was his standard answer, but for some reason he felt this boy needed more than a pat response.

'It's true that when I'm standing in a spot where I'm about to make a *noike* arrangement, the scene pops into my head. It's only there for a moment and I can't let it escape from me. If I want to reproduce what I see in my head, I need to hurry. To do it quickly, you need to master the technique, which is why I practised so much. At first, the image would disappear while I was working, and that would frustrate me.'

'Wow.' Jin was impressed. 'Speed.'

'That's right. You need speed so that fleeting image doesn't escape you.'

The boy considered this, his eyes once more resembling mirrors.

'Excuse me if this sounds rude,' Jin said, 'but isn't flower arranging a sort of contradiction? You cut things from the natural world, bend them and so on, and set them up to look as if they're alive. Don't you sense the contradiction in that? To intentionally kill something and then make it appear as if it's alive?'

The boy's tone was so matter-of-fact, it startled Togashi. The boy might seem innocent enough on the surface, but underneath was an unexpected level of maturity.

'I do feel that,' Togashi admitted. 'But our existence is contradictory to begin with, since it's premised on having to kill something in order to live. Eating – the basis of our survival – is based on that. The pleasure in the act of eating is but a fine line away from being sinful. Whenever I do *noike* arranging, I do feel a sense of guilt and sinfulness. Which is why I endeavour to make that moment of arranging the very best it can be.'

Togashi paused for a moment.

'A make-up company states it on their ads, don't they? *Make every second, every life, beautiful*. I think each moment is eternal. The opposite is true, too. Creating the supreme moment means that, as I arrange the flowers, I get the strong sensation that I'm living it. And since that moment is eternal, you could say I'm living eternally.'

Jin gazed upwards, as if taking in the meaning of Togashi's words.

'Umm. *Ikebana* and music are similar,' he said.

'Really?'

Jin gently laid the scissors down on the tatami and folded his arms.

'In terms of reproducibility, it's the same as *ikebana* – just one moment. You can't keep it in this world for ever. It's just that one moment, which vanishes. But that moment is eternal, and when you're reproducing it, you can live in that eternal moment.'

Jin looked at the tip of the branch that Togashi was arranging. There was a pattern of leaves on it, the last of the autumnal foliage.

'Umm—' Jin murmured to himself. 'Then bringing music out is—?'

'Excuse me?' Togashi asked.

After a moment Jin looked back at him.

'I promised my piano teacher that I would take music out of its confined space indoors, and bring it out somewhere bigger.'

Togashi was bewildered.

Take music out. Togashi didn't know much about the music world, but wasn't it a bit rare for such a young man to consider things like that?

'I'm guessing you don't simply mean things like outdoor concerts and such,' Togashi asked.

And the boy said, 'I think it's different. We did lots of performances outdoors, but that wasn't it. I still haven't been able to take it outside.'

Shaking his head, he picked up the flower-arranging scissors again and stared at the glistening blades.

'When you arrange flowers, Mr Togashi, the branches and flowers are alive. As if they're totally unaware they've been killed.'

Togashi flinched at the word *killed* but couldn't take his eyes off the boy gazing at the scissor blades.

'One moment, and eternity and . . . Reproducibility—'

Unconcerned that Togashi was staring at him, the boy continued to focus on the shining blades.

I Want You

IT WAS DARK OUTSIDE the window when she awoke, the pane of glass distorting the view.

A cold rain seemed to be falling, and she felt a chill creeping in.

Mieko shivered despite herself.

The first rain of winter. That's how it used to feel.

The last day of round three was about to begin, and it promised to be a big day.

She'd long passed the peak of exhaustion and was experiencing a sort of high. Today was the last real judging they had to do, and she felt pumped, her emotions a mix of anticipation at being released and of knowing she'd miss it after it was all over.

That's right, she thought. *That's how it is.*

I always feel like this when a competition is winding down.

The sense that, though there were certainly little cliques and differences of opinion, she and the other judges, having shared so much time together, had become like comrades-in-arms.

As if they'd literally fought a battle together.

There were so many older judges, which made her feel a bit of an underling, and they were all, as a whole, hardy people. If they hadn't been, they never would have made a go of a business that required people to listen to music. Their generation of musicians, who'd survived a century of war, were, at their core, unshakably tough.

Mieko exchanged a quick greeting with the other judges and strolled into the concert hall.

As always the first person she spotted was Nathaniel. She realized she always sought him out.

He was a man she used to love, a man she'd spent years with. She still had residual feelings for him, and every time she saw him, she felt a faint ache inside.

Nathaniel quickly took his seat, and she knew he was lost in thought.

What was he thinking about? His pupil's future? The wife he'd divorced and his beloved daughter? Or the orchestra he'd be conducting next week?

No, she knew it was none of these.

Mieko took her own seat and shook her head.

It probably wasn't only Nathaniel, but the other judges, too, who were surely thinking along the same lines.

Would Jin Kazama make it to the finals? More accurately – would they *let* him reach the finals?

Mieko could think of little else they might squabble over. The other pianists worthy of reaching the finals would be decided as a matter of course.

The judges sat down in their seats, quietly waiting for the performance to begin.

But Mieko knew. They might pretend to be calm, but there was an expectancy there.

She could tell they were secretly looking forward to Jin's performance, wondering what that trickster would come up with next.

Mieko couldn't deny that she, too, was excited. Like a child waiting to unwrap a present, trying to be patient, she wondered what he was going to pull off this time.

From the very first round, opinion on Jin had been clearly divided between those who supported him and those who were adamantly opposed. Somehow he'd managed, as if treading on thin ice, to make it this far down a narrow, treacherous path.

What struck her was that as time passed the number of his supporters slowly increased.

Even among those judges who'd initially experienced a physical revulsion to him, there'd had been a growing sense of wanting to hear him play again. Those who'd shown a clear disdain towards his playing were, almost despite themselves, now reluctantly expressing the hope of hearing him one more time. They were already fans.

Who in the world *was* he?

What was he?

Mieko knew even his supporters found it hard to figure him out. They'd heard him perform twice but were still puzzled as to how to react. And Mieko was one of them.

While she still felt abashed for, in Smirnoff's words, *committing apostasy* regarding Jin, it was also an unmistakable fact that she was drawn to his playing. Yet she still questioned her judgement of him, and remained unsure whether she may have been taken in by something fraudulent.

And the judges were dimly aware of how devious and frightening Hoffmann's trap was.

They knew, too, that whether they allowed Jin to reach the finals or not would reveal *their* own stance as musicians.

Mieko could picture Hoffmann smiling, that strangely impish, satisfied grin.

Back at the Paris audition, Mieko thought, *we were all neatly caught in his trap. A fuse had been laid out, linking that competition and this one.*

We were all so fascinated by the wonderful packaging we didn't notice what a powerful bomb lay inside the box.

The bomb that Hoffmann had set had a long, long fuse attached.

He had prepared this while he was still alive – no, this went back all the way to when he first started instructing Jin Kazama. Mieko didn't know when he'd lit it, but the fuse continued to burn patiently, inch by inch, to the point where it would end in a major explosion.

The ones to have picked up that box were these very judges here.

What a gift.

The flame on the fuse was snaking closer and closer.

Should they throw away the box without opening it? Or stamp out the lit fuse?

Or should they hold on to the box and release an amazing firework display?

Mieko couldn't help picturing Hoffmann, even now, coolly appraising them.

Nathaniel must be the one who sensed that gaze the most.

So what are you going to do? *You?* You, as a *musician*?

These questions were being posed to each and every judge, like a knife blade pointing straight at their forehead.

It was likely Hoffmann wouldn't have objected if they threw the box away. If at the last minute they decided, 'Nah, this won't do,' and stamped out the fuse, the most he would have done would be to give a little shrug.

If he saw them throw the box aside, and cover it with a blanket, fearful of the explosion, he would probably have stridden right over, picked up the box and left without a word.

As he had said, it was entirely up to them whether they would see Jin Kazama as a *gift*, or as a *disaster*.

Mieko brought her bottle of mineral water up to her mouth.

She was surprised at how parched she was.

Wow, I really am tense. What is going on?

She gulped down another mouthful.

There is one thing I'm sure of. Mieko wiped her mouth and leaned back in her seat.

If we do eliminate Jin Kazama today, sometime in the near future I'll have to learn to live with that, as one of the judges who cut him from the competition.

THE CONCERT HALL FILLED TO capacity almost as soon as the doors swung open.

Their eyes glittering with excitement, the crowd jostled for good seats.

Aya and Kanade, along with Masaru, were relieved they were able to find places at the back.

The hall grew stifling with a suppressed excitement and fevered anticipation.

'It's packed already.'

'Things are finally getting pretty lively.'

Aya and Masaru whispered to each other, but there was already an invisible barrier between them, between the one whose performance was over and the one who was yet to perform.

'You're lucky, Ma-*kun*, to be able to sit back and enjoy the rest of the third round.'

'Sorry about you being the very last one, Aa-*chan*.' Masaru shot her a wry smile. 'But being the pianist whose performance wraps up a competition – that isn't something you get to experience very often. You're here the longest.'

'I guess that's one way of looking at it.' Aya flashed her own wry smile.

The one who can enjoy the competition the longest. And can fully savour it. To turn that around, though, it also meant being the one who suffered the most.

'Where's Jin, anyway?'

Aya was a bit startled. 'I don't see him. He's always off in that corner over there.'

Kanade, too, looked around. 'He prefers being in the aisle to a seat.'

'He said he can concentrate on listening better there.'

'He wasn't here last night, either. Maybe he's off practising?'

As she listened to Masaru and Kanade, Aya felt strangely uneasy.

I'm so out of it. I don't feel like I'm aware I'm the last one to go on. What am I so preoccupied about? Aya tried to pinpoint the source of her unease, but she just felt detached, and was puzzled by her lack of emotion.

To fully savour it. It was true she'd discovered what a competition was all about. The pleasure of listening to such a variety of pianists, and learning about their different backgrounds.

But this idea of *savouring* it was different from how Masaru meant it.

You're here the longest.

He meant it as a competitor, as a musician. Savouring the battle itself.

I'm different from him, Aya thought. *I wasn't* savouring *it all as a competitor, but as a listener.*

Aya felt her mood sink even lower, as if gravity was pulling her straight down in her seat, yanking her into the abyss.

Why in the world am I here, anyway?

That was the question she'd been avoiding all this time.

The clamour of the audience faded and Aya was seated there in the hall, alone.

Being up on stage *was* fun, for sure. It felt good to play in front of an audience.

And I could see Mother. And fly off into space.

I've just been running away, pretending not to face my own fears. I know that now.

So it was a valuable experience. I could really feel, all over again, how wonderful music is.

But so what?

Aya was astonished at how much she'd lost interest in being a competitor.

Music will always be a part of my life. And I'll never stop performing. That is for sure. But that, and this competition I'm in right now, are not organically connected. There's a disconnect somewhere, and I don't feel this competition's linked to my musical life.

Aya felt a sudden chill. She could picture herself, the competition over, saying, 'Well, that was fun. I'd like to go and hear another one,' and leaving the concert hall.

But why was that so frightening? She was confused.

Wasn't that enough? That was the type of person she was, yes? And she liked that type, someone who viewed a competition she herself was playing in as basically a very long and enjoyable concert.

But was that OK?

*

It's OK, another part of her said, the voice sounding a touch desperate, hysterical.

You accomplished what you needed to do. You let Prof. Hamazaki avoid embarrassment, didn't you? The audience loved you, and reporters even came to interview you. You saved face, and lived up to expectations, yes?

But was that true? A voice of doubt kept nagging at her.

So what am I supposed to do now? Aya didn't notice she was damp with a cold sweat.

The bell rang, the audience scurrying to their seats, but none of it registered with Aya, only the gravity pulling her deeper down into her seat.

THE FIRST PIANIST WAS A Korean man. Tall and charismatic, with a Rachmaninoff-centred programme that perfectly displayed his technical prowess.

'Wow, he really is pretty flashy, isn't he?'

'He wasn't like that in the first and second rounds.'

Kanade overheard Aya and Masaru whispering to each other. And she agreed.

There were all types of competitors, some who were slow starters and only came into their own as the contest progressed. This young man had peaked at just the right moment in the schedule. Making it to the third round must surely have boosted his confidence, too.

'He's really cool,' Kanade whispered to Aya.

'Yeah, he's going to be popular.'

Many in the audience must have agreed, for when his performance was over girls screamed their approval.

The next competitor was Korean, too. A young woman, the type who made you fully relish the music.

Those who'd made it to the third round were all at a level where they each made you think: *This is the one*.

This girl was barely twenty, yet there was a maturity to her playing.

So young, yet she had such a sober, restrained style, Kanade thought, impressed.

'She's great, too.'

'They're all so good.'

How amazingly talented Aya and Masaru must be to stand out in such a group, Kanade thought.

And don't forget Jin Kazama.

She could sense that the audience was looking forward to him.

Yesterday it was Masaru they had eagerly awaited, but today it was Jin.

That unique atmosphere of his, that unique sound.

It was all so sensational, yet she felt, suddenly, uneasy at how excited she got. His was such an unusual talent, one she couldn't put into words. She felt captive to his sound, yet when it was over she couldn't say what it was that held her so in thrall.

Kanade was still struggling with what to make of him, something that seldom happened to her.

She scanned the audience stealthily for Jin.

Dark shadows filling the corners of the hall.

Today it was standing room only from the morning on.

Where was he?

The Jin whom Kanade was so concerned about was at the very back of the auditorium.

He'd woken up early and, unable to sit still, had wandered about in the rain outside, then slipped into the concert hall just moments before the performances began, joining those standing, and squatting down among them.

He hunched forward, swaying as he listened to the Korean girl's ardour.

Yeah – that part's really nice too.

He was with the girl, off in her musical world.

This part was a castle, it seemed. Inside an ancient building.

A solid, tranquil world. A calm air about the place, the accumulation of years. The girl had on a classic dress and was completely immersed. Seemingly unaware that Jin was right beside her.

Jin gazed around him.

Stone walls. Inlaid wooden flooring.

Lamplight flickering.

Hmm – a historical place. Something from olden times in Europe, maybe.

Jin felt someone was calling him. He left the girl's side. His consciousness was gradually transported somewhere else.

Outward.

He left the castle and went out to a wide-open space.

Soft grass underfoot. A broad grassy plain.

Off in the distance he spied Maestro Hoffmann. Fingers linked behind his back, walking along, head slightly down.

To the outside. To the outside.

How was he supposed to take it outside? Take music out into the wider world?

Jin ran after his teacher.

Maestro Hoffmann, wait!

The wind was blowing, and he felt the sunlight on his cheeks.

He could sense the light, but the scene was unclear.

Hoffmann halted and turned his head. Jin caught a glimpse of his face, but then his teacher turned and walked off again.

And then he heard a *snip, snip*.

Jin stopped running and looked in the direction of the sound.

Togashi was cutting branches. He was snipping off pussy willow at a furious pace with his razor-sharp flower-arranging scissors and gathering it in his arms.

As quickly as I can. So they don't notice they're dead.

Eternity is one instant, and one instant is eternal.

Jin opened his eyes wide.

There was a roar of applause.

Before he realized it the girl's performance was over, and she was bowing deeply. The applause swelled even louder.

The heavy doors behind him whooshed open, and Jin hurriedly got to his feet. He was caught up in the crowd streaming out into the lobby.

Outside. Outside.

He walked vacantly over towards the floor-to-ceiling windows.

You could feel the cold beyond the glass.

A chill rain fell outside, and people were popping open umbrellas as they exited.

It's winter already, he thought.

Jin laid a palm flat on the glass. It was much colder than he'd expected, and instinctively he pulled his hand away.

As he watched, he was still on that grassy wind-swept plain, the two scenes merging into one.

Maestro Hoffmann was far away now, about to vanish in the mist.

What should I do? And how? Jin asked the far-away figure of Hoffmann.

He had played the piano outdoors with Hoffmann, but that was different. There was no sense of freeing music. It was fun, but that wasn't what Hoffmann had meant by *Take it out*.

'Have you ever felt that way, Maestro?' Jin once asked him.

Hoffmann smiled, and said, 'I have, though not very often.' He then gestured with one hand, as if pinching something between his fingers.

Jin looked for the exit. He wanted to breathe in the fresh air.

The automatic door slid open, cold air rushing in.

The chilled, damp air outside.

The scent of winter.

Jin quietly began to walk off.

The concert hall was part of a larger multi-purpose building, and you could walk almost to the station without getting wet. Only the stone paving in the plaza directly in front of the hall, which lacked a roof, was wet from the rain.

Jin gazed up at the sky.

There was no wind, the rain was falling softly.

In the distance, there was a low rumble of thunder.

Winter thunder. He felt something bubble up from deep within him.

He couldn't see any lightning.

The grey rain inscribed dark lines as it fell.

Under the covered walkway the rain blew in sideways, making Jin's cheeks feel clammy.

Take it outside.

Even as the cold rain lashed at him, Jin still felt as if he were locked up somewhere. The impatient, anxious feeling he'd had ever since he woke up.

Where should he go? Where should he take it?

He took off his cap, put it back on again, and carried on walking.

There was a long tunnel leading to the station.

Under the fluorescent lights, pedestrians had folded up their umbrellas. Jin joined them.

I want to go out, somewhere expansive.

The damp-smelling tunnel was stifling.

This isn't it.

Jin started to hurry.

He emerged from the tunnel, almost running.

Out into the empty plaza in front of the station.

Jin came to a halt, out of breath.

The station loomed above, the sky wider now.

The grey, blank sky spread out above him. No hint of light.

He stared vacantly up at it.

The rain quietly tapped against his cap. The world filled with the whisper of the rain. Car horns blared, and hawkers clamoured, yet the rainfall was so very quiet.

The honeybees aren't flying today, he thought.

I can't hear that buzzing sound I miss.

Where is the Maestro now?

TAKUBO, THE STAGE MANAGER, WAS startled when he spotted the boy rooted to the spot in the wings, looking like a ghost.

On stage the pianist before Jin Kazama was in the middle of his performance.

'Is anything the matter, Kazama-*kun*?'

Takubo tried to question him calmly but got no reaction.

Usually the next performer waited in the green room, where they could practise, and they would be summoned only when the previous performer had left the stage.

Some arrived early, some practised until the very last minute – there were all kinds – but in Jin Kazama's case he did almost no warm-up practice and told them he preferred to listen to the other competitors' performances from the concert hall, so they were used to him not appearing until just before he went on.

Some thoughtful person must have let him go backstage early, but clearly something was wrong with him.

Even when Takubo addressed him, Jin's eyes remained unfocused.

His hair was tousled – nothing unusual about that – but his head and shirt seemed wet from the rain.

Takubo quietly went over to some staff members. 'Could somebody get me a towel?' he asked.

He handed it to Jin. 'You can use this to dry yourself,' he said, but the boy was unresponsive.

He had no choice but to take Jin by the arm, walk him over to a corner of the wings, and towel off the boy's hair himself.

The feeling of the boy's tousled, soft hair reminded Takubo of his own son back when he was little.

How long has it been, he wondered, *since I dried off a child's head like this?*

He was filled, for some reason, with a bittersweet nostalgia.

'Kazama-*kun*, are you OK? Are you feeling ill?' Takubo whispered in the boy's ear. It seemed to startle him – Jin's eyes widened and began to dart around.

Takubo put a finger to his lips to signal they had to be quiet. 'We're backstage,' he said.

'Is it my turn?' Jin looked surprised.

'Not yet. The competitor before you is not yet halfway through.'

Jin was silent for a moment, then let out a big sigh.

He seemed to have finally returned to the real world, his eyes no longer blank.

'Sit over there.'

Takubo pointed to a small stool and the boy obeyed. Head wrapped in the towel, he sat, lost in thought. His eyes had a look in them that Takubo had never seen before.

He was so focused it was almost frightening.

Thankfully he apparently wasn't feeling ill, or panicky.

Takubo felt relieved. Later he'd have to check with the staff about why Jin had been allowed backstage so early.

For nearly thirty minutes Jin sat perfectly still.

Always full of surprises, this one, the stage manager thought.

Takubo cast a few glimpses at him, and glanced out at the stage.

The final piece of the programme was over.

Takubo opened the stage door, and smiled at the young Russian, whose face was flushed as he took in the roar of applause.

There was nothing else like the joy of seeing a performer's face at this moment, Takubo thought.

The applause didn't let up.

They wanted an encore, and the young man, with an abashed smile, went back out on stage.

One more piece, I suppose.

Takubo glanced over at Jin. The boy was staring at a point on the floor, and hadn't budged an inch.

Takubo realized that neither the cheers, nor the applause, had registered with him.

While congratulating the returning competitor, Takubo was still aware of the boy sitting in the darkness of the wings.

What could he be thinking? And what was he seeing?

Takubo felt uneasy as he heard the audience stand up and noisily head for the exits.

Asano, the piano tuner, came over.

'Hello,' he said, as Takubo motioned with his head at Jin Kazama seated there.

'What's the matter with him?' Asano asked the stage manager.

'I have no idea. He seems lost in thought.'

'But I need to tune the piano – the pianist before him really pounded away at it.'

Jin would be using the same piano as the young man who'd preceded him.

'Kazama-*kun*. Kazama-*kun*.' Asano approached Jin and crouched down next to him.

'Oh, Mr Asano.'

Jin looked down. His expression was calm, and Takubo told himself it was going to be OK.

'So, how would you like me to tune it today? I'll tune it any way you prefer.'

Asano smiled at him, and Jin thought it over for a moment.

'. . . I'd like the sound to reach heaven,' he said.

'What?' Asano and Takubo both said at once.

With a serious look, Jin pointed upwards.

'Make it so Maestro Hoffmann can hear it.'

His voice couldn't have been more earnest.

Asano staggered back a step, then hurriedly straightened up, and gulped.

'Meaning what, exactly?'

'Soft,' Jin replied. 'The opposite of a crisp sound, if you would.'

AYA EIDEN WALKED INTO THE green room and quickly changed into her dress.

This one was red, almost scarlet. Her third outfit already.

She recalled the red dresses Jennifer Chan had worn. They were all so amazing, she thought. Where did she buy those, anyway? Or did rich people have them made to measure?

Aya pictured the silver dress hanging in the wardrobe back at the hotel. The dress she was saving for the finals.

But would she have the chance to wear it?

She took no time at all changing and applying a light touch of make-up. The dress had draped sleeves, which made it easy to move her shoulders and arms. She kept on low-heeled shoes for the time being, though, and would slip into her dress shoes backstage.

Aya looked in the mirror, rotated her arms and nodded in satisfaction.

She too had done hardly any warm-up practice.

I have to hurry back to the hall to catch Jin Kazama's performance.

To avoid standing out in the dress, she decided to wear a black cardigan over it and get to the hall just minutes before the performance started.

She felt more nervous waiting for Jin's recital than for her own. With her own performances she knew what she was going to do, and they seemed to finish before she realized it.

I'm betting on him, she suddenly thought.

But betting *what*, exactly?

What do I want from that genius? Whatever I hope for from him, that's my *problem and has nothing to do with him. Yet I am trusting in him for a ray of hope, beseeching him even now.*

She clasped her hands together and squeezed hard.

It was an odd sensation.

Now that she thought of it, she'd been feeling this way since the initial round.

When she'd heard Jin Kazama's first performance, she felt she wanted to play too, to be with him. The same happened in the second round.

She was able to play her own *Spring and Ashura* because he played his, she thought. His performance stirred up the smouldering embers that lay in her darkened heart.

She was where she was now, it was fair to say, because he'd pulled her along. But what about after this? After the competition, and the days to come. Her future, her life in music. A sense of anxiety, close to fear, was creeping up on her, like a prickly burning sensation on her back.

She couldn't explain this feeling that neither Masaru nor Kanade could alleviate.

But somehow Jin Kazama could allay that anxiety for her. She felt this instinctively and trusted him.

He might pull me back, might create a reason for me to come to grips with the real world of music.

Deep down inside she'd been waiting, for a long time, for a spark. *So – I beg you*, Aya said, her words directed at Jin.

Please – bring me back. Give me the reason to return to that harsh, wonderful world.

As she wished for this, another part of her smiled ruefully, thinking, *You're pretty bold, aren't you, asking that?*

In the mirror she saw a young girl's face with a crooked smile.

So what do I do if his performance doesn't live up to my expectations? If I'm disappointed, let down. Does that mean I go ahead and quit?

The girl in the mirror wore a sarcastic smile.

All you've been doing is blaming others. Relying on other people. You're not a real musician after all. Look at Masaru. Even Kanade, and the other pianists.

They've decided to spend their whole lives as musicians. With no doubt in their minds. But you're no musician. Have you ever been one, up till now? You leave your fate up to others, so are you really ready to dedicate your whole life to music?

The prickling sensation turned into a sharp stinging pain.

That's why I'm betting it all on this! she shouted at the girl in the mirror.

Masaru is wonderful, and Kanade – I respect her so much, how earnest and sincere she is towards music. The two of them have qualities I don't have. It makes me feel jealous, guilty. A little inferior.

I admit it – I'm totally mixed up. A scheming girl who blames others for everything. But I want to play too!

Aya stared at her pale face in the mirror.

She felt her heart pounding, cold sweat breaking out at her temples.

Far off a bell sounded.

She looked up at the clock on the wall. She lifted the hem of her dress and hurried out of the green room.

'Kazama-*kun*, it's time,' Takubo said quietly.

Asano was on tenterhooks as he gazed at Jin.

The piano tuner had become a fan of Jin, and as Jin walked out into the light of the stage Asano saw him off almost with a prayer.

As thunderous applause rang out, Asano felt he was seeing a vision.

Beyond the doors was an expansive field.

A high sky. Distant white clouds. A deserted land.

And in that deserted place Jin Kazama, standing tall, was walking by himself.

Heading towards the distant horizon.

Along an untrodden path.

Where are you going? Asano called out as he watched the boy disappear beyond the doors.

Jin Kazama seemed a little different from the previous two occasions he'd been on stage.

He didn't rush up to the piano and start playing as if he couldn't wait. Instead he walked steadily towards it with a serene look.

Goodness – is he nervous? That would be unusual, Mieko thought at first.

He's looking at something far away.

Performers on stage were always solitary, but he looked even more alone.

But why? Mieko asked herself.

Standing by the piano, the boy bobbed his head in a quick bow.

The applause stopped, the audience held its breath.

The boy sat down. He glanced upwards for a moment.

The audience, too, sensed something was different.

The boy was murmuring something to himself.

Words of prayer? Or just talking to himself?

If, at this moment, Mieko could be beside him on stage, maybe she would hear him speaking to Hoffmann.

The boy grinned.

Mieko was startled.

And he began to play.

THIS WAS PROBABLY THE FIRST time Masaru had heard an Erik Satie piece played at a competition, and he doubted he ever would again.

The witty piece 'Je te veux' or 'I Want You'. A light, exhilarating waltz.

The simple melody immediately transformed the concert hall into the streets of Paris.

The clink of glasses at a café, the chatter of the clientele.

Jin's music was so smart. He was so young, yet his interpretation of Satie's chic was so mature, so knowing.

This little piece was a prologue to the hour-long programme.

Very gradually he did a ritardando—

And suddenly launched into the next piece.

A famous piece, 'Spring Song', from Mendelssohn's *Lieder ohne Worte*, or *Songs Without Words*.

What a vibrant change of scenery.

They were suddenly in a fragrant flower garden.

Lustrous spring blooms, and birds singing.

So lovely.

What a visual performance, overflowing with colour.

Next came Brahms. The Capriccio in B Minor.

The touch here became freer, unfettered. This too, was a short, smart piece, filled with melancholy, yet with a hint of humour. Tricky to perform.

This scene would be all blue, wouldn't it, Masaru thought and closed his eyes.

Scenery tinged with blue. A lakeside mansion, maybe, with the locals in traditional costume dancing in the big hall. He could see the women up on their toes.

This was no longer a performance in a competition.

Masaru admired what Jin was doing but was also stunned.

It was as if he were spinning out melodies, making them up as they came to him. It was an odd sort of live performance, with one tune beckoning the next.

Yes, this was less a concert or a recital than a live performance.

The Brahms ended as if it had been conjured away to another concert hall.

Jin lowered his hands on to the keys again.

Then a gasp sprang up from the audience.

Erik Satie. Again.

The hall was abuzz, confused.

Jin Kazama had begun playing 'I Want You'.

From the smile on his face, this was clearly no accident. He was fully aware that he was repeating the first piece in his programme.

What is going on here?

Masaru was dumbstruck, but also worried for Jin.

Wouldn't a performance that didn't stick to the programme he'd submitted in advance be a violation of the rules? Competition rules were quite strict, after all.

What if Jin were disqualified?

How could a talent like this be kicked out?

Masaru felt a cold sweat spring up.

Was Jin not even thinking how nervous this was making the audience?

Up on stage, Jin wore an innocent smile as he worked lightly through Satie again.

A premeditated crime? Or did he think this was within the bounds of the competition rules? Or else—?

The second playing of Satie slowed down, before he unhurriedly launched into his next piece.

Debussy.

'Pagodas', the opening piece of his suite *Estampes*, or *Prints*. Next to the Japanese title, which meant *Tower*, was a notation that referenced pagodas.

Clearly Debussy must have had an Oriental image in mind.

The scene immediately switched.

A large, old painting in a period frame.

A village at twilight. Sticky, Asian subtropical humidity. You could almost smell the grass, the scent of the hot wind blowing. An ancient pagoda.

You felt gravity pull the scenery off the stage and into the audience.

As Kanade listened, a part of her also wondered if he was breaking the rules.

This was a competition. How would the judges react to hearing Satie twice?

Plus the second performance of Satie hadn't been complete. Halfway through, it faded out into the next piece. A medley was what this was.

Still, her heart was stolen away by the undulating aural scene Debussy had created, and she was carried somewhere far away.

Who cares about rules? Kanade ended up feeling.

The amazing thing about Debussy's music was that, every time she heard it, she was surprised again by its melodic originality. It made her heart flutter, and she felt it anew each time. The same thought always came to her: *Claude Debussy, you are indeed a genius.*

An ancient pagoda – the scene of that faded Western painting suddenly sped up.

Nostalgia – was that what you'd call it? Water deep down at the bottom of your heart, in a deep, dark place, was being stirred by an invisible force.

Debussy's unexpected acceleration completely *carried away* the whole audience to another dimension.

Jin Kazama's dynamism stood out all the more. Kanade felt goosebumps.

The increased volume from pianissimo to fortissimo was beautifully delivered. This wasn't showing off, but an instinctive playing with sound that happened before you were even aware of it.

As if a racing car had suddenly, without a sound, accelerated to top speed.

A quietly unfolding drama, gathering an incredible momentum.

The music shifted to the second piece in *Estampes*, 'Evening in Granada'.

The audience was transported in a moment to a world redolent of Islam.

The word *Granada* conjured up all sorts of associations. It was in Andalusia, in southern Spain, a region where Christianity and Islam had intersected. The clear, dark blue sky was being absorbed by the gathering twilight. The white pillars, evenly spaced down a hallway, were steeped in the glow of the setting sun, and the word *infinite* came to mind.

The rhythm of the habanera. Women with raven-dark hair, clutching fans, dancing.

Something here, too, raised its head from the sea of emotion lying deep within. An uneasy, cheerless late afternoon.

Twilight, where the blessings and curses of life merged.

It was completely imbued with this.

A rose madder hue lay over the audience as this evening light shone down from the stage.

Kanade was riveted to her seat.

Something like a huge wall of energy was thrusting out from the stage, literally pinning her to her seat.

She felt parched and hesitated even to breathe.

Until the scene switched.

The third piece of *Estampes*, 'Gardens in the Rain'.

The temperature suddenly dropped.

The madder-red light that had been shining down on the audience dissipated, whisking them to chilly France.

To a lush garden wet in the afternoon rain.

The sky suddenly dimmed, with gusts of moist wind, raindrops.

The wind grew more blustery, shaking the trees, the rain striking leaves and flowers, making them bow lower, lower and lower.

Children scattered, trying to dodge the rain, a dog scampering beside them.

Oh – it's raining.

The audience's eyes were glued to the stage, gazing at the rain falling on the garden.

Small puddles began to form.

Water dripped down from the eaves.

On the cobblestone street the rain had formed a rivulet, a grey stream gushing downhill.

Kanade felt cold raindrops splashing on her cheeks.

AFTER THE VIBRANCY OF DEBUSSY, Jin Kazama dived straight into Ravel's *Mirrors*.

The audience was already used to this style of his.

And strangely enough, it didn't feel uncomfortable.

In this boy's mind, *Estampes* and *Mirrors* were connected. An association between their scenery?

Nathaniel Silverberg hadn't paid much heed to how the boy had repeated Satie.

Someone among the judges might call him out on that, but they'd deal with that if it came to it.

Nathaniel was focused instead on probing what was running through Jin Kazama's mind.

He'd noticed this in his two earlier appearances, the unique approach the boy took to the pieces he played.

These days the trend was to focus on the composers themselves, as pianists tried to discern their intentions and align themselves more closely with them. This approach looked to a piece's origins; pianists tried to figure out what sort of image the composer had in mind and researched the historical background and the composer's personal source of inspiration.

But Jin was the exact opposite. He was intent on drawing the piece closer to *him*, which would provoke the ire of professionals and pedants.

No, that wasn't it. What he did was to make the piece a part of *his* world. Reproducing his own world through the music, making any piece he played part of something far larger.

Five scenes reflected in a mirror.

'Moths', 'Sad Birds', 'A Boat on the Ocean', 'The Jester's Aubade', 'The Valley of Bells'.

Jin was drawing out the scenes that Ravel had written. And the scenes Jin evoked were large-scale. These were not mere images that had come to his mind, but it was if he were painting the scenes up on stage. Moving the whole piano into the landscape, immersing the audience.

Playing Ravel was difficult. Focus too much on technique and your scope narrowed and you ended up with tunnel vision. Jin, though, nimbly leapt over that trap.

Every time Nathaniel heard Jin play, he was blown away by his technique. He had extraordinary technical skills, yet they sounded so natural they didn't draw attention to themselves. As if these weren't skills he'd struggled to obtain, but ones he naturally possessed, as if by right. His ability was close to instinctive, something that a mechanical term like *technique* couldn't convey.

A truly eccentric boy.

Nathaniel was completely swept away.

The boy took the audience into his own space, somewhere unexpected.

Nathaniel suddenly found himself on a plain stretching out towards the horizon.

Maestro Hoffmann?

Somehow Hoffmann seemed to be there in the distance.

What you were aiming for. By teaching this boy—

Was it this?

Hoffmann seemed to smile.

THE FIFTH PIECE OF *MIRRORS*, the deeply contemplative 'The Valley of Bells', quietly drew to a close, and for the third time Erik Satie's 'Je te veux' rang out.

It was clear that by now Jin Kazama knew he was intentionally breaking the rules. These Satie repeats formed a promenade holding his recital together, creating a breather for the audience.

He shifted over to a Chopin impromptu.

As Aya Eiden hovered among the standing-room-only crowd, a strange feeling came over her.

As if she were up there on stage with Jin, one with him.

As if she were up on stage herself – as if she herself were playing.

No, that's not it. It's as if I'm up there on stage, standing beside the piano, talking with him as he plays.

He looked over at her, shot her a quick smile.

Do you love the piano?

She nodded. *Yes, I do love it.*

How much?

I don't know. I love it so much I can't even say.

Seriously?

He flashed an impish smile and carried on with the Chopin.

What? Do you think I'm not telling the truth? Aya glared at him for a second.

I don't know. It's because you look confused.

Really?

Yeah. Not when you're up here playing, but when you get off-stage, you always look confused.

He'd seen right through her, she thought.

I really love the piano, he said.

How much? Aya's turn to ask now.

Let me think . . .

Jin Kazama glanced up into space.

I love it so much that, even if I were the only person in the world, and there was a piano out in an open field, I would want to play it for ever.

The only person in the world.

Aya looked around her.

A deserted plain spreading out as far as the eye could see.

Wind was blowing and distant birds were calling.

Light poured down from the sky.

A deserted, barren place, yet one that somehow made you feel content.

Even if there's no one else to hear?

Yep.

Can you call yourself a musician if there's no one to hear you?

I don't know. But music is instinctive. Even if there was just one bird left in the world, it would still sing. Isn't it the same?

I suppose. The bird would sing.

Right?

Jin Kazama's light touch. A melodic line that sounded as if he'd just now improvised it.

Don't you want to sing? he asked.

He looked sideways at Aya.

I wonder . . . if I do. I don't know.

Aya squinted in the light.

When I see you play, I do want to sing. I was able to get back on stage thanks to you. Without hearing you perform, I may never have played.

Really? The boy shrugged.

Really. That's why I don't know. Whether I want to keep on singing or not.

I don't think that's right. The boy shook his body.

What isn't?

I think you and I are the same. You just saw yourself in me.

The same?

Yeah. Music is an instinct. It's the same for you. Which is why we can't help but sing. I think if you, too, were all alone in the world you'd still sit down at the piano and play.

Me?

A warm wind was blowing from somewhere. Aya ran her fingers through her hair.

Yeah. Absolutely.

*

I wonder.

I'm positive. Jin Kazama laughed. *Trust me. We flew together to the moon the other day, didn't we?*

You're right. We did. Aya laughed too.

So I'm telling you – trust me.

If you say so.

Yes. I'm telling you, so you can't go wrong.

He broke into a broad smile and carried on.

AYA SUDDENLY GOT HOLD OF HERSELF.

Jin Kazama was up on stage.

His figure was wavering, seemed blurred.

Wondering why, she put her hand to her face and discovered she was crying.

Before she realized it, tears were streaming down her cheeks.

Thank you, Aya whispered silently.

Thank you, Jin Kazama.

She wiped away her tears.

JIN KAZAMA'S FINAL PIECE.

Saint-Saëns's *Africa: Fantasy for Piano and Orchestra*.

Originally a ten-minute piano concerto.

Fascinated by Africa, Saint-Saëns had written the *Africa* theme in 1889 on the way to the Canary Islands, off the western coast of the continent, and then completed it two years later.

With a unique melody that revealed the exoticism Europeans sought in Africa at the time, the piece was said to actually incorporate a motif from a Tunisian folk song.

If you looked at Jin Kazama's programme for the third round, your eyes would surely be drawn to one point in particular, where in the column listing composers it said *Saint-Saëns / Jin Kazama*.

In other words, Jin himself had arranged the piece, which would make this the world premiere.

What kind of arrangement had he created to make this the finishing touch to his one-hour recital?

Masaru waited excitedly to find out.

The Chopin impromptu drew to an end, and after a brief pause Jin Kazama began, with a tremolo, playing the suspenseful introduction originally composed for violin.

The audience tensed up.

The left hand, further down the keyboard, played the melody.

Heavily layered chords, building to a crescendo, the motif repeating.

It's coming, it's coming.

The thrill of expectation for a masterpiece.

The audience was instantly riveted, the hall crackling with electricity.

It was gorgeous, catchy, Masaru felt.

A pleasing, exotic melody. A brisk, rhythmic phrase, exchanged between the hands.

This is great, he thought. *I want to play this too.*

His honest response to it. Just imagining himself beating out that melody and rhythm, he could predict how happy it would make him.

A real concert tune, a piece that was entertaining to the max – with an arrangement that was astonishingly creative.

In a corner of his mind, a different Masaru coolly analysed the arrangement.

Usually when you adapted a concerto for solo piano, you put together the orchestral and solo parts so the whole was as close as possible to the original score. When you did the opposite, arranging a piano piece for orchestra, you also dismantled the piano part and apportioned it to various sections of the orchestra. Compositions where both the orchestral and solo-piano versions were famous, such as Mussorgsky's *Pictures at an Exhibition* and Ravel's *La Valse*, usually followed this pattern.

But Jin Kazama's arrangement was something else.

*

Certainly he'd seized hold of the essence of the orchestral motif, but you could also tell he was trying to make this into a piano piece that stood on its own.

The exoticism that Saint-Saëns felt, and how he evoked an African rhythm – one that human beings sensed primally, deep down inside their very core.

The joy of rhythm.

The scales in the development, flowing over and over from high to low notes, high-end trills, low-end chords. These merged into a groove that anyone would enjoy.

What does his score look like? Masaru tried to picture it.

When you read the score, would you see what a great arrangement it was? Or did it take a live performance to make that clear?

Was he even playing it the way he'd arranged it? Masaru found it all rather mysterious.

The arrangement was persuasive – it was Jin's own, after all, plus the live-concert experience made it stand out all the more – but that tiny phrase, the motif he could only call a *flicker*, wasn't found in the original.

Was he, by chance, *arranging* it even now as he went along?

It certainly felt like it.

Aya had a complete turnaround, from quiet tears to feeling herself soaring over the vibrant hues of the African landscape.

The African colours that Saint-Saëns must have intended, the sounds of Africa, the scenery, all of it projected down towards her from the stage. She didn't need to go up on stage, for what was up there came to her. At this very moment the audience *became* Africa, as if a rumbling, dry wind was wafting over them.

Jin Kazama was smiling.

As if to show Aya, he raced alone across a vast tract of land.

We'll all be left behind. No, Jin Kazama is swallowing us up into his *universe – not a black hole but rather a universe that is pure white. It will absorb us all.*

No longer the bright, stern deserted plain of a moment ago, but an Earth filled with light.

The glittering melody, and rhythm, were enveloped in dazzle.

Dance! Dance!

Aya spread her arms wide as she tried to catch the downpour of light.

Letting instinct take over, giving rein to her soul's desire for pleasure.

More – more! *I want more light, more colours, more sound.*

Hands spread wide, held upwards, she stretched up to the skies.

Jin Kazama, I think I know who you are.

Aya gave herself up to the vortex of colours, the shower of light.

MIEKO COULDN'T BELIEVE HER EARS, nor her eyes.

It felt as if her face was being pounded by the pressure of the sound.

Her skin actually felt the kick, the pain.

How is such a huge sound possible?

Or is what I'm feeling just my imagination?

She could feel herself breaking out into a cold sweat.

This groovy feeling – the feeling swelling up from beneath.

Was he playing swing?

No – it was a real piece by Saint-Saëns.

It was just like a four-beat piece played at a live-music club, the backbeat accent just barely contained.

But – how? How could it be?

The impulsive pleasure bursting inside her had nothing to do with a classical-piano competition.

NATHANIEL SILVERBERG WAS FEELING THE same way.

This sensation: a warmth welling up in your gut, the feeling that the blood in your veins had reversed course. What in God's name *was* this?

He felt afraid.

In awe of this unknown *object* ruling the stage.

This young boy, eyes closed, grinning, was taking everyone in the hall to hell, though a hell not at all far from heaven. Nathaniel felt a chill run down his spine.

Where are you going, son?

Nathaniel realized his question wasn't directed at Jin so much as at himself.

Maestro Hoffmann, where is this boy taking us?

No, that's not it, another Nathaniel called out.

Where do I want to go? What am I doing here, sitting here in this judge's chair in a competition on an island in the Far East?

Nathaniel was mystified.

What's seated here is a raw, naked ego.

What was here, listening to Jin Kazama's piano, was not a member of the judging panel, not a musician, but a nameless, non-attributable lump of pure ego.

Why do I feel it this way now? I've never felt like this before.

Jin Kazama's piece moved towards the final cadenza.

How many arms does this boy have, anyway?

A massive sound, as if he were striking the keys all at once.

Is this actually in the score?

Or is it improvised?

As these thoughts brushed his mind, Nathaniel, the judges, indeed the entire audience, were being overwhelmed by this wave of sound, as if bulldozed aside, swallowed up, hauled this way and that.

We're going to be stranded! Nathaniel yelled out to himself.

But by this time the piece was over.

Jin Kazama sat there, a blank look on his face, the piano no longer making a sound.

Yet everyone was still hearing it.

Steeped in his cadenza that still filled the hall.

Inside Nathaniel, too, the music remained.

It was a strange tableau. The performance was over, yet the pianist, the audience, everyone sat drained and unmoving.

This must have lasted for some thirty seconds.

Jin Kazama suddenly found his feet.

The audience finally broke free from the spell and began to move.

The young man bowed deeply, holding his head low for some time.

The air was filled with silent admiration.

And then, predictably, the hall was battered, as if by a storm, for some five whole minutes, with screams and applause that could only be called *frenzied*.

The Island of Joy

*H*OW MANY TIMES HAVE *I stood on this spot?*

And how many times will I stand here in the future?

I mean, how much do I really understand about what it means to be here?

'Eiden-*san*, perhaps you'd care to sit down?' the stage manager asked. Aya had been standing frozen in the wings.

She smiled but appeared to turn down the offer.

Seeming to grasp what she meant, the stage manager nodded and silently withdrew into the shadows.

Aya turned towards the stage and straightened up.

The wild enthusiasm aroused by Jin's performance was ongoing – there was encore after encore. The final pianist's performance was thus delayed by ten minutes.

The audience was limp, as if the competition was already over.

Aya picked up on this but didn't care.

I just want to stand here.

Before I go out under the bright lights, I want to stand here, savouring the meaning of it all, the joy, the dread.

Until now, I've always stood here without any special feelings. Simply waiting my turn. And when the time came, I'd go out and play.

Never afraid. But not excited, either.

She'd only considered it a place to wait.

She'd heard stories and seen it depicted in documentaries. How even leading figures in classical music, world-renowned maestros, felt nervous as they waited in the wings, trembling in fear, some even troubling those around them by insisting until the last minute that they didn't want to go on, didn't want to play.

Even in college, and at other competitions, she'd caught glimpses of this. People staring up into space, turning pale, twisting and turning their bodies, desperately trying to overcome the fear, as they waited their turn.

Aya had never experienced *stage fright* herself, so she'd always observed this objectively, as a scene playing out before her. She could understand being tense, but *terrified*? That she couldn't fathom.

Why be afraid? Isn't everyone here because they want *to be? Isn't that why they're here? So why be so terrified of it?* she'd muttered at some point.

For Aya it was a simple question, but she couldn't forget the shock on the face of a friend who happened to hear her say this. And at that moment, she understood – that this was something she shouldn't have said. *Other people are different*, she thought.

No – it's me *who's different.*

But here, for the first time, Aya felt in *awe*.

Aya tried repeating the word to herself.

Awe.

She remembered a moment long ago, when she'd just started learning.

When she was sitting beside a window, listening to the sound of rain.

Rain was falling on the tin roof, beating out a strange rhythm, and this was the first time she noticed the *rain horses running*. The moment she heard, quite distinctly, the horses gallop as they charged across the skies.

In the hush of the pouring rain, I saw horses galloping.

This is the same feeling I had then.

The moment she realized that the world ran on secret principles unknown to her, she'd felt a disquiet for what lay outside that window, high up and far away.

The moment she understood the world was filled with an overwhelming beauty that she – no, maybe *no one* – understood, she was surprised at her very smallness and insignificance. But at the same time, she felt awe.

So – I've had this feeling before. From the moment I first heard music in nature.

She thought she could hear horses' hooves on a tin roof in the rain – her eyes widened as she looked restlessly around.

This was the first time she'd felt these things so vividly, as if she could grasp them properly. Maybe this was what they meant by an *awakening*?

The murmur of the audience conversing, of the stagehands working backstage, the awareness of all this flowed around her body like an astonishing melody.

She shut her eyes.

WHAT SHE WAS EXPERIENCING NOW was totally different from the despair she'd felt during the first round.

That felt like so long ago, and when she looked back on it now, she'd been so naïve. She'd been struggling to justify herself. Aya flinched when she thought about it, blushing at the memory.

In the past, she'd been well aware how puny and insignificant she was, though hadn't she then gone on to think she'd become something significant just because she'd turned twenty? But she'd been lost in a swell of conceit that she was making music, that she understood music.

How utterly stupid I was! I was so much wiser than that when I was small, and really understood the world.

I never grew up at all. I just saw what I wanted to see, only listened to what I wanted to hear. The mirror only reflected what worked to my advantage.

I didn't even do a decent job of listening to music.

A bitter taste rose up inside her.

I boasted how wonderful music was, how I was going to spend my life immersed in it, yet I did the opposite. I took advantage of it, looked down on it, steeped myself in bog-standard music. I made my peace with it, thinking that was the easy way out. Thinking I was different, I didn't even really enjoy music.

The more she thought about it, the more it made her shiver.

Kanade and the others believed in her, urged her to compete, but her attitude back then, and later when they were picking out dresses – how shameful, ungrateful, how brazen it had been.

Aya let out a small sigh.

She despised her stupidity.

And when she thought about how Kanade and others never gave up on her, despite all her conceit, how good they were to keep believing in her, she could only see herself as an even greater idiot.

And to think – it took me until the end of the third round to realize this.

She smiled bitterly to herself.

It's not too late, is it? Aya asked herself.

Listen, whether or not it's too late, the fact is you haven't done anything yet.

Jin's voice.

Ask me after you've stepped out on stage.

That makes sense, Aya thought.

No use asking if my music's any good before I play anything.

Where could Jin Kazama be? If the audience found out where he was, they'd mob him, so maybe he was hiding somewhere.

Or maybe, since he didn't usually stand out, he was strolling around the lobby as always, wearing his signature cap.

What about Ma-*kun*?

Her chest suddenly tightened.

Ma-*kun* was so very earnest and sincere about his music, and in comparison her attitude couldn't be ruder.

Maybe he'd run off? Maybe he'd felt awkward. He wanted to take on music properly, make his way in it, and maybe he was just too dazzling for her.

Though he did keep his promise to their teacher, and to her.

Promise me you'll play the piano?

She remembered the lanky boy nodding back.

I kept my promise to our teacher and to you, Aa-chan.

I'm such an idiot. I know nothing. I understand nothing. No . . . thing.

Aya let out another low sigh.

I'm scared. Scared to death to go out on stage. Can I play anything? Do I have an ear? I'm frightened about whether I have anything worth listening to.

She felt her whole body tremble.

I'm frightened – but I'm also elated, Aya admitted.

I'm excited by the unknown. What will I do out there? What will I be able to create? I'm burning to know more than anyone.

The bell signalling the end of the interval rang out, startling her out of her reverie.

From the wings she could hear the buzz in the audience.

Having your performance wrap up a competition isn't something you get to experience very often, is it? she heard Masaru say.

She'd felt nothing then, but now she felt her heart beating faster.

You're right, Ma-kun. *This* is *a pretty thrilling experience.*

She could sense the packed concert hall, the level of emotion out there – the exhaustion, the dashing of expectation, the sense of duty, of needing to hear every performance to the bitter end.

Jin Kazama has won over the audience, right? Aya thought. *So I guess I'm just a little extra thrown in. Which, in a way, makes things easier.*

She took a deep breath.

The feeling of being awakened never left her, of the world stretching out for ever and ever.

Behind her, the staff in the wings fell silent. The moment had arrived, the bustle of the audience, too, had stopped.

'Ms Eiden, it's time.'

From the side a hand reached out and the door opened.

Everything grew bright.

Before she knew it, Aya was smiling radiantly.

Let the music begin.

As SOON AS THE AUDIENCE glimpsed her face, you could hear them gasp.

And naturally Akashi Takashima was one of them.

What's that expression? he wondered.

She's smiling.

Not the kind of smile he'd seen before – not a forced one for the public, but a luminous, relaxed smile.

Like the look on people's faces after a downpour, when they see the sun break through.

Aya sat down on the stool and gazed at a point above the piano.

What could she see?

Akashi felt something bitter suddenly rise up in him.

I wanted to go there too. I wanted to see what she's *seeing.*

Maybe I did *catch a fleeting glimpse of it.*

I want to go on. Want to go on playing.

Akashi silently shouted out to Aya at the piano.

That feeling he had while on stage – his body filling with music, of it overflowing out of him. That feeling of being utterly enriched, filled with omnipotence, that no matter how much music kept coming, there would always be more. Once you went through that, there was no escape. You couldn't help wanting to feel it again, and again.

I want to be there. In the same place as Aya Eiden.

I've never wanted anything so badly in my life.

It's as if my skin is tingling, covered in a membrane of cold flame.

For me, the competition is over.

At least I thought so.

I felt a sense of accomplishment, felt refreshed. I thought I'd be satisfied, able to go back to my everyday life.

But that's not how it has turned out.

Akashi realized, with a twinge of pain, how naïve he'd been.

It was only exhaustion that made him think that, the lethargy he felt after all the hours he'd spent preparing.

This was only the beginning.

With a feeling close to fear, Akashi was sure of it.

He held back the desire to cry, but the moment he heard Aya quietly playing the opening notes of Chopin's Ballade No.1, his feelings, bottled up for so long, came gushing out.

BALLAD.

Aya had happened to flip through a music dictionary once and had come across this definition: a sentimental love song played at a relaxed tempo.

Which was pretty much the idea most people had of ballads.

You always included one or two of them in an album. In a concert you played them as a solo to give the other band members a break. To be an artist you needed a few songs like this, songs for lovers to listen to, nestled close, lost in each other.

That was the image of ballads, wasn't it?

But Aya felt that in the past what was meant by *ballad* was something a little different. Something closer to a folk song (and here the term was different from its use in Japan, its original meaning being closer to *minyo*, or indigenous music) – songs that sang of actual events or simple sentiments.

The four ballades (or instrumental 'ballads') that Chopin had composed were, she felt, situated somewhere in the middle, between the older meaning and the more contemporary one.

Songs were once a means of holding on to memories. They were epic poems, performed in place of written historical records.

But later, songs became less about what had *taken place* than what was being *felt*, expressing more universal emotions.

Aya found Chopin's ballades conveyed what it was to be a child, singing children's songs, with the kind of loneliness of being human.

And this is exactly the loneliness I feel right now as I play, she thought – the unavoidable loneliness every person feels from the moment they're born into this world.

Chopin's ballades were so melodious, so catchy, that they felt like they'd always been around, but George Sand had described how much Chopin had struggled to compose them. Aya felt touched by how even a genius like Chopin toiled to compose. Many works that seemed to have come effortlessly, from the first inspired phrase to their completion, involved an unseen agony and struggle. But that was only to be expected. If the effort that went into composing them was plain to the listener, they would lose their power.

This sadness lay deep within the wavering flow of time, a feeling we normally pretend isn't there, the sadness that adheres to everyday life that keeps us too busy to feel it. Even if a person experiences enviable peaks of happiness, a fulfilled life, all happiness still carries with it the loneliness inherent in being human.

Aya knew she shouldn't think too deeply about it, for once you did you were shattered, with the knowledge of human weakness. She'd always tried to avoid this fundamental *loneliness*.

Which is exactly why you *had* to sing – about this loneliness, the happiness and unhappiness of a life that is but a fleeting, transient moment in time.

Believe that people hundreds or thousands of years ago must have felt the same.

Believe that people hundreds or thousands of years in the future would feel the same.

What one person can do is so limited, the time they're allotted so very short.

In my puny, short life I encountered the piano, spent so much time with it, and now I have people listening to me play.

How much of a miracle is that? Aya asked herself. *How much of a miracle is it that, every moment, each sound reaches these people who just happen to be living at the same time, who just happen to be assembled in this space together? It's frightening to think about it; it makes me tremble all over.*

I am, right now, in awe, frightened, trembling.

Yet – that makes me happy beyond words.

It is all so precious. So very heart-rending.

Buffeted by these complex emotions, Aya was also calmer than she'd ever been before. From the moment she was waiting in the wings until now, she had the sustained feeling she could see into every inch of the hall – no, even *beyond* the walls of the concert hall to take in the entire world – and she felt totally level-headed, her mind crystal clear.

A doubt suddenly crossed her mind.

Was this just a momentary occurrence? Or a sensation she'd have whenever she performed?

She hadn't a clue.

Even now, when she had a clear view of everything, she honestly had no idea.

This was, for Aya, uncharted territory.

THE AUDIENCE, TOO, WERE SHARING the same awe and trembling.

Not so much sharing the music as sharing the heart-rending affection Aya had towards the humanity beyond the composition.

Masaru sat, mouth agape, gazing at her.

She'd done it again – taken another leap forward. Her face today was completely different from how it had been the other day.

The impetus for this was Jin Kazama's performance, Masaru thought, a bit unhappily.

The credit belonged to that boy genius.

Each and every note Aya touched went straight to your heart.

Aa-chan, *you're a goddess. You've sprouted wings.*

Masaru was half stunned.

She is, right before my eyes, at long last reaching for the heights.

She'd pulled ahead of him again. *How hard am I going to have to work now to catch up?* he wondered.

Now he knew she would never abandon music again. The relief that they could be in the same place was, however, short-lived, as he feared she would go somewhere out of reach to him.

Aa-chan *is astonishing*, he thought, feelings of pride coming a beat late.

He knew that Kanade, too, beside him, was proud of her. Kanade, who trusted her ear for music, who'd always been sure of Aya's talent since she was a young girl. How proud must she be of all that now?

Like waves receding, the ballade quietly came to an end.

Silence.

With Jin Kazama the audience knew he'd launch straight into the next piece, so they held back their applause.

But in Aya's case she was so steeped in her own world that she didn't stand up, and the audience, too, had not yet awoken from her world either, and didn't feel the need to clap.

They sat quietly waiting for the next piece.

Aya straightened up.

A sudden change of gear: an elegant, dazzling work, with an appealing structure and technique. One of Schumann's *Novelletten*.

What a marvellous piece, Masaru thought. *I want to play that next time myself.*

He felt tears pricking his eyes.

Where did they come from? This wasn't exactly a piece that made you cry.

But the urge only grew stronger. His chest began to heave.

Masaru was filled with the sense that he and Aya had taken a long journey together. Over a long, long time. As if he'd finished reading the last chapter of an epic novel.

*

*Aa-*chan, *neither of us has lived very long, but before we saw each other again, we were both travelling in far-away places, like planets on different trajectories around the Solar System that later come round again.*

Masaru sighed.

She's back. For real.

Somehow the image of Aya and himself as children came to him, again and again.

Aya tugging him by the hand, Aya leading him to Mr Watanuki's place, Aya wailing and dejected when he moved away.

His parents' surprised faces when he told them he wanted to learn the piano.

The face of the music-college student who tutored him – composed and sober at first, but clearly bowled over when he heard Masaru play.

The first time he set foot in the conservatory.

His audition at Juilliard.

The day he was first introduced to Nathaniel Silverberg.

What are all these memories? I'm not about to die, am I? Is this what they mean about your life flashing before your eyes? The thought helped him hold back his tears.

He realized with a start that he wasn't alone, that most of the audience around him were also fighting back tears. Some were quietly wiping them away.

He thought he was crying because of Aa-*chan*. But that wasn't it. Was everyone weeping at the *Novellette*?

Beside him, Kanade was crying, too, but she didn't wipe away her tears. She sat there silently, tears sliding down her cheeks, staring fixedly at Aya on stage.

Emotions continued to build, even with a piece as cheerful as this. One after another, they consumed you. Stunned to acknowledge they had so much pent-up feeling inside, the audience watched silently. Not watching what was in Aya, but what, through her, was in *each one of them.*

Masaru continued to gaze at her. Just a young girl with a bright smile.

So why are we all crying? Especially when she's performing so happily like this, so lightly?

He saw her face after they had first met up again at the competition, her doubtful-looking face in front of the lifts.

Her face as her eyes and mouth opened and she called out, 'Ma-*kun*?'

Her face when she felt anxious, her helpless face, her face when she glared, when she smiled and let down her guard.

Nathaniel Silverberg's surprised face, too, came to him, when he was first introduced to Aya.

Masaru could tell how much Silverberg wanted to give him a piece of his mind but had restrained himself. It was obvious what he'd wanted to say: 'This isn't the time and place to fall in love with a rival! You don't have time to be infatuated.' But Masaru knew the woman who was standing beside his teacher. She was Silverberg's ex-wife, and Masaru was also aware that his mentor wasn't about to say anything when he himself still seemed to have feelings for her.

Masaru observed, and understood, his teacher better than Silverberg could ever imagine.

Before he knew it, Masaru was inwardly addressing his teacher.

Mr Silverberg, I may well lose to Aya. Actually, she's gone way past the level of winning or losing. Plus there's someone else you have to consider. Jin Kazama.

You told me to win, to grab first place – and that's what I planned to do. But if they're my rivals, it's not going to happen.

And you must think so too, right?

Even as he carried on this inner monologue, Masaru realized this, too, was a means of containing his tears.

Ah – my God.

Unable to hold them back any more, he quietly wiped his cheeks.

Even as the *Novellette* gently came to an end, Aya still didn't stand. Eyes closed, a smile playing about her lips, she sat unmoving.

The audience followed suit.

Silence. Her world unbroken.

Seriously? You're going to let one of the Novelletten, *of all works, make you cry so much?* Masaru asked himself bitterly.

The next piece was a more legitimate tear-jerker, the centrepiece of the programme, the heavyweight composition Brahms's Piano Sonata No. 3.

Masaru smiled as he watched Aya lift her fingers to play the opening chord, but was then thrown by how the scene suddenly blurred.

If I'm already crying at the beginning, he thought, *how am I going to hold out for the rest of the thirty minutes?*

BRAHMS'S PIANO COMPOSITIONS CAME AT the beginning, and the end, of his life as a composer.

The solo pieces in particular were composed early on in his career.

Brahms composed the Piano Sonata No. 3 in F Minor when he was twenty, and it was the last sonata he ever wrote.

Though written so early, it was packed with the elements later listeners associated with him – the gravitas of his sound, the imposing stance of the piece, the overwhelming Romanticism.

The sonata was a form he had to grapple with as a composer, and one could fully understand how he never wrote another sonata, for this piece was such a bold, major work.

Aya Eiden, performing it, was the same age, twenty, that Brahms was when he composed it.

Twenty during Brahms's time wasn't the same at all as twenty nowadays, in terms of experience and circumstances. A twenty-year-old today was no more than a child compared to a twenty-year-old from the era he had lived in.

Which meant that, no matter how much of a child prodigy

or genius you might be, Brahms was the one composer you could never truly play unless you'd reached a certain level of maturity as a person.

Brahms alone.

Nathaniel Silverberg had to admit that the time to retract that opinion had arrived.

That premonition had come to him the moment Aya Eiden had begun to play the Chopin Ballade No. 1.

He realized he was listening to her not as one of the judges, but as just another member of the audience, and he was certain now that when he heard her Brahms, he would rid himself of that opinion entirely.

The girl genius's resurrection drama.

He was well aware, of course, of her background.

But that wasn't who this girl before him was now. Even when she was no longer performing she must have, unconsciously, continued evolving. Yet her evolution during the days of this competition had been extraordinary. With each piece, and each day, he felt he was witnessing her grow ever more confident in her own music.

Every single note born of her fingers was deep, and consequential. You could feel her breath reaching every corner of the pieces, yet somehow she remained an anonymous figure, allowing the music to retain its universality.

What a strange thing music was.

It was just one small individual up there performing, and the notes created by those fingers were here one moment and gone the next. Yet what was there was almost the definition of the eternal.

The wonderment of a living creature, with a finite life, creating the eternal.

Through that fleeting, transient moment of music, one was in touch with eternity.

Only genuine performers made him feel this.

And the person before him was, without a doubt, one of them.

Aya Eiden shut her eyes and quietly waited.

The audience did the same. There was no applause after this piece either.

And then she began to play.

The dynamic melody of the introduction.

The opening of this piece was liable to come across as grandiose.

But there was no danger of that now.

From the very first note it was clear her interpretation was brimming with truth. A sense of security and expectation filled the hall, as the audience understood this was a pianist they could relax with and entrust everything to.

She has the strength to make us feel calm.

And she speaks for us all, as she so modestly relates the trajectories of our lives.

What we wanted someone to know. What we never could say. What we repressed as we lived our day-to-day lives. What we could feel, yet couldn't put into words—

She related all of this – like a *miko* priestess at a Shinto shrine – suppressing her own self while truthfully relating everything.

This quiet recitation continued as the second movement began.

Countless lives, spoken of simply.

As they watched her, the audience were examining themselves. Their lives up until now, the paths they had taken, witnessing all of this projected there on stage.

There were some who were, no doubt, witnessing Aya Eiden's life as well.

Nathaniel was one of them. It was as if he were watching a movie – a scene of her performing overlaying a documentary film about her life.

Her early life as a precocious child prodigy. The amazement, fervour and anticipation of those around her. Hectic days, always on the road.

A death in the family and dejection. Abuse and slander heaped upon her, the feeling that the whole world was against her.

A long silence.

Her relief and confusion as she withdrew from the front lines to live a *normal* life.

Did that give her peace of mind? Or did she taste, instead, a bitter disappointment?

Was she tired of life so early? Did she hide away from others?

Did she experience both heaven and hell far earlier than anyone, come to distrust others, and feel herself empty and hollow?

She may very well have experienced all of this.

But then she came back. And once again something began to well up inside her.

At first it must have been just an uncertain trickle.

But the flow became a constant stream, then a torrent. Slicing away the banks, flowing over hills and fields, surging on its way to becoming a huge river flowing towards the estuary.

The third movement.

Here the melody changed to a dramatic scherzo. Where one's life unfolds.

She hadn't been in a competition for years.

She must have been quite frightened. With all those curious eyes and jaundiced looks focused on her. She couldn't give an ordinary performance. The only thing permitted her was to be overwhelming.

More than anything she must have felt fear of herself. Would she really be able to play? Was she determined enough to return to the stage?

For even the most experienced veteran pianist, the stage was both a sacred and a terrifying place. Knowing that, a person who stepped away from performing for a while and then returned had to possess an unwavering determination and power that far exceeded what they'd had the first time they were up on stage.

She must have had her doubts.

When he saw her with Masaru, he sensed some confusion, some uncertainty, within her still. She didn't seem to have really grasped the fact that she'd returned to the stage. It struck him that she was undecided about being a musician.

But then she was reunited with Masaru, whom she herself had discovered, and who had grown into an amazing musician.

Nathaniel's feelings were complicated. Even now he believed that Masaru would win the top prize, and that Aya's appearance as a rival would serve to inspire him. But at the same time, there was no doubt that Masaru was one of the factors in the great evolution he'd seen taking place in her.

The shock must have been unimaginable for her – to meet up again with someone you had always been far better than, and had introduced to the piano, who now surpassed you as a musician. If that didn't spur you on to compete, what would?

As a performer, Aya's sensibility was closer to Jin's than to Masaru's. This may well have been the first time she'd met someone so similar, whose genius was equal to, or perhaps exceeded, her own.

Geniuses are only influenced by those they recognize as equals. There are things that only geniuses can understand about each other.

Just as Nathaniel and the other judges were affected by Jin, so Aya must have been too. He could well imagine her being even more shocked than they were.

And finally, she got serious.

No, it was more that she had rediscovered where she belonged.

In the fourth movement of the Brahms, she did some soul-searching.

Deep, deep reflection, a bird's-eye view of everything up until now.

She could now see things she couldn't before. Hear what she couldn't hear before. Keenly aware of her smallness, her stupidity, her immaturity.

Her audience sat with bated breath. They could see, up on stage, her life, their own life, countless lives, and an eternity that they could touch only now, at this one moment in time.

Aya's own life, and each life watching her. All of these souls' trajectories had finally converged in the present moment.

The fifth, and final movement.

The melody slowly climbing as it headed towards the climax.

An estuary was near. Beyond that, the wide, open sea awaited. Every person could feel a breeze on their cheeks that was unlike anything they'd felt before.

Soon. Very soon, we will emerge into an incredible open space.

There will be no going back. The person I was yesterday is no more.

Incomparable challenges unlike anything we've experienced await us. Yet so does incomparable joy.

The self I will be from now on will shout out a resounding 'Yes!' to my life.

AYA PUSHED DOWN ON THE final chord.

Her upper body, still hunched over the piano, suddenly straightened and she got to her feet.

As if following suit, the audience leapt as one to their feet, screams of approval shaking the hall.

Up on stage, the girl looked surprised and simultaneously totally blank.

The standing ovation didn't subside, yet there was one more piece still remaining to be played.

Aya bowed, smiling, over and over, and then sat down.

The applause finally faded, and the audience too, took their seats.

Aya sighed lightly.

This was literally the final piece of the long haul of the competition.

Debussy's *L'Isle joyeuse*, or *The Island of Joy*.

WHAT AN AMAZING BIT OF luck that this would be the last piece, Kanade thought.

Aya had decided the programme herself, Kanade recalled. She'd got advice from Papa and her professors, of course, but the programme she submitted was the one she'd first decided on.

Aya probably wasn't conscious of it, but this programme was perfect, as it anticipated both the road back to her career, and her evolution over the course of the contest.

Kanade remembered Aya's expression as she brooded over whether or not to be in the competition.

Aya herself must have had a premonition of this resurrection drama. Wasn't it exactly because of this that she'd hesitated to participate? At the same time, as a musician she coolly and strategically put together her programme.

L'Isle joyeuse began with a brilliant trill.

It was said that Debussy conceived of the piece on a trip, an elopement really, with Emma, the woman who became his second wife, but Kanade had also heard that he had finished it a year before the two of them set off.

Either way, as the title reflected, the piece was an expression of joy and exaltation. A dazzling work, filled with a sense of euphoria.

And Aya herself, playing it, was filled with warmth. She really did give out a bright light.

The joy of making music. The joy of being at one with the audience. The joy of having perfect command of her talent.

Aya's euphoria was more than shared by the audience.

Kanade too felt herself filling with joy.

She's back.

The thought brought on fresh tears.

Kanade felt triumphant.

See? I was right after all!

Papa, I was spot on.

Kanade wanted to stand up and shout out to the world.

I was right! I won!

THIS *ISLE JOYEUSE* WAS AMAZING.

Mieko focused, wide-eyed.

Aya Eiden looked noticeably larger up there as she continued to astonish the judges.

To think that she could hold them all in such thrall when this was the very last performance, when everyone was completely exhausted.

It's up in the air now, isn't it, who the winner will be?

Mieko was dying to catch a glimpse of Nathaniel Silverberg's expression, but she stopped herself from glancing over at him.

Aya had been a lap behind the others, or so they'd thought, but she'd gradually sped up and now, with this last spurt, had suddenly pulled out ahead, Mieko thought.

It had been a long while since she'd seen someone evolve so much in such a short time. Well, in fact, it might be the first time ever.

This girl was, indeed, a genius. A frightening thing, being a genius.

Mieko had known several geniuses in her time, but with Aya she'd witnessed another, different type entirely. There was a different feeling of scale from what you gleaned with Masaru or Jin Kazama. A sense of uncanny depths.

The judges must be satisfied with this wonderful conclusion to the competition, Mieko thought.

They must feel themselves blessed to have such worthy pianists.

A sudden thought came to her. That *bomb* Hoffmann had set meant . . . what did it mean?

Yes, they'd all been pondering this, all along – where exactly was the arrow aiming that Hoffmann had let fly?

From the days of the Paris audition when that boy first appeared.

From when she heard that incendiary performance.

For sure, that boy with his letter of recommendation from Hoffmann had made a splash with his trickster style of performance, firing up the audience and stirring up debate among the judges.

I felt tested, worrying whether I had an ear for music any more. I felt played, by my irritation at Jin Kazama, my assessment of him, my own wavering opinions.

However—

Was Hoffmann aiming, as Smirnoff had suggested, at the music-education establishment by throwing an unorthodox boy genius into the mix?

At first glance, this seemed the most likely interpretation. Was making high-profile judges quake in their boots the reaction Hoffmann had been hoping for?

I am presenting Jin Kazama to you all.

He is, literally, a gift.

Most likely a gift from heaven to us all.

She heard Hoffmann's voice in the words of his letter of recommendation.

It isn't he who is being tested, but me, and all of us.

It's up to all of you – all of us, rather – to decide whether we see him as a gift, *or as a* disaster waiting to happen.

As Mieko listened to *L'Isle joyeuse*, she was listening to Hoffmann's voice too.

I am presenting Jin Kazama to you all – presenting.

What she was seeing right now was the answer.

A pianist who embodied an explosive joy. Someone who had evolved during the competition and truly blossomed because of him.

That was it.

It's not musical education that Jin Kazama has exploded. Jin Kazama's performances were the catalyst that made truly individual ability blossom, not conventional performances or those that simply relied on superb technique. *This* was the bomb that Hoffmann had set.

The result was this very genius's performance being played out right now.

I hadn't realized, Mieko thought.

We've already received all kinds of gifts. *Not* disasters *at all. Hoffmann's present to us, in a most-welcome form.*

Mieko was moved to tears. Not just because Aya's performance was so exquisite, but because Hoffmann's last wishes had so clearly come true.

I didn't realize, she thought again.

One after another the figures of the other pianists overlaid that of Aya, joy gushing out as she performed – Jin Kazama's recitals, Masaru's and Hoffmann's, all overlapped in her mind.

Each and every one of them was a *gift*.

How lucky could a person be? Could anything be more joyous than to sit here and to feel all this?

L'Isle joyeuse REACHED ITS CLIMAX.

The joy of performing, of hearing genius, the joy of this being handed down.

We are, Mieko thought, truly on an *island of joy*.

Everyone, without exception, receiving the *gift* of music.

The final phrase.

Rising upwards on the scale.

Then, in a single breath, descending.

After finishing the Brahms sonata, Aya had stood up unconsciously, but not this time.

Now, filled with a look of firm conviction, an incandescent smile on her face, Aya sprang purposefully to her feet.

Magnificent applause brought the celebration to a finish. Applause for the pianists, for the audience, for the judges, for everyone.

The battle, over some eleven days, was at an end.

All that was left now was to make the final selection.

Battle without Honour or Humanity

THE AIR FELT SO LIGHT.

Standing among the crowd spilling into the lobby, Masami felt so liberated a sigh escaped her.

Even the camera in her hands felt light.

Everyone looked relieved, she thought.

Or dazed, maybe, and worn out. What an intense time it had been.

She was waking from a dream. Over nearly two weeks they had shared the lives of almost one hundred competitors – it had been a profound, impassioned time. She felt a solidarity with them all, as if they'd been through a war together.

Her body couldn't take any more, though. No more piano competitions for her for a while, she decided. Yet – a part of her wanted to go through it all over again.

She spotted a familiar face and called out.

'Takashima-*kun*!'

For a second, Akashi looked blank, then he turned around.

'Oh!' He paused before collecting his thoughts. 'It's finally over. You worked so hard,' he said.

'No, that would be *you*.'

They nodded to each other, the shared empathy of comrades-in-arms.

'I'm just getting started,' Masami said. 'And I have a lot of editing to do, too.'

'Right. You still have the finals to go.'

As they walked across the lobby, they gazed at the crowds streaming through the many wide-open doors.

'Everyone seems to be leaving,' Akashi said.

'Most of them. It'll be some time before the judges' announcement. I'm sure some of them will come back later. Are you going to stay for the announcement, Takashima-*kun*?'

'Yeah. My turn's long over, but since I did take part, I really want to hear the results.'

'It really was worth listening to it all. I feel stuffed.' Masami stretched. 'That girl at the end – wasn't she incredible? I've never had that kind of experience before. As I listened, all these images came back to me – childhood memories, my parents' faces, my family—'

Far-off memories resurfaced, and a stinging sensation, a tingling deep down, that made her want to cry.

Masami glanced closely at Akashi, who was listening quietly.

He held her look, his eyes red.

'What's the matter? Did I say something to upset you?'

'No.' Akashi laughed, waving a hand dismissively, and looked away. 'That's not it. That's not it at all.'

But there was no doubt about it – he was in tears.

'What's wrong? Did something happen?'

'It's nothing.' Akashi smiled but kept his face turned away.

Masami couldn't figure it out. Tears of regret that he'd failed to make the third round? Pent-up frustration only now escaping?

She thought this over, making sure not to look at him.

Did I say something insensitive? Was it because I praised the final pianist? Or other pianists?

As she worked on this assignment, she saw how everyone watched what they said, and Masami had herself grown cautious.

She didn't realize Akashi's tears were flowing because he'd been so moved by what she was saying. Even Akashi himself didn't understand why.

Masami's comments about Aya Eiden had simply made him happy. The fact that someone like Masami, who didn't normally listen to classical music, shared the same emotions filled him with joy.

I'm so glad I competed, he thought. *So glad I put up with everything this past year. Glad I was a part of this.*

These feelings welled up all at once, and more tears began to flow.

Masami spotted someone she knew and went over. Relieved, Akashi continued to wipe away his tears in a corner of the lobby.

Nobody's looking at me, are they? he hoped. *What am I doing crying at my age?* He continued to weep, stealthily, feeling a bit ridiculous, but also treasuring his reaction.

He spotted her in an instant.

A girl in jeans and a sweater, fresh-looking with no make-up, probably having just washed it off. Akashi found himself making his way quickly over to her.

'Thank you,' he said.

Aya Eiden looked up.

Was she really this tiny?

Akashi was taken aback.

The girl before him was a gentle-looking twenty-year-old, with large eyes. Unforgettable, luminous eyes.

'Thank you so much, Eiden-*san*,' Akashi repeated.

Aya looked blank.

'Thank you for the wonderful performance – thank you for coming back.'

A sudden emotion appeared in Aya's eyes, as if she'd just now understood something.

And those wide eyes quickly filled with tears.

Akashi found himself tearing up all over again.

Why, he didn't know. All he knew was that Aya, that both of them, shared similar emotions, and were crying for the same reason.

Aya's face crumpled. She suddenly clung to Akashi and began to sob.

Her fingers squeezing Akashi's arm were unexpectedly strong.

Akashi felt his own tears gushing.

What a strange situation, they thought, as they clung to each other and cried their eyes out. Yet these tears, oddly enough, felt good, uplifting.

They knew people around them were watching.

'What's wrong, Aa-*chan*?' a voice asked.

It was Masaru Carlos. Beside him was a girl with long hair, and, together, they walked over.

Akashi and Aya sniffled and wiped away their tears, neither of them able to speak.

Masaru and the girl looked at the crying pair, but realized it hadn't been sparked by any particular trouble, that Akashi hadn't made her cry, that it was simply the two of them bawling like a couple of kids. Masaru and the girl exchanged a look.

Akashi and Aya took each other in, their faces both flushed, and burst out laughing.

'I'm so sorry about that.'

'My apologies. I don't know what came over me.'

They both started speaking at once, then simultaneously clammed up. They doubled over, laughing.

'My apologies,' Akashi said. 'I was in this competition, too, and have been a fan of yours for a long time.' Akashi began to introduce himself, but Aya cut him off.

'You're Akashi Takashima. I love your playing.' Her big eyes sparkled.

'You – you remember my name?'

'I do. And I want to go to your next performance.'

He shivered, as if a cold chill had run through him.

'Well – see you.'

'I'm sure we'll meet again.'

'Who's that, Aa-*chan*? Are you friends?' Akashi heard Masaru and the girl ask as Aya turned to them.

Akashi stood rooted to the spot.

This is, indeed, a beginning, he thought.

A warmth engulfed him.

This competition is the start. I have, at long last, begun my life as a musician.

KANADE GLANCED AT HER WATCH – 8.42 p.m.

According to the original schedule, the finals announcement should have happened just after eight. But with all the fervent calls for encores, the performances had run over, and the announcement was rescheduled for eight-thirty.

Aya had heard that the judging at the Yoshigae International Piano Competition didn't usually drag on, and sure enough all the official statements so far had taken place on schedule.

Aya and Kanade exchanged a glance.

They'd gone to a coffee shop by the station to relax, but they hadn't kept an eye on the time and, before they knew it, the announcement was due. The three of them had then rushed back to the hall.

Aya was quite familiar with everyone by now. Away from the stage, released from any pressures, every face reflected relief and tiredness, and a sense of liberation.

Most of them seemed like ordinary students again. All so young-looking, very different from when they'd been up on stage. But with the judging taking so long, a sense of frustration and tension gradually settled over the lobby.

The place was a-buzz with something ominous.

The media had gathered, and the lights and microphones had been set up for the announcement, but there was no sign of the judges themselves.

'Something's up.'

'You're right.'

As each minute ticked by, a feeling of unease began to grow, infecting them all.

'Do you think they're arguing about something?'

'What would they argue about?'

A staff member hurried down the stairs and all eyes landed on her.

She was pale, and looked preoccupied. Apparently unaware of everyone's gaze, she crossed the lobby to speak to other staff members. Their faces clouded over.

The officials finally dispersed.

'What's going on?'

Aya and the others had watched all this closely, and then someone started whispering.

'. . . disqualified.'

'They said it was a disqualification.'

'Someone seems to have been disqualified.'

'What—?'

'Why?'

Masaru glanced at Aya and Kanade.

He knew they were all thinking the same thing.

Any way you looked at it, it had to be Jin Kazama.

The fact that he hadn't stuck to his programme but had repeated the Erik Satie piece. And not the whole piece, but an excerpt he'd picked out.

Aya's face stiffened.

'You really think he's been disqualified?'

Masaru was silent, his eyes neither denying nor affirming it.

Aya couldn't bring herself to speak Jin Kazama's name. She felt if she did that it would all come true.

So disqualifications really did happen?

Kanade felt a faint irritation.

'Where could he be right now?'

The boy himself was nowhere to be seen. Certainly he didn't have the faintest idea that he'd been disqualified.

Aya's heart was pounding.

It just couldn't be true. *Disqualified?* The boy who played so magnificently? Who brought her back to the stage? *No. No.*

She felt the ground beneath her giving way.

Masaru looked at her face, took a deep breath. 'OK,' he said, and spread his hands wide. 'We still don't know anything. It might be somebody else. There might be some other reason.'

'Like what? Can you think of anything?' Kanade sounded sceptical. 'Everyone kept exactly to their allotted time, and no one was stopped for going over. Can you think of a reason for it being anyone else?'

Her question left Masaru silenced.

They were all at a loss for words. Disqualified.

Jin had come all the way from Paris to Yoshigae, and now the whole time he'd spent here would be for nothing. It wouldn't count on his CV as experience in a competition. It would be as if he had never taken part.

Aya thought of the time she'd spent with Jin, all the conversations they'd had.

The image of his innocent smile spun round in her head.

This couldn't be happening.

She felt a panic she'd never experienced before. Even if it had been happening to her, she could not have been more shaken.

Amidst the clamour around them they heard his name being repeated again and again, like ripples spreading out.

*

'They said Jin Kazama has been disqualified.'

'What—? The Honeybee Prince?'

'DQ'd. That's what they're saying.'

'Because his performance broke the rules.'

The collective unconscious was a terrifying thing.

Before they knew it, this had turned into an established fact, and the place was buzzing, everyone certain it was true.

As more people walked into the lobby, it was clear they soon picked up on the news as well.

'What—? Really?' they heard people gasp. The lobby was soon in an uproar.

And still no sign of the judges.

The media had leapt in, cornering staff members, grilling them. But the staff seemed as much in the dark as everybody else.

It was already nine p.m.

People shuffled randomly about the lobby. Exhaustion and impatience lay heavily, and gloomily.

'Still, they're really taking their sweet time about it,' Masaru muttered.

'Could such a disqualification take so long?' Kanade said.

Just then a figure popped up in the lobby, the one thing that was giving off any light. Aya's eyes were drawn in that direction.

'Oh—' Aya said, and Masaru and Kanade followed her gaze.

'It's Jin.'

Jin realized everyone was staring at him. He came to an abrupt halt and started to shrink back.

Aya remembered the first time he appeared on stage, how the tumult of applause had startled him.

The boy gazed around the lobby.

Aya sympathized. He had no idea what was happening.

'Kazama-*kun*, over here,' Kanade said, motioning him over.

The boy caught sight of the little group and, looking relieved, made his way across.

But all the stares followed him, and he ducked down a bit awkwardly.

'What's going on? Did I get cut?' he asked Aya.

Aya shook her head.

'They haven't made the announcement yet.'

'What? And it's this late?'

The boy looked over at the clock on the wall.

'Hey, where have you been all this time?' Aya asked.

The boy looked confused. 'I was watching my teacher as he was working.'

'Your teacher? You mean for piano?'

'A florist, the one whose home I'm staying in.'

'A florist? Is that your teacher?' Kanade looked taken aback.

'Yeah.' Jin Kazama nodded. 'He had a job to do today, and he let me join him. It was a bit far from the centre of town, so it took a while to get there and back. I was sure they'd made the announcement a long time ago.'

Aya and Kanade glanced at each other in astonishment.

Of course, with all the performances over, he was free to do as he wished.

'So, what's going on? Everybody seemed to . . . be looking at me.' Jin Kazama glanced around him. By now, people had gone back to their own conversations.

'There's some kind of problem, apparently,' Kanade ventured, doing her best to sound calm.

'Problem?'

'They're saying someone got disqualified.' Kanade glanced at Masaru.

'Disqualified? You said *disqualified*?'

The boy looked up at Masaru, seeking an explanation.

'I've been disqualified myself once,' Masaru said quickly. 'I played a piece that wasn't allowed and got DQ'd. You can get disqualified for things like going over the time limit, too.'

*

Jin Kazama looked at Aya, only half convinced.

Avoiding his gaze, Aya faltered, trying to get some words out.

Jin looked suddenly in shock.

His eyes widened, his face grew visibly pale.

'No!'

His anxious expression made Aya and the others even more upset.

They'd never seen such a look on his face before.

Jin Kazama's lips quivered.

'*Me?*'

He looked at each of them in turn, his face fearful.

'I'm disqualified? Is that why they were all staring at me?'

'We don't know yet,' Aya and Masaru said at the same time. 'It seems like someone's been disqualified, but we haven't heard who.'

'But they're all looking at me. They must think it's me, right?'

The boy looked despairingly around him, plainly confused. He gazed searchingly at Aya's face, as if the answer was written there.

'I'm telling you we really don't know. No one's announced anything.'

'Was I cut, then?' the boy said blankly. His eyes no longer focused on anyone. 'That means my dad won't buy me a piano . . .'

'What?' Aya asked.

Won't buy him a piano?

A stir rippled across the lobby.

The judges had appeared on the upper floor.

There was a commotion as more lights came on and the emotional temperature in the room shot up.

The judges steadily descended the stairs.

Kanade tried to read their faces. They all looked quite placid.

It didn't look as if there had been some terrible problem. Most of them appeared quite satisfied.

Olga Slutskaya, the chair of the judges, had been the first down the stairs, and a staff member handed her a microphone.

The mic switched on with a *pop* and a hush descended on the lobby.

'Ladies and gentlemen, thank you for your patience.'

Despite the prolonged time they'd taken, Olga appeared unruffled, exuding her usual stately sangfroid.

'I'm happy to announce the results of the third round. It wasn't easy to arrive at a decision, but we are very happy with the final results.'

She continued with her standard comments, reminding those who didn't get through that they shouldn't view this as a negative judgement on their musicianship or on themselves as individuals, and not to be discouraged but to continue to devote themselves to their music.

Of course, for the press, and the competitors waiting there, her words barely registered.

Olga was well aware of this. She saw how impatient and fretful everyone was, and she seemed to be deliberately stringing them along.

She gracefully put on the glasses hanging round her neck.

'Now, as to the reason for this unprecedented amount of time spent on our deliberations . . .'

Olga paused for a moment.

'Something unforeseen arose that, unfortunately, led to one pianist being disqualified.'

So, it was true after all, people whispered. Aya felt Jin Kazama, beside her, tense up.

She lightly rested her hand on his shoulder, and he gazed at her dejectedly.

Aya looked in his eyes and nodded, as if to say, *Don't let it get to you*.

'It took time to confirm all the facts, and then to review the case once more, and we sincerely apologize for the delay.'

Olga gave a curt little bow and then opened up the sheet of paper in her hands.

Confirm all the facts. What did *that* mean? Kanade wondered. Would you really use that term when someone's disqualified?

Olga took a deep breath.

'The following six people will advance to the finals.'

The lobby grew still again.

All eyes were fixed on her hands, the lobby filled with a painful silence.

Aya and Jin Kazama edged closer to each other.

Was it just her imagination, or did it really take an unnaturally long time for Olga to read out the names?

The lobby was enveloped in an uncanny quiet. Olga stayed composed throughout, and it definitely felt as if she was deliberately drawing out the suspense.

'No. 19, Kim Sujon.'

A cheer rang out. A young man, face flushed, pumped his fist a couple of times.

'No. 30, Masaru Carlos Levi Anatole.' An even louder cheer this time.

All eyes turned towards Masaru, who gave a half-hearted smile, his expression not easy to read.

'No. 41, Friedrich Doumi.' More cheers.

Already half of the names had been announced.

Three to go. Aya nestled closer to Jin Kazama and he to her.

'No. 47, Cho Hansan.' Cheers and screams.

Aya felt herself tense up. *Here we go*. The announcement of the next name frightened her, and she couldn't take it.

Olga's lips moved.

'No. 81, Jin Kazama.' A loud shout rang out from the crowd – a shriek or a cheer, it was hard to say, but the roar shook the lobby.

Aya felt the space around her open up. She felt strangely liberated. Bright, and buoyant.

She and Jin turned to each other, disbelieving. Aya heard Olga's calm voice go on.

'And finally, No. 88, Aya Eiden.'

She lowered the sheet of paper in her hand and peered at the crowd.

Aya found it hard to connect this with herself. Cheers

continued to ring out, the excitement unabated. Olga stood coolly erect amidst it all.

Sound and time finally returned.

'We did it! All three of us passed!' Masaru said in a strained voice and raised both hands in a cheer. Aya at last felt a warm joy welling up.

Jin Kazama's face looked wan and careworn.

'We did it!'

Aya and Jin hugged each other, wry smiles wreathing their faces, while Masaru and Kanade just looked relieved.

'Gosh – all that worry for nothing.'

'A little too thrilling, if you ask me!'

They were finally able to make light of it.

Aya wasn't sure who to be thankful to, or for what exactly, but words of thanks were what came to her.

Thank you, thank you, thank you, for letting Jin Kazama pass.

After the initial excitement and shock had settled down, people started to ask aloud, 'Well, then, who was disqualified?'

As composed as ever, Olga stayed silent, but in the end she reluctantly gave in to the pressure and began to speak again.

'There was one other competitor we have been discussing, particularly whether their points were high enough to reach the finals, who, after the third round, fell sick and went home. This competitor did not properly inform the competition office of this, and it took quite some time to ascertain where they were. We finally did establish that the competitor had indeed returned to their home country, had had an emergency appendectomy, and would be unable to play in the finals.'

'Oh – is *that* what it was?'

'And we were sure it was . . . you know—' Aya heard people say and felt them glancing over at Jin Kazama.

Olga waited until the crowd had seemed to accept this before carrying on.

'Congratulations to those of you who have reached the final round. All of you are truly wonderful musicians. For those in the final, be confident and give it your very best. Following these announcements there will be a get-together with the judges, and I urge you to make use of this opportunity. Thank you, and we will see you all again at the finals.'

Aya and her group started to stretch to ease the tension.

Masaru let out a laugh. 'I've never been so tense in my life!'

'Right?'

'I'm so, *so* happy!'

Aya and Kanade hugged.

Jin Kazama had finally regained his innocent smile. 'Wow, I feel like that took years off my life. I have to let my father know.'

Kanade found a quiet corner of the lobby.

Masaru's cell phone rang.

'Yes?' Masaru answered and signalled to Aya with his eyes.

It was from the competition office, confirming the schedule of rehearsals with the orchestra.

Jin Kazama and Aya's cell phones began to ring – their official call.

I'm in the finals. I really did make it, Aya thought.

Aya wordlessly expressed her thanks.

To whom, though, she couldn't say.

In the lobby, pinned to the wall, were row after row of photos of the pianists.

Another flower-shaped ribbon had already been attached to each of those in the finals.

Only six of them had three ribbons.

Akashi Takashima gazed at them, his heart full.

His own photograph had only one, but he had no regrets.

Jin Kazama had made it to the finals, and no one could deny that these six were fully deserving.

Akashi sighed deeply.

For him, the competition had been a good one, a meaningful experience.

At first his attitude had been to join in and get it over

with. With this he'd planned to finally sort out his feelings about music.

But what he came away with was, frankly, a feeling of courage. After listening to so many performances, and being on stage himself, he was determined now to live out his life as a musician.

Well, maybe I should be getting back now, he thought.

He'd turned round and was walking away when his cell phone rang.

Who could that be?

It was from the competition's main office. A number he'd probably soon delete.

'Hello?' he responded uncertainly.

'Is this Mr Akashi Takashima's phone?' he heard a woman's voice ask.

'Yes, this is Akashi.'

'I'm calling from the office of the Yoshigae International Piano Competition. May I ask where you are right now?'

That's a strange question.

'I'm in Yoshigae. I was planning to go back to Tokyo now.'

'I see. Do you think you can be here on the final day of the competition, on Sunday the 24th?' the woman said, in a business-like tone.

'The final day?'

Akashi was even more baffled. That would be the second day of the finals. Of course he planned to come back to listen, but why was she checking?

'Yes, I'm planning to attend the performances in the finals.'

'I see. I'm glad to hear that. So will you also be here at the awards ceremony?'

'Awards ceremony?'

'That's correct. While the judges were deciding on the final six, they also discussed the recipients of other awards. As a result of their conversations, you've been awarded an Honourable Mention Award, as well as the Hishinuma Prize.'

'What? What did you say? An Honourable Mention Award and—?'

'And the Hishinuma Prize,' the woman repeated.

Akashi paused while he let this sink in.

'By Hishinuma Prize, you mean—'

'Yes. It's a prize awarded by Maestro Tadaaki Hishinuma to the pianist with the most outstanding performance of his piece *Spring and Ashura*.'

'And that's . . . me?' Akashi almost shouted.

'Correct. Congratulations.'

He felt as if he could detect a smile for the first time in the woman at the other end of the call.

Heart racing, he bowed deeply to the unseen woman.

Me? I won the Hishinuma Prize? His performance of *Spring and Ashura* had beaten Jin Kazama's and Aya Eiden's?

And the Honourable Mention Award. An award given to a pianist who, though they didn't make the finals, made an impression and was seen as someone with a future.

Akashi was left bursting with joy.

Now he knew for certain.

He could make it as a musician.

'So, WHAT ABOUT JIN KAZAMA?' Mieko asked Masaru.

Masaru shrugged. 'He's gone back to his host family. He said he still has to help out his teacher.'

'His teacher? Who's working with him now?' Mieko asked. Nathaniel, standing beside her, perked up at the mention of the word *teacher*.

'No, it's not for piano,' Masaru said, looking a bit troubled.

'Not for piano? Then is it for solfège, maybe? Or composition?'

Aya, standing beside him, smiled wryly.

'It's for flower arranging.'

'Flower arranging?!' Mieko and Nathaniel exclaimed in unison.

'A friend of his father's owns a large florist's and is a noted *ikebana* practitioner. Jin said he's learning flower arranging from him.'

'What?'

They were standing in the banqueting hall of the hotel, where the judges and competitors were enjoying an amicable evening get-together. All that remained was the finals – the six pianists each playing a concerto with the orchestra – and everyone was enjoying a feeling of release.

Dotted around the hall, groups of some of the remaining competitors were each huddled up with a judge, listening raptly to them.

'Boy, oh boy. He really defies expectations, doesn't he?' Nathaniel shook his head. 'The judges were looking forward to speaking to him, but he's already left.'

'Is that right?' Masaru asked. 'We were all sure that Jin Kazama had been disqualified.'

'Not a single judge discussed whether he should be disqualified. He's really special. Even the judges who were against him at the beginning have become fans.'

Masaru nodded his approval.

'You're OK with that, with a rival making it?' Silverberg prodded.

Nathaniel looked into Masaru's eyes, and Masaru laughed.

'Why wouldn't I be? Winning without Jin Kazama in the running wouldn't be any fun.'

'Ah hah – such spirit.'

This evidence of Masaru's solidity and self-confidence made Mieko and Nathaniel exchange a look and a smile.

'It really is—' Aya murmured. 'It really is great that Jin Kazama is still in the running.'

Goodness me, Mieko thought. *Aya's expression has transformed completely. There's a serenity about her you might even call bold.* The confusion she'd shown when they last met had vanished.

Mieko gazed at her, dazzled by the transformation.

For a judge, witnessing a moment like this in a young musician's life was an unparalleled joy.

'OK, but don't let your guard down,' Mieko cautioned. 'The finals are going to be intense. Everyone's on a roll, and any one of you could win.'

Masaru and Aya exchanged a look and laughed.

All they cared about at this point was their own individual performance. Competing didn't seem to be on their radars.

But it was true – the top prize was up for grabs.

Six finalists.

There was a tendency to think that, with the finals, the main judging was over and that it was now just a matter of confirming the ranking, but playing with an orchestra could have a great impact, and the previous impression given by a performer could be overturned completely. It was entirely possible that, even with a string of wonderful performances behind them, it could all backfire.

'I'm looking forward to it,' Mieko said, and shot Nathaniel a pointed glance.

Do you think your star pupil can win?

Nathaniel knew exactly what Mieko's look meant.

'Yes, I'm looking forward to it,' he said, echoing her words.

They might be smiling, but their eyes weren't and they knew it.

The Finals

Orchestra Rehearsals

THE MULTI-PURPOSE FACILITIES IN which the Yoshigae International Piano Competition was taking place housed three concert halls.

A mid-sized, 1,000-seat hall, where the first three rounds had been held.

A smaller, below-ground hall, with 400 seats.

And then the largest concert hall with some 2,300 seats.

The finals were to be held in the largest of the three halls.

The concertos and order of performance were as follows:

Kim Sujon (South Korea): Rachmaninoff No. 3
Friedrich Doumi (France): Chopin No. 1
Masaru Carlos Levi Anatole (US): Prokofiev No. 3
Cho Hansan (South Korea): Rachmaninoff No. 2
Jin Kazama (Japan): Bartók No. 3
Aya Eiden (Japan): Prokofiev No. 2

The conductor for the finals with the Shintobu Philharmonic was Masayuki Onodera, a mid-tier conductor in his late forties.

Onodera had quite a lot of experience, though accompanying pianists for a competition was much harder work than anyone could imagine.

The soloists were amateurs, and it wouldn't do for people ever to say the orchestra had been at fault – that they hadn't followed the competitor well enough or worked hard enough to draw out their best performance. And with the Yoshigae being such a large-scale, internationally known competition, the responsibility was especially onerous.

Preparing for the finals was gruelling. There were dozens of concertos on the list of eligible works. They were all famous, standard concertos, well within the repertoire of a professional orchestra, but since some were more difficult, they had to review them all so they could be prepared.

The six finalists had each selected a different concerto, which, for the orchestra, was both something to be thankful for, and also not.

Onodera had once conducted in a competition where of the six finalists four had chosen Beethoven's *Emperor Concerto*, while the other two both played Chopin's Concerto No. 1. The audience must have grown bored, and by the fourth rendition of the *Emperor Concerto* the orchestra, too – consummate professionals but only human after all – was sick of it. Keeping an orchestra motivated was a tough task, he recalled.

Following up four performances of the Beethoven concerto with Chopin No. 1 was, to be honest, also annoying. It might be a famous piece that all pianists longed to play, but for the orchestra there were several concertos from the standard repertoire which they found tedious, and Chopin's No. 1 was one of them. In the finals of a Chopin competition there was only a choice between Chopin's No. 1 and No. 2, and no matter how much Chopin was the pride of his country, and no matter how much you loved his music, it must have been pretty torturous for the orchestra. Onodera secretly sympathized.

The six concertos this time were major works, many of them challenging for both the pianist and the orchestra.

Onodera had got background information on the finalists from the stage manager, Mr Takubo. What Takubo told him about the competitors' attitude backstage, and his observations on their personalities, had been invaluable.

Naturally he'd already checked their CVs, whether they'd ever played with an orchestra before, and had listened to their third-round performances.

A CONCERTO WAS A GENRE where experience meant everything. You couldn't understand this unless you had gone through the challenges involved in playing with an orchestra.

When performing on stage, though, you were hearing live instruments up close, and they were at varying distances from you. As you listened from *inside* the ropes, so to speak, the work you thought you knew felt like a different composition altogether. Your sense of timing, too, could easily be thrown.

Twice in the finals of earlier competitions, Onodera had experienced a concerto coming to a halt mid-performance. In one case, the pianist became so engrossed in his playing – panicking, you could say – that he didn't listen to the orchestra and became totally out of sync. One whole bar off, to be precise.

In the second case, the pianist didn't feel confident that his performance level matched the orchestra, and his playing became steadily quieter. If the soloist's sound decreased, the orchestra would naturally lower their own volume, trying to hear him, and the overall sound level would drop. Finally, it got so low the piece didn't hold together, and both the soloist and the orchestra ground to a halt.

The rehearsals this time had proceeded smoothly, however, and the orchestral players looked relieved.

The pianists, as Takubo had informed him, were all outstanding, with five of the six already having experience with an orchestra. After four rehearsals, there'd been hardly any issues at all. They each had their own style, naturally, and though quite young there was a maturity about them, especially one of the pianists from yesterday's session, Masaru Carlos Levi Anatole. The orchestra had been completely entranced by him, certain they were witnessing the emergence of a new star.

THEY WERE NEARING THE END of their break.

The orchestra players filtered back in twos and threes.

They'd finally landed on the single pianist with no experience at all with an orchestra. Jin Kazama from Japan.

Although Onodera was looking forward to the rehearsal, he was admittedly a little anxious. Kazama's third-round performance had been magnificent, but he was worried that perhaps he was the self-centred type who wasn't made for playing together with an orchestra.

What's more, he'd chosen Bartók's Concerto No. 3.

Score in hand, Onodera considered how best to approach it.

A first-time pianist, playing Bartók, threw up some high hurdles for them. There was a lot of negotiating that would have to take place between soloist and orchestra, and if they didn't listen carefully to each other, things could become sticky. The main issue with Bartók was to get the correct timing between the two. Bartók was known for his extended melodic lines.

As Onodera walked into the hall, he saw the piano tuner still tinkering.

And he'd been expecting Jin Kazama to be already practising.

The tuner shot occasional glances out at the auditorium.

'How's this?' he called out.

'Good.'

Onodera looked around and spotted a boy seated at the rear of the hall.

What the—?

Onodera's eyes widened in surprise.

He was sure it had been a staff member he'd seen, but then realized it was Jin Kazama. What was he doing over *there*?

'It's basically OK, but I won't know until the orchestra comes in. Mr Asano, could you come back here and check out how it sounds?'

'OK—'

Onodera couldn't believe what he was seeing.

He'd heard from Takubo that the boy had an excellent ear, but he'd never heard of a pianist and a tuner communicating so closely.

The tuner spotted Onodera and bowed.

'Sorry, we'll be done soon,' he said.

Onodera nodded and placed his score on the music stand.

The orchestra players filed in, and when they were all assembled the tuner stepped down to the seats.

Jin Kazama shuffled forward and leapt up on to the stage.

'Hi, I'm Jin Kazama. I'm really looking forward to playing with all of you.'

'I'm Onodera. I'm looking forward to it as well.'

The leader of the orchestra greeted him, too, and shook his hand.

What a nice-looking boy, Onodera thought.

Naïve, rough around the edges, exuding something completely natural.

'So, how shall we proceed? Shall we play through the whole concerto? We could highlight the entry points that need precision timing.'

But to all these suggestions, Jin Kazama only shook his head.

'I have a request,' he said.

The boy's big eyes looked straight at him, and Onodera felt his heart beat faster.

'Of course.'

Some nerve this boy had.

'I'd like all of you to play the third movement.'

Onodera was taken aback.

'What? Just the orchestra? What about you?'

'I'll listen to it from the back.'

Jin Kazama leapt down from the stage and trotted down the aisle to the rear of the hall.

Onodera and the leader of the orchestra looked at each other.

What was he doing? Testing the power of the orchestra? That didn't sit well with them.

'OK – please go ahead!' The small figure of Jin Kazama waved.

Onodera put on a generous smile, nodded to the orchestra and took up his baton.

The musicians, with raised eyebrows, readied their instruments.

The third movement of Bartók's Concerto No. 3.

A brilliant tutti, the highlight of the piece as it swelled gloriously into the finale.

The orchestra put their all into it.

You want to see what we can do, son, well, we'll show you. Show you what sound we can produce.

A massive fortissimo.

You think you can square off against this volume? When the solo comes in and we have to reduce the power, we'll have the last laugh.

Onodera could sense these feelings in the orchestra.

The nearly seven-minute-long third movement came to an end.

Onodera turned around and saw Jin Kazama and the tuner whispering.

He found it hard to believe this guy was really a finalist.

'*Thank you—!*' Jin Kazama called out as he trotted back and jumped nimbly up on stage.

Wow – that was quite a leap.

Before he knew it, the boy had made his way quickly through the orchestra.

Onodera wondered what he was doing when the boy began pulling chairs aside, shifting music stands, repositioning the musicians.

'I'm sorry, but could you move over here?' He even asked the double-bass players to shift.

They smiled quizzically and shrugged.

Some of the musicians were clearly none too pleased.

The boy, though, looked nonchalant.

'But if I change position, it's going to make it hard to play,' the tuba player muttered.

The boy spun around.

'The floor there is warped. I think they must have repaired it a few years ago, probably using some plywood as backing. So that part of the floor is heavier, the density different. So if you stand on top of that the sound won't project well.'

The tuba player looked up, a perturbed expression on his face.

The boy, unruffled, walked over to the piano and sat down.

'I'm sorry, but please run through the third movement once again. Mr Asano? Could you please check out the balance?' the boy called out to the tuner at the back of the hall, then looked up at Onodera.

Onodera nodded back and, as instructed, picked up his baton. The players, looking perplexed, took up their positions.

There was a moment of silence.

The boy played the low, opening trill.

His sound is so immense.

Their eyes lit up. What a powerful sound. It flew directly into your ears, so clear and striking.

Onodera twitched his baton on the first beat.

Like a conditioned reflex, the orchestra leapt in as one.

They were immediately in gear.

A rising phrase in dialogue with the woodwind section. The brass came in, followed by the low thump of the timpani.

The piano solo.

A robust, confident rhythm.

The orchestra was pulled along, as if dragged by some unseen locomotive.

The piece moved onwards steadily, led by the piano.

What a uniform, full-bodied sound. The strings joined in.

No!

Onodera couldn't believe what he was hearing.

The orchestra had done the first run-through at high volume, but their sound was much louder now. And pulled by Jin Kazama's piano, their volume was still increasing.

The players' expressions looked serious – no, *frantic* would be closer to the truth. Desperate not to be left behind by Jin Kazama's piano.

Onodera noticed something else.

The balance was far better than before.

The low notes dovetailed nicely, reverberating in one neat layer.

The boy's voice flitted across Onodera's mind.

The sound isn't projecting well.

The chairs he'd moved, the music stands, the instruments. Did he really catch all that? With a single run-through by the orchestra?

Finally, they headed towards the climax.

It wasn't so much that they were performing as being *made* to perform. As if their arms were unconsciously moving.

Was the brass section really this strong? Hadn't he always pointed out to them how they needed more punch, that they lacked something?

A rich sound from the horns. The piano, not backing down for a moment.

The final scale.

Jin Kazama, as if bulldozing aside snow, raced up the keyboard, the acoustic pressure overwhelming.

And now the tutti.

The brass rang out, the air quaking, tingling.

What a thrill.

For a second, Onodera forgot himself.

The sounds from all sections of the orchestra converged at a single point in the air, leaving behind a brilliant reverberation.

Conductor and orchestra were speechless – then they heard someone clapping.

Pulling himself together, Onodera turned around – the piano tuner was applauding.

The boy called out, 'Mr Asano, how was it?'

'It was fantastic. Perfect.'

'Maybe it should be a little softer?'

'No, that's just right the way it is.'

'Really? Then, can I ask you all to play again from the top?'

Jin Kazama gazed up at the conductor, and for a second looked worried.

The musicians were staring at him, pale-faced, as if he were some rare species of animal.

'Um, is something – wrong?' Jin Kazama asked, but none of them replied.

Fevered Days

THE DOORS WERE THROWN open on either side, and people poured eagerly into the lobby.

This wasn't the mid-sized concert hall they'd grown used to over the past two weeks, but the much larger main hall. To get there they climbed a wide, plush, red-carpeted staircase.

She might be imagining it, but it seemed as if people's expressions, and outfits, were more vibrant than before.

The first day of the finals was an evening event. Outside it was completely dark.

'I see – so this is what the finals feel like—' Aya said, impressed, as she gazed around the concert hall.

Up on stage the orchestra was arranged to encircle the piano.

Staff members were walking around, getting things ready, and the tuner was absorbed in some last-minute adjustments.

Kanade, who'd experienced numerous competitions, both as a performer and as a spectator, nodded.

'Aya-*chan*, this is your first competition other than junior-level ones, right? This is what the finals are like.'

'It does feel special,' Jin Kazama, seated next to them, murmured.

'I really can't believe it's your first international competition, and first finals, for the both of you. You guys are pretty lucky, that I can tell you.' Kanade looked impressed.

'Mmm—' Aya kept muttering, as if searching for the right words to describe this special atmosphere. 'It's like – I don't know – you prepare for so long, suffer so much hardship to climb to the top of the mountain, and finally scramble over the last ridge, totally out of breath, and you feel a sense of real accomplishment. But the thing is, what comes after isn't easy. You've got to watch every step as you descend. Do you know what I mean?'

'What're you talking about?' Kanade asked.

'I get it, I totally get it,' Jin Kazama said, nodding at Aya. 'Once you reach the top, your nerves are shot.'

'Stop it, you guys. You've just got to hold out a little longer and stay psyched for the finals.'

Kanade slapped Aya and Jin on the shoulder.

But she knew how they felt.

There were a lot of competitors who, after making it through the intense pressure of three rounds, were left feeling deflated. It was hard, even for professionals, to maintain their motivation over the long haul.

'So where's Ma-*kun*?'

Jin Kazama looked around the hall.

'As you might expect, he's skipping the first performance and is in the rehearsal room warming up.'

'Rachmaninoff No. 3 is so long, isn't it?'

Kanade glanced down at the programme.

Rachmaninoff No. 3, which the first pianist was due to play, was nearly fifty minutes long.

Aya giggled.

'What're you laughing about?'

'I was remembering what Ma-*kun* said about Rachmaninoff No. 3, that it's a piece dripping with the pianist's self-consciousness.'

'He really said that?'

Still, wasn't Aya being a little too relaxed about things?

'By the way, why did you choose Bartók's No. 3?' Aya asked Jin. 'Was it your choice? Wasn't there any other concerto you wanted to play?'

Kanade had wanted to ask the same question. With technique like Jin's he could have played any concerto he liked.

'At first I wanted to play Schumann,' Jin said.

'The A Minor?'

'And I was thinking of writing my own cadenza at the end of the first movement.'

'Really? The famous one?'

'But my teacher told me I shouldn't intentionally be picking a fight.'

'Hoffmann?'

'Um.'

Aya let out another giggle.

There was no doubt that Jin Kazama's virtuosity would allow him to ad lib a piece as much as he wanted to. It might say *Cadenza* on the score, but the accepted practice was to play existing cadenzas. Playing your own cadenza, one you created, was almost taboo.

'You did your own arrangement for *Africa*, too, didn't you?'

Kanade knew exactly what Hoffmann meant by *intentionally pick a fight*. There were many in the world of classical music who felt that adding your own phrase to a piece was utter blasphemy.

'Um. That's why I gave up on playing Schumann and was wavering between Prokofiev No. 3 or Bartók No. 3.'

'Really – then you might have overlapped with Ma-*kun*.'

Jin Kazama made a gesture of great relief, and both Aya and Kanade laughed.

It was surprising to learn that even a major talent like Jin Kazama didn't want to duplicate Masaru. Which only reinforced the notion of what a tremendous talent Masaru was.

A *natural and eccentric genius* like Jin Kazama was the type that was easy to understand. Masaru, just as much a genius, wasn't. Talking to him over the last few days, Kanade thought he came across as very balanced. He possessed a superior talent, no doubt, but also gave you the sense of being an *ordinary* person. Even if he wasn't in music, he would definitely be exceptional, for someone with his talents could embrace any field.

'Hmm . . . So what made you decide on the Bartók?' Aya persisted curiously, peering at Jin.

'It was simple, actually. I figured the Prokofiev No. 3 would be a popular choice but that no one else would choose the Bartók.'

'As simple as that?'

'Yep.'

'You know, Ma-*kun* did say you're kind of Bartókesque yourself.'

'Bartókesque?'

'Yeah. Though I couldn't say exactly how.'

Kanade could understand what Aya was trying to say.

Jin Kazama's natural qualities, his unexpected change of rhythms, did make you feel he had an affinity with Bartók.

'So what about you, Aya? What made you choose Prokofiev No. 2? Why not No. 3?' It was Jin Kazama's turn to ask, his expression innocent.

Aya and I probably have the exact same look on our faces now, Kanade mused.

Just before Aya left for the competition, Kanade had remembered how this piece was the last that Aya was due to have played in public.

Until then she'd performed an enormous repertoire.

Her eyes met Aya's and without a word they smiled at each other.

Jin Kazama looked back and forth between them.

'It's my . . . homework, I guess,' Aya said.

'What?' Jin Kazama asked.

'It was my homework, this piece. From a long, long time ago.'

'Oh.'

'And tomorrow I'll finally be able to hand in my homework. It's taken long enough, though. No, actually, it seems like such a short time.'

Aya's eyes seemed to be scanning something far away.

I've been waiting for this, too, for such a long time. The day that Aya would be back on stage, and I can sit in the audience and hear the piece she was supposed to play back then.

Kanade mulled over Aya's words. 'It's taken long enough, though. Yet it seems like such a short time.'

The bell rang, signalling the start of the performance.

'OK, let's check if it's true what Ma-*kun* said, that Rachmaninoff's No. 3 really shows a pianist's ego spilling all over the place.'

'Ego spilling? What does that mean?' Jin Kazama asked.

Aya turned to him.

'Don't you know? Even Ma-*kun* knows and he lives in New York.'

'I've hardly ever been to school.'

'You haven't read Japanese manga?'

'Not really.'

'I'll tell you after the performance. Think about it in the meantime.'

'OK.'

It was Kanade's turn to giggle now.

The lights went down, and silence descended.

ORCHESTRAL PLAYERS STROLLED IN FROM either side of the stage to the sound of gentle applause.

Now came the tuning up.

From out in the audience Akashi Takashima longingly watched the scene unfold.

His expression bespoke a quiet confidence.

There was a moment of silence, then the stage door opened and the pianist and conductor walked on.

It was the Korean Kim Sujon, wreathed in a smile.

Throughout the competition he'd worn only black, and today too he was neatly decked out from head to toe in black.

Some fan girls gave a little shriek.

The pianist looked out on the audience. He was tall to begin with, but now seemed an even larger presence.

I get it, I totally get it, Akashi said to himself. *Little by little, you come to understand what you're doing and where you are.*

It was interesting how watching a soloist take on the might of an orchestra allowed you to gauge their stature as a performer. Not their physical size, but how it brought out, starkly, the power of the individual. Now you could see their real gravitas as musicians: their strength, their breadth.

The young man settled himself on the stool.

He was still for a moment, as if making certain of where he was.

Then he looked up at the conductor.

A moment of eye contact.

He began to play. A simple melodic theme, with a touch of pathos.

Rachmaninoff's No. 3 was one of the heavyweights. Whoever was playing it would need a certain scale and strength to handle it.

This pianist had chosen well. Akashi stared up at the young man in black.

Affinity with a piece was an interesting thing.

Akashi felt his forte lay in classical period pieces, more charming works like those of Mozart, but people seemed to enjoy his interpretations of contemporary works as well. Something unconscious within him must respond to them, some essential element of which he himself was unaware.

This guy was tough. He must have really trained his core.

I bet he attended a music academy in America, too. Akashi had once dreamt of studying abroad, too, but he'd felt that he wouldn't be good enough to keep up.

But now he was feeling it was OK that he hadn't. Wasn't it perfectly acceptable not to go to Europe, the *centre of Western music*, and instead allow musicians to study in their own country?

He had stayed in Japan for his studies and had taken part in the competition while still working full time, but still his music was, one way or another, rated highly. Didn't that mean that this era was coming soon? The era of the ordinary musician?

A sort of vague notion had started to take shape within him now that the competition was in its final stages.

The pianist was in the middle of a highly intense passage, with the orchestra surging along beside him: the Rachmaninoff, like some dazzlingly huge edifice.

Compared to concertos Nos. 1 and 2, with their perfectly shaped structure of introduction, development and denouement, there were places in Rachmaninoff No. 3 that came across as a little too heavy.

After the great popularity of No. 2, Akashi mused, people must have demanded that he write more of the same, works that offered the listener one big musical hook after another.

Akashi compared it to how, after a Japanese song became a big hit, people wrote songs in a similar vein, recycling the hook. In Rachmaninoff's time, the same thing must have been at work. It wouldn't have been at all strange if Rachmaninoff himself had wanted to create a work so chock-full of memorable moments and with a dazzling melody that it could become the centrepiece of a recital. He was, after all, a hugely popular pianist himself, in search of as much killer content as he could find.

So when you heard Concerto No. 3, it came across as mosaic-like, creating the impression of a series of connecting hooks. It was one turning point after another.

This meant you had to be in an extremely serene state of mind to play it. If you became carried away, you could lose control and the performance would tailspin into an embarrassing, floundering mess. This particular soloist cleared all the hurdles.

His mysterious, cool air neatly kept the Rachmaninoff in check, preserving its magnificence, all in an understated manner. For all that, it was still truly a tremendous piece.

Akashi stared as the pianist displayed the most transcendent technique.

He remembered the first time he'd seen the score, a mass of black notes, an endless succession of chords for both hands. How on earth could anyone ever play it?

This young man on stage was here after thousands – no, *tens* of thousands – of hours spent in practice, and the thought moved Akashi. He felt a kinship with him.

The orchestral players behind him, and the conductor, had all spent a dizzying amount of time since they were children in lessons, in music, in search of that supreme moment.

Breathtaking, was Akashi's honest reaction.

He was witnessing the miraculous coming together of such a massive amount of time and passion, right here, right in this very moment.

Suddenly, he felt fearful.

What kind of job was it to be a musician? What sort of vocation was it, anyway?

Vocation – that was the perfect word for it. It really was a calling, a living *calling*. It didn't fill your stomach, didn't last. To devote your life to something like that, the only way you could describe it was as a *calling*.

What kind of path is this I've chosen?

He felt a chill run up his spine, and found it hard to breathe.

A harsh road to follow, but there's a joy to be found in it that doesn't exist elsewhere. I am part of the flow of musical history, Akashi thought.

Even if I'm but one drop that flows away in an instant, I want to be part of that flow.

Shouts and cheering. With a start, he realized the concerto was over.

The pianist, flushed and with a radiant smile on his face for the first time, stood up.

In the orchestra, the strings waved their bows in appreciation.

After a moment, Akashi, his face dreamy, joined in, eagerly applauding.

THE INTERVAL WAS A SHORT fifteen minutes.

A bell rang out, urging the audience back in.

The next pianist was a young man from France, short, with curly blond hair. After the previous competitor, tall, dark and all in black, this pianist conveyed a bright, pastel-coloured impression as he came out on stage.

There was an air of lightness about him, totally different from the earlier soloist.

The concerto he chose was Chopin No. 1.

Of all the heavyweight concertos in the finals this had to be the most popular.

As soon as the piano began, Aya thought, *Hmm, now that's intriguing.*

Individuality was the word. Unexpectedly elusive and subtle, yet substantial.

Yes, unique mannerisms. Slightly unusual articulation.

This French pianist was not the type who stood out much,

had never been the subject of speculation or rumour. He'd made slow and steady headway in international competitions, though up until now he had never given the impression of having any obvious individuality.

Yet from the moment his fingers touched the keys, Aya sensed an extraordinary singularity.

The judges, who'd listened to hundreds, thousands, of pianists, would surely discern what the audience could not, an *individuality* that the soloist himself was probably not even aware of.

This competitor's Chopin concerto was unique.

Sometimes pianists would drastically change the tempo, or forcibly add pauses to express their personal approach. But with this pianist, the pauses, and tempo, were truly genuine, a part of his own unique *voice*.

If you played it just as it was written, it tended to sound sluggish, and even a bit tedious.

There were few parts of this concerto where the pianist had to consult with the conductor, and timing-wise it wasn't difficult. The orchestral backing was a perfect accompaniment to the piano, so if you simply paid attention to your fellow musicians, you wouldn't make any mistakes.

Which is why pianists felt they had to intentionally amplify and intensify their interpretation, otherwise the performance might lack any drive or thrill. But if the *intensifying* was too deliberate, the whole thing would end up sounding impatient and rushed.

Aya was swept along with the dialogue between piano and orchestra.

Chopin's No. 1 was pretty stunning after all, was her true impression.

She recalled Akashi Takashima's face when he'd called out to her the other day.

It felt so strange, that empathy. The conviction, and euphoria, they'd shared.

She'd never experienced that before – crying with someone she'd never met before.

He'd planned to play Chopin No. 1, too, she recalled, if he had made it to the finals.

Oh, I wish I could have heard his Chopin, she thought.

That scene came to her.

Wait a sec. The scene she'd just imagined of Akashi Takashima performing had to be a premonition of a future event, a moment yet to come.

I can hear him playing.

Aya gazed up at the Frenchman on stage.

I can hear Akashi playing Chopin.

This was the true joy of classical music. Imagining someone else playing something, how they would approach it. It thrilled her to think it. The joy of seeing, before one's very eyes, how a work performed for many years could be remoulded under each performer's distinctive touch.

If Ma-*kun* played Chopin No. 1, it would be so romantic. The girls would be moved to tears, and fall for him all over again.

Now if Jin Kazama played it, the Chopin would be tricky, magical, *fascinating*.

And if it were *her* . . .?

It had been ages since she'd considered something like this.

If it were me, this is how I'd play it. This is how I feel this piece—
A nostalgia overwhelmed her now, threw her off balance.

It's true that seeing Jin Kazama at this competition, listening to him, being with him, made me feel that I want to play too, Aya thought. *I want to make music. Play the way he does. I want him to bring me back to the stage*.

It had been ages since she'd wondered, *How would* I *play this piece?*

Aya felt drained.

I could play it like this. Or maybe like this . . .

So – it's OK to make music as if it's as natural as breathing.

Her whole body felt buoyant at this sudden insight.

Music has its history and its rules, but at the same time it constantly needs to be renewed. And that's something I should discover again for myself.

Suddenly she saw a scene opening up before her.

As if a breeze was blowing down from the stage, straight towards her.

I can do this. I can keep on playing—

She'd never felt so sure of anything in her life.

This wasn't some eager *I'll do it* excitement, neither was it a kind of vague *that would be nice* hope. But rather a taken-for-granted certainty that *this was going to happen*.

Up on stage the pianist was finishing the relaxed second movement, not playing it with the approach most people tended to employ, but with a lighter, playful touch. He was now moving on to the dynamic third movement.

His fingers flew across the keyboard, coquettishly, a bit deviously.

This is fantastic! Aya thought happily.

The vigorous finale came to an end, and as the pianist stood bowing to thunderous applause, Aya had an ear-to-ear smile the equal of his.

In the wings, Masaru let out a long breath, then inhaled deeply.

Human breathing wasn't a matter of inhaling then exhaling, but the opposite – exhaling, then inhaling.

When a baby was born into the world, it cried out loudly. The first thing it did when it emerged was to exhale.

And when someone died, they *breathed their last*. In their final moment they breathed in.

When Masaru competed as a high jumper, he tried all sorts of breathing techniques. Breathing that builds up power. Breathing that calms the nerves. Breathing that helps you focus on the here and now.

The mental image of exhaling as if crawling into some deep, dark place, moving from the depths of your body to the depths of the Earth. And the image of breathing in the countless particles of energy scattered about the world, the glittering particles of light.

What I'm doing is gathering all the fragments of music scattered about in the world and crystallizing them inside me. Music fills my body and, filtered through me, goes out again into the world as my music. It isn't that I'm giving birth to music. I'm the intermediary through which music returns *to the world*. And a concerto was like a large-scale music session in which the notes were already determined. It was exactly because it was all prescribed that interpretation could be infinite.

Masaru watched the orchestral players file in.

He was the last to play that day, and after two performances the audience was feeling relaxed, and chatting.

He closed his eyes and felt that shining spot beyond the heavy doors.

As the orchestral tuning up faded out, a strange, unrivalled hush descended.

Mr Takubo and the conductor beside him gave him a smile – calm, encouraging.

Masaru gave them a broad smile back.

'Time.' The fourth occasion Mr Takubo had said this to him.

Masaru stepped out into the light, and the hall rang with applause.

Masaru could feel the love washing over him.

During rehearsals he felt he'd *won the approval* of the orchestra. This had now risen to a conviction that he was *loved*.

Right now, I'm the happiest I've ever been.

Prokofiev Concerto No. 3.

The tranquil opening by the woodwind. Something was beginning, something great and wonderful. The timpani beat out a light rhythm alongside the strings, stirring up anticipation and rising in a crescendo.

Then the piano entered.

Masaru always smiled at this moment.

He'd talked with Aya about it; Masaru always pictured outer space at this instant.

The world of *Star Wars*. The lines of text scrolling off into the galaxy.

Fleets of Star Destroyers whizzing around in space. The whole work gave him the sensation of floating.

Among the more famous concertos, Prokofiev No. 3 was notorious for its insane number of notes. Masaru didn't mind the process of matching up the myriad pieces of Prokofiev's massive jigsaw puzzle. Linking up the complex melody lines was a joy akin to riding a roller coaster.

Prokofiev composed ultra-contemporary music, for sure. Even free-form jazz couldn't come up with melodies like this. Masaru couldn't help but wonder what imaginary scene this amazing melody-maker held in his head when he composed this.

Masaru always found it miraculous how these musical stars, these masters who created the classical-music genre, popped up one after another in each era, composing so many masterpieces that even now were unrivalled.

Human evolution happened explosively, a massive surge with a variety of *original* things appearing all at once. Not gradually but appearing all at once in the same period.

The same phenomenon had occurred in a certain age in the world of music.

And what did it give humankind? From ancient times, people and music have been closely intertwined, but for what purpose?

I don't know.

Even when playing like this, enveloped, immersed in sound, he still didn't know the reason.

Though one thing was certain – there was an endless joy in it, a pleasure, and wonder.

A competition, finals, winning a prize – these trivial concerns had completely vanished, far off into space.

So why? Why *am I playing?*

Why did music evolve like this?

Masaru felt himself continuing to evolve.

Strange to think of things like this in the middle of a performance. To be on stage, and thinking about human evolution and the evolution of music.

What did you find yourself thinking about?

His friends who weren't musicians often asked him, 'During a performance, what are you thinking as you play?'

It felt as if he was musing about all sorts of things, but also nothing at all. There were times when different feelings passed through him, emotions he couldn't articulate, while at other times he was, from start to finish, beside a quiet, still lake.

Today it was the evolution of humankind and of music that he was thinking about.

Of course, a part of him was also coolly analysing the situation. *The orchestra is on great form today*, he thought. *Being the third pianist on the first day of the finals suits me perfectly.*

Suddenly the answer came to him.

Music must have originated alongside humans to help them evolve into spiritual beings, different from other creatures. And so they evolved together – humans and music.

What he meant by *spiritual* was different from its meaning in Christianity and other religions. He didn't mean it arrogantly, that human beings were lords of all creation. As long as they lived on this vessel that was the Earth, all living creatures should be of equal value.

Yet if these beings called humans added something that allowed them to escape the burden of being human . . .

And *making music* was the most appropriate thing to enable this, wasn't it? Music, transient, here one moment and gone the next. Enthusiastically pursuing this, devoting your life to it, was akin to a magic that separated humans from other creatures.

Now *that*, he felt, struck at the very heart of it.

The smile never leaving his face, Masaru raced along in tandem with the orchestra, about to reach the dazzling, note-filled third movement.

THE SILVER DRESS, THE LIGHT in the wardrobe illuminating it.

Aya gazed intently at the outfit waiting for her.

'Is something wrong with the dress?' Kanade asked.

Aya hurriedly closed the sliding door and gave an embarrassed smile.

'I was just thinking that the day I will finally wear it has actually arrived. It has sort of got to me.'

They'd listened to the first day of the finals, had dinner with Masaru, and come back to the hotel.

'That Ma-*kun*, he looks so relaxed it makes me jealous. His performances are all finished, and he can sleep well tonight. I envy him.'

'Once again you're the last to perform, Aya-*chan*.'

'Yep, gonna wrap up the show.'

Aya held a clenched fist up high and Kanade watched her.

Her look, so filled with affection, Aya thought. *So much like my mother*.

'It seems like so long ago that we picked out the dresses.' Kanade walked over to the sideboard, dropped a tea bag into a mug and poured in hot water.

'I never imagined that this day would come.' Aya flopped down on the bed.

'You were still unsure of yourself then, Aya-*chan*. You made it clear how demoralized you'd become.'

'It's a little embarrassing to remember.' Aya scratched her head.

'And now we can finally hear your Prokofiev No. 2.'

Such a long time had passed since that day she'd fled from the stage.

'I am so, so happy that you took part in the competition. And that you made it to the finals,' Kanade murmured, as if sighing.

Her voice pierced Aya to the quick. She suddenly leapt off the bed, startling Kanade.

'Thank you so, so much for taking care of me for so long. I've been so stupid, so dense. I'm so sorry, too, thinking of your father, for me being such a dunce.'

Kanade looked surprised, then grinned. 'You don't know what I mean.'

'What?' asked Aya.

'When I said *I'm so happy*, I meant I'm happy because I'm relieved to know I wasn't wrong.'

'What do you mean?'

'The thing is – I've always known I have a good ear. To be honest, I was wondering what I'd do if you didn't make it to the finals. If that had happened, I'd be wondering: *Was I wrong? Am I hearing wrong?*'

'Oh, I see.'

'So, it's for *me*. I was happy for *myself*.'

Kanade rested a hand on her chest.

'I don't mind telling you this now, but I promised myself that if you made it to the finals, I'd switch to the viola.'

'Seriously?'

'Yep. I thought that if my intuition turned out to be correct, I'd officially switch instruments.'

'I had no idea . . . Does your father know?'

Kanade shook her head.

'No. I haven't told him yet. He can't decide for me. I have to make up my own mind. I'll tell him after the competition's over.'

'I'm glad I didn't know earlier. That would have made me even more tense.'

'Hah hah. Thought it might.'

The two of them sipped their tea.

'So, Aya-*chan*,' Kanade asked, 'what are your plans after the competition? Are you going to do some concerts like you used to?'

'I don't know,' Aya said, inclining her head. 'Though I'll tell you what. Just wanting to doesn't mean I can. But still . . .' She was quiet for a moment. 'If there are people who want to hear me perform, I'd like to play for them.'

Kanade's face lit up. 'Really?'

The two smiled in silence at each other.

She's back to the front lines of music.

'I should be grateful to Jin Kazama.' Aya looked up at the ceiling.

'Jin Kazama? What about Ma-*kun*?'

'To Ma-*kun* too. To all of them.'

'Jin Kazama's going to get that piano he's been wanting, since he made it to the finals.'

'Oh, that's right! I wonder what kind he'll get. He can tune it, too, which is great.'

'Perhaps he'll build his own.'

'A Jin Kazama homemade piano. He does seem clever with his hands.' Aya chuckled. 'I'd like to go to a Jin Kazama concert,' she said. 'Do a joint concert with him.'

'That would be fantastic. Let's plan it. I bet people would come.'

'In Paris and Tokyo.'

Kanade looked at her watch. 'We should go to bed. It's getting late.'

'You're right. I can't hang out like this. I've still got a competition final to get through.'

THE FIRST PIANIST OF THE second day was a Korean, Cho Hansan, playing Rachmaninoff No. 2, a flamboyant piece that in Japan was seen as the pinnacle of concertos. Its structure and dramatic opening captured the audience from the start.

Different from the previous day's Kim Sujon, the all-in-black pianist who'd played Rachmaninoff No. 3, Cho Hansan was only eighteen, still with a boyish air about him. His performance, though, was noble and stately. He took an orthodox approach, not swayed by trends.

Masaru relaxed at the back of the hall.

I don't see Kanade, he thought. *Maybe she's with Aya?*

It had been quite some time since he'd listened to music like this all by himself.

He could enjoy the final three competitors' performances without worrying about his own. He could look forward to seeing his friends, Jin Kazama and Aya Eiden.

Friends.

Masaru felt a bit strange thinking that.

He'd known Aya years ago, of course, but he'd got to know Jin and Kanade only at the competition. Otherwise, he probably never would have met them.

Rivals? Of course, but it didn't feel like that. *Friends* was more like it.

It was because they were all thrown into the same high-pressure situation, that they could become friends. But . . . wasn't that exactly what real friends were all about?

They might go their separate ways later, but they'd always be connected. No matter where they were in the world, his thoughts would always be with them.

He had a hunch: *With Aa*-chan, *though, I hope we won't go our separate ways. I'll always want her to be close.*

He was confident that they would see each other again.

So, what was the final decision going to be? Masaru snapped back to reality.

I think I'll be in the top three. I'm not sure I'll win the top prize, though.

But I'm pretty sure the Audience Award is mine.

Masaru considered this calmly.

During the finals, each member of the audience could vote for the one pianist who impressed them the most. And the one who garnered the most votes was given the Audience Award.

Of the three performers yesterday, I think I got the most votes by far, but today the vote might be split. If that's the case, that's to my advantage.

As the audience applauded, the conductor and next finalist walked across the stage.

Some day I'd love to play this piece.

But I can't play it yet. I don't want to yet.

I'll play it only when I'm satisfied I can. When the time's right. That's how much this piece means to me.

From the moment it was first performed, Rachmaninoff No. 2 had been wildly popular.

Back in the day, popular songs weren't written down. These days, a concerto was considered *classic*, but at the time it would have been cutting edge, the latest of the *pops*. It was a time when the vast majority of people only heard music performed live. People who heard this piece live for the first time – imagine how moved they must have been, how thrilled.

It could make you jealous, Masaru thought. How lucky those people were who'd been present at its first performance.

Was that kind of excitement a thing of the past? Masaru considered this.

Was it no longer possible to experience the joy of hearing a new piece live for the first time ever?

In a world where one new song after another appeared and was instantly transmitted around the world, why couldn't one recreate the experience of hearing the premiere of Rachmaninoff No. 2 once again?

Masaru didn't dislike so-called *contemporary music*. Most of it was dissonant, hard to keep time with, the performers and the audience both needing great patience, with any clear melody scorned, all musical value turned upside down. But still, it could become interesting if you really listened.

But Masaru felt this kind of music had reached a dead end, the way it mistakenly looked down on melodic music as something that anyone could do to stir up the emotions of the listener. There was something not right about making lack of popularity a point of pride.

Would another *classic* ever be composed? Masaru thought this all through as he was enveloped by the first movement of Rachmaninoff No. 2.

The old masters were, of course, totally astonishing. Their existence, the pieces they composed, were veritable miracles. The same circumstances would never arise again. He knew that in the present, an era of endless information and instant access to every kind of music imaginable, it would be difficult for such a miracle ever to reoccur.

But it wasn't out of the question, or impossible. It was only the spell cast by prejudice and preconception that prevented more *classics* from emerging.

And if that's the case, then I—

The idea hit him.

Some day, I'll *do it.*

Some day I'll play the first performance of a Rachmaninoff No. 2 for the new century.

Once I make a start, someone will follow.

No – the world was always in sync. It wasn't just him – there must surely be lots of other musicians, below the radar, thinking the same thing. Once somebody started it, everyone would join in, and it would become a full-fledged movement. Once again, people would be able to enjoy a brand-new piano concerto. Once again, that would be what people talked about.

Masaru was lost in thought for a while.

Before he knew it, he saw the pianist on stage playing Rachmaninoff No. 2 as merging with himself. What was being played there was Rachmaninoff No. 2, but at the same time it wasn't. It was the piece yet to be, the future Rachmaninoff No. 2 that Masaru would create.

A shiver went through him, a strange quivering. He trembled at the weight of this future responsibility, this expectation for the future, and for himself.

They were already in the third movement, he suddenly realized.

The audience's expectations rose.

Probably most of the audience here knew the piece. But knowing it only made them eagerly anticipate the high point all the more. Masaru's heart beat faster. And as always it struck him: *What a truly emotionally rousing melody!*

It could be performed thousands, tens of thousands, of times, and this melody would never ever wear thin. It moved you, no matter how many times you heard it. It struck you right in the heart.

The highest form of human achievement was music. This is what he thought.

Human beings might have dirty, repulsive aspects to them, but out of the sordid swamp that was humanity – no, it was precisely *because* of this chaotic swamp – the beautiful lotus flower of music would bloom.

We have to let that lotus bloom for ever, nurture it to become a bigger flower, more innocent and beautiful. That's how we can endure being human. And it will be our reward.

It was said that lotus seeds could sprout even after a thousand years.

There might well be buried seeds even now, in this age, that were still dormant, seeds waiting for the chance to bloom—

An image came to Masaru, of lotus flowers blossoming everywhere he looked.

He wasn't sure if it was true, but they said that, when lotus flowers open, they make a cheerful, explosive *pop*.

Pop, pop – cheery sounds echoing across the world.

Immaculate pink flowers blossoming everywhere.

The scenery suddenly brightened.

Each and every flower would light up the world.

The light would transform into little round orbs that rose into the air.

Thousands of lights, ascending one after the other into the sky.

Masaru was entranced.

Are they above the stage?

No, it feels more like they are in the sky far above.

Balls of glittering light floating softly, bumping into each other, pushing and jostling.

So bright. So wonderfully bright.

Masaru was astonished.

As Rachmaninoff No. 2 reached its climax, the lights came together as one.

God, it's beautiful. Where is *this?*

If he told Aa-*chan* what he'd just seen, what would she say?

*What? You ascended to heaven, Ma-*kun*? So – you're a Christian?*

He could picture Aya's dazed, curious face, and he smiled.

No, I'm not a believer, Masaru answered Aya in his imagination.

*Maybe I'm more dangerous than I thought. Compared to Jin Kazama and Aa-*chan*, I thought I was the sensible one.*

Masaru sat there grinning to himself in the roar of thunderous applause.

THE STAFF WERE BUSTLING AROUND on stage, moving chairs.

'Is this where it should go?'

'Look for the tape on the floor.'

The audience watched, wonderingly, exchanging glances.

But Aya, at the very back of the hall, knew exactly what it all meant.

The orchestra was going into its *Jin Kazama shift*.

She'd noticed how in earlier performances the stagehands had subtly repositioned the other pianos, a move that had to be at Jin Kazama's direction.

Jin Kazama's ear was special, unique.

It was often said that Japanese people could hear noise as music, but his sense of hearing surpassed that by far.

But what in the world was he listening to? How far did his hearing extend? And what did it sound like to him?

His ear was so good that even Aya, when she was with him, was in awe.

She recalled the sheer shock when she'd first heard him, at the music college, playing Chopin's Étude No. 1.

And ever since then, every time he performed he gave Aya the little push she needed. Inspired her. The fact that she was standing here now was thanks to him.

So she was determined to hear his performance. In order to live from now on as a musician.

Aya had changed into her final outfit – a simple silver gown.

It had become her habit by now – to throw on a cardigan over her dress and stand at the back of the hall before her own turn to play.

Aya felt a tingling sensation.

She needed Jin to give her one more strong push.

Aya knew for certain that more than any other spectator or judge, more than anyone else in the hall, she was the one waiting most eagerly for Jin's appearance.

The person who's gained the most from being in this competition has to be me.

I don't know if I'll ever share a stage with him again. Or experience this inspiration, the encouragement, I feel from listening to him perform before I go on.

The thought made her shiver.

Please. This is the last thing I'll ask.

Let me listen to Jin Kazama's *Bartók No. 3. And let me play* my *Prokofiev No. 2.*

She felt as if she were praying.

The bell rang, signalling the start of the performance.

The hall was still astir as the orchestra drifted in. The players shuffled into their seats, smiling, relaxed.

Even greater applause burst out as the conductor and Jin Kazama came on stage.

Jin's face, wreathed in a natural smile, glowed faintly, as if the spotlight was on him alone.

This boy doesn't realize that he's carrying my life on his shoulders.

Aya found the thought a bit comical, and felt sorry for laying this heavy burden on him.

She felt, though, that he noticed this weight, and nonchalantly shouldered it.

Jin Kazama settled himself on the stool.

The conductor loosened his shoulders, rotated his neck. Clicked his baton twice on his stand.

An intimate, singular silence fell on the hall.

The quiet, ripple-like trill of the strings came in.

The hushed introduction.

The melody from Jin Kazama. The utter clarity of that first note, she knew, was enough to awaken the ears of the entire audience, herself included.

How would you describe it? Like a clear voice singing outside in a forest.

Jin had wanted to play Prokofiev No. 3, he'd said, but since it was so popular, the process of elimination led him to Bartók No. 3. From the first note, she knew it was the right choice.

With Bartók you felt as if you were outside, walking through pristine nature, a capricious breeze wafting over you.

Hungary, Romania, Slovakia. Bartók was also a collector of folk music from Eastern and Central Europe, and his melodies carried a local flavour no other composer had. The sombre colours of a forest, the hues of the wind and the water.

Coupled with Jin Kazama's special wildness, this evoked an unusual swell of sound. No other competitor could produce this effect. His sound was the *sound of nature*. When he'd played 'St Francis of Assisi's Sermon to the Birds', you couldn't help feeling as if the birds were actually chirping.

Originally, people had heard music in nature. What they heard became a musical score, and a composition. But with Jin Kazama he was *returning* a piece back to nature. Taking the music the audience heard here and returning it once more to the world. He created this sensation with his unique sound, and the strange improvisatory impression he gave, even when everything was written down note for note.

In Aya's mind there coexisted the Aya who was analysing and the Aya who gave herself up to the music. And there was one more. The Aya-as-performer wondering how *she* would play it.

In the best performances it was incredible how, even with a piece you knew well, it felt as if you were hearing it for the first time. And amazing, too, how you could understand completely what the piece was really *all about*.

The adagio of Bartók's second movement. The orchestral introduction, relaxed yet sober. As if one spied a deer slowly making its way through a cluster of trees in a forest.

A morning mist has risen, it's slightly chilly, and a mysterious air lies taut over the world.

Still not dawn, there's a bated-breath stillness all around.

Aya too was walking in that cold morning mist.

She was no longer an analyst, a spectator or even a

musician, but simply Aya, relaxed, wending her way through the forest.

The cold droplets felt good against her skin. Dried branches cracked underfoot.

Through the milky mist, light flashed in.

It was still dark though the day promised to be sunny.

The deer's ears pricked up and it raised its head.

It had noticed something approaching in the distance.

From high above a bird called out. Chirping, singing. Flapping its wings as it passed overhead. The morning mist slowly cleared and there was Jin Kazama at the piano.

Andante. At a walking pace.

His body moved from side to side, as if riding in a comfortable, swaying gondola.

Hi, Aya. How am I doing? Jin Kazama gave a small smile.

*Not bad. You've trained the orchestra well. Very different from how Ma-*kun *trained them. How'd you do it?*

At rehearsal I got them to play on their own. And then got them to move the music stands, and the bass instruments, the tuba and the rest.

I think it's great you went with the Bartók. No one else can play Bartók like this.

Jin Kazama gave a happy laugh.

I promised Mr Hoffmann, you know.

Promised him what?

Promised to take music out into the world.

Really? I see. No wonder you can produce such a magnificent sound.

So have I managed it?

Um. I'd say so.

I hope so. But I've still got a long way to go.

Jin Kazama tilted his head just a fraction.

His eyelashes sparkled in the morning light.

I talked with Mr Hoffmann about it, how the world is filled with so many sounds, yet music is kept shut up in a box. He said in the past the whole world was filled with music.

I totally get it. They'd hear music in nature and write it down, but nowadays no one hears it any more but, instead, it's shut away inside their head. They think that's music.

Right. That's why we talked about taking this trapped music back to where it first came from. He and I wondered how to do it, we tried all kinds of things, but neither Mr Hoffmann nor I could figure it out. He's gone now, but I promised to keep on trying.

So that's your motivation, is it?

I suppose. I haven't thought too deeply about it, though.

Sounds good to me. Since you can take a wonderful morning walk like this.

I know, right?

Jin Kazama laughed.

I thought you could take music outside, too, together with me.

Me?

Um. Return music to the world.

Well, I hadn't thought about it. But I want to help out.

Thanks.

OK.

Aya leaned against the piano and thought it over.

It's true, up till now I've always been given things by music. We all thought music was supposed to give to us. We never gave anything back. We just ingested it, without ever being thankful. It's time to start giving back, I'd say.

Aya looked up at the sky.

The bright sky. Distant birds were flocking and gliding.

We have to say thanks. To this world filled with music. The blue of the sky touched her heart.

Jin Kazama gazed quietly at Aya.

Then you promise?

I do.

That's good, but there's another promise you need to make.

Meaning?

Show it to me. After this.

After this?

With the Prokofiev No. 2.

The two of them briefly locked eyes.

Show me today, *after I've finished. Proof that you'll keep your promise. Show me you intend to.*

Jin Kazama's round, boyish eyes, like those of a small deer, grew visibly larger, drawing closer to her.

You promised, remember—

Aya was startled back to the present, as the third movement of Bartók No. 3 was beginning.

Jin Kazama raced up the keys with his brilliant scale. Bartók's exciting, dynamic world gloriously swelling, fast, thrilling.

What a sound the orchestra was producing. You could almost feel the acoustic pressure against your face.

Aya was taken aback.

Even with all that overpowering sound, Jin Kazama's piano rang out – clear, distinct. What in the world was going on?

The dialogue between piano and strings. Neither one giving an inch.

The audience was swept along, on the verge of being swallowed up by the performance.

You promised, remember.

The brass, percussion, woodwind, strings, the piano, Jin Kazama, Aya, the audience, the concert hall, Yoshigae – all of it resounded with music.

As the music stopped and the hall was filled with the cheers of the audience, in Aya's head there was only Jin's voice, like the ping of a ringing bell, repeated over and over.

OUT IN THE AUDIENCE THERE was a strange mix of exhaustion and sense of achievement now that the end was near, after the hundreds of hours they'd spent here.

The competition would soon finally be over.

And from that moment, something new would begin.

How many people here realize that? Kanade vaguely thought.

I've been waiting so long for this day, this moment.

Not that she'd been conscious of it, yet in a corner of her being, she'd known that some day it would arrive.

Kanade was no longer tense.

Throughout the competition she thought she was much more nervous than Aya. It was precisely because she wasn't performing that she grew so anxious. In truth, every time Aya played it wiped Kanade out.

But as Aya performed – in the first round, the second and the third – bit by bit this tension eased.

To the point where now I can even say I feel relaxed, she thought.

And I'd been thinking I'd be on tenterhooks until this final performance – especially this fated Prokofiev No. 2.

But now she felt utterly tranquil.

She was wholeheartedly looking forward to it.

And truthfully, this was partly due to Jin Kazama.

Because she was certain that if Jin Kazama gave a great performance, so would Aya.

Chance encounters were a strange thing. Kanade couldn't help thinking that it was destiny, and a miracle, that had brought Aya and Masaru together again. And Jin Kazama.

The three of them met, just as they were supposed to. For each of their sakes their meeting was necessary, inevitable. Remove one person from the equation and this moment would never occur.

I no longer have to wait, Kanade thought.

She sat back in her seat, letting it all go.

Once Aya's performance is over I can get up and start down my own path. Aya's restoration was mine as well. The chance meeting of those three was a fated meeting for me too. Perhaps I was a part of it.

BACKSTAGE, AYA WAS QUIETLY WAITING.

She no longer had that omnipotent feeling she'd had before her third-round performance.

She now felt utterly calm.

Suddenly she understood that the two moments were linked – this moment, and the moment years earlier when she'd also been waiting in the wings to play Prokofiev No. 2.

It was as if her younger self at that time was also with her now.

Maybe I should be feeling afraid? Was that trauma I experienced?

I felt that day there was nothing there for me. The grand piano on stage looked more like an empty grave.

There was no music. My music had vanished.

I remember that distinctly.

OK, but what about now?

The stage door was still closed, the black box not visible. That toy box that used to be stuffed full of surprises. The one which, on that day, looked so empty, so desolate.

Aya retraced her emotions during the competition.

In the wings in the first round, the second, the third.

What was I thinking about as I stood here? When I stepped out on stage, how did that black box look to me?

She thought hard but couldn't recall any more.

It was all so long ago.

I am back now. I wandered, lost all these years, but now I'm finally on the road I was meant to be on. Not on some moss-covered side path, but the wide, main road everyone is heading down. Wide, yes, but not an easy road to travel. Competition is fierce, and far ahead, a trackless field awaits. Everyone has to carve out that path on their own.

The stage door opened.

The orchestra filed on in groups, absorbed on to the stage with a ripple of applause.

Ah – music was filling the air as the leader struck an A on the piano and the orchestra began to tune.

Aya closed her eyes.

Stillness. Silence.

She felt the whole world gathering right in the centre of her forehead.

'Ms Eiden, it's time,' the stage manager said quietly. She could detect a smile somewhere in his tone.

'All right,' Aya replied.

A warmth rose up inside her.

So very warm, a little sweet and heart-rending. Very much like tears.

Before she knew it, Aya was on stage. Surprisingly loud applause broke out, washing over her.

And she saw the black box, quietly illuminated by the overhead lights.

Aya calmly gazed at it.

This was no toy box.

And it was not empty.

The contents are here. Here, inside *me.*

And this place is already filled with music.

I know, right? Aya said to Jin Kazama, out there somewhere.

Right? This world is already *filled with music, isn't it? Not just in here. We have to give music back to music.*

I'm right, aren't I?

There was no answer from Jin Kazama.

Aya shook hands with the leader of the orchestra and stood beside the grand piano.

The applause was so fevered it sounded like the performance was already over.

Aya smiled broadly, bowed deeply and sat down.

The conductor smiled. They exchanged the smallest of nods.

OK, let's make music.

My music. Our music.

And the baton came down.

Love's Greeting

'So, WHAT WAS THE Maestro intending, after all?' Nathaniel said.

'Good question. I don't know.' Mieko shrugged. 'Maybe it doesn't really matter now.'

'No way.' Nathaniel looked at her reproachfully.

'Besides, isn't it enough that at least we know Jin Kazama wasn't a disaster, but a gift?'

Nathaniel looked caught off guard.

'A gift? You're saying – he was a *gift*?'

'Well, *I* thought so. Wasn't he, in the end? A gift to your beloved pupil, too.'

Nathaniel thought it over. 'Hmm. I guess you're right.'

'He reinvigorated the competition. And those wildly unpredictable performances of his made Masaru's seem more regal in contrast.'

'I suppose they did . . .'

'He was like a catalyst, impacting other competitors. Even her.'

'You mean Aya?'

'Yes.'

'Her performances were outstanding.' Nathaniel looked serious. 'The Prokofiev No. 2 in the final, too. She could very well have won.'

'Yes. I never imagined tearing up quite so much at the No. 2, that's for sure,' Mieko said. 'I'm happy she's made a comeback.'

'You think she'll go back to performing?'

'I heard she said she'd like to, if she gets any requests. And I think she already has.'

Mieko pictured the girl's fresh-faced expression.

'Chance meetings are a strange thing. I never imagined that she and Masaru were childhood friends,' she said.

'Didn't you get the feeling Masaru's madly in love with her? Shouldn't we tell them? Pianist lovers never work out. Tell them to look at *us*.' Nathaniel chuckled. 'Good grief, now I even have to worry about who he's going out with. Not what I expected.' He sighed, but there was a hint of happiness in his expression.

They were in the hotel bar.

The place would be closing soon, and all the clientele had left.

Behind the counter the bartender was wiping a glass.

The awards ceremony was over, and the media had come and gone. The pianists and staff would no doubt sleep well tonight.

As the two of them sat there drinking they, too, felt relieved and lethargic. Mieko gave a little stretch.

'With every single competition I think I never should have taken on such a tough job. Yet the moment it's over, I feel – and this might sound odd – as if it wasn't such a bad assignment after all.'

'Especially when the competitors are so appealing.'

Nathaniel took a sip of whisky.

'In other words,' he said, placing his glass on the counter, 'we're having an unfinished dream. A dream that somewhere out there is some amazing music we've never heard. That the young person who possesses that sound will appear.'

'I think Maestro Hoffmann felt the same way.'

A gift.

I present to you all Jin Kazama.

Well, we got the gift all right, Maestro.

Mieko raised her glass in a little toast.

'What's that for?' Nathaniel asked.

'Cheers.'

'To whom?'

'Maestro Hoffmann.'

'Ah – I see.'

He raised his glass.

'So what are you planning for Masaru?' Mieko asked after a short silence. 'Will you enter him in another competition? He's ready for anything.'

'I wonder.'

Nathaniel inclined his head.

'Even before I could congratulate him, he told me *I want to carry on studying*. Especially composition.'

'Composition?'

'Yeah, he's mentioned it before a couple of times. There's still a lot he has to study about classical music, but he said he eventually wants to perform his own works.'

'That's ambitious.'

'He said he hopes concert pianists can premiere more new works.'

'Hmm. Now *that's* an interesting idea.'

She suddenly pictured Jin Kazama on a street corner, performing.

Passers-by stopping, eyes sparkling as they listened.

What was this image?

'Maybe that's the way to go for them. Jin Kazama, I know, could definitely play original pieces. His arrangement of Saint-Saëns' *Africa* was an eye-opener.'

'Definitely. What's great about his performances is that they make you want to play the pieces yourself.'

Nathaniel looked down at his hands.

'I feel as if I want to play the piano for the first time in a long while.'

Mieko gazed down at her own hands.

'I know. And me,' she said. 'He made me want to run off and find a piano. These days you've just been conducting and producing, haven't you?'

'That's true, I have. But nobody can predict what that boy might do. What'll he be up to two years from now? I wonder.'

'Who will be his teacher?' asked Mieko.

'Maestro Hoffmann apparently selected a few people at the Conservatoire to guide him.'

'He was placed third, so he'll finally get that piano he's been hoping for.'

Nathaniel smiled wryly. 'His whole set-up was highly irregular to begin with.'

'For him, irregular is regular. Nothing's changed since the Paris audition.'

'*Now* you people can brag a little, since you're the ones who discovered him.'

Mieko laughed loudly, as if forgetting completely how angry she'd been after his audition.

'I'm detecting a little too much pride here.'

The bartender brought over the bill, the signal they had to leave.

'So,' Nathaniel murmured as he signed the slip, 'have you thought it over?'

'Hmm?' Mieko asked as she stood up.

'I'm sure you can remember what I asked you at the start?' He gazed steadily up at her.

Mieko felt her heart tighten a little.

'Were you being serious?'

'What do you mean? Of course I was!'

'I'm shocked,' Mieko said.

Together, they walked out of the bar.

'I'm with someone, you know,' she said.

'But how serious are you about him? I mean, he's not your husband.'

'True.'

A feeling was tugging at her. After all this time there was still something about Nathaniel that resonated, deep in her soul.

'This would be after you get that divorce mess sorted out, I imagine?'

'So – I can hold out some hope?'

Nathaniel was so openly thrilled that Mieko had to smile.

'Well, let's meet again,' she said.

'I have a concert next month in Tokyo, so we can see each other again soon.'

This man, I tell you . . . Mieko tutted to herself. Always trying to set the agenda and rope me in. She really missed that about him. She felt unexpected tears welling up, but steadfastly held them back.

'Will you text me?'

'Absolutely. I'll save you a seat at the concert.'

At the bank of lifts, Nathaniel gave her a small wink.

The two of them silently studied the changing floor numbers above the lift doors.

And now we'll both go back to our own musical lives, Mieko thought as she watched the numbers light up.

Back to our lives. To our music.

Music

THE OCEAN LOOKED CALM in the dawn light.

The gentle lapping of the tide carried in the chill air.

The boy was standing at the water's edge, listening.

I might never come back here again.

He blew hot breath on his frozen fingers.

Winter was coming on. He could feel it.

Today was the finalists' concert and tomorrow he'd be off to Tokyo. After giving another concert there, he'd have to get back to Paris.

There was no wind. The ocean was frighteningly still.

But – listen. Can you hear it?

He closed his eyes.

If you listen, the world is filled with music.

Right, Maestro? the boy asked.

The sunlight pouring in. The clouds swirling lazily across the sky.

A swarming orange triangle, flickering and shape-shifting on the horizon.

What is that? Something dense, filling the world.

The boy opened his eyes.

Isn't this what we call music?

He considered this for a while.

Something sparkling landed at his feet. A tiny, swirled conch shell, perfectly shaped, like a jewel.

He picked it up between his thumb and forefinger and held it up to the sky.

'The Fibonacci sequence,' he murmured, and grinned.

Suddenly he wanted to laugh out loud.

The world is overflowing with so much music. I'll take it outside, and help fill the world.

I have friends now, friends who will help.

The boy spread his hands wide and breathed in deeply.

From somewhere he heard the buzz of honeybees.

Where were they from, those bees? Paris? Alsace? Or maybe Lyons?

Oh, that's right. The buzzing I can hear is the sound of life being gathered together. The very sound of life itself.

I have to go back. To the place where I can hear that sound. That sound gives me strength.

The boy stretched, then spun around.

He began to run as fast as he could.

Music. It meant *the art of the gods*. A fertile *muse*.

The boy himself was music.

He himself, every move he made, was music.

Music was running.

In this astonishing world, music itself raced through the morning stillness and, in a flash, was gone.

Results of the Sixth Yoshigae International Piano Competition

First Place
Masaru Carlos Levi Anatole

Second Place
Aya Eiden

Third Place
Jin Kazama

Fourth Place
Cho Hansan

Fifth Place
Kim Sujon

Sixth Place
Friedrich Doumi

Audience Award
Masaru Carlos Levi Anatole

Honourable Mention Award
Jennifer Chan
Akashi Takashima

Hishinuma Prize (Japanese Composer's Performance Award)
Akashi Takashima

RIKU ONDA is a No.1 bestselling author in Japan. She grew up in Sendai and attended Waseda University, where she played the alto saxophone in a student band. A book lover from an early age, she left an office job to try her hand at writing. In 1991, Onda won an award with her first novel, and became a full-time writer soon after. In 2003, after overcoming a fear of flying, she visited the UK and Ireland, and later lived in South America, where she reported for NHK television on Mayan and Incan culture. As her father was a music enthusiast, Onda grew up listening to classical music and played the piano from an early age, discovering Western rock and jazz later. In 2017, her novel *Honeybees and Distant Thunder* was awarded both the Naoki Prize and the Japan Booksellers' Award, the first time a novel has won both. It became an instant No. 1 bestseller in Japan, going on to sell several million copies, and was later made into a highly successful Japanese-language film.

PHILIP GABRIEL is Professor of Japanese Literature at the University of Arizona. He has translated numerous works by Haruki Murakami, including *Kafka on the Shore* (winner of the PEN/Book-of-the-Month Club Translation Prize) and the short-story collection *First Person Singular*. He has also recently translated the novels *The Travelling Cat Chronicles*, *The Forest of Wool and Steel* and *Lonely Castle in the Mirror*.